Praise for *The Notorious Pagan Jones*:

"[A] well-paced historical thriller. Scary in all the right places, with a strong setup for the sequel."

—*Kirkus Reviews*

"Fast-paced and furious, this work will be a certain hit with those who love historical fiction, Hollywood, and stories of redemption."

—*School Library Journal*

"Noirish writing blends the blinding spotlight of Hollywood, the sexy world of espionage, and a smattering of real-life events and figures to create a fast-paced spy thriller."

—*Publishers Weekly*

"This is a well-plotted balance of Hollywood glitter and international political conspiracies during the Cold War, and the historical backdrop is meticulously set. Pagan is a smart, charismatic heroine given depth by her struggles with alcoholism."

—*Booklist*

"With a hint of Hollywood glam, mystery and a time period unique to the YA genre, Berry treats readers to a can't-miss story. She finds a winner in Pagan, creating a Marilyn Monroe–like teen actress with a tale that will appeal to younger and older fans alike."

—*RT Book Reviews*

**Available from Nina Berry
and Harlequin TEEN**

**The Notorious Pagan Jones series
(in reading order):**

The Notorious Pagan Jones
City of Spies

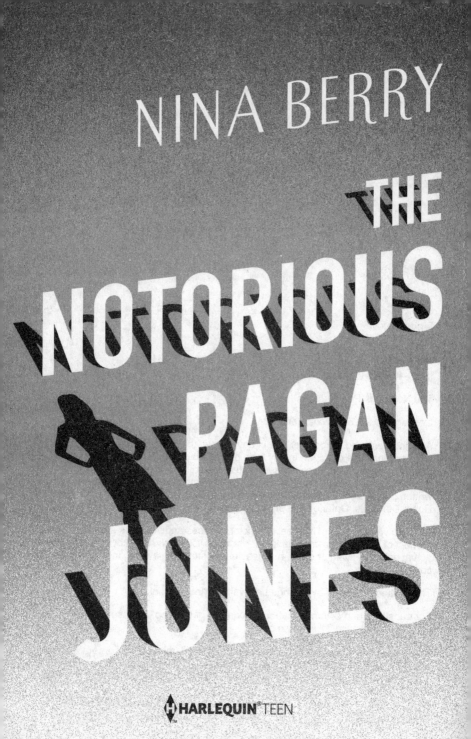

NINA BERRY

THE NOTORIOUS PAGAN JONES

HARLEQUIN® TEEN

Recycling programs
for this product may
not exist in your area.

ISBN-13: 978-0-373-21190-6

The Notorious Pagan Jones

Copyright © 2015 by Nina Berry

www.HarlequinTEEN.com

Printed in U.S.A.

For Natalie Downing

And for all who struggle with addiction

"Hollywood is a place where they'll pay you a thousand dollars for a kiss and fifty cents for your soul."

—MARILYN MONROE

"Berlin. What a garrison of spies! What a cabinet full of useless liquid secrets. What a playground for every alchemist, miracle worker, and rat piper that ever took up the cloak."

—JOHN LE CARRÉ

CHAPTER ONE

FORMER STARLET LANGUISHES IN JUVIE!

Receives Visit from Mystery Man in Black

Time in solitary goes by with unbearable slowness when you've killed every member of your family. With nothing for Pagan Jones to do but pace the five steps back and forth between the walls of a former broom closet, it wasn't surprising that all she could think about was blood and shattered glass and her baby sister's final scream.

At Lighthouse Reformatory for Wayward Girls, a summer Saturday night usually offered up a group dinner of canned beef stew followed by a *Lawrence Welk* rerun. But here in solitary, Pagan had only a hard narrow cot next to a seatless toilet, a sink, and four blank walls reflecting back her darkest thoughts.

Miss Edwards herself came bearing a tray of congealing food in her bony hands. Her heavily starched black uniform rustled as she set the tray down on Pagan's cot. Waitressing creamed corn and meat loaf would have normally been beneath her. But from the smirk on those narrow lips, Pagan could tell Miss Edwards had made an exception so she could take in every moment of Pagan's humiliation.

It took every ounce of Pagan's self-control not to grab the woman's skeletal upper arms and shake her, but then she'd never know what had happened to her roommate after their aborted escape attempt the night before. She swallowed down her anger and asked, "Could you tell me, please. What happened to Mercedes?"

Miss Edwards lifted her narrow shoulders in a sad little shrug.

Horror threatened to close up Pagan's throat. Mercedes couldn't be dead. "You have to tell me if she's okay, at the very least!" It came out louder, more desperate than she wanted. "What happened?"

The matron's shark-like smile widened. "What makes you think you deserve to know?"

Pagan fought back a flush of shame. She didn't deserve anything. She knew that. She'd earned a fate far worse than two years locked up in Lighthouse. But ever since the night she drove her cherry-red Corvette off Mulholland Drive, killing her father and younger sister, a kind of claustrophobia had closed in. It wasn't a fear of enclosed spaces. More like a need to know she had a way out of any situation. As soon as the judge had sentenced her to reform school, the remorseless itch had taken hold. Any situation she couldn't extricate herself from felt like the end of the world.

She'd tried to be good her first few months in Lighthouse. She'd stuffed down her anxiety, bitten her nails, and annoyed Mercedes by constantly pacing their tiny room like a lion in the zoo. But inevitably the necessity to get the hell out, to prove she had a choice, had become unbearable.

So she'd started planning her escape, and Mercedes had asked to come along. Their careful, months-long strategizing had soothed Pagan's anxiety, but their climb over the barbed wire fence had been interrupted by Miss Edwards's inmate enforcers. By the time those girls had sauntered up, Pagan had made it to the other side of the wire. Mercedes had not.

Mercedes had ordered Pagan to go, but then Susan Mahoney pulled a knife. No way would Pagan have left her best—her only—friend behind to face that alone. She'd climbed back over the fence and dropped into the fray only to be pummeled nearly unconscious by Phyllis Lawson and Grace Lopez.

That didn't matter. What mattered was that Susan had viciously stabbed Mercedes in the shoulder with her stiletto just before the guard rushed in, gun drawn. Pagan had heard nothing about her friend's condition since they'd carried her away, trailing blood.

"You'll be here in solitary for two weeks," Miss Edwards said, her beady eyes happily taking in Pagan's shaking hands. "One meal a day. If Mercedes survives, she'll get the same. I've asked the judge to review both your cases. He could decide to extend your sentences past your eighteenth birthdays. I hope you're both eager to see how they deal with escape attempts from adult prison."

That was enough to shred Pagan's attempt at detachment. "They can't do that! It was my fault, not Mercedes's—"

Miss Edwards didn't let her finish. "You may have noticed," she said, backing toward the door, where a guard waited in case Pagan got any ideas, "I had them take away your shoelaces, your girdle, and your belt."

Pagan had noticed, and she knew why. "I'd never try to kill myself," she scoffed.

Miss Edwards's shiny upper lip curled in disbelief. "Why not? Your mother did it and didn't even leave a note."

Pain ripped through Pagan as if Miss Edwards had stabbed her perfectly manicured nails into Pagan's chest and pulled out her heart. It took all of Pagan's training as an actor to keep her face blank.

Obviously, the matron of Lighthouse had never lost anyone she cared about to suicide or she would've known that, once it happened to you, you would never go down that road yourself. It led only to darkness. Not an expansive velvet black like the sky at night. No, this was a suffocating, heavy dark, a nauseating mass that dragged you down to drown. Once that weight landed on you, all you could do was to keep holding it up, hoping it wouldn't touch anyone else.

The weight clouded her mind again as the door locked behind Miss Edwards. The matron had taken the single bare lightbulb with her and left Pagan with only the line of light slithering under the door. Pagan fixed her eyes on it as she lay down and clenched her fists against the smothering black, the pain in her head, and her racking worry about Mercedes.

She woke up sometime later knowing only one thing. She was getting out.

Her headache had dimmed, and Miss Edwards had not thought to confiscate Pagan's bobby pins. There was no time like now, now, now. Remembering how Mercedes had showed her to bend the pins into a tension wrench and pick, she got busy with the lock.

Luckily, because the solitary cells had once been closets, there was a keyhole on her side of the door that she could rake. Once out of this room, she could sneak into the parking lot and maybe crawl into the trunk or backseat of a car. Outside the walls she could find the hospital where they'd taken Mercedes.

She focused on the lock, ear to the door. The tension wrench gave a bit to the right, so she slid the pick in and began tapping the pins in the lock. There. That one. Push *that* one down and—

A key was shoved in from the other side, pushing her pick out of the cylinder. It dropped to the floor.

No time to be terrified. She felt the floor frantically for the pin and palmed it as the door opened to reveal the rigid form of Miss Edwards, silhouetted against a shaft of morning light.

So. The night had passed.

The narrow crimson lips turned up in a tight smile as the small glittering eyes took in Pagan's flushed cheeks and the curl of her fingers as her hands slid behind her back. Quick as Pagan had tried to look nonchalant, wreathing her face in habitual resentment, Miss Edwards was no fool.

"Your right hand, please." She held out French-manicured fingers.

Trying to hide or drop the pins would only delay the inevitable. Pagan all but threw them into Miss Edwards's palm and braced herself.

The painted mouth curled. Miss Edwards put the pins in her pocket and pulled out a pack of Lucky Strikes and her favorite lighter, a silver Zippo engraved with the Ace of Hearts in red. The "students" at Lighthouse weren't allowed to smoke, and Miss Edwards took pleasure in flaunting her privilege in front of them. She drew out a cigarette, put it between her lips, and formed words around it. "Adult prison's too good for you."

"Would you be sad to see me go?" Pagan was pleased at the insouciance in her voice, because her knees were watery, her throat tight. Every fiber in her wanted to demand how Mercedes was doing, but she'd rather die than endure another smug, withholding smile.

Miss Edwards had just had her hair done, the roots retouched to a glowing blond much like the fashionable color Pagan's had once been. She was wearing eyeliner today, winged out at the corners like Marilyn Monroe. "It's always a tragedy when a young life takes the wrong turn." She flicked the Zippo and lit her cigarette. "Which brings me to why I'm here. You have visitors." She exhaled the smoke into Pagan's face.

Those last three words turned Pagan's next smart remark

into something like a hiccup. She struggled to keep her face blank. Only immediate family members were allowed to visit "students" at Lighthouse.

"I killed all that was left of my family." Her voice was thicker than she liked. The smoke smelled like her old life, and she tried not to suck it in with a deep, appreciative breath. "Are you making an exception for second cousins once removed?"

Miss Edwards's heavy eyelids lowered in a look of self-satisfaction that made Pagan's hands curl into fists. "These men have Judge Tennison's permission to see you," she said. "I sent my request in to him yesterday to reconsider your sentence. Perhaps this has something to do with that. Come." She pocketed the Zippo and click-clicked down the hallway without looking back.

Pagan followed slowly through the still-open door into what the students called the Haunted Hallway. Its adobe walls stretched thirty feet down then turned right, but through some trick of acoustics if you stood at this end you could hear the slightest whisper taking place around the corner another thirty feet, where the hallway ended near Miss Edwards's office and the stairway descended to the first floor. If a girl desperately needed to hear word of the outside world, she'd volunteer to mop this hallway to try and catch a sentence or two as it bounced up the stairs, passed the office, and rebounded around the corner.

Pagan hurried after Miss Edwards, using her fingers to comb her dry, overgrown hair into a semblance of neatness, stuffing down a desire to plead for more information. The hallway stretched on forever. The walls around her were scuffed gray, the barred windows allowing in brief glimpses of azure sky, a dusty green palm frond swaying in the breeze. Nine months here had been an eternity. Prison would be infinitely worse.

She tried to swallow, but it was as if the bent bobby pin had lodged in her throat. She'd figured on a beating, bread and water, some solitary at worst. And she'd gotten exactly that.

But what if that was just the beginning of her punishment? The escape attempt had happened Friday night. This was Sunday morning. Surely judges didn't come in on the weekends to change the terms of a juvenile's sentence.

But maybe what was about to happen was justice. Pagan had done far worse things than try to escape a reformatory. Maybe she deserved what she was about to get.

Miss Edwards stopped at her office door, her mouth turning ever downward as she laid one hand on the knob.

"Just because I'm allowing this doesn't mean you're special," Miss Edwards said. Her resentful tone set off further warnings in Pagan's busy brain. Why was the matron frustrated now instead of triumphant? "You're thinking that you're better than me, aren't you? You still think you're a movie star. You're famous. You're somebody."

"I killed my father and sister." Pagan's voice was flat. "So the last thing I could ever feel is that I'm better than anyone. Even you."

Miss Edwards's frown deepened. Effort flickered between her painted eyebrows as she tried to figure out how a statement of such humility could come out sounding like an insult. Pagan was good at ambiguity; it was part of what had made her such a good actress. In the past nine months, that skill had proven vital. That and Mercedes's friendship.

Miss Edwards turned the knob. Pagan squared her shoulders and lifted her chin, the way she always had before auditions, trips down the red carpet, or courtroom entrances. Her mother would have approved. Even if facing your own execution, best to meet it with a serene smile and excellent posture.

The doorknob under Miss Edwards's hand jerked back. She lost her grip and grabbed the door frame to stop herself from falling. A fresh cloud of gray-blue cigarette smoke wafted over them from the room beyond.

"Do come in." The low, masculine voice was not one Pagan recognized. A shaft of sunlight filtered through the smoke, blinding her, until a slender young man in an exquisitely cut black suit and narrow tie moved forward. He was tall and wore no hat, his dark hair slicked back, one unruly lock spiking over his forehead. He stood with one hand on the door, as relaxed as if he were welcoming them into his own home.

Only his eyes were turbulent, a dark blue. They swept over Pagan with speculative calculation and something darker she couldn't identify. Goose bumps ran up her arms.

She was staring at his mouth and pulled her gaze up, shaking off a sudden blankness in her thoughts. It had been nine months since she'd seen a man other than the gatehouse guard, but she couldn't let that distract her. The crews on her movie sets had called her One-Take Jones in the early days because of her composure and professionalism. That was before she'd started drinking. Now that she was sober, that girl was still inside her, somewhere.

"The notorious Pagan Jones." The dark-haired young man held out his hand. "My name is Devin Black."

She slid her hand into his. It was warm, the grip firm. "I'd say it was a pleasure, Mister Black, but I don't like lying to strangers."

Amusement curved one corner of his mouth. He kept hold of her and leaned in, his voice soft. "Lies are best saved for those we love."

Her heart hammered once, twice. At this range his eyes glittered like shards of stained glass shaded from indigo to azure. They locked on to her, taking her in.

He pulled away. The moment might never have happened but for the electricity still prickling over her skin.

He cast his indifferent gaze at Miss Edwards, who was hovering like a storm cloud. "That will be all. Thank you."

Dismissed from her own office, Miss Edwards puffed out her narrow chest as if about to spew fire. But Devin Black was already ushering Pagan inside. The door clicked shut behind them.

DESPERATE FORMER MOVIE STAR OFFERED SHADY DEAL

Mystery Man Knows More Than He Should

"Here's a familiar face." Devin Black pulled out a seat for Pagan facing the small well-dressed man with gray, thinning hair who occupied Miss Edwards's imposing black leather chair. He was the one generating all the smoke, puffing nervously on a cigarette and tapping the ash into a coffee cup.

Pagan stared and didn't sit. This was no hearing. She had no idea what this was. "Jerry?"

Jerry Allenberg stood, which didn't add much to his height, and stubbed out the cigarette with agitated little shoves. "Pagan. It's been a long time. Please, have a seat. I've got something important to talk to you about."

Pagan lifted her chin to stand taller. "So you've come to visit me after all. Tell Satan it's time to put on the cashmere coat and mittens."

Jerry stroked his fedora, which sat soft and gray as a cat on the desk. "You're my client."

"Former client." Anger surged as Pagan narrowed her eyes at him. "I got the notice of termination from the agency, Jerry. That was one piece of mail they made sure I received while in custody."

"I'm sorry I couldn't be there for your trial." Jerry took another cigarette out of a gold case and tapped it on the desk, feeling his pocket for a lighter. "And I'm sorry about that notice. It wasn't kind."

"No, but it's what big Hollywood agents do when their clients kill people, right?" Pagan watched as Devin Black leaned in with a silver lighter to ignite Jerry's cigarette. He flicked the lid shut on the flame, and Pagan caught a glimpse of red on one side. As he pocketed it, the design became clear—a silver Zippo lighter with the Ace of Hearts engraved in red.

He couldn't possibly have the same exact lighter as Miss Edwards. Which meant…

Her gaze flew to his face. He caught the movement and locked eyes with her. That corner of his mouth was curving up again, only now he looked like a mischievous boy who'd gotten away with something.

Who *was* this guy? Pagan hadn't even seen him come close to Miss Edwards, so how the hell had he gotten ahold of the lighter Pagan had seen her deposit in her skirt pocket just moments before?

"I never meant to hurt you, Pagan," Jerry was saying. His lips trembled slightly as he drew on the cigarette. "It was the shareholders who insisted on letting you go. Not me."

Pagan forced herself to look back at her former agent. He was a part of this, too. But somehow she thought he didn't quite know who he was dealing with in Devin Black. Either way, something about the situation was making him sweat. "You look nervous, Jerry. Don't worry. I didn't bring my shiv."

Jerry exhaled a short laugh in a gust of smoke. "I see they haven't ironed the smart aleck out of you yet, kid."

Pagan's legs were wobblier than they should have been. Something beneath her feet was shifting. She didn't know what it was yet, but it was big. She slid down into the hard chair facing Jerry. "I'm the bad influence here. The others are just thieves and truants, not killers."

"What happened to you was an accident." Jerry took the cigarette out of his mouth with his index finger and thumb, smoke trickling from his nose. "You were a child, a girl who lost her mother in an unimaginable way. We all should have seen it coming a lot sooner."

Pagan had heard those words before. "Instead you gave me a brand-new Corvette for my sixteenth birthday, and I used it to drive Daddy and Ava off a cliff. Thanks a lot, Jerry."

Jerry looked up sharply, the veneer of concern falling away. "You can't blame me for what happened. I didn't stick the bottle of vodka in your hand—"

"Jerry." Devin's low voice was a warning.

Jerry shut his mouth, lips tight. He stubbed out the second cigarette next to the first one like he was smashing a cockroach.

Pagan looked back and forth between the two men. Jerry was one of the most powerful men in Hollywood. Nobody talked to him that way, yet Devin Black had just gotten away with it.

Pagan cocked her head toward Devin. "Who is this character, Jerry? His suit's nicer than yours, so he can't be your new assistant."

Jerry cast a sideways look at Devin and felt for his cigarette case again. "He works for the studio."

"Nobody from any studio would interrupt Jerry Allenberg like that and still have a job five minutes later." When Devin shrugged and didn't reply, she asked, "What have you got on him?"

Devin shoved himself away from the wall, picked up Jerry's cigarette case off the desk, took out a cigarette, and offered it to Pagan. "What I have on Jerry, Miss Jones, is a deal for you that's going to make you both a lot of money. He wants you back as a client, because the studio needs you to star in Bennie Wexler's new comedy."

Astonishment bloomed through Pagan, followed by relief. Her fears of someone coming to put her in prison weren't going to happen. At least not yet. This was some Hollywood scam. But why torment her with an impossible scenario?

She ignored the offered cigarette. "Bennie Wexler hates me. Before that he hated my mother. He kicked her off the set of *Anne of Green Gables*. The man won a statue for Best Director, but you're saying he's going to direct his next movie—" she spread her hands wide, taking in all the beige-walled, barred-windowed dreariness around her "—here? Because, in case you forgot, this is my vacation home for the next year and a half."

"The movie shoots in West Berlin." Jerry rested one blunt-fingered hand on a pile of paper in front of him. "The judge has agreed to let you out of here, if you sign this contract to do the film and agree to a court-appointed guardian."

Pagan lowered her lashes to mask her anger. "Jerry, Jerry. It isn't nice to tease."

"It's no joke." Jerry exhaled noisily, blowing the smoke upward. "The studio really wants you on this project." He glanced at Devin Black, who nodded, as if in approval. "You're still under contract to them. I don't know who pulled the strings, but if you agree to do the movie under the conditions spelled out here, Judge Tennison will grant your parole. It's a supporting role, but it's good. It's funny, and it suits you. Bennie starts rehearsal in Berlin in three days, so be a good girl and say yes now."

Nothing he was saying allayed her suspicions, and she hadn't been a good girl for years. "Three days? What happened—did the original actress get killed or something?"

"Worse. Pregnant." Jerry reached under the contract to

pull out about a hundred pages held together with brass fasteners. "You'll like the script. Bennie's usual mixture of farce and heart. You'll play the teenage daughter of an American businessman living in West Berlin who falls in love with a Communist from East Berlin."

He laid the script in front of her. The cover read *Neither Here Nor There.* Written by Benjamin Wexler & I. S. Kopelson. Universal Pictures.

Pagan stared at the familiar logo, not blinking. This was actually happening. It made no sense. But it was real.

Jerry coughed, and she realized a long silence had elapsed. She pursed her lips in cool consideration, even though her blood was beating hard through her veins. "So, you're saying that after the movie is over, I won't have to come back to Lighthouse?"

Jerry's chest rattled with another cough. "After the shoot you'll have to report weekly to a parole officer until you turn eighteen. But you'll be free."

Pagan erupted out of her chair with such force that Jerry flinched back and Devin Black straightened from where he was slouching against the wall. She paced to the door and back and halted, then grabbed on to her chair. She didn't like that she needed something to steady herself, but after so long in confinement, after worrying about Mercedes, and thinking they were going to put her in a real prison, the prospect of imminent freedom was the most terrifying thing of all.

The last time she'd truly been a part of the real world had been the worst time of her life. It made solitary seem like a cozy nest.

"Judge Tennison called me a menace to society in front of every reporter in town." Her voice was hoarse. She cleared her throat. "He said Hollywood was a festering pit of sin, and he cast me as lead sinner. Why would he give a damn what the studio wants and let me out?"

Jerry shrugged, casting another sideways look at Devin. "Everyone has a price, even a judge. Or maybe he saw the light. We'll never know for sure."

"Beyond that," she went on, "the whole world knows I'm a disgrace. Tabloids make up lurid stories of my exploits behind bars. Why would a studio risk giving a decent role in an award-winning director's next big movie to me?"

Jerry shook his head. "A young lady accepts that the men in her life know what's best for her. I'm the closest thing you have to a father—"

He didn't get to finish because Devin Black cut in, his voice casual. "Haven't you heard? Bad publicity sells even more movie tickets than good publicity. People are curious. With you in the movie, it's a guaranteed blockbuster."

He wasn't wrong, but she knew better than to trust him. Pagan gave him a cold smile. "And why is it, I ask myself, that Jerry Allenberg is taking orders from a kid in a Savile Row suit who's young enough to be in college, maybe even high school? I'm sorry, Mister Black. But I'm not signing anything until my lawyer looks it over."

Devin Black's eyes danced over her in a way that made her conscious of the uneven neckline of her uniform, of her sagging stockings and scuffed sneakers. "I hear you're in solitary confinement for two weeks because you and your roommate nearly escaped."

At the mention of Mercedes all her assumed coolness fell away. "Do you know how she is?" Her voice shook. "Did she make it?"

"Make it?" Devin asked, his voice sharpening into a crisp, almost-British tone. "You mean they didn't tell you?" He shot a blazing look at the door, behind which, no doubt, Miss Edwards still waited, then placed a warm hand on Pagan's upper arm. "Miss Duran is doing well and is out of the hospital. They brought her back to the infirmary here this morning."

Relief washed over Pagan, so acute, so powerful that she had to blindly find the chair and sit again. "Thank God, thank God," she said under her breath. It wasn't really a prayer. Or maybe it was.

"There's no need to worry about your roommate any longer," Devin said, stepping closer to her. Was he trying to reassure her some more? Or was he moving in for the kill? The contradictory signals were dizzying. "So, if you take this job, not only will you get out of here forever, but we'll make sure your friend gets the best of care, spends no time in solitary, and no extra time will be added to her sentence. You can give this to her." He picked up Jerry's gold cigarette case and handed it over. Jerry didn't protest, and it sat heavy in her hand. "If you say no, you'll go back to solitary and what happens to Miss Duran is anyone's guess."

Pagan regarded him steadily. He wanted her dizzy—to keep her off balance, and to get what he wanted. She took his long-fingered hand and pressed the cigarette holder back into his palm. "In that case, my answer is definitely no."

Devin looked down at the shiny metal, lips curling ruefully. "Definitely no?"

Pagan nodded. "Definitely." It hurt to refuse. But if he was trying to extort her into cooperating, the whole situation had to be too good to be true. She had a funny feeling she'd be safer getting beaten by Miss Edwards here at Lighthouse. She'd learned that if you gave in to a threat, all you'd done was ensure more threats down the road.

Devin's eyes were thoughtful. "You're not the only one to ever make a mistake, you know."

She studied him. Where was this going? More misdirection? "Believe me, I know," she said. "I live with a hundred and fifteen mistake-prone teenage girls."

Devin went on as if she hadn't spoken. "Make a big enough mistake early in life and it can destroy everything," His words were like Susan Mahoney's stiletto, slicing into her, conjuring up her own countless errors.

But he wasn't looking at her. His eyes were staring off at some faraway place, somewhere raw, somewhere that made him ache. "Ruin enough lives and you'll ruin yours."

It sounded personal. What lives had Devin Black ruined? Or was this another cunning attempt to pull her in?

"But if you're very lucky, sometimes, someone offers you a second chance." He turned back to her, smiling. "And if you're smart enough to take that chance, it's just possible that the thing you long for most, that thing you crave more than anything, will happen."

Pagan sat very still, not wanting to give away how his words affected her. She couldn't put a name to it, but he'd touched a place inside her she hadn't known was there. "Tell me, Mister Black," she said. "What do I crave more than anything?"

"Redemption." His voice pulsed with a passion that echoed in her mind. "This is your chance."

Redemption. That was so far from possible that it hadn't even occurred to her. She searched the riotous mess in her brain, the thousand conflicting feelings and thoughts that only alcohol had ever silenced.

In A.A. they called it *recovery.* That was a much more manageable word. *Redemption,* with its vaguely religious overtones, promised a slate wiped clean, a complete deliverance that was too much to hope for. She couldn't hang on to that, because it would never, *could* never happen, no matter what strange hunger for it the complicated Devin Black seemed to have.

"Sounds more like a chance to be bullied and blackmailed." She shook her head with finality. "Thanks, but no thanks."

"I see." Devin swallowed hard. Was that regret in his eyes?

But then he swiveled with sudden grace, scooped up the contract and script on the desk, and dumped them into a sleek briefcase. "Let's go, Jerry."

Puzzlement crossed Jerry's face as Devin snapped the briefcase closed. "But you said—"

"Pagan Jones can't take a chance," Devin interrupted, sliding the briefcase off the desk. "After all she's been through, I understand." He glanced at Pagan, who was glaring at him. "Wasn't your mother born in Berlin?"

Her scowl became uncertain. "What? Yes. After my grandfather died, my grandmother moved to California with Mom when she was around two."

"Berlin's a strange place these days," Devin said. "Divided between Communist and capitalist, with thousands of East Germans fleeing across the border to the West every day. The rumors are that the East Germans won't wait much longer to do something drastic. I thought you might want to see where your mother was born while you're shooting the movie, find your grandparents' former home, before everything changes. By the time you get out of this place, it may be too late."

The knuckles of Pagan's hands, gripping each other, were white. "You think something big's going to happen over there?"

Jerry drummed the desk with his fingers. "In June, the leader of East Germany said he has no intention of building a wall."

Devin gave him a knowing look. "Walter Ulbricht studied politics under Joseph Stalin. Trustworthy he is not. Every other part of East Germany is cut off from the West. And the East Germans have just completed construction of a rail line that completely circumvents Berlin. How long can they continue to allow their best-educated citizens to flee?"

Pagan was only half listening as Jerry asked another question. Whether by accident or design, Devin Black had touched on the only real mystery left in her life. She knew all too well why Daddy and Ava were dead. But when Mama took her own life, she hadn't left a note. She'd never mentioned suicide and had shown no signs of depression. Up to the end she'd been the same: cheerfully in charge; planning the next move in Pagan's career; pushing Ava to practice her piano three hours a day; organizing the next fund-raiser for the German-American Heritage League.

So every day since she'd died, Pagan still asked the question: Why? Why had Mama abandoned them? Every day the wound reopened, fresh and painful as the moment it had happened.

After Mama was gone, movies and photo shoots had kept Pagan busy. She had even fallen in love. But only alcohol had closed up the wound. For a little while, at least.

Psychiatrists had told her that her mother's suicide wasn't her fault. They said it had nothing to do with her. But how could they know that for sure? They hadn't spent long hours on a movie set watching Mama, a frustrated actress, act out Pagan's dialogue for her when she messed up a line. They hadn't heard Eva and Arthur Jones arguing late into the night about how Pagan's latest bump in salary might not cover that month's bills. Everything—the big house in the hills, Ava's private school, Mama's designer clothes, Daddy's cars—they all would continue to exist only so long as Pagan was perfect.

Pagan knew all too well that she was nothing but a collection of flaws, a rich stew of defects, a ratatouille of failings and weakness. And in lieu of another explanation, she couldn't help thinking that maybe that's why it had all come crashing down and Mama had died.

Maybe.

Maybe not. The shrinks didn't understand how the uncertainty about *why* Mama had wanted to die gnawed at Pagan. If Pagan could find the answer to that question, she might truly come to understand that this one thing, at least, was not her fault.

Maybe that answer lay in the place Mama was born. Berlin.

Now here was a chance, not just to get out of this horrible place, to be free, but to explore an unknown corner of Eva Jones's life. A chance that would not come again.

"I'll do it." The words split open something that had long been closed inside her. She stayed very still, hoping she wouldn't cry.

The two men, in mid-conversation, stopped speaking. Devin Black's long-lashed eyes held a knowing look that should have bothered her, but didn't.

He'd succeeded in manipulating her this time. But it didn't matter, not in the long run. What was important was that soon she'd be able to hunt down the answers she needed, whether they were in Berlin or somewhere else.

"I said, I'll do it." She gave them her best *I'm practicing patience* look.

With a flourish, Devin put the briefcase on the desk and unsnapped the clasps.

Jerry took out the contract and laid it in front of Pagan. "Are you sure?"

Devin Black shot him a suppressing look. "An excellent choice, Miss Jones. One I'm sure you won't regret."

She took hold of Miss Edwards's best fountain pen. "Worry about your own regrets, Mister Black. How soon do I get to see Mercedes?"

Devin peeled back the top pages of the contract to show her the signature line. "Why not immediately? Then we'll send a car for you at four o'clock this afternoon. You'll spend the night in your own home. Tomorrow you'll fly to Berlin."

"Very well." Her mother had often used that phrase, and Pagan enjoyed the way it sounded coming from her own lips. She ran her eyes over the last page of the contract. It looked like standard language, except for a clause about her being on parole and having *a court-appointed guardian with all the power of a parent on hand during the film shoot and thereafter at the court's discretion.*

"My father's lawyer is going to be at the film shoot?" she asked. At their confused looks, she added, "He's my court-appointed guardian, and it says here—"

"A new guardian will be appointed," Devin said.

She looked back and forth between them. "Who?"

"You'll be the first—or the second—to know," Jerry said.

Which probably meant it would be someone the studio approved of, to keep an eye on their investment. That chafed, but given her history it was hard to blame them. She leaned down and signed her name. Devin Black's eyes followed her hand, watching as the jagged lines of her signature formed.

"Never thought anyone would ask me to sign a contract again," she said. "The world is a very strange place."

"You have no idea." Jerry stuffed the contract into the briefcase. "Go pack your things."

She went to the door and turned. "What if I'd put on weight?" she asked. "Or sprouted a million pimples? Or cut off all my hair?"

Jerry darted a glance at Devin Black. "Enquiries were made."

She nodded. Of course. "I imagine Miss Edwards is very bribable."

"You'll learn that anyone can be made to do just about anything," Jerry said, grabbing his hat with an angry swipe.

"You're walking back into a different world than the one you left nine months ago." Devin Black slid himself between her and the door so that he could open it for her, as if they were coming to the end of a formal date rather than an exercise in blackmail. "Have you kept up on the news? There's a new president, a new attitude, and new fears."

Pagan took a few steps into the hallway, her heart lifting. She'd be leaving this place today. It was really happening.

A shiver overtook her and she wrapped her arms around herself to make it stop. She couldn't tell if she was thrilled or terrified.

Miss Edwards waited just down the hall, bony arms crossed. Pagan ignored her and tilted her head up at Devin Black. "I keep up on the news that matters, Mister Black, thanks to Ed Sullivan reruns and old copies of *Photoplay*. Elizabeth Taylor's going to be Cleopatra, the new Dior suit dresses are divine, and everyone's twisting again with Chubby Checker." She flashed him a genuine smile. Warmth was spreading through her, a feeling perilously close to happiness. "Is every hit song getting a sequel now?"

Devin Black loosed the first spontaneous grin she'd seen from him. "Why not? I can't wait to hear 'Cathy's Clown Gets a Job under the Big Top.'"

Caught by surprise, Pagan laughed. Devin's smile widened, lighting up his face and the whole dreary hallway, a thousand times more genuine and charming than his earlier studied elegance.

"How about 'Fallen Teen Angel'?" Pagan said. "That could be my theme song."

Devin loosed a hoot of laughter, nodding at her knowingly, as if to say *touché*.

"I think," Miss Edwards's icy voice cut in, "I'd better get you back to solitary, young lady."

"That won't be necessary, Miss Edwards." Devin's grin soured into something formidable as he turned to her. The playful boy vanished behind the man's sharp gaze. "Miss Jones will be going to the infirmary immediately to see Miss Duran, where they will be allowed to converse in private for at least an hour."

The color drained from Miss Edwards's face. "Oh, I… Is Mercedes back? I hadn't heard."

"You know very well she's been here since last night," Devin said. "It's a shame you didn't bother to inform her worried roommate. I'm sure the judge will find that detail of my visit quite illuminating."

Miss Edwards's countenance became positively chalky. "No need for that, Mister Black, I'm sure. I've been and will be happy to abide by the judge's orders, of course. But I'm a busy woman. I can't be expected to—"

"When Miss Duran is released from the infirmary," Devin said, in tones that brooked no further discussion, "she is to be allowed all of her normal privileges. Her attackers are being removed to a more appropriate facility as we speak. If we hear of any further injury to or issue with Miss Duran, we will take further action." He paused. "Action you may not appreciate."

How could a mere studio executive know these things and wield such power? Still, it did Pagan's heart good to see fright fill Miss Edwards's perfectly lined eyes, to watch the lips in their expensive red lipstick press themselves together as if pushing back a desire to plead or to protest. "I understand," the matron said.

Devin's smile was chilly. "Meanwhile, Miss Jones will leave this facility for good at four o'clock this afternoon. See to it her things are ready when the car arrives."

Miss Edwards opened her mouth, but Devin Black simply

stared at her, and the woman shut her lips again. It was like magic.

He turned to Pagan and took her hand again to shake it. "The studio will make all the arrangements. Welcome back, Miss Jones."

She pressed his strong fingers with her own firmly. "Thank you." She slid her eyes to Miss Edwards. "For everything."

He held her hand for a long moment. Her heart was hammering, but that didn't mean anything. She was just out of practice when it came to boys. Well, she'd mend that soon enough. Carefully, maintaining composure, she removed her hand and walked out of the office, into the hallway.

"Wish me luck, Jerry," Pagan said over her shoulder. "I'll do the same for you."

"Good luck, Pagan," Jerry said, adding under his breath, "We're both going to need it."

The hallway. As she moved down it after the erect form of the headmistress, Pagan slowed, remembering how the strange acoustics of the bent corridor sent sounds bouncing from one end to the other. If she hovered in the sweet spot for a moment, she might catch some of Jerry and Devin's private conversation.

They were speaking now, but she couldn't distinguish the words over her own footsteps and Miss Edwards's. Miss Edwards, at least, was in front, her back to Pagan, and pulling away rapidly. Pagan slackened her pace and softened her footfalls.

"You're not as cool a customer as I thought, Jerry." That was Devin. He sounded different. More clipped, or something. It was hard to tell from the hallway echo. "Next time, don't smoke so much."

"Next time?" Jerry's voice got louder with alarm. "Why should there be a next time?"

Devin's voice moved farther away. He must be heading toward the stairs that led down to the first floor. "You never
know."

"Keep up!" Miss Edwards's command cut through her
thoughts. Pagan began walking again, straining to hear more.

Jerry was saying, peeved, "One drink and she could sink
the whole thing. And that girl has a lot of reasons to drink."

Pagan was nearing the next bend in the hallway, after which
she wouldn't be able to hear any more. Miss Edwards had already turned the corner, so Pagan dropped to one knee and
slowly tied her sneaker laces.

"Go home, Jerry." Devin Black's footsteps trotted lightly
down the stairs, nearly out of range. "We got what we wanted."

His steps faded into nothing. A moment of silence.

"Who," Jerry asked of the empty echoes, "is we?"

TEEN JAILBIRD'S FIRST TASTE OF FREEDOM IS BITTERSWEET

But Reunion with Best Friend Is Simply Sweet

Mercedes was asleep when Pagan got to the infirmary, so she sat down quietly next to the bed and stared at the wad of bandages wrapped around her friend's shoulder.

That was where Susan Mahoney's stiletto had slid into Mercedes. It had made a sickeningly slick noise as she'd yanked out the thin, shiny blade. Blood had dripped from the knife's tip as Susan had poised it over Mercedes's throat.

Stop thinking about that, stop! The important thing was that Susan hadn't succeeded in finishing off Mercedes. She was going to be okay.

Pagan focused on her friend's relaxed left hand, studying the smooth brown skin and clear nails. They were cut short, but not too short. Pagan had begun to keep hers the same length after Mercedes had explained that you needed enough nail to effectively rake your enemy's face or neck to draw blood. But let the nails grow too long, and they'd bend back or snap during a fight, which not only hurt but might distract you at a crucial moment.

Not exactly something Pagan's manicurist had chatted about, back in the day. Life in Lighthouse had been horrible, but it had taught her a few things Hollywood couldn't. Not just how to put your body weight into a punch or how to choke down canned meat for dinner, but things like how to know when someone meant you harm, and how stay in the moment. Mercedes had impressed upon her that if you let too many thoughts of the past or fears of the future cloud your thoughts, you might not survive the present.

All those lessons might come in handy if she was going back into the real world.

If she was going to stay sober.

Mercedes's eyelids fluttered and snapped open. Like Pagan, she slept lightly and woke all at once. It was one of the many things they'd been surprised to find they had in common.

"Hey," said Pagan. She wanted to squeeze Mercedes's hand, but she refrained. M didn't care for sentimental words or physical demonstrations of affection. "You're doing great."

The brown eyes studied her, crinkling a little at the corners. "Thanks," Mercedes said. Her normally smooth, deep voice was scratchy but calm. "For saving my life."

Oh, right. Pagan had so thoroughly avoided thinking about how Susan Mahoney had almost succeeded in stabbing Mercedes a second time, how the big redhead had aimed for the throat, that she had also blanked out how she herself had stopped it. Her vision had narrowed down to the freckled hand holding that stiletto, and a strange conviction had taken over.

Not this time.

Somehow, despite her own injuries, Pagan had fought her way to her feet and propelled herself into Susan, tearing her off Mercedes before Pagan had blacked out.

"Thanks for not dying," Pagan said, her voice hoarse but steady.

Mercedes let out the barest breath of a laugh. "Anytime." Her gaze traveled over Pagan and the room they were in, empty except for the bed and some medical equipment. "It's not like the witch to lock us in here together."

"We're not locked in," Pagan said. "We're free. Well, free of solitary anyway." As Mercedes listened, frowning, Pagan told her all that had happened that morning, stumbling a little as she tried to convey the bizarre dynamic between Devin Black and Jerry Allenberg.

"I'm hoping I can call you from Berlin," she said. "So if Miss Edwards tries to retaliate against you at all, you let me know."

"I'll be fine." Mercedes was dismissive. "It's your situation that's radioactive, so you better call me."

"It's just a movie shoot," Pagan said, sounding as casual as she could. "It's not life and death."

Mercedes slanted her eyes at Pagan in her best *who are you kidding* look. "First thing, you go to one of those meetings."

"A.A." Pagan shifted uneasily on the bed. "Yeah."

"Yeah?" Mercedes raised her eyebrows. "You promise me you'll go?"

Pagan waved one hand airily. "I'm fine, really."

Mercedes's brown eyes took on an implacable look. "Promise me you'll go to a meeting."

Pagan looked at her best friend, her only friend, and said reluctantly, "If there's time, and if they have meetings in Berlin, I'll go."

"If, if!" Mercedes made a tsking sound with her tongue. "Just go."

"Okay, okay!" Pagan threw up her hands. "Can I hang out here with you for a bit longer before I leave, at least?"

Mercedes relaxed. "Who's going to tell me crazy stories about the guests on *Ed Sullivan* after you're gone?"

"You won't need *Ed Sullivan*," Pagan said. "I'm going to

send you every single brand-new tabloid magazine I can lay my hands on."

"Coolsville," Mercedes said, looking sly. "I can read what they're saying about you."

The tiny windowless room they'd shared felt so empty without Mercedes. Miss Edwards had brought Pagan the suit she'd worn the day she walked into Lighthouse, but it was now too big in the chest and the hips. Prison was apparently an excellent dieting tool.

Now the suit looked like something another girl would wear. Pagan wasn't sure who that girl was—a spoiled drunk movie star or a sad orphan going off to juvenile detention—but she wasn't either of those people anymore, and the outfit was all wrong. After they allowed her to shower, she folded up the suit and her old white gloves and left them behind for Mercedes to trade, donning her saggy garters, stockings, and scuffed flat shoes under the scratchy gray Lighthouse uniform for the last time.

She didn't take anything else with her. As Miss Edwards clomped angrily in front of her toward the front door, Pagan paused to listen to the voices of the girls in the distant classroom, now reciting geometry proofs. Their chant faded behind her as she walked out the double doors and the sunshine hit her face.

All the snappy last words she had prepared to say to Miss Edwards fled her brain the moment she gazed up at the azure sky. Hot, dry August air swept through her hair. After nine long months, she was free.

At the bottom of the steps lurked a long black limousine with fins like a shark. Leaning against it with the passenger door open beside him was Devin Black.

He pulled the door open wider. "Ready to go home?"

Home. Without a family waiting for her, she didn't know what that meant anymore.

In a blink everything seemed oppressive—the heat; the hard yellow light; the empty, waiting house that still held Ava's stuffed animals and Daddy's golf clubs.

And the car. It wasn't remotely red or a convertible, but the thought of getting in it made her queasy. Nine months since the accident, and the memories were waiting there, circling like vultures.

"What are you waiting for? You can't stay here." Miss Edwards's voice sliced through the dread. "Even if you're not ready to go."

Pagan glanced over her shoulder. Something about Miss Edwards's condescending smirk made the big scary world out there a lot more appealing. "Thanks ever so much for all your kindness." She bestowed a wide, fake smile on the woman. "I'll be sure to mention you in my first magazine interview."

Miss Edwards's face froze. Knowing that she probably looked more like a war refugee than a movie star in her stained uniform and ponytail, Pagan nonetheless did her best model sashay down the steps. The dark depths of the car swallowed her. She didn't look back as Devin got in after her and slammed the door.

Inside it was air-conditioned. She sank back into the smooth, deeply cushioned black leather seats as the driver stepped on the accelerator and they glided away. The limo's velvety bounce was nothing like the low-down rumble of her Corvette, and she began to relax. Low storefronts and empty, fenced yards flashed past as they headed west. She was free.

Or was she? The unreadable expression on Devin Black's face wasn't reassuring.

"Does the car bring back bad memories?" he asked, his voice mild.

"The car?" Dang, he was perceptive. She'd have to be careful around him. "It's no big deal. I'm cool."

He leaned forward and opened a small cabinet set into the partition between them and the driver. "Something to drink?"

She stared at the tiny refrigerator. The luxury of it being here, inside a car, reminded her of her old life. Limousines, movie premieres, and fridges full of alcohol. She'd never appreciated it, or feared it, the way she did now. "Got a Coke?"

"Sure." He grabbed a bottle and used an opener to remove the cap. She took it and sipped, her first taste of Coke in months. It was delicious and icy cold.

Devin reached into the breast pocket of his coat and pulled out a red-and-white pack of cigarettes. "Smoke?"

Winston. Her brand. This guy had done his homework. But why? She took the unopened pack, and the plastic wrap crackled in her hand. She could almost taste the smoothly acrid smoke and feel the filter of the cigarette between her index and middle fingers. All she needed was a martini in the other hand. Cigarettes and alcohol went together like drive-in movies and making out. One without the other just didn't make sense.

"Thanks," she said. "I'll save these for later."

He nodded and removed his sunglasses. In the cool dark of the limousine interior, his eyes were shadowed. "The plan was to take you directly home. We got permission from Judge Tennison to air out your house. The studio has sent over a designer with some clothes for you to choose from, with a hairdresser and manicurist on standby. Is there anywhere you'd like to go first?"

"You mean, like a record store?" She tucked the cigarettes away in her skirt pocket. Maybe one day she could face them without a drink. "I wouldn't mind seeing what's new from Ray Charles."

"We could do that if you like. Or is there some sort of organizational meeting you should attend?" When she looked at him blankly, he added, "The Friends of Bill W?"

Pagan nearly did a spit take with her Coke. "A.A?"

He regarded her, his face neutral, and said nothing.

Of course, he meant well, and she had promised Mercedes. So she'd go. She really would. But certainly not with Devin Black tagging along. She'd attended exactly two meetings of Alcoholics Anonymous between getting out on bail after her arrest and being sentenced to Lighthouse. Everyone there had been her parents' age or older. They'd tried so hard not to stare at her that she'd felt both conspicuous and invisible, like a ghost no one wants to admit is haunting their house.

"I'm fine," she said to Devin Black. It came out sharper than she intended.

"If you say so." He couldn't keep a slight tone of skepticism out of his voice. "You should know that the studio has assigned me to make sure you get to Berlin without incident."

Which meant he'd been assigned to keep her off the bottle. Resentment flared. "What I drink is none of the studio's—or your—business."

He didn't drop his gaze. "We have a considerable investment in you."

She stared right back. "You knew the risks when you brought me into this."

Unexpectedly, a slow smile spread over his face, as if he couldn't help it. "The risks. And the rewards."

He slid stormy blue eyes over her, and a warm flush stole up her neck to her cheeks. She hadn't blushed for a boy since the last time she'd seen Nicky, her first and only boyfriend. She'd forgotten how exciting it was to get flustered like that.

"The reward of seeing me look like a fugitive from a chain gang?" She made her voice tart, which helped the flush subside. It wasn't as if she could truly be attracted to Devin Black. He was a studio minder, her jailer. He might be useful for now, but he was her adversary.

"You're talented enough to make any role believable." At her incredulous look, he leaned forward and said, "No, really. I remember seeing that they'd cast you in *Leopard Bay* as a homeless street girl and I thought, *That will never work*. But it was an astonishing performance. For once they gave the right person the Golden Globe for most promising newcomer."

The role in *Leopard Bay* had been her most challenging, something to be proud of before her career devolved into fluff like *The Bashful Debutante* and *Beach Bound Beverly*. By then, she was too busy hanging on Nicky's arm and getting down to some serious drinking to worry about the quality of her movie roles. If they'd all been as rigorous as *Leopard Bay*, her drinking problem might have been noticed—by her father, by her fellow actors, by the studio. Maybe things would have been different.

"I was more excited about getting the BAFTA," she said. "As far as I know the British Academy can't be bought, unlike the Hollywood Foreign Press."

He smirked. "As far as you know. What was it like to work with Richard Burton?"

Pagan looked out the window, remembering a brooding, pockmarked face, a warm presence. "He's even more charismatic in person, but he was sort of sad. He caught me sipping from his hip flask one day, and all he did was take it away from me very gently and shake his head." *Leopard Bay* had been shot not long after her mother died. She'd started drinking in secret. "He helped me practice my Welsh accent."

Pagan shook off the memory. Time to learn more about the mysterious Mister Black. "Where are you from?"

"New York." He eased back into the leather seat and

stretched out his long legs so that they almost touched hers. "Born and raised."

"You don't have a New York accent," she said. "You sound like me." Pagan had been coached in elocution from an early age. Once her career as a baby model had taken off, her mother had made sure she grew up trained in how to speak, move, sing, and dance. She now spoke with a nondescript American accent, instead of sounding like a California girl.

"Education drills out the quirks," he said with a shrug. "But I don't have your gift for mimicking accents."

After the barest pause, he gave her another smile. It was warm. Deep. But she didn't blush this time. That pause, that fraction of a second, before he flashed her that smile, opened up a part of her brain she hadn't used in months, years. The smile was perfect. His eyes even crinkled at the corners exactly the way they should. But Pagan knew it was fake, because she was trained to know.

Devin Black was acting. Behind his seeming spontaneity lay an iron control.

Pagan curved her lips into a shy smile to simulate her own coy response, her mind racing. Liars were a dime a dozen in Hollywood. She herself was one of the best. But Devin Black was more than a liar. He was dangerous.

Strange forces were at work. And for her own sake, she had to unmask them.

Devin Black wasn't the only one who could flirt to get what he wanted.

"You're a New Yorker, so you must have been to the Stage Deli over on Houston," she said.

The Stage Deli was on Seventh Avenue, not Houston. If Devin was indeed from New York, he'd know that. "My dad and I ate there all the time when I was shooting that musical in Manhattan. He had the pastrami sandwich five times in a row."

Devin's blue eyes narrowed slightly. "Katz's Deli is on Houston. The Stage Deli's on Seventh."

"Oh, Katz's!" She lifted one palm to the sky as if asking heaven to return her brain. "That's what I meant."

So Devin knew New York. That didn't mean he wasn't lying. She scooched an inch closer to him on the leather seat. "We'll be stopping in New York on the way to Berlin probably, right? What's the hot new thing on Broadway these days?"

He tilted his head, musing. "I was hoping to see *The Happiest Girl in the World*, but it closed in June."

"I was hoping to *be* The Happiest Girl in the World." She gave him a rueful smile. "Then my life turned into *West Side Story* in a hurry."

"Have you heard from Nicky Raven recently?" he asked, his voice deceptively light.

Nicky. Just the sound of his name squeezed all the blood from Pagan's heart. Born Niccolo Randazzo, Nicky sang smoother than Sinatra and could swing like Louis Armstrong. Nicky, with his thick brown hair swept back in a wave, those flexible lips that had kissed her so many times, and that slightly crooked nose lending his boyish face a tougher cast. Just the sound of his name sent everything inside her swirling upward like a dust devil.

The first time she'd seen him, he'd been swaggering past Stage 12 on the Universal lot, singing his latest hit, "Sunlight on Her Face." His dark eyes had lighted upon Pagan as she'd walked past, and he'd stopped dead, taken her hand, and said, "Hey, beautiful. I'm gonna marry you."

He'd asked her to dinner on the spot, and with her father's permission, they'd dined that night at The Brown Derby. It was the first of many long, romantic evenings together.

She caught Devin Black's assessing gaze and stifled the tumult inside her. He'd asked her about Nicky to see how flustered she would get, to test her weak spots. It was cold-blooded…and smart as hell.

Or maybe he wanted to know if she was over Nicky—for himself.

"Not recently." Her voice was a study in nonchalance. "Has he put out a new album or had a hit single lately?"

"Not that I noticed." Devin gave her another appreciative look. "Perhaps he's run out of inspiration."

She leaned in close, wishing she had a lower neckline to deploy or at least some lipstick. "Perhaps you and I should take in a show when we hit New York."

He inclined toward her, a smile playing around his mouth. It looked genuine. "There's only time for dinner, but I know a place…"

He stopped, as if catching himself, and his smile straightened into a resolute blank. "At the airport we can get a decent meal before we get on the plane for Berlin."

Although his voice was pleasant, the already refrigerated air took on a chill. Without moving a muscle, Devin Black had become as remote as the waning moon.

But she'd gotten to him. Pagan leaned back in her seat, suppressing a smile. He'd warmed to her for a moment, the same way he had when they'd discussed sequels to popular songs. He'd probably pulled back because he was worried about losing his job if she beguiled him too thoroughly. But with a little work, she might transform him from prison warden to adoring acolyte.

"Perhaps once we get to Berlin, you could show me around," she said, her voice soft. "I've never been there."

He didn't turn his head to look at her. "Once we get to Berlin you're going to be very busy trying not to get fired off the first movie set you've been on since you quit drinking. Better to concentrate on that."

Rage flooded her. Had she been completely mistaken, thinking he found her attractive? Or was he the type of jerk who lashed out when he couldn't have what he wanted? Either way, he was utterly disagreeable.

"I was a better actor drunk than you are now," she said. It was a stab in the dark. He was performing in some way, and he didn't have to know she couldn't figure him out.

He gave her a cold smile. "Think how splendid you'll be now that you're sober."

Sober. What a dismal word.

Uneasy silence settled between them. She sipped her Coke. The car turned north on La Brea and slid past the old Chaplin studios.

A cherry-red convertible overflowing with laughing people zoomed past them, radio blasting a raucous song she didn't recognize. Pagan suppressed a sigh. A few months ago that had been her. She and Nicky had been drunk on love and success, and other things. He'd driven her down Sunset Boulevard, singing along to his own voice as his number one single played on the radio.

Another car went by, and she was afraid to look out the window to see who was driving it. Nicky could still be in Los Angeles, for all she knew. She tried to picture running into him now, ten months after he'd stopped calling. She imagined a look of pity crossing his face when he saw her, the disgust he'd try to keep from his eyes. The same dark eyes that had once held so much love, so much desire.

She was real gone over Nicky still. Good thing she was going to Berlin, far from anywhere she and Nicky had ever been.

A need to run, to move, to get away from this car, from Devin, from everything, pushed through her like a wave.

As they turned west on Hollywood Boulevard, she pressed

the switch for the automatic window to bring it humming down. Warm dry air rushed over her face, and she stuck her head out. So what if Devin thought she was crazy? She needed to breathe.

She closed her eyes as the wind whipped her hair back, pushing against her eyelids. Shadows pulsed over her, dimming the sunlight briefly. She opened her eyes to look at the palm trees towering above, slipping past like signposts.

She turned her head to gaze back east down Hollywood Boulevard. As they rose up an incline and her hair lashed at her face, she caught a glimpse of Grauman Theater's swooping Chinese roof. She'd hoped to have her hand—and footprints— added to the greats already enshrined in the concrete there. No way that would happen now.

They crested the slight hill and headed down again. Grauman's disappeared from sight. Mansions and gardens lined the road. The Hollywood Hills rose, brown from the summer, to her right. Up there, on the narrow curves of Mulholland Drive, was where she'd crashed her Corvette. Where Daddy and Ava had died.

She didn't want to run or let the air breeze over her anymore. The wind—or something else—had scoured that need out of her. She pulled back into the stillness of the car and shoved her hair back into place. Devin Black sat unmoving, not looking at her as they turned right onto Laurel Canyon.

Not long now. She'd be back home. Where she had nothing but the spirits of the dead to comfort her.

BEDRAGGLED STAR GETS OVERDUE MAKEOVER

But Manicures Can't Lay to Rest Ghosts from the Past

As Devin Black held Pagan's own front door open for her and she walked into the high-ceilinged entry, three women with perfectly coifed hair and identical black pumps bustled down the stairs to introduce themselves.

So much for ghosts. The house was full of actual people. Pagan was too overwhelmed to catch their names, but she did hear the words *manicure, makeup,* and *haircut,* and that was enough to distract her from the sight of Ava's grand piano draped in a huge white cloth in the music room, from the gilt-framed photos of her mother, father, and sister on the mantel.

The beautician, who had very shiny red hair, didn't give her time to dwell on anything, guiding her into the master bedroom, where her father had slept, and stepping into the master bathroom before pausing to look expectantly over her shoulder.

Devin Black was there ahead of them, by the side of her father's bed, squinting up at the small, brilliantly colored painting of a woman in a garden that her mother had hung in a place of honor on the wall.

"Do you like it?" Pagan asked. That painting was one of her favorite things in the world. The dazzling smudges of scarlet, violet, and orange flowers led to a path strewn with lilac and golden sunlight where the suggestion of a woman in a dark blue dress stood, holding a white parasol.

It reminded Pagan of her grandmother Katie, her father's mother, and her vibrant garden in Maine the last spring they visited, shortly before she'd died of stomach cancer.

"Exquisite," Devin said, peering closer at the thick swirls of paint. "It's a Renoir."

Pagan was surprised. "That's what the man who gave it to Mama said." She paced closer to it. "I figured he had to be lying."

Devin's eyes continued to travel over the intricacies of the painting. "Was this man a relative of yours?"

"I don't think so." Pagan frowned, trying to remember. She'd been eight years old when the man had come to visit. She'd forgotten about him until just now, but he could be a link to her mother's past, back in Germany. "Doctor somebody. He was very tall and commanding. But his voice was nasal and whiny. He stayed with us for a couple weeks, so Mama must've known him well."

"Where did he go after he left here?" Devin asked.

"I don't know. He was waiting here till he caught a boat somewhere," she said. Devin was staring at the painting again. It was mesmerizing. "I love it, but it's got to be fake."

"No." Devin's voice was meditative, almost dreamy. "Renoir painted it the summer of 1873 when he was staying with Monet."

Pagan stared at him. How could a studio publicity hack know so much about art? "Are you an artist?" she asked.

"What? No!" He laughed. "I've just been fortunate enough to see a number of works by the great Impressionists up close."

"Did you work in a museum?" she asked. "Or do you moonlight as an art forger?"

The laughter in his eyes died, replaced with a wariness and something that almost looked like pain. She was about to apologize for she knew not what when he gestured toward the bathroom and the sleek redheaded stylist. "Linda, my dear, do what you can with this creature."

Devin vanished, and Pagan was left in her parents' bathroom, made unfamiliar by a large hair dryer set up over a hard chair next to a serving table covered with rollers and twelve different shades of pink nail polish. Linda was already mixing something that smelled like peroxide in a little bowl.

"First we make you blonde, then we do a wet set, and Carol can do your nails while you dry," Linda said. "How's that sound to start?"

Pagan caught sight of herself in the mirror—the stiff, bedraggled, ash-colored hair, the unruly eyebrows, the chapped lips and too-big brown eyes that looked lost without mascara. Her mother would never have approved.

"That sounds like heaven," Pagan said.

Linda, who couldn't have been much older than Pagan, popped her gum and offered her a pack of Fruit Stripe. "The studio told me to do your hair exactly the way it was in *The Bashful Debutante*, just so you know. Chin length, curled under and blondest of the blond. Sorry if you were hoping for something else."

Pagan unwrapped a cherry-striped stick and bit down on it slowly. The sweet, fake-fruit flavor flooded her mouth. She would have killed to have a pack of gum just a few hours ago in Lighthouse, and here it was now, offered to her freely. Funny how reform school made you appreciate things everyone else took for granted. "Anything will be better than how it is now."

Linda chewed her gum with a casual sassiness that was fun to watch. Maybe Pagan could use the mannerism for her character. "No offense," Linda said, "but it's a mess. So you just relax. Magic Linda can fix anything."

"Oh, so you're my fairy godmother," Pagan said. "I've been waiting for you to show."

"Bippity boppity shampoo," Linda said with a grin, pointing at a tube of Lustre-Crème. "Right after we make you a real blonde again."

As Linda brushed and sectioned off Pagan's hair, readying it for the peroxide, Carol came in and lifted Pagan's right hand to examine her fingernails. "I like to keep them short," Pagan said. She probably wouldn't need to scratch anyone's eyes out on the movie set, but prison habits died hard.

As Carol set her hands to soak and Linda began painting peroxide into her hair, it took her back to being in the makeup chair early in the morning before the day's shooting began on a film. Makeup artists knew everyone's secrets—who had acne and who had a toupee, whose red eyes were due to too many uppers and whose were caused by an all-night argument with their spouse. All the best gossip happened there.

"So I'm dying to know what's hot on the radio now," Pagan said. "Last new song I heard was 'Georgia on My Mind,' for crying out loud. What's Ray Charles's latest?"

Carol shrugged. "Search me, but that Pat Boone is dreamy."

Linda made a face. "I like that Bobby Lewis song you hear all the time now, 'Tossin' and Turnin',' even if he can't move like Jackie Wilson."

"Nobody moves like Jackie Wilson," Pagan said. "Elvis tries, but…"

"Oh, Elvis!" Linda wiggled happily, snapping her gum. "That boy is killer diller. I'd play backseat bingo with him any day of the week."

"Linda!" Carol admonished with a grin and began filing Pagan's nails.

"What's the latest from Nicky Raven?" Pagan asked, her voice bland, her face a study in casual.

Linda inhaled sharply, her hand with the peroxide-loaded brush stopping in midstroke. Carol's grip on Pagan's hand tightened.

"Nobody cares about that guy anymore," Carol said a bit too forcefully, and ducked her head down to keep filing.

"Yeah," Linda chimed in. "He's no Elvis."

So much for any attempt to fish news of Nicky out of them. She had thought they'd be eager to get the "real" story on her famous thwarted romance, but that pesky Devin Black must have given them a gag order. Fine. She could play that game.

Carol gestured at the bottles of nail polish and said into the awkward silence, "I hope you like pink, 'cause that's what they told me it had to be. But you can pick which one."

"That one's pretty." Pagan pointed to a rosy shade with her free left hand. "So, was it Devin Black who told you how to do my hair and nails?"

"No." Linda had finished applying the peroxide solution and was folding Pagan's laden hair into a plastic cap to sit until it lightened. "It was the head of makeup at Universal, Josie McIntyre. She said she'd discussed your look with Bennie Wexler."

"Oh, of course," Pagan said. "I remember Josie." She did, too—a nosy, middle-aged woman with an amazing ability to make your nose look slimmer or your eyes bigger. Pagan had been hoping these girls could give her more insight into the role Devin Black was playing in her life. But it sounded like *Neither Here Nor There* was being handled like any other movie.

So the evidence continued to support the fact that Devin was just a junior publicity flack charged with ensuring Pagan didn't make any trouble for the film. But Pagan had met a lot of executives in her time, and Devin Black was from a different planet entirely.

"Oh, my God, have you seen the clothes Helen is laying out for Pagan to try on?" Linda took the cap off Pagan's hair and prepared to wash out the peroxide and apply the toner. She placed a hand on Pagan's shoulder and looked at her in the mirror. "The studio got some special designer things for you. I heard Helen telling Devin. Didn't hear which designer, but he told her to get something specific for you, and the head of costume pulled a lot of strings to get it."

Carol let out a little squeal. "Oh, can't wait to see what it is."

"Oh, me, too!" Pagan widened her eyes to look excited and kept her fingers splayed so as not to mess up her manicure as Linda guided her to stand and go over to the sink.

The next couple hours with Linda and Carol crawled by as Pagan racked her brain, trying to figure out why Devin Black would ask for a particular outfit for her, and what it could be. If it was from a well-known designer, it couldn't be something too strange or revealing, though her mind went to all sorts of weird places trying to picture what sort of clothes a sleek, well-dressed man like him would have demanded for her. She tried not to tap her fingers and ruin the polish as she sat under the dryer with her newly platinum hair pinned up in big rollers.

Finally, her eyelids were lined with winged black and her eyebrows were darkly penciled high at the arch over her wide brown eyes. Dots of foundation and blush had been blended over her moisturized face, then a quick fuss with the contouring brush, new pink coral lipstick from Lournay, and lots of powder.

Pagan stared at herself in the mirror. It was as if she'd gone back in time. Her cheeks had lost some of their baby roundness in the past year, but they were gently flushed, and once again her hair glowed softly white gold against her pale face, setting off her dark eyes and brows.

It all looked so natural, so real. All the illusion needed now was the right clothes. She thanked Linda and Carol, then let them follow her toward her own bedroom, where Helen waited with a movable rack of clothes on hangers and several things laid out on the bed.

Pagan glanced around the familiar room. She hated its pale lilac walls, the high white canopy bed piled with pillows and stuffed animals, the shelves lined with pretty dolls in frilly dresses, classic children's books, and official portraits of the family taken over the years.

What if I just painted everything black? she thought, and immediately felt guilty. How disrespectful to wipe away all of Mama's efforts to showcase the perfect little girl's life.

Her eye landed on the last family photo Mama had been in. They were all smiling dutifully in front of the Christmas tree. Next to it was a framed shot of Pagan, grinning on Clark Gable's arm as she held up her Golden Globe award.

Mama had died shortly after that Christmas photo was taken, and Pagan had been so tipsy at the Golden Globe Awards that she'd tripped over her long gown and was hustled into a limousine by her publicist, sent home before the parties were over.

It was all so far away, as if it had happened to someone in a book, not to her. Clark Gable had died of a heart attack last year, and the attorneys had put her Golden Globe and BAFTA in a vault.

The fake glossiness of it all made her a little sick. Then she caught sight of the creation laid out on the foot of her bed and gasped.

Helen, a tall former model type dressed in a sleeveless red shift, clapped her hands together in delight. "Yes! It's the Dior suit dress Mister Black insisted we get for you. Isn't it spectacular?"

It was more than spectacular. It was perfection. Somehow Devin Black had obtained a brand-new suit dress from the house of Dior. The rich dark brown wool was sewn to look like two pieces—a full flared skirt that hit around the knee belted wide and tight at the waist, and a body-hugging bolero jacket with a crew neck, two almost invisible chest pockets, and three dark shell buttons down the front. But it was really all one piece, a dress so chic and modern she could barely breathe.

She watched Helen unbutton and unzip the dress for her and remembered now. She'd mentioned the Dior suit dresses offhand to Devin Black when they'd first met. The design was new that year, available only to the very rich and privileged. Soon they'd be copied by the department stores, but for now they had to be special-ordered from Dior at an exorbitant cost. It hadn't occurred to Pagan to request one for herself. She couldn't imagine how Devin Black had gotten it here in just a few hours.

As she pulled on the girdle—Lord! How she hated those things—and clipped her stockings to her garters, she couldn't figure out how to feel about the dress. Was it a kindly gesture, meant to welcome her? Or was it a display of power, a sign that he was paying attention to her every word and could conjure anything he desired at a moment's notice?

Knowing what little she did of Devin, it was both of those things. And more.

She didn't look at herself in the mirror until the dress was fully zipped, her feet were slipped into a pair of kitten-heeled Dior pumps, and soft black leather elbow-length gloves were slid on over the dress's tight sleeves.

The women were shaking their heads in appreciation, eyes wide. She stepped up to see her reflection and stilled. The

dress was more than flattering—the warm brown comple-
mented her eyes, the skirt tapered to make her waist look
impossibly slender, showing off her calves and knees, and the
bolero jacket widened at the bust to give her curves where it
counted. This was a dress meant to make things happen, to
let her move through the world with confidence and grace.

Her throat tightened. Could she ever be that girl in the
mirror again?

Something dark moved in the reflection, and she whirled.
Devin Black was leaning against the bedroom doorway, arms
crossed, regarding her. One corner of his mouth deepened ad-
miringly. "Glad to see it fits."

Pagan opened her mouth, not sure what to say, gratitude
and resentment battling inside her.

Helen made a tsking noise. "Mister Black, please! Girls only
in the bedroom!"

Devin gave her a little bow and faded down the hallway.

Pagan's eyes filled up, threatening to send mascara dripping down her cheeks.

"Excuse me," she muttered, and ran into her bathroom,
shutting the door and grabbing a tissue. The girl in the mirror looked uncertain now, overwhelmed, and not nearly mature enough for her outfit.

She took another tissue out of the box sitting on top of the
toilet tank and had a sudden memory—of sliding a half-empty
pint of vodka into that tank, about a year ago. She had concealed bottles all over the house, but that was one of her best
hiding places. However much the maid scrubbed the bowl,
she never bothered with the tank. No one did.

*I'm not going to take it. I'm not going to drink it. I just need to
know if it's still there. That's all.*

Breathing a little harder than she should, Pagan removed
her gloves and lifted the top off the toilet's tank.

Nothing. No bottle of vodka. Just clear water, rods, valves, and the float.

She let the tank lid fall back into place with a clang, then her knees buckled and she sat down on the lilac bath rug.

Someone had found the bottle and taken it away. After the accident and the discovery of her ridiculously high blood alcohol level, her father's attorney had probably had a team go through the entire house to get rid of any damning evidence.

She wiped her eyes carefully and blotted her wet cheeks with some toilet paper. She looked down at the fluffy lilac rug and a tiny laugh escaped her. How ridiculous she must look.

Get off the floor in that Dior, Mama would've ordered, and then would have looked blank when Pagan laughed out loud at the inadvertent rhyme.

She climbed carefully to her feet, smoothing the skirt of her splendid new suit dress. It was unblemished, beautiful.

She looked at her face in the mirror. If she schooled it just right, she almost looked happy.

And she had a job to do. Mama would approve of this refusal to give in to insecurity. Where had Mama gotten that strength, and why had it crumbled so disastrously?

She threw away the tissue and put her shoulders back, chin up. She looked good, strong, thanks to the perfect structure of the dress.

Clothing wasn't magical. There were no fairy godmothers, and she hadn't been transformed. But no way was she giving up the Dior suit dress. One day she'd make it fit, inside and out.

In Daddy's office there was a safe. Once Devin left for the night, Pagan would see what she could find inside. She was on a mission in Berlin. Not only to revive her career, but to learn more about Eva Jones, and maybe, just maybe, feel as happy as she looked.

KILLER STARLET REFUSES TO SHACK UP WITH GUARDIAN

Need to Escape Prompts Drastic Measures

The door to Daddy's study was locked. Pagan rattled the doorknob again, not believing it. Daddy had never locked the office after Mama died; it was she who had kept the girls out, saying she didn't want them spilling things on her important papers. Daddy had liked having them in there, settling Ava on his lap to act as his secretary or helping Pagan build a fort out of books.

It was late, but Devin Black was unaccountably still here. Pagan found him lounging with rather too much ease on the sofa in the living room, feet up on her mother's rosewood coffee table, reading the *New York Times*.

"Can I have the key to my father's office?" she said. "It's locked for some reason."

He didn't look up from the paper. "I don't have the key."

She stared at him. He kept reading. She pressed down the irritation of being kept out of a room in her own house and put on a smile. More flies obtained with honey and all that nonsense.

"Who would lock it?" She arced her voice up to sound puzzled. "Daddy never locked it."

The paper rustled with his shrug.

She'd changed into the silk pajamas and robe Helen had included in what they called her "trousseau." For a moment, she imagined herself a frustrated housewife talking to her indifferent husband in a silly Rock Hudson comedy. "I do need to get in there and go through a couple of things. Who do you think would have the key?"

He folded down one side of the paper to look at her. "The trustee to your estate, I imagine."

"Oh, right." She sat down on the tasseled ottoman in front of her father's favorite leather chair. The room still smelled like Daddy, of cigars and leather and citrus trees. She blinked, forcing her thoughts back to her plan. "That's Daddy's lawyer, Mister Shevitz. A bit too late to call him tonight, I guess."

"I guess." Devin slapped the paper back up and continued reading.

Pagan stared at his Italian leather shoes on the coffee table. "Speaking of it being late, isn't it time you went back to your own lair?"

"This is my lair, for tonight," he said from behind the paper. "I'm in the guest room."

She found herself on her feet, her face flushing against all her efforts at control. "You can't stay here!"

He laid the paper on his lap and folded his hands over it. "Oh, but I can. I'm your new court-appointed guardian."

"But..." She didn't like how this information was agitating her. "You're a kid! You're too young to be anybody's guardian."

"Not according to Judge Tennison."

"That doesn't make any sense." She rounded the edge of the couch, rattled down to her bones. "I just met you today. You've got no connection to my family, no history of trust or...of anything!"

He cocked an eyebrow at her. "There's no need to get flustered. I won't be lurking in your closet all night. Or sharing your bed."

Heat shot up her spine. He was goading her now, and she wasn't about to cooperate. She calmed her voice down to a level of rational concern. "What if the tabloid magazines found out that you and I spent the whole night alone in my house?"

He appeared unworried at the prospect. "They won't."

"What if Linda, Helen, or Carol sell that information to a journalist?"

That thought seemed to entertain him. "They won't."

"What if *I* sold that information?"

His eyes narrowed. "You wouldn't."

"Why not?" She smiled. "It's not as if I have a reputation to protect. Think of the delicious headlines—Killer Starlet Shacks Up with Her Blackmailer."

"I offered you an opportunity—" he began.

"So you'd get an opportunity with me?" she finished.

"Don't flatter yourself." He put the paper back up and ran his eyes over the print, but she knew he wasn't reading a word.

"And in Berlin?" she pressed. "How are you going to keep your court-appointed guardian eye on me there?"

"You'll have your own room at the Hilton," he said.

"But you'll be in the room next door."

He smiled, confirming her guess. "It's new, but the Hilton's already the best hotel in town. They have a restaurant on the roof with a great band that plays on fine summer nights."

"Good," she said, and walked decisively toward the door. "The music will cover your scream when I shove you over the edge."

He laughed as she ran up the stairs to her room. She slammed the door, taking fierce pleasure in the wall-shaking crash. Oh, he was irritating. But that would only make her focus more on how to get around him. He had to sleep some time.

She brushed her teeth and got in her fluffy white bed at 10:00 p.m., then turned out the light, wide-awake and determined to stay that way. She rolled from one side of the huge bed to the other, punching the pillows piled around her. Back in Lighthouse, Miss Edwards had confiscated her only pillow, a pathetic, paper-thin affair half filled with feathers from anemic birds. So Pagan had spent the past nine months sleeping without one. She'd dreamed about having all her pillows back. But now their lift and softness crowded oddly around her head. Quietly, she shoved one after the other onto the floor then lay back flat, listening for Devin's footsteps.

She snapped awake at midnight at the sound of a lock clicking into place. She sat up. It sounded like a lock on her door. But it couldn't be. She'd already locked her own door, from the inside. Fully awake, she tiptoed over to her door, listening as Devin's steps faded down the hall and vanished into the guest room. She unlocked her door, turned the knob, and gently tugged.

It didn't budge.

She pulled harder, fumbling for the key to make sure it was really unlocked. Her fingers met a smooth plate of metal above the doorknob. *What the hell was that?*

She flicked the light on her bedside table to life and stared at a brass plate she'd never seen before, newly installed over the doorknob. Someone had installed a dead bolt on the exterior of her bedroom door.

Not someone. Devin Black. He'd locked her in.

Towering, head-clearing rage surged from her heart and out of every pore.

She wasn't a criminal. Well, if she was, she'd served her time. This was her house now, and she had every right to come and go as she pleased. How dare Devin treat her like his own personal prisoner? Guardian or no, he'd gone too far.

He thought he'd boxed her in, giving her no choice. Well, he'd learn soon enough. If you were willing to go far enough, to think hard enough, there was always a choice.

She donned a pair of pants and hoisted up the largest window overlooking the oak tree outside, glad to note the window was still well oiled and silent. She'd used it this way many times over the years, usually to sneak out to see Nicky.

The tree branch looked farther away than she remembered, but she'd been drinking back then. If she could bridge the distance between window and branch after chugging vodka, she could sure as shooting do it sober. She grabbed the house keys, shoved several pins into her hair, and lifted herself onto the sill.

In a blink she was straddling the branch and climbing down the tree, finding all the old handholds like good friends, waiting. As soon as her feet hit the ground, she sped down the side yard and entered the house again through the back door using her own key, careful to lock it again behind her.

Sit on that, Devin Black. She padded through the kitchen and down the hall to Daddy's office door. Using the bigger bobby pin as a tension wrench, Pagan slid it into the lock the way Mercedes had taught her.

Two minutes later, the last pin clicked into place and Pagan turned the lock. The aroma of her father's cigars hit her like a blow. It lingered, but Daddy was gone.

She clenched her fists, her newly pink nails biting into her palms. *Focus.* She had more important things to do here tonight than wallow in self-pity.

She made herself walk right up to her father's leather chair and sit down in it. Daddy had opened the safe in front of her many times. She pulled aside the fake wainscoting on the lower part of the wall that concealed it and put her fingers on the dial.

Eleven and a turn left, then six, then two turns to the right, then forty-four. Pagan's birthday. It was a stupid, sentimental number to use for a family safe, but her father had been that kind of man. How he and her hardheaded mother had ever fallen in love remained a mystery to Pagan.

The safe clicked open. She angled the desk lamp to shine into it and began piling file folders onto her lap. After the car crash, life had been too scary and hectic for Pagan to think about going through her father's papers. Mister Shevitz had handled what needed to be done. But if there was anything to be found on Mama, Daddy would have put it in here.

Her hand hit the metal floor, and she stuck her head down to make sure she'd gotten everything. A lumpy rectangle threw a shadow near the back wall. She leaned in to pull it out.

There were two bundles. The first was wrapped in plastic and secured with rubber bands. Green glinted under the wrapping. A large stack of one hundred dollar bills.

Bless Daddy for keeping an emergency stash of cash.

The second bundle was an envelope full of folded paper, bound together with an older, nearly rotted rubber band. When she slid her index finger under it, the band snapped and flopped away like a dying fish.

The envelope was unsealed and yellowing at the corners. Pagan lifted the flap and carefully pulled out a stack of folded stationery on heavy white paper. Letters. She unfolded the first one with the care of an archaeologist unrolling an ancient papyrus.

Handwriting in black ink slanted across the paper in a jagged scrawl. She didn't recognize it. Her breathing quickened as she read the first two words: *Liebe Eva.*

Her mother's name, Eva, with a casual German greeting in front of it. Pagan understood enough German to know that *Liebe* was, at the very least, friendly. It didn't have to be more than that.

But it could be.

Why in creation would her father have kept letters to her

mother from someone in Germany? At the top the date was written: *30 Juni 1952*. In European fashion, the day came first, then the month and year. June 30, 1952. Pagan had been seven years old. She'd turned eight that November.

She turned the expensive, textured paper over to see the signature. *Hochachtungsvoll, Rolf von Albrecht.*

Yours truly, Rolf von Albrecht?

Outside the office door, a floorboard creaked.

"Daddy?" she breathed, and caught herself.

Oh, God. For one wild moment she'd thought that sound was her father, coming home late. The urge to tear open the office door and throw her arms around him was almost overwhelming.

Steady, Pagan. No, it had to be Devin Black, patrolling her house in the middle of the night. He must be feeling as restless as she was. Thank goodness she had shut the office door when she came in.

Resentment of him and his control over her movements, her time, her life, bubbled up inside.

Damnable Devin might have all the power of a parent, but she'd sneaked out of the house on her actual parent, Daddy, plenty of times. Years of memorizing scripts had given her an ironclad memory for words on a page and the terms of the contract she'd signed were clear. The court-appointed guardian had to be *on hand during the film shoot and thereafter at the court's discretion.*

Well, she wasn't on the shoot, yet. She could give Devin Black a merry chase and still abide by the contract. She'd arrive in time for the movie, but on her own terms. Maybe by the time Devin caught up to her in Berlin, he'd realize he couldn't treat her like a child.

Pagan grabbed her father's empty briefcase, stuffed the files and the bundle of money inside, and closed it with two quiet clicks of the clasps. She'd finish reading the papers later.

She made her way carefully to the door and pressed her ear against the wood. Outside, wooden stairs squeaked. Devin was heading back up to his bedroom.

She let him get farther up before she silently opened the office door, listening. The faint footsteps continued above her, down the hall, back toward his room. His door rasped open. She waited for the soft thud of it closing before she tiptoed up after him. She was prepared to pick the dead bolt to get back into her own room, but there was no keyhole, just a latch she could flip. Moving in silence, she reentered her bedroom and began to pack.

At 5:00 a.m. she opened her door and looked back at the lilac bedroom. Pillows lay scattered all over the floor, except for the three she'd stuffed under the lacy white coverlet to look like her own sleeping body.

Devin Black would come to wake her up in a few hours. He'd be concerned when she didn't respond and even more concerned when he saw the door wasn't locked. He'd probably push his way into the room to throw back the coverlet. Then he'd see how she'd fooled him. He'd see her packed trunks still in the closet, waiting for transport to Berlin. He'd curse her when he saw that her smallest suitcase, the new Chanel purse, and the Dior suit dress were gone.

She was wearing that fabulous outfit now, her purse full of Daddy's money, his papers in her bag. She was slick and chic and lighter than air. She floated downstairs and out the door. Through the clear air of the summer morning, she glimpsed the cab she had called waiting for her at the end of the drive. Let's see Devin Black catch her now.

RUNAWAY FALLEN STAR TRAVELS FIRST CLASS

Freedom Brings New Dangers

As the cab drove past the Episcopal Church on Hollywood and Gardner, Pagan swiveled her head to stare at the small group of people smoking outside. So they still had A.A. meetings there early in the morning.

Should she ask the driver to stop? She had promised Mercedes, after all. But then they were half a block, then a full block away and there was no point in turning around.

And she didn't need a meeting. Dodging Devin Black had given her a high no glass of vodka could compete with, and she didn't want to miss the early flight from LAX to New York.

Instead she made the driver pull over at a newsstand on Sunset, where she bought every silly tabloid magazine they had—*Photoplay* and *Screenland*, *Modern Screen*, the *National Enquirer*, and *VIP*. Plus *Life*, *Time*, *Seventeen*, *Vogue*, and anything else that looked juicy.

She'd read them on the plane, then mail them special delivery to Mercedes. She'd loved hearing Pagan's insider stories about the celebrities on the magazine covers. Together they'd read every tattered copy of every old magazine in the reformatory.

The cab swept past the new *War of the Worlds*–looking

Theme Building in front of the airport and up to the terminal by 6:00 a.m. Pagan carried her own bag to the ticket counter and asked about a flight to Berlin with a stopover in New York. Without Devin's ticket in hand, she'd have to buy her own. Thanks to Daddy's money stash, that wasn't going to be a problem.

Devin had told her they were booked on TWA, so she went to the Pan Am counter. Better not to run into him on the plane. But Pan Am's flight straight to London had already departed, and they confirmed that all the direct flights to New York were sold out, so she settled on a plane change in Chicago. It didn't get her to New York in time to see a Broadway show, but the agent did help her call ahead to get a room at the Waldorf-Astoria that night, with a flight to Berlin the next morning.

Once on the plane, she settled into first class, happy the seat next to her was empty, until she realized that the stewardesses in their light blue uniforms and flat round hats were serving drinks. Alcoholic drinks.

In her suit dress, Pagan knew she looked much older than sixteen. It would be so easy to wander over to the tiny, exclusive first-class lounge before takeoff and order a Bloody Mary. Later there would be caviar and toast served on bone china, with maybe a glass or two of champagne.

To distract herself, she pulled out the stack of magazines. She made a note to read the article in *Time* on the Cold War, then scanned the covers of the fun magazines. According to *Screen Stories*, Liz Taylor's plans for life were Full Speed Ahead! *Movie Teen Illustrated* had a Special Elvis Issue, and *TV Star Parade* featured Annette Funicello's Tips for Teens: A Miss *Should* Kiss.

No kidding, Pagan thought. How else are you supposed to have any fun?

Then she caught the names *Nicky Raven* and *Pagan Jones* in large print on the next magazine cover, and her heart stopped.

She dropped the other magazines on top to cover it up, and looked around to see if anyone had seen it, or noticed her. But the other first-class passengers were gathered in the lounge, clinking glasses. Adult laughter filtered down the aisle, and a stewardess passed, bearing a tray of canapés.

What was her name doing on a magazine cover? She'd been out of the public eye for months, and Devin had gone to great lengths to keep her release from Lighthouse under wraps. Whatever else he was, Devin Black struck her as someone who could keep a secret.

Which meant she'd have to look at the magazine cover again to see what was going on. One by one, she slid the other magazines aside until she revealed the *Star Insider* again.

Her heart leaped into her throat when she saw Nicky on the cover. He wore a morning coat and top hat and was running down the steps of a church holding the hand of a pretty blonde girl in a long white dress and veil while people on either side of them threw rice.

That's me, she thought. *That's us.*

But it couldn't be.

Nicky had stopped calling after the accident. She hadn't heard from him in nine months. So what the hell…

She looked at the cover again and the words on it came into focus. Nicky Raven Marries Pagan Jones Look-Alike! Exclusive Photos and Interview with Bridesmaid Inside.

Pagan's heart was running a crazy race inside her chest. Images fought for space in her head. Nicky kissing her naked shoulder. Nicky singing "I love you," in her ear, soft and low. Nicky shouting "Hey, beautiful! I'm gonna marry you!"

She forced herself to look at the cover, to really see it.

Nicky was married.

To someone who wasn't Pagan.

To someone who looked like Pagan.

Hands shaking, she picked up the magazine and riffled the pages till she saw a photo of a convertible Rolls-Royce pulling away. Nicky was waving from the backseat with his other arm around the blonde woman in white. The Rolls had a sign on the back that said Just Married, and strings of tin cans fixed to the bumper.

Pagan squeezed her eyes shut, trying to come up with some other explanation. Nicky was starring in a movie where his character got married; Nicky was doing a photo shoot to advertise a particular designer or tailor; Nicky's new album had a song about getting married, and these were possible photos for the cover.

She forced her eyes open and ran them over the print of the article. The information didn't register at first, until she saw a phrase in the interview, spoken by the bridesmaid: "People need to stop comparing Donna to Pagan Jones. Donna's much prettier and sweeter, and she certainly never killed anyone. Nicky loves Donna for who she is, not who she looks like."

Pagan stared into the accompanying close-up photo of Mrs. Donna Godocik Raven. She was taller than Pagan, as tall as Nicky in her heels. Her eyes were blue instead of brown, her nose more upturned, her face more heart-shaped. But otherwise, she did look like Pagan.

Probably a nondrinking version with no deadly car crashes on her résumé.

According to the chipper magazine copy, Donna was nineteen and an up-and-coming actress, with a few small supporting roles in Paramount films to her credit. She and Nicky had met "thanks to mutual friends."

Friends. Ha! More likely their mutual publicists.

Nicky's reputation must have been tarnished by his association with Pagan after her conviction. It could only help him to be seen dating a clean-cut young woman who wasn't Pagan.

But did he have to marry her? Pagan had last spoken to Nicky a few hours before she'd crashed the Corvette. His last words to her had been, "I love you, Pigeon."

Pigeon, his pet version of Pagan. She hadn't liked it at first. But later she'd basked in the way his smooth baritone caressed its vowels. Love could change anything. While she'd been in Lighthouse, she would've taken a month in solitary just to have heard him say those words again.

But he'd never called, never visited.

There were no quotes from Nicky in the article. It was mostly fluff about the wedding dress and statements from Donna's friends and family. Then Pagan caught sight of Nicky's mother Octavia and his three older brothers clustered in the back of a photo, and the stone in her chest turned into an anvil. The wedding was real. Mrs. Randazzo was a warm, no-nonsense Italian-American widow, and despite Nicky's success, she still lived in the family's same small apartment in Brooklyn. Nicky visited her three or four times a year without fail. The family was very close, and Pagan had loved becoming part of it once she'd started dating Nicky.

If Mrs. R and Nicky's brothers had traveled all the way to the Church of the Good Shepherd in Beverly Hills to attend this wedding, it was the real deal.

Pagan threw the *Star Insider* aside and tore through the other gossip magazines, looking for more coverage. She found it in three other places, each with very similar photographs, but no further information other than how well Nicky's new single was doing on the charts. So he *did* have a new song out. Finally, in the fourth magazine, she found the date of the wedding: August 5, 1961.

Just three days ago.

While Pagan and Mercedes were planning their escape from Lighthouse, Nicky had been getting married.

What if she'd escaped one day earlier and called him? Would he have gone through with this marriage?

She shook her head at herself. *Don't be thick.* Nicky would never have taken her call. Immediately after the accident, she had called him a hundred times. He'd never answered his phone or called her back. Why would it be any different now?

It was still hard to believe that he hadn't had the guts to formally break up with her after all they'd been to each other. It was unlike the Nicky she'd thought she knew. She couldn't help being angry about it, but she always came back to the horror of what she'd done. How could anyone want to see her or speak to her, let alone be her boyfriend, after that?

"Champagne, miss?"

A blue skirt and jacket swayed into her peripheral vision, and a pretty dark-haired young woman bent her knees to lower a tray bearing several flutes buzzing with champagne.

Pagan automatically took one of the flutes and sipped. Bubbles tickled her nose. The faint burn of the alcohol singed her tongue.

So delicious. So familiar.

So…wrong!

She abruptly set the glass back down on the tray so hard, some of the golden liquor sloshed out.

The stewardess caught the edge of the tray to keep it from tipping. "I'm sorry. Can I get you something else?"

"No," Pagan said. "No, I'm sorry. Thank you."

See, she still had everything under control. She could find out the boy she loved was married and even accidentally taste alcohol without giving in to temptation.

Further proof A.A. was unnecessary. She was cool.

She tried to smile at the stewardess. The woman turned her

own lips up with professional grace, then her gaze ran over Pagan's face, and the smile faded. Her eyes widened in recognition. Her mouth, professionally lacquered in coral lipstick, parted, then closed, then parted again.

"How about a Coke, honey?" she asked, low and kind. "Or we carry Sprite now, too. It's like 7Up."

Pagan swallowed. The pity in the woman's face came close to undoing her self-control. "A Coke would be great. Thanks."

This time the stewardess's smile was small and real. "Coming right up."

She strode away, and Pagan took a tissue out of the beautiful black patent leather Chanel bag and quietly blew her nose. Very quickly, the stewardess brought the Coke in a bottle with a glass full of ice on the side, as well as some crackers and cheese.

"Eat a little something, too, maybe?" she said. "We won't be taking off for another ten minutes or so."

"Thank you." It came out very low, almost a whisper.

The stewardess patted Pagan's shoulder. "Just let me know if you need anything, mmkay?"

Pagan nodded, and the woman left her alone. She managed three crackers and a square of cheese before she set the food on the empty seat beside her, got up with studied composure, walked down the aisle, and locked herself in the tiny lavatory to cry.

By the time she hit Chicago's Midway Airport, Pagan had full possession of herself again, but she kept her sunglasses on. Her skin was buzzing with the anxiety of being recognized, of how people's reactions might undo her. She distracted herself by tapping back into her anger over the nerve of Devin Black. Maybe his failure to keep tabs on her would get him fired. Someone else would be assigned to be her minder.

Anyone would be better than him, even if he was cuter than Elvis Presley.

She'd devoted far too many thoughts to Devin, so she forced him aside by finding a lonely seat in the first-class lounge at the airport and pulling out the files from Daddy's safe for another look.

Looking again at the signature on the letters to her mother, Pagan drew a blank on the name Rolf von Albrecht.

She turned the paper over again and saw the date.

1952...

Something jolted from her memory. That had been the year the Renoir-giving German Doctor Someone had visited. Maybe Doctor Someone was Rolf von Albrecht.

The tall, skinny man with the squeaky, nasal voice had stayed with them in the winter of '52 for a couple of weeks, barely speaking to anyone except for Mama, and then mostly in Daddy's office with the door locked. He'd departed quietly the morning after a late-night, knock-down fight between her parents, never to be seen again.

Pagan focused on the unfamiliar language in the letter. She'd been pretty fluent in German once upon a time thanks to her early years speaking to Grandmama, but after many years away from it, the German-reading part of her brain stop-started like a rusty engine.

Fortunately, most of it was in simple language, and the more she read, the more German came back to her.

But the letter was weirdly benign and boring. Whole paragraphs consisted of sentences like *As summer arrives, I find myself wishing it was November again.*

Pagan had been braced for evidence that her mother had somehow betrayed her father with this Rolf von Albrecht guy. Instead, it was nothing but sunny days, back pain, and roast turkey.

All the letters were like that, stilted and dull, filled with memories of anonymous landscapes, walks in the garden, and purchasing tickets to the opera. The relentless banality was oddly chilling. No one would write letters this pointless every week for months.

No one would have kept something so meaningless in a safe.

Unless… The thought was ludicrous. But what if there was more going on, literally, between the lines?

She shoved away the memory of the taste of that champagne by plunging into an attempt to find some sort of cipher in the letters. But two hours later, safely ensconced in first class on the plane to New York, she'd found no obvious code or hidden message. If there was any truth to her instinct, finding proof was going to take a lot more work, and right now her stomach hurt. So she put them and her own boring file away.

She was doing the same with Ava's folder when a photograph fell out of it into her lap.

Pagan threw her gaze up toward the airplane's ceiling, not wanting to see her younger sister's face.

Ava had been twelve when she died, blonder than Pagan, but people said she wasn't as pretty because she was more serious and smiled less. The truth was that Ava had been beautiful because she didn't smile when she didn't feel like it. Pagan could only dream of being as confident as her little sister had been.

Pagan swallowed hard and looked down at the photograph. It lay sideways on her lap—a shot of Ava at age three seated next to seven-year-old Pagan on the piano bench. Pagan had both arms around her sister and was grinning ear to ear as she squeezed her tight. Ava, taking the hug for granted, stared down at the piano keys, chubby fingers already reaching for a chord.

Dang it, she was not going to cry again.

She hastily put the photo back into its folder and continued going through the others. She'd learned how to conjure tears on cue for her movie roles, and she could damn well do it in reverse now.

She came to the last folder, labeled *Eva Murnau Jones*.

Murnau. That had been her mother's maiden name. Eva's mother's name was Ursula, her father's was Emil. That was everything Pagan knew about that side of her family.

She opened the folder and paged past bank statements and the dull, posed pictures of Mama with her hair freshly done. Near the back of the file lay a white-bordered photo, smaller, grainier, and very different from the rest. In it a handsome blonde woman around thirty years old stood in front of a worn stone building. She was smiling, holding a swaddled baby in her arms.

Pagan flipped the photo over. In fading script someone had written: *Ursula mit Eva, 1924*.

Grandmama and Mama had moved to Los Angeles in 1925, so this must have been taken in Berlin when Mama was an infant. Pagan scanned the photo for anything that might identify where it had been taken, but there was no street sign or building number, just a glowering winged griffin carved in stone over the door.

There couldn't be more than one building with that design in Berlin. Funny how that's where she was headed now.

Maybe it was nothing. But all of a sudden, more than anything, she wanted to walk the street where her grandmother had held her infant mother, maybe even explore the building where Mama had lived. She didn't know what going there might tell her, but any tiny glimpse she could get into her mother's life or her mother's mind was precious.

All she had now of her family was the past.

As she plunged into reading the script for *Neither Here Nor There*, two people across the aisle began glancing over at her furtively, whispering. She sank back against the plane's round window and lifted the script to block her face.

Fortunately, the script was smart and funny, mocking both capitalism and socialism at every turn. Pagan was slated to play Violet, a flirtatious teenage Southern belle who caused havoc wherever she went. She swiftly fell in love with a handsome young Communist and secretly married him, much to the horror of her family, particularly her rabidly capitalist father. Although James Brennan, former star of gangster movies and expert tap dancer, was the star, her role wasn't far behind his in size. Jerry Allenberg had been right about one thing at least—this was a pip of a role, and she'd better not mess it up.

She let everyone else get off first at Idlewild Airport. She stepped out the door onto the metal bridge under the vast, saucer-shaped overhang, and the warm humid air was enough to make her remove her gloves and unbutton the top of her dress. The metal rungs clattered beneath her heels as she walked toward the gleaming terminal.

It was past eight o'clock at night, and she was hungry again. Time to catch a cab to the Waldorf and order some room service. Maybe a big juicy steak. She could get the concierge to mail the stack of magazines to Mercedes at Lighthouse, with a note to say hi. Maybe it wasn't too late to call M. She had to tell someone about Nicky and that Donna woman.

Thinking about Nicky being married again literally made her heart ache. As she entered the terminal, Pagan pressed one hand against the painful spot. She was too young to have a heart attack, wasn't she?

"Hello, Pagan."

She jerked her head up, hand clutching the fabric at her throat.

A slim figure in a perfectly tailored black suit detached itself from the shadows and stepped into a pool of light.

Devin Black was in New York, waiting for her.

BATTLE OF THE SEXES WAGED FROM NEW YORK TO BERLIN!

Divided German City May Never Be the Same

The maître d' swept his narrowed gaze over Devin and Pagan. When he looked up, he was smiling. They had passed some unspoken test. "Welcome to the Panorama Room," he said. "Do you have a reservation?"

"Do we need one?" Devin stepped closer and slid a folded bill into the man's ready left hand.

"Not at all!" The maître d' slipped the money into the interior pocket of his suit jacket. "This way, please!"

He led them across the polka-dot carpet around the perimeter of the dimly lit circular lounge, to a table overlooking the restaurant's sweeping view of the curving interior of the Pan Am Terminal. Taking hold of one of the transparent Lucite chairs, the maître d' slid it back and bowed a little toward Pagan. "Mademoiselle."

Pagan sank down on the cushioned seat as Devin sat opposite. Below them the white expanse of the new terminal spread like some adult version of Tomorrowland. On a Tuesday night, the place was quiet, the baggage check-in empty. Ladies in Pan Am blue rested their elbows against the white seat-selection counter, talking in low voices. A few waiting passengers smoked in rows of square padded seats, feet up on coffin-shaped tables. Beyond the outer wall, or rather, a curtain of glass, skycaps waited for arriving passengers on a wide concrete porch.

A white-coated waiter arrived to turn their water glasses over and give them menus. Devin waved him away. "I'll have a salad with vinaigrette and a flank steak, medium rare."

Pagan's simmering frustration and anger at being tracked down nearly boiled over. That was exactly what she wanted to order. She pondered snatching a menu and making them both wait for a good long time while she pretended to decide, but she was hungry. "I'll have the same," she said.

The waiter put the menus under his arm with a flourish. "And to drink?"

She looked Devin dead in the eye. "Water."

Devin smiled. "As the lady said. And please let the cook know we have to catch the flight to Berlin in an hour."

"Yes, sir. I'll put your order at the top of the list." The waiter gave a little bow and hustled off.

Pagan kept staring at Devin. "I know how you did it."

He stared back. "And I know how you did it."

That almost threw her, but she plowed on. "Somehow you arranged for every seat on every direct flight to New York to be sold out, which forced me to do a stopover in Chicago. That delayed me long enough to let you get here first."

His blue eyes narrowed. "Your father had a bunch of cash in his safe, and you knew the combination."

"And you have your own boatload of cash—enough to buy up every empty seat on every plane to New York," she said. "The benefits of working for a big movie studio."

"You know every creaky board in your house," he said.

She shrugged. "The benefits of a misspent youth."

He opened his hands as if releasing all control. "Perhaps all this was meant to be."

"Nicky used to say that all the time, about the two of us," she said with heat. "We were 'meant to be.' Turns out he was full of baloney, and so are you."

His expression got serious. "So you heard about Nicky."

She shot him a poisonous look and said nothing.

He studied her, eyebrows furrowed. "I wanted to break that to you gently."

She took a sip of water to calm herself. "Nicky told me he would marry me the first day we met. I told him I'd never get married, but he didn't believe me. Nobody believes me."

"He's a romantic." Devin's voice was dry. "Romantics believe what they're saying when they say it. And they believe it just as much when they say the opposite a few days later."

"He had rheumatic fever when he was a kid, and it damaged his heart." Pagan took another sip of water, watching Devin's face closely. He didn't appear surprised, even though Nicky's condition wasn't public knowledge. "It makes him want to live every moment to the fullest. He doesn't pussyfoot around. He jumps right in."

"And you think he jumped into the first girl who looked like you and married her." Devin considered the prospect. "Probably. He's a fool."

"I was his girlfriend for nearly a year," Pagan said, not ready to forgive Devin yet for tracking her down. "What does that make me?"

"Young," he replied.

"When you are so old and wise." She eyed him, seated so comfortably across from her in his pricey suit with the sophisticated air of a man twice his age. He was awfully cagey, Devin Black. He must have a lot to hide.

Time to find out more about this so-called legal guardian of hers. She needed leverage if she was ever going to truly escape him. She made a wild guess, based on nothing more than instinct. "Coming from a rich family makes you pretentious, not more mature."

He smiled skeptically. "Whereas growing up in Hollywood makes you down-to-earth?"

She waved aside this attempt to insult her, intent on wringing some kind of admission from him. "No studio pays press agents enough to have custom-made Savile Row suits," she said. "Did your mother pick it out for you?"

His smile broadened. "Mother can't be bothered with my suits. She's too busy ruling her little kingdom of wealthy socialites." He shrugged the elegant shoulders of his jacket. "You're right, of course. I had no idea you were so observant."

So his mother was still alive, and he referred to her as "Mother" rather than "Mom." A distant, formal relationship then.

The waiter was approaching with their food. She moved her water glass aside. "And your father? Does he rule that tiny kingdom by her side? Or is he like my dad was—just happy to be on the team?"

Devin's face went blank. The emptiness there was so profound, a chill ran down the back of her neck.

Then the waiter was at the table, putting down plates of rosy butterflied steak filets and snowy white mashed potatoes dolloped with chunks of golden butter.

Devin picked up his fork and knife, contemplating his food with anticipation, and the moment was gone.

"Looks good, doesn't it?" He nodded at the waiter. "Thank you."

He began cutting the steak, and she took up her own utensils, waiting for a response to her question. But he only made a small appreciative sound as he took a bite. "I always eat here if I'm stuck waiting for a flight," he said. "Better than the Clipper Club."

The warm rich smell wafting up from her plate was making her mouth water, so she cut into her steak. But she made a mental note: Devin didn't like discussing his father. That relationship held some kind of secret pain for him, and knowing that, she'd gained a tiny victory. He knew so much about her, it was only fair that she find out more about him, and she resolved to dig further into this whole father issue of his when she could.

The filet melted between her teeth. She groaned involuntarily with pleasure. She hadn't tasted anything so delicious in months.

"See?" Devin cut himself another neat piece. "Did you want sour cream for your potatoes?"

She had practically forgotten sour cream existed. "Oh, yes please!"

As he signaled the waiter, she realized that for a good five minutes she hadn't thought about Nicky Raven and his new bride. Maybe that's just how Devin Black had wanted it.

The Dior suit dress withstood the trip to Berlin without a wrinkle, but by the time they landed Pagan was very much looking forward to getting out of it and into a nice soft bed, faraway from everyone on earth, particularly Devin Black.

While on the plane, and with a showy flourish to demonstrate how she was ignoring him, Pagan had plunged into an article in *Time* about the Cold War.

She'd found herself caught up in the article in spite of herself. Nothing like the serious threat of nuclear war to grab your attention.

A defeated Germany had been divided into four parts after the Second World War, each part governed by a different Allied nation—the United States, England, France, and the Soviet Union. They'd similarly divided up the German capital, Berlin.

But the alliance soured fast after Soviet leader Joseph Stalin effectively took control of all the countries east of Germany, as well as a big chunk of Germany itself, now known as East Germany.

So the other three powers remained huddled in the three quarters of Berlin that had been given to them, surrounded on all sides by the new country of the German Democratic Republic, or East Germany as Westerners liked to call it.

The man now in charge of that country, Walter Ulbricht, had been tight with Stalin, and even more than the Soviets, maintained rigid control of every aspect of daily life—from the price of bread to what people could read and say.

Well, that was glum, restricting, and oddly familiar. Pagan's biggest hit, *Beach Bound Beverly*, would never have been made in East Germany—too frivolous. Also, the East German government spied on its citizens all the time, so even if you managed to get your hands on something "decadent" like a Dior suit dress, you could never wear it out or the government would punish you.

This Walter Ulbricht guy sounded a lot like a balding, grumpy version of Mama.

Pagan giggled, then caught herself guiltily. Mama had been warm as well as firm, and Pagan loved her. The world had seemed to bow to Mama's control. Pagan had been safe with her around, and Mama had taught her many useful ways in which to navigate the strange world of Hollywood. That was one of many reasons her suicide had cast Pagan so adrift.

But Mama had been a perfectionist—overseeing Pagan's every word and gesture, grooming her meticulously for success, managing every tiny detail of her career. Pagan had barely been allowed to breathe out of her mother's sight. As long as Pagan was perfect, the family would get to keep their fine house in the Hollywood Hills, and Mama would be happy. One mistake could ruin them.

All of that effort had paid off. Pagan had become a star. She hadn't made any mistakes until Mama died. After that it had been the secret stashes of alcohol that soothed her anxieties instead of her mother's firm hand on her shoulder.

Maybe Ulbricht's approach was paying off for East Germany, too. Maybe he loved his people the way Mama had loved Pagan. Pagan couldn't be sure, but she doubted it. You couldn't mold millions of people the way you could your own child.

It was for the best that Mama hadn't been in charge of an entire country. Every little girl would have been forced to walk for thirty minutes each day with a book on her head, and every husband would have been lectured regularly on how to fold the morning newspaper just so.

Hours passed, and Devin sat next to her the whole way. He never seemed to sleep. She would nod off, then jerk up her head to find him alert and reading the latest editions of the New York and London newspapers. He was polite; he knew when to speak and when to be quiet, but he was there.

They changed planes in Frankfurt to Air France, one of the airlines with permission to fly into Berlin's Tegel airport. By then Pagan was so tired and grumpy, the plane could have been a flying palace and she would have found something to complain about. Devin Black just kept reading, taking one of the German language journals from the stewardess with a smile. By the time they reached Berlin, fatigue had smudged dark circles under his eyes, but he seemed alert. Pagan decided he was either a robot or one of the aliens from *Invaders from Mars*.

Tegel airport had a dreary, military air, and men in French uniforms stamped their passports. A chauffeur was waiting in a large Mercedes-Benz. The sight of the car set off the usual jitters in Pagan, echoes of the accident, but as she had with the cab to LAX, she shoved them into a dark corner of her mind and made herself get in. As they left the airport with the rising sun at their backs, her nerves calmed and she could look around.

The car sped down a tree-lined road with the blue-gray River Spree on the left. The streets were busy with foot traffic, motorcycles, and cars, but Pagan couldn't help noticing the number of armed men in uniform either walking or stationed on various street corners. A vivid reminder that West Berlin was a lone island surrounded on all sides by the hostile Communist East Germany.

"We're in the French sector of the city at the moment," Devin said. "But we're staying in the American sector at the new Hilton. It's very close to the Tiergarten, which has grown back nicely since the war—"

"It sounds lovely." She interrupted him in a repressive tone. "Perhaps after I've gotten some rest far away from you, I'll give a damn."

"You can rest," he said, his voice calm in a way that only irritated her more. "But I won't be far away."

She turned to look at him. "What does that mean?"

"It means I can't trust you." His voice was bland, but his face carried a warning.

"I never promised you anything—" she started to say.

"You signed a contract," he said, voice getting sharper, "which includes a clause stating that you have a guardian, with all the authority of a parent. Deviate from my orders and you could go back to prison."

"I'm not your child," she said, just as sharp. "Or your slave, or your wife."

"You're my ward," he said. "You're on parole, and it's very easy for me to make a call to the judge."

She lapsed into fuming silence, her head abuzz with fatigue and fury. Maybe some of this was her fault. Fine. But why, when boys broke the rules, did they get called "rebels" and "hotheads," while girls were "bad"? Pagan being a nice little girl hadn't kept Mama from dying, so she'd done what she wanted after that. She saw no reason to change now.

There had to be a way out from this new Devin-bound prison, an escape. That's what alcohol had always provided, and without that tool available to her, she had to find a new way to be free.

Devin had too much power over her. But he also had secrets—there was more to him than just some minor studio executive. If she could decrypt the riddle that was Devin Black, she might find her freedom that way.

They drove past a crowd of people lining up in front of a warehouse-like building. Thousands of men and women in neat summer clothes were carrying suitcases and shepherding children. Pagan remembered what she'd read about the mass exodus of people from East Berlin and craned her neck to see if these were indeed immigrants from East Berlin. No way was she going to ask Devin a question now. She glimpsed a sign: *Réfugiés/Flüchtling.*

"That's the French sector processing center for refugees," Devin said as if she'd asked him aloud. His voice was friendly as ever. "The city gets nearly two thousand a day. The other borders with East Germany are closed, so Berlin's the last place of escape. For now."

She didn't reply as the car entered a wooded area. Up ahead loomed a column that glinted gold on top. She leaned forward to look up at it through the windshield and caught sight of a glittering winged statue with arms outstretched.

"The Victory Column," Devin said, still in his best tourist guide voice. "But the Berliners call it *Goldenelse*—Golden Lizzy. The Prussians erected it last century to commemorate their victory over the Danish. But by the time it was done, they'd also defeated Austria and France in other wars, so it covers a lot of victories."

Pagan said nothing as they circled the monument's red granite base. A lot of wars had come and gone since then. The Germans sure wouldn't be erecting a victory column to commemorate the last one.

The parkland gave way to newly constructed buildings, some still with scaffolding. "Still rebuilding," Devin said. "From the war."

Pagan stared. Sixteen years later they were still rebuilding?

It was one thing to read about World War II, another to see how people's lives were still affected by it here. No wonder Berliners were fond of Golden Lizzy, their angel. They needed one.

Pagan could've used an angel, too, a few times in her life, but how could her tiny little troubles stack up against what Berlin—what all of Europe—had been through? Hollywood seemed like the center of the universe when you were there, making movies, attending award shows, reading about yourself in the paper. But Berlin was a reminder that in the big-budget epic of the history of the world, Pagan was nothing but an extra.

The Hilton was sleekly modern and sparkling behind its subdued but gracious facade. Pagan blearily followed the bell-boy and her luggage up to her room. When Devin stopped at the door next to hers and let his bellman take his luggage inside, relief overtook her. So she would get time to herself after all. And if she needed to, she could walk quietly past his door and he'd be none the wiser.

The room turned out to be a suite. She gave the bellboy five dollars, apologizing in German that came out better than she expected that she didn't have any German marks. He replied in perfect English that dollars were better anyway.

Then she was blessedly alone, wandering from the large living area with its low-slung sofa and large curtained windows looking onto the Tiergarten to a set of double doors that led to a room with a queen-size bed and adjoining bathroom.

She kicked off her shoes and began unzipping her dress. Lovely as it was, she couldn't wait to get it off and crawl into the fluffy red-and-white bed, which, as usual, had way too many pillows. She unsnapped her garters, yanked off her stockings, and walked barefoot over the thick carpet to investigate another set of double doors. They opened up to reveal a second bedroom, complete with its own bed and bathroom.

She stood in that doorway, frowning. Why would they give her two bedrooms? In the distant past her mother would have stayed there, but the studio had no reason to be extra generous with her now.

There came a chunk and a scrape—a key turning in a lock. She turned to see a door she hadn't noticed before in the opposite wall. It opened, and Devin Black stood framed there. She could see a portion of his unlit room behind him.

She grabbed the gaping hole in the side of her dress, where she'd unzipped it, strongly aware of her bare legs and feet. "Is that how you're going to keep watch on me, unlocking the adjoining door between our suites?"

"Not at all," he said, and, picking up his suitcase, he walked a few steps into her suite to set it down. "That room is just for show."

Her face flushed, scalding hot. "But…but…"

"I left you alone in your bedroom in Los Angeles, and you chose to run away," he said. "I don't make the same mistake twice. Thank you for saving the bedroom closest to the exit for me."

Words failed her. She fled to her bedroom, slammed the door, and turned the lock.

Through the wood she heard his low laugh. "Sleep tight," he said.

STARS SNUB PAGAN JONES!

Communist Co-Star is Entranced

Breakfast the next morning was of the very silent room service variety. How bizarrely domestic to sit across the tray table from Devin, sipping coffee and eating eggs while he, the picture of ease and elegance in another splendid Savile Row suit, his dark hair combed perfectly back, read the *International Herald Tribune*. Pagan couldn't help staring at his deft hands as they poured her coffee. Unbidden, the thought of those skillful hands on her skin flashed into her mind. But that was only because she missed Nicky. Still, her cheeks burned. She needed to refocus on something, anything.

"How old are you?" she asked Devin, not caring how abrupt it sounded.

He set down the paper and looked at her. His eyes were darker today, a stormy blue closer to the navy of his suit, and they took a moment to slide over her, taking in everything from her teased updo to her new green Givenchy dress.

The effrontery of the frank assessment made her flush. What was it about him that made her acutely aware of the brush of her blouse against her collarbone, of the taut line of her garter as it bit into her thigh?

"Old enough," he said.

She gave it a moment, staring back at him. "Well. I'm not old enough to be sharing a suite with a man, or boy, or whatever you are."

His hand, bringing the cup of coffee to his lips, paused as a surprised smirk took over his mouth. "Nicky Raven thought you were."

Her already aggravated temper ignited. He had a world of nerve, bringing up her ex-boyfriend as if he knew her, as if all of her secrets were his playthings. He wasn't the only one who could play that game. He'd revealed just enough by now for her to use it against him. Whatever wounds he carried must have happened when he was quite young. She took a stab.

"Nicky's younger at heart than you are, or ever have been," she said.

His smirk switched off. He set his cup down with a hard click and looked away, a line appearing between his brows.

"One old soul recognizes another." His voice was insouciant, but she'd hurt him. And she was glad. She also knew exactly where to strike next.

"Tortured soul, you mean," she said. "And yes, I do recognize another. But whatever your father's sins, they aren't my fault, so stop taking it out on me."

His gaze flew to hers with an uncharacteristic flash of anger. But behind that she saw something else—something bleak and inconsolable. The depth of it bounced her smugness away.

He lowered his eyes, spiky dark lashes brushing his cheek, and snapped the paper back up between them.

After a moment: "I'm nineteen," he said.

The way he said it was some kind of admission, though she wasn't sure of what. Had she won this round of whatever game they were playing?

"Okay," she said, because she had nothing else. He was

younger than she'd imagined, and so much younger than he seemed.

Given his reaction to her remark about his father, some guilt-ridden heartache must lie buried in his past. But she felt oddly mortified. She'd glimpsed a part of him he never wanted anyone to see. Nobody knew better than Pagan how much that could wound.

A ponderous silence settled over them both. So Pagan pulled out the script for *Neither Here Nor There* as a distraction. She'd studied it in detail over the past twenty-four hours, but it never hurt to have a refresher.

She forced herself to reread the very first words at the top of page one:

Dialogue speeds should be in excess of 100 mph on the curves, 140 on the straightaways.

That was Bennie Wexler's typical way of saying he wanted the pace to be rapid-fire, but coherent. So she mouthed her lines to herself as fast as she could, finding the places where she was most likely to mangle the words and making little hash marks next to those paragraphs to remind herself to enunciate clearly.

Devin finished the paper and folded it up neatly. "Are you ready for the table read today?"

She looked at him over the top of the script. The boy had nerve, checking up on her preparation as an actress.

"Yep," she said.

One dark eyebrow went up as he lifted his coffee to his lips. "Really?"

She went back to reading. "Yep."

"You've memorized your lines?" Skepticism dripped from his voice.

Even when she was drinking at her worst, Pagan had never dropped a line, so Devin Black could get bent.

"Here." She tossed the script at him.

With a sudden catlike move, he caught it in his left hand. "What's this?"

"Test me. Pick any of Violet's dialogue and give me the line before."

"And you'll know the line that comes after?" He pressed his lips together, mouth turning down in consideration. "All right, then." He set down his coffee and opened the script to a random page. As he read, his voice became thicker; it sounded older, and slightly affronted. "'Where did you find that guy? He doesn't even wear socks!'"

Pagan summoned her best Southern accent, dripping with honey and love-struck enthusiasm. "'He doesn't wear underpants, either! Isn't he the most?'"

Devin burst out laughing. The genuineness of it almost made Pagan laugh, too, but he quickly tamped it down with a small clearing of his throat.

"Okay, so the script is funny," he said, avoiding giving her the credit as he thumbed through the script. "Let me find a tough one." His eyes traveled over the pages. He cleared his throat and read, "'How about that?'"

He looked at her over the top of the script, a direct challenge.

Pagan glowered at him. Although he'd cheated, taking the line from the end of a previous scene, she knew which line started the next scene. So she channeled her inner Violet Houlihan, she of the moonlight and hot running hormones. "'His name is Niklaus, but I call him Klaus.'" She sighed dreamily. "'It reminds me of Santa.'"

Devin nodded, reading the next line as if deeply puzzled. "'You like to pretend he's a fat man with a big white beard?'"

"'No, silly!'" Pagan said with a dismissive little wave of her hand. "'Because every time I unwrap him it's like Christmas!'"

"And cut." Devin let the script fall closed. "All right. You might be ready."

"Your timing's terrible," she said, taking the script back. "And your impression of a middle-aged mother of three needs work."

He shook his head at her, half smiling with some secret amusement sparking behind his eyes. "But my imitation of a nineteen-year-old American man is spot-on."

The mood between them had not improved by the time the chauffeur drove their long black Mercedes down tree-lined streets toward the center of town. They passed the battered-looking Brandenburg Gate with its six grand columns and smaller annexes on either side, a four-horse chariot riding victoriously forever on top. The black, red, and yellow flag of the Communist German so-called Democratic Republic crowned it all.

Pagan peered through the window and saw the large white signs in English, Russian, French, and German: You Are Now Leaving British Sector.

Round Volkswagens, rectangular Trabants, and cobbled-together motorcycles and bikes zoomed toward the looming gate, slowing as the stationed East German *Volkspolizei*, or People's Police, in their lumpy olive uniforms scanned their license plates. Those with approved types were waved through. Others had their papers checked.

"The gate is actually in East Germany?" Pagan asked as the car continued past it along the river. They were staying in West Berlin for the shoot. "It still looks damaged from the war."

"It's better than it was," Devin said. "The Russians cooperated with the West for a while to restore most of it. This whole town was one big pile of rubble when the Allies were done. You can still see piles of what used to be buildings on the Eastern side."

"I wonder which sector my Mother was born in," she said, "back before there were sectors."

"Do you have an address?" he asked.

"No." She hesitated, not wanting to confide more. But what if he could help? She had nothing to lose. From her purse, she pulled the photograph of her youthful grandmother in front of the building with the glowering griffin. She'd decided to carry it with her in case she found someone appropriate to ask about it. The stash of letters from Rolf von Albrecht she had left hidden in her suitcase. "This is all I have."

Devin took it carefully, read the back without comment, and removed his sunglasses to scrutinize the photo. "No street name," he said.

"But the building behind her is pretty distinctive."

He nodded. "A native Berliner might recognize it."

"If it's still standing," she said as he handed the photo back.

"Your chances are maybe fifty-fifty, unfortunately," he said.

It was a lovely clear August morning, and the car slowed as it pulled into a parking lot. "You look a lot like your grandmother," he said. "Do you have any photos of your grandfather?"

A good question. "No," she said. "I remember asking Mama about that when I was little, and she seemed sad not to have any. He died of polio when she was a baby, before they came to the US."

"I might be able to find his death certificate for you, although the war made a mess of many city records," he said. "What was his name?"

Pagan stared down at her new low-heeled pumps, frowning. She'd just seen her grandfather's name in her father's files, but still it didn't leap to mind. Her mother had never known him, and her grandmother had never spoken of him—a curiously blank entry in the family history.

"Emil," she said as it came to her. "Emil Murnau."

She looked up to catch a strange, triumphant look in Devin's eye. The cold satisfaction in it lifted the hair off the back of her neck.

In a split second, his expression transformed into a tolerant smile. He was simply doing her a favor. "Emil Murnau," he repeated as if memorizing it. But Pagan knew he'd heard the name before. "I'll see what I can find," he said.

"You're very generous." She schooled her voice to stay bland even as her mind churned with chaos and calculation. Why would Devin Black or anyone else give a damn about her long dead grandfather? And how could that possibly have anything to do with Devin's apparent ability to blackmail everyone from Miss Edwards to Jerry Allenberg? Was he looking for some kind of family skeletons so that he could continue to manipulate her. Or...?

The driver put the car into Park and hustled to get her door. Devin didn't wait for him and let himself out. As she stared at his custom-made suit, his Italian race-car driver sunglasses, his perfect haircut, she realized that all of his actions—the blackmail, the manipulation, the flattery—it was all directed toward one goal: to get her to act in this movie.

But why? Why tempt her with her mother's mysterious past to get her on a movie? And why *this* movie? *Neither Here Nor There* was funny and smart, yes, but it wasn't going to win any awards or break box office records. Why fly her out at the last minute to shoot a comedy in a divided city on the brink of nuclear war?

"Come on now." Devin was standing outside the car, ducking his head down to peer at her, still stewing in its air-conditioned depths. "They won't bite."

"The girl I replaced," she said flatly. "The original actress slated to play Violet. Who was she?"

He'd put his sunglasses on, and she couldn't see his eyes, but his shrug looked natural. "Some nobody," he said.

"Did she really get pregnant?" she asked jokingly, but secretly half-serious. "Or did you have her killed to get her off this movie?"

He smiled. "I'm a fan of yours, but even I have my limits."

"Never mind." She scooted forward, putting those disturbing thoughts on hold for later consideration. Whatever Devin Black's agenda, this was her chance to restart her career. She wasn't going to let him or anyone else mess that up.

Pagan took his offered hand to help her out of the car, but released it as she stood and straightened the lapels of her green Givenchy dress. Its classic lines, along with her pearl necklace and gloves, made her look older and thus more responsible. Bennie Wexler had bad memories of their last time working together, but she'd been only eleven years old. Fashion was just one of the tools she planned to use to win him over.

Another black Mercedes had pulled up. A tall, broad-shouldered young man with thick blond hair and a broad-browed, high-cheekboned face that would break more than a few hearts stepped out and smiled at her. His teeth, even and white, flashed, and for a moment she thought she was back in Hollywood. Everything about him, limpid green eyes, powerfully built body, smoothly tan skin, dimpled chin, all screamed *movie actor.*

"Miss Jones!" He strode over, holding out his strong right hand. "Thomas Kruger. I'm thrilled to meet you."

His English was excellent, but laced with a German accent. This had to be her costar, the boy who would play the Communist hunk Violet fell in love with. As her hand disappeared inside his, she found herself smiling back at him. No shadow of concern or judgment lay behind his sparkling eyes. He was dazzled to meet her, and his open friendliness came as an enormous relief. She hadn't realized how worried she'd been about what her fellow actors would think of her. "The pleasure's mine, Mister Kruger. I'm looking forward to working with you."

He bowed slightly and held out his arm to her, as if he were about to walk her into a ballroom. "Call me Thomas, please."

"And you must call me Pagan." She hadn't heard of him before, but given that he was from Germany, perhaps he was better known here than in the United States. As she slid her arm through his, they turned to walk stride for stride toward the glass door to the building together, as naturally as if they'd always been friends. "We'll be getting to know each other very well, after all."

"It will be my privilege," he said. "I'm such a big fan of yours."

"Thanks so much!" It never failed to tickle her when people said that, especially if they seemed as genuine as Thomas. Maybe this shoot wouldn't be an exercise in humiliation, as she'd feared. If Bennie Wexler and her fellow actors were half as nice as Thomas, she'd get through it all just fine.

She waved a desultory hand back toward Devin, who had fallen in behind them. "Do you know Devin Black?"

Thomas glanced briefly over his shoulder, not really bothering to look. His voice was dismissive. "We've met, yes."

The obvious snub seemed to amuse Devin. "Hello, Thomas. How are you today?"

Thomas didn't turn his head again. He and Devin were of a height, but Thomas's bulkier suit and muscular shoulders made Devin look knife-thin. "I'm well, Mister Black. Very well indeed."

Interesting that Devin had called Thomas by his first name, while Thomas resorted to "Mister Black." Even Thomas Kruger wanted to keep the man at a distance.

They were ushered to the elevator and up to the tenth floor, which housed the film's production offices. A receptionist waved them into a large conference room. A magnificent view of the city gleamed through the windows.

Pagan let go of Thomas and ran over to see as much as she could. "Oh, look, you can see the Tiergarten and the Brandenburg Gate from here. Which means that—" she pointed east "—must be East Germany."

"That is indeed my home," Thomas said, walking to stand beside her. "We call it the *Deutsche Demokratische Republik*, of course. Or as you say, the GDR, the German Democratic Republic."

"You *live* there?" she asked, then realized how bad that could sound and said, "I'm sorry. I never thought Hollywood would've had enough sense to hire an actual Communist to play a Communist."

He laughed. "Please don't be sorry. Sometimes it still surprises me that I live there." He pointed at the Brandenburg Gate, easily spotted near where the trees of the Tiergarten ended. "If you go through the gate and take the Unter den Linden—see that street with the four lines of trees?—take that to Alexanderplatz, that more open area there, then go north—" he pointed left "—about ten blocks and you're in my neighborhood."

"I'm sure your wife keeps a lovely home," Pagan said, ignoring the amused presence of Devin Black, now lounging in a chair near the middle of the conference table behind them. It wasn't subtle, but saying that phrase to a man never failed to get her the information she wanted. She didn't really care whether or not Thomas Kruger was single, but it was fun to flirt with someone right under Devin's nose. She slid a glance at him to assess his reaction, but he was busy putting cream in his coffee, a satisfied smirk on his lips.

"Well, my mother does that for me now," Thomas said, just awkwardly enough to show that he wasn't a native English speaker. "I'm not married. I live with my mother and younger sister, Karin." He smiled down at Pagan, eyes shining as he spoke of his sister. "She became eleven just last month, and she's an even bigger fan of yours than I am. Don't tell the Party Chairman, but I take her to the movies and buy her magazines whenever we are able to come to West Berlin."

"Don't tell the Party Chairman, but we plan to corrupt you to our evil capitalist ways before the shoot is done." Bennie Wexler burst into the conference room and opened his arms wide to them both, grinning. Although Bennie was six feet tall with a contented pot of a belly, his balding head, pointy ears, and mischievous eruptions of energy lent him an elfin quality. "There you are, my beautiful young movie stars! Come give your uncle Bennie a kiss."

Pagan and Thomas moved over to him as one. Bennie favored Pagan first, taking her shoulders firmly in his hands to kiss her lightly first on one cheek then another. He had large black-rimmed glasses over his small eyes, which missed little. A known clotheshorse, he wore an expensive gray cashmere sweater over a crisp white shirt and checked tie, and he smelled of coffee and turpentine. Bennie collected paintings and dabbled a bit in the art himself. She remembered the sharp odor well from the weeks she'd spent with him back when she was eleven, on the shoot for *Anne of Green Gables*. The shoot where Bennie and her mother had quarreled about something. Whatever it was, it had gotten Eva Jones banned from the set.

"Wonderful to see you again, Bennie," she said. "Thank you so much for bringing me onto this film. Really." She took a deep breath and smiled, not wanting to get too emotional. "It means a lot to me."

He patted her shoulders as his eyes darted over her, evaluating her. "I'm glad to have you, my dear." He squinted at her slightly as he added with a bit more emphasis, "Be good for us, and we'll be good for you."

Translation: Don't start drinking and muck this up.

The back of her neck got hot, and she hoped her cheeks weren't burning. Bennie continued to stare at her, waiting.

"I promise you have nothing to fear from me," she said.

"Good," he said, his faint Austrian accent hardening the *D* at the end to a soft *T.* "Here, I will introduce you."

As he pulled her fellow actors over to say hello, it became clear that they all knew each other well. She was the newcomer. The rest of the company had been in town for a week, rehearsing without her.

That, at least, was not her fault. She couldn't be held responsible for the other actress's pregnancy.

But no matter whose fault it was, the other actors weren't nearly as welcoming as Thomas Kruger. The movie's star, pugnacious sixty-year-old James Brennan, with his excellent toupee and large white teeth, wouldn't even shake her hand. He grunted at her, narrowed his eyes, and moved past her to sit at the head of the table.

Brennan was notoriously cranky and a stickler for professionalism. No doubt he feared Pagan was still a drunken flake whose shenanigans would drag out the shoot.

Indeed, Brennan's fiftysomething costar, Adele Franklin, said it directly as she limply shook Pagan's hand, fingering her diamond necklace with her other hand. "You won't be causing any trouble on the set now, will you, my dear?"

Pagan smiled with all the fake niceness she could muster,

searching for the best way to respond. Luckily, Bennie interrupted, clapping his hands twice to announce:

"All right, my cherubim and seraphim—the time has come! Take your seats! Adele, darling, you are here, of course..." Bennie steered her next to Brennan, placing the two biggest stars in their assigned seats. Coffee and croissants on little plates were dispensed.

Matthew Smalls led Pagan to her seat. He was Bennie's first assistant director, a short, slender, no-nonsense middle-aged man with teak-brown skin. He stood out in an otherwise all-white cast and crew, most of them local Berliners.

But Bennie Wexler had fled the Nazis in the thirties and lost his parents to the concentration camps. He didn't truck with prejudice or other "horseshit," as he tended to call it. Matthew Smalls had been his assistant director for the past ten years because he ran the set with a calm competence and natural authority that kept things moving smoothly and allowed Bennie to do his job.

Pagan made a note to befriend Matthew, since the first assistant director, even more than your costars or the director, could make your life comfortable or hellish during a shoot. So she smiled and thanked him as she found herself between Thomas Kruger and Hans Petermann, who played a Communist party official.

"You, over there!" Bennie gestured impatiently at Devin Black, seated at an unassigned middle chair. "Studio flacks at the far end of the table, please."

Devin bowed his head and moved with good grace to the end of the room, where he took a seat that wasn't even at the table but in a row behind.

Next to Pagan, Thomas uttered a private, satisfied little laugh, even as he drummed his fingers nervously on his script.

"I take it Devin Black's annoyed you as much as he's annoying me," Pagan said, keeping her voice low so that only Thomas could hear.

"He's…" Thomas started to say, his voice full of some strong emotion. But then he caught himself and looked down, a muscle in his jaw tensing. "I've met worse."

So Thomas was afraid of Devin for some reason, too. Pagan was burning to find out more about her mysterious keeper and why he wanted her here, now.

But that would have to wait. The last of the group was seating themselves, and Bennie was about to start the script read. Instead, Pagan took off her gloves and tapped her fingers next to Thomas's, keeping time with his. Their fingers improvised a little dance around each other, and he grinned at her.

"You're going to be great," she whispered. "But it helps to imagine everyone at the table naked."

Thomas chuckled, and his tanned skin flushed slightly as his gaze zoomed around the table at the Hollywood elite. "We have that trick in German theater, too."

"You're a theater actor?" She shook her head as if that was a shame. "Then I'm afraid you're overqualified for this."

He laughed softly again, casting her an appreciative but rueful glance. "I do wish that were true."

"And so we begin!" Bennie said, and silence fell over the table. Cigarette smoke rose in a gray cloud overhead as actors in their designer finery puffed nervously and fingered their scripts. Crew members in slouchier pants and rumpled shirts made notes in the margins of theirs. "We have at last the final piece of our puzzle with us today. She was gracious enough to come to us at the very last minute for this role, a role we are lucky to have her play—Miss Pagan Jones as Violet Houlihan."

Tepid applause greeted this introduction. Pagan smiled and nodded around the table as if it were a standing ovation. Traditionally at table reads, the director presented all the actors with speaking parts, but everyone else had met before, and Bennie was impatient to start.

"We will begin with shots of the lovely town in which we find ourselves. A town divided by politicians, but not divided in spirit—Berlin," said Bennie, his clipped voice taking on a more mellifluous, storyteller's flourish. "The voice-over of American businessman L. T. Houlihan begins our tale…"

James Brennan, barely glancing at his script, spoke his voice-over line. "'For all that it's a divided city, life in Berlin's pretty normal, I guess. The Eastern side is still covered in rubble. But I had a plan to change all that…'"

Violet didn't appear until page twenty, so Pagan had time to sit back and react to the script as if for the first time. As James Brennan's capitalist character blustered his way through the story, lying, swindling, and bamboozling everyone from the Communists he was selling to, to his mistress, to his wife—all so that he could get a promotion—she began to see just how clever Bennie had been.

On the surface the film was critical of the Communists, showing them as backward, narrow-minded, hypocritical zealots, who longed for the luxuries of the West even as they decried them as decadent. But the main American businessman character L. T. Houlihan was the entertaining embodiment of Western rapaciousness, duplicity, and greed. No one escaped unscathed in Bennie Wexler's cynical universe. Her own character, she was just now realizing, was the epitome of privileged American youth: blinded by lust; self-centered; and naive to the machinations of her double-dealing elders, which meant she'd grow up to be exactly like them.

By the time her entrance came, she was truly excited to be playing the role. The movie was more than a fluffy comedy, deeper than a farce, and she was lucky to be in it.

As her character flirted and sashayed her way into the

movie, the people at the table begin to relax in relief. During her first scene with Brennan's character, the chuckles began, and by page forty, when she first introduced him to her "fiancé from socialist heaven," the laughs were coming with nearly every line.

Thomas turned out to be better than she'd hoped. Actors with his kind of good looks usually relied too much on that to carry them through. But Thomas was bigger than life when he spoke, too, and perfectly in character—resentful of authority, crazy about her, and dumb as a stump. As the two of them idiotically discussed the "finer" points of relations between East and West, the room erupted in hilarity. By the end, with them married and Nicklaus the Communist completely compromised by the deceitful West, Bennie was beaming at her. As he read "'The End,'" the room burst into applause. Pagan clapped, too, her blood humming with a high she'd forgotten about, the feeling of creative people coming together to make something great.

"Thank you, ladies and gentlemen," Bennie said, and everyone stood, gathering their things. "Be sure you get a copy of the production schedule. We'll see those of you in the scenes tomorrow on set. Pagan, my dear, come here for a moment."

"See you tomorrow," Thomas said quietly, pulling back her chair to help her up. "And thank you."

"Thank you!" she said, smiling up at him as she put on her gloves. "We're going to have so much fun."

The crew said "hello" and "great job" to her as she sidled past them toward Bennie. James Brennan and Adele Franklin nodded, still frosty but at least acknowledging her presence. Maybe, just maybe, she could pull this off.

Bennie took her hand as the room emptied. Devin, subtle and sleek as a panther in the shadows among the glittering, chattering actors, took Thomas by the elbow as they left, pulling him aside in the lobby for a quiet word. From the expression on Thomas's face, he wasn't happy about it.

"You are so very talented," Bennie said to her. "I'm sorry the last movie we were on together was…difficult."

"That's all right," Pagan said, blushing at his compliment. "Mama wasn't always easy to get along with. I just have to tell you, Bennie, this script is so smart and so funny—I know how lucky I am to be here."

"Good," he said, releasing her hand, his eyes narrowing at her behind the thick lenses. "Good. Because there's another thing I must tell you. You're going to kill in this part, and you will be welcome to play it just so long as you remain sober and don't cause trouble."

The smile on Pagan's face faded. She clasped her hands together to stop them from shaking. "I understand." It was all she could think to say.

"Normally I don't care what actors do off-set, but I know damned well you were high as the moon during shoots, for years. You're also underage, on probation, and responsible for two deaths, so if I catch you taking even one sip of alcohol on or off the set…" Bennie jutted his chin out for emphasis. "Just one sip!" His finger stabbed up at the ceiling with each word. "I'll fire you. Do you hear me?"

She was shrinking back, terrified. Not just of him, but also of how his anger sent a stab of need through her. The need for a drink. She shoved the desire back and made herself square her shoulders, to look him in the eye. "I hear you. And I promise you. It won't happen."

"We'll see," he said, unrelenting. "And don't think your friend can protect you." He gestured at Devin, over in the lobby. "I don't care what the studio says, I don't care how far into the shoot it happens, or how much it inflates the budget. One drink and you're out."

PAGAN JONES'S MYSTERIOUS GUARDIAN: SECRETS REVEALED!

How Far Will She Go to Uncover the Truth?

"I think you scared Bennie," Devin said.

By the time Pagan had visited the costumer to try on dresses and shoes and let her take Pagan's measurements, it was nearing lunchtime. They were in the Mercedes headed back to the Hilton. Pagan had withdrawn to the farthest corner of the black leather backseat and was staring silently out the tinted window.

Devin was, as usual, seated upright, long legs crossed, sunglasses hiding those all-too-perceptive eyes. They hadn't spoken for the first few minutes, and she'd been grateful for the silence. She just had to concentrate. That's all it took. If she put her mind to it, she'd stop fantasizing about asking the driver to take them to the nearest bar.

"*I* scared *him*?" She recoiled deeper into the seat. "So you heard what he said to me?"

"I was too far away to hear, but it was pretty clear from the look on his face." As she stirred, agitated, he added, "Don't worry. No one was looking."

"Oh." It was odd to be grateful to Devin. "Then you should know it was him who scared *me*."

He shook his head. "You were so good at the table read, you gave him hope. Hope is terrifying."

She uncurled a little at the compliment, but only a little. Sometimes people complimented you just to soften you up for the follow-up punch to the gut. "I can think of worse things than hope."

"Not for Bennie," Devin said. "He's a cynic. Hope makes him, for a brief time, an optimist. And nothing scares a cynic more than that, because they're so certain they'll be disappointed. You made him think today that his movie might be great, that you'll be great in it. And now that you've given him that hope, he's petrified you'll destroy it."

She pictured Bennie's squinty eyes. She heard again the venom in his voice. "Scared and angry is still angry," she said. "If I make one mistake, Bennie said, if I drink, he'll fire me, no matter what. He doesn't care what you and the studio might try to do about it."

"Then it's simple," he said. "Don't make a mistake."

"Maybe for you," she said, resentment of him rising. Did he have any idea how lucky he was to be able to have a drink and not even give it a second thought? It wasn't fair that she had to worry about it every second of every hour of every day.

"I didn't say it would be easy," he said. "The simplest things are usually the most difficult."

Back at the hotel Devin stopped in the lobby to pick up his messages while Pagan decided reading boring letters was better than thinking about martinis, so she went upstairs and pulled out the letters she'd found in her father's safe.

There it was again, the too-neat signature *Rolf Von Albrecht*, addressed to *Liebe Eva*, along with his relentlessly mundane remarks about his life.

She looked at every sheet again, becoming more certain

that there was no way anyone would write twenty letters full of this drivel without a very good reason. Squinting, she held up the paper to the lamp, but no nearly invisible squiggles appeared between the even lines of script. She put the paper close to the hot bulb of her side table lamp to heat it, but no lemon juice ink manifested a secret message.

Then, on the last letter, dated 1 November, 1952, a week before Pagan's eighth birthday, she found something written in smaller, tidier script.

Someone else had jotted down another date, 20 April, 1889, in the margin of the letter. It wasn't easy to tell with just a few strokes of ink to go by, but it looked like her father's handwriting.

April 20, 1889. The date had familiarity to it, as if something important had happened in history. Maybe she was imagining it because it was so long ago. Anything that had happened before the war seemed like ancient times. She ran through the little she knew about that era from her days being tutored on set—Queen Victoria, railroads, the Wild West. None of those things or April 20, 1889 had anything to do with the letters or with November 1, 1952. But then why had her father carefully written it there?

She heard Devin open the door to the suite and hastily hid the letters in her suitcase. A glance at the clock told her it was nearly 10:00 p.m. back in California, and if she was going to call Mercedes, she'd better do it now. She changed into comfier Capri pants and a sleeveless cotton top, grabbed the hotel phone and walked it on its long cord into her room of the suite. Devin was reading several slips of paper, probably messages he'd picked up at the front desk. She was dying to peek over his shoulder at them, but he was too smart to let her do that.

She shut the door to her room and dialed the international

operator, hoping that Devin's instructions to cater to her and Mercedes still held Miss Edwards in thrall.

A minute later, Mercedes said, "Hello?" in a puzzled voice.

"M!" Pagan shouted. "Didn't the Bitch Queen tell you it was me?"

"Hereje!" Pagan's heart swelled as she recognized one of her friend's favorite nicknames for her. "How are you? How is the world?"

"It's crazy, of course." Pagan lay back on the bed, phone to her ear, completely happy for the first time in forever. "How's your shoulder?"

"I'm out of the infirmary. So far the *puta barata*—" Mercedes's favored cusswords for Miss Edwards "—just ignores me, so that's okay. I have to keep my arm in a sling, but should be out of it in a week. Got the whole room to myself for now. It's like having a mansion, so it's like being you."

"I know you miss me," Pagan said, grinning. "I'm in a luxury suite in the Hilton in Berlin, if you can believe it. But—" she lowered her voice "—Devin Black is sharing my suite!"

"He's in the same room?" Mercedes sounded surprised but not shocked. She wasn't easy to scandalize.

"No, separate bedrooms and bathrooms. He says he needs to keep an eye on me."

"Sounds slippery," Mercedes said. "Can you lock your bedroom door?"

"Yeah," Pagan said, lowering her voice even further. "It's weird because he doesn't scare me that way, exactly, but..."

Mercedes exhaled a skeptical laugh.

"Okay, so he's hotter than Alain Delon driving a black convertible in *Death Valley at noon*," Pagan admitted. "He's like a combination of complete gentleman and devious scoundrel."

"Have you searched his luggage while he's out?" Mercedes asked.

Pagan smacked her hand on top of her head. "No, but what a great idea! I haven't had a chance yet, but—"

Three quiet knocks on the bedroom door sent her leaping several feet in the air in surprise.

"Pagan?"

It was Devin, of course. Pagan put a hand to her hard-beating heart. "Hang on one second, M." Louder, she said, "Come in!"

The door opened enough to allow Devin's dark head to peer into her room. His restive gaze found her on the bed, and although his expression did not change, she became conscious of how she was half lying on her bed with him standing only a few steps away.

"I'm going to make a call from downstairs," he said.

She nodded, as if impatient with his interruption, but secretly she was intrigued. "Okay."

"After that we should get some lunch. I know a good place in the French sector."

"Sounds great," she said.

He started to close the door, then stopped and shot a glance back at her. "I'll have an unobstructed view of the lobby," he said. "Just in case you decide to take a stroll without me."

Damn. He was thorough.

"Wouldn't dream of it." She gave him a big fake smile.

"Uh-huh," he said, dubious. And shut the door.

"That was him, right?" Mercedes said.

"Oh, my God, M, things are weird…" Pagan quickly gave her a synopsis of her suspicions of Devin—how he couldn't be a studio executive, how he seemed to know about her long-dead grandfather, how everything he'd done had been to get her here, on this movie in Berlin, for who-knows-what reason.

"That city is dangerous," Mercedes said. "Since I learned you were going there, I snagged a *New York Times* from the guard, and everybody's worried the Commies will do something there that'll start World War Three."

"Yeah, but what's that got to do with me?" Pagan asked. "It doesn't make any sense."

"They're gonna make me leave you any second now. Curfew at ten. So I'll tell you what you do," Mercedes said. "That Devin boy is gone now, so you search his room. You've got to be fast, so don't look in the obvious places like the main compartments of his luggage or his suit pockets. Look for false bottoms in the suitcases, between the mattress and the box spring, and go all the way under the bed if you can."

"Under the bed?" Pagan's heart was beating hard. "Wouldn't the maid find something if he put it there?"

"No, no. You get under the bed, on your back, like a mechanic checking a car, and you see if he slid anything between the bottom of the box spring and the bed frame. It's a hotel, so he won't be able to hide things behind false walls or under the floorboards."

Mercedes was only seventeen, but growing up in the female clique of a Los Angeles gang had taught her some fascinating things. "Wow, okay. I will." Pagan stared at the door to her bedroom, not wanting to get off the phone with this, the one person on Earth she trusted. "Thanks."

"Okay, so, before I go. Did you go to a meeting like I asked you?" Mercedes's voice was casual.

Pagan hesitated. It would be so easy to lie, and then M would be satisfied and she wouldn't have to deal with her disappointment. She'd lied so often to Daddy, and it hadn't bothered her once. But she'd never lied to M before, and that was a part of the unspoken bargain of their friendship. What if Mercedes found out she'd lied and stopped being her friend? She couldn't imagine that. Mercedes was all she had.

"Pagan?" Mercedes said, tone sharpening.

"There hasn't been time yet," she said.

Mercedes exhaled in frustration on the other end of the line and she rushed to explain. "I flew out of LA early yesterday and had the table read for the movie today. We just got back. And we start shooting tomorrow. But I haven't had a drink. I'm fine."

"That's great, but you need to go to a meeting," Mercedes said.

"Why?" Pagan said. It came out angrier than she intended. She swallowed hard, pushing her voice down into a semblance of reasonableness. "I can handle this, M. I haven't had a drink in ten months, and I'm not about to start now. Not when I've finally got a chance to act again, a chance to find more about Mama…"

"You can't handle it," Mercedes said, unrelenting. "And you telling me that you can, shows me that you have no idea what you're doing."

"But I am handling it!" she said. "You have no idea how hard this is, but I'm doing it, M. I'm doing it! Don't you trust me?"

"I've been around addicts, Pagan. They're only trustworthy when they're sober." Mercedes's tone was harsh, and she broke off, as if reining in her feelings. "But at least you didn't lie to me about going to a meeting. Listen to me, Pagan." Her voice had gone dead serious. "Strange and maybe dangerous things are going on around you. You have to keep sharp. And that means no drinking. To make that happen, you have to use every resource there is."

Pagan leaned into the phone, wishing her friend was there and also wishing she'd never made this phone call. "That's what I'm doing."

Mercedes was quiet for a moment. "No, you're not."

"Mercedes…" Pagan's throat was tight. "I know you want

what's best for me, but you've got to let me figure this out myself."

Another pause. Mercedes never spoke until she was ready. "You're right," she finally said. "It's not up to me. I hope you figure it out, *Hereje*."

Pagan bowed her head. She could do this. She would keeping powering through and make Mercedes proud.

A voice on the other line said something Pagan didn't catch. "I've got to go," Mercedes said. "And you need to go do what we were talking about earlier. You know I miss you, right?"

Pagan's eyes got watery, but she choked it back. "I miss you, too."

"Call me!" The words were a warning, and Mercedes hung up.

Pagan put the receiver on the cradle and walked the phone slowly out of her bedroom, back to its place on the side table in the suite's common area. It was quiet, empty. The door to Devin's bedroom was closed.

It would be locked. If she was going to do this, she had to do it now, fast, before he finished his phone call in the lobby and came up to get her for lunch.

Pulling two hairpins from her updo, she strode to his bedroom door and turned the knob. Yep. Locked.

She slipped one bent pin in as the tension wrench and quickly figured out which way to torque the lock. The second pin slipped out of her sweating fingers, and she had to fish it off the carpeted floor while keeping the tension wrench in place. Every second of delay could bring Devin in at just the wrong moment. She couldn't help turning to stare at the door to the hallway.

Should she lock the security dead bolt on that door? If Devin came in unexpectedly, he'd be shut out, and it would give her time to look innocent.

Or would double locking the door just arouse his suspicions? She had no justification for doing it. Did she?

Damn it! *Stop overthinking and just do it.* She stuck the second bobby pin in the lock and found the most stubborn internal gear faster than she'd hoped. In thirty seconds the lock was open, and she was inside Devin's bedroom.

She paused, running through Mercedes's instructions in her head as she surveyed the place. It was annoyingly neat. Of course the maid had made the bed and refreshed the towels in the adjoining bathroom, but Devin had left nothing draped over the back of the chair or on the floor of the closet.

Her eyes lingered on the bed. So that was where he slept, just a few feet away from her. It was so strangely intimate, their arrangement in the suite, and even more so now that she had violated his trust and broken into this inner sanctum.

Stop it! Stop being distracted and get searching. But where? He'd closed up his suitcase. There were no papers, no money, no cigarettes or matches or anything on the side table.

Best to do the toughest spot first. Under the bed. She was glad she was wearing pants as she lay down next to the bed and poked her head under, just as Mercedes had said, like a mechanic under a car.

It was dark under there. She didn't see anything immediately, and as her eyes adjusted, she ran her hands over the underside of the bed. Her updo, rubbing along the carpet, started to come down. The dirt on the metal frame stuck to her fingers.

Muffled laughter and running footsteps in the hallway outside. She froze. A trickle of sweat ran down the side of her forehead, over her ear, and down her neck.

She looked down the line of her own body and saw her legs sticking out from under the bed like the Wicked Witch under Dorothy's house. She curled up, pulling her legs from view.

Then she told herself not to be stupid, shoved her legs out long again, and kept running her hands over the box spring above her. Hiding was no better than being found. If she wasn't immediately available when Devin walked in, he'd start searching, and under the beds was the obvious first place to look.

The footsteps outside padded past their room, taking the laughter with them. She sent a mental thank-you to whatever gods took care of thieves and kept touching along the metal struts of the frame for anything that wasn't the box spring.

When she hit something smooth and leathery, at first she didn't believe it. But as she carefully ran her hands over it again, she realized it was some sort of briefcase, shoved between the metal crossbars of the bed frame and the wooden part of the box spring.

Throwing caution to the wind, she pulled the briefcase out of its hiding spot and scooted out, back into the light of the bedroom, then sat up next to the bed to assess.

It was indeed a hard burgundy leather briefcase, thinner than any case she'd seen before, with two silver clasps and a combination lock.

Damn. How did you pick open a briefcase? She tried to click the clasps, just in case he hadn't set the lock, but no luck. Devin was thorough.

She didn't have time to pick it. He could be back any second. But the fact that she had found it tucked in such a secret place was a strong indication that Devin Black had something—maybe a lot of things—to hide.

She slid her top half back under the bed and shoved the briefcase back where he had put it, adjusting its angle to what she thought it had originally been. Then she was up and on her feet, head spinning.

What else? Where else?

She opened the drawer of his nightstand. Nothing. She slid

her hands under his pillows and between the mattress and the box spring. Zilch. A quick glance at the closet showed her nothing but several ridiculously gorgeous suits and neatly hung belts. His upright suitcase was also locked.

Was there anything he hadn't thought of?

She was about to head back out the door to see if she could lock it behind her when a thought struck her. There was one hiding place she herself would choose if she needed one in a hotel room.

She turned on her toe and ran into Devin's private bathroom, ignoring the toothbrush and Pepsodent, the old-fashioned straight razor and shaving cream and the light hair pomade. She went right to the toilet, removed the extra roll of toilet tissue in its knitted cozy sitting on top, and lifted the lid off the tank.

Lying in the clear water at the bottom was a black plastic bag.

Her pulse tap-dancing, she spared a glance back at the bedroom. She'd closed the door to give herself time if he walked into the suite, but again, that wasn't much help. Just being in here was damning.

He'd been gone for at least twenty minutes. How much longer could his downstairs phone call possibly last? She should probably shut the tank lid and come back later.

To hell with *should*. She stuck her hand in the cold water and pulled out the black plastic bag. It was surprisingly heavy. With her other hand she grabbed a towel off the rack and placed it on the counter to catch the water dripping from the plastic bag.

The bag was sealed with a kind of plastic zipper. She fumbled with her wet fingers, then got it open to find another plastic bag inside. She opened that bag, which was dry, and reached in.

Her fingers hit cold metal and glass.

Glass? She pulled out a small test-tubed sized bottle with a cork in it. Something dark, about the size of her thumbnail, rattled inside it.

She held it up, trying not to let it move around and make any noise. The object inside the tube was made of metal. It looked as though it might have once been cylindrical, but some great force had warped it. It made no sense but it sure looked like a spent bullet.

She put it aside, reached back in the bag, and pulled out a gun.

BATTLE OF THE SEXES BECOMES ALL OUT WAR!

Brute Force or Sneaky Deception: Which Will Win the Day?

Pagan dropped the gun. It thumped onto the towel-covered counter and lay there, gleaming. The barrel was a very shiny silver. The grip was black.

She stared at it, suddenly dizzy, as if she'd discovered herself standing on the edge of a precipice. When she looked down, she couldn't see the bottom.

A gun?

But no matter how long she gaped at the gun, it remained a gun. A semiautomatic .22 caliber pistol, in fact. She'd learned enough from her shooting instructor on *Young Annie Oakley* to know that.

She leaned in closer, not touching it. It carried no identifying marks, no manufacturer's name or serial number. She wasn't sure, but that seemed odd. She didn't know enough about modern guns to tell who had manufactured it. Her training had been mostly with rifles and shotguns.

What the hell was Devin doing with a gun? And why was it hidden in the tank of his hotel toilet?

She snapped herself upright. She'd been gaping at it for too long. She dropped the spent bullet in the second bag along with the gun and zipped it up, sealed up the first bag, and plopped it back in the same corner of the toilet tank.

A doorknob click-clacked.

She stiffened, listening as if her life depended on it.

Maybe it did.

The main door to the suite ticked open.

Devin was back. She grasped the edges of the heavy porcelain tank lid and hoisted it back into place, taking care so that it didn't clank.

"Pagan?"

Devin's voice. Dang it, she was sunk.

She whipped the towel back onto the rack and tiptoed to the bathroom entrance, staring at the shut door of Devin's bedroom. He must be right outside it.

"Pagan?" His voice was more irritated now. His footsteps, soft on the carpet outside, moved over to her bedroom. She heard him knock and rapidly open her door. "Ready for lunch?"

She ran to the door of his bedroom and put her hand on the knob. If he went inside her bedroom, there was a chance she could slip out of his room unnoticed and act like she'd just walked in herself.

She turned the knob with aching slowness to keep it quiet and gently cracked his door. She could see Devin's slim form now coming swiftly back out of her bedroom muttering something that sounded like "Bollocks."

Odd. Not a swear word most Americans used… Oh, dang, he was heading right toward her!

Too late. She'd never escape without being seen.

She shut the bedroom door and ran back into the bathroom. Maybe if he couldn't find her, he'd go out to look for her, giving her time to escape.

The bathroom was hellishly small. The claw-foot bathtub was in the "sit down and soak" European style, with no shower curtain or sliding doors to screen her. The only place he might not find her at a glance was behind the door. Cursing herself silently for taking so long to search, she switched off the bathroom light and slid behind it. Devin would notice that his bedroom door was unlocked, but she half-hysterically told herself maybe that would lead him to think she'd been kidnapped, or that the place had been robbed.

Over the uneven sounds of her own breath she heard him slip his key into the lock of his bedroom door.

She couldn't see what was going on, but she didn't hear the door open or Devin's footsteps enter the room. Nothing.

Was he coming in or not?

She'd been holding her breath. She forced herself to exhale silently, putting her hands up against the smooth wood of the bathroom door to stop it from banging her in the nose if he pushed it open. If he found her here, what was she going to say? How could she possibly justify being in his bathroom after breaking into his room?

An iron hand gripped Pagan's raised right arm. She gasped as he wrenched her out from behind the door, arcing her toward the tub.

She twisted her wrist against his thumb and slipped free, stumbling back into the tub, but managing not to fall into it. She opened her mouth to speak, to let him know it was her.

He threw a punch at her face.

She flinched back and got her forearm up in time to deflect it, but the power behind the punch rattled her bones. Dim light limned an angle of his implacable face. There was no sign of recognition. He couldn't see her in the dark.

Terror pushed her past him, toward the bathroom door, but he grabbed her wrist with fingers like steel bands and twisted. Pain shot through her as he spun her around and shoved her bent arm up behind her back, brutally pushing her face first against the wall. The entire line of his body pressed up against hers. Her hair was tumbling down, sticking to her neck and her lips. The heat from him burned a line down her back from shoulder to hip.

Enough! With sudden fury, she slammed her heel onto his instep.

He grunted in pain. But his grip on her wrist did not slacken.

She was pinned to the wall, helpless. His chest was heaving in time with hers. She prepared an earth-shattering scream for help.

Then: *"Pagan?"*

He let her go so suddenly, she nearly collapsed.

But this time he caught her, gently, by the shoulders.

"Oh, my God," he said. A line of light from the cracked door showed his eyes, wide with horror. Locks of dark hair spiked down over his forehead. "I'm so sorry." He set her back on her feet and slid his hands down her bare arms, feeling for injury. "Did I hurt you?"

Still trying to catch her breath, she brushed her hair out of her eyes and mouth. "I'm okay, I think. But my wrist…"

Before she could finish the sentence, he was holding her wrist in both of his hands as delicately as if it were a baby bird. "Did I break it?"

"I don't think so." He was probing the bones of her arm for signs of injury.

Something about the way he handled her, softly stroking the thin skin on the inside of her wrist, combined with the ebbing of adrenaline, was turning her knees to water. She wanted to fall into him. She wanted to run away.

"It's okay," she managed to say.

He reached over, eyes never leaving her, and flicked on the

light. He put one hand up to her cheek. "Your face. When I pushed you against the wall. I didn't mean to…"

His fingers were warm. His mouth was only a foot from hers. Waves of heat pulsed through her with every breath. After all the tension of searching his room, waiting to be caught when he came in, their heart-stopping clash, and now this—her head was buzzing. His scent lingered on her skin where he'd grabbed her, clean leather and rain on tobacco leaves. She wanted to press herself into it, to drown in it. The temptation to do that, to lean into him, to breathe him in and feel his strength surrounding her expanded into a drastic ache. She swayed.

Concern creased his forehead. "Come sit down," he said.

She allowed him to guide her out of the bathroom and sit her down slowly on the edge of his bed. Hard to believe that just a minute ago she'd been underneath that same bed. The only place left to go was in it.

What was wrong with her? She bowed her head, as if to keep him from reading her mind.

"How do you feel?" he asked, feeling her uninjured wrist for her pulse.

She tugged away from him and sat up a little taller, taking a deep breath. "I'm okay," she said. "I'm… I just am not used to fighting men for use of the bathroom."

He let her pull away without quarrel and stood up, staring down at her with a look she couldn't decipher. "I thought you were an intruder. I'm sorry."

"I know," she said. "It's my fault."

"I could have hurt you very badly," he said. "Why didn't you answer me when I called you?"

The question was like a bucket of cold water, bringing her back to the strange new reality. He looked so young with his hair falling in his eyes, a faint sheen of sweat from their fight on his forehead. He could've been a normal teenage boy, instead of a man with a hidden gun and an even more secret agenda for her here in Berlin.

When she still didn't respond, he took off his jacket and walked over to the closet. The taut muscles in his shoulders moved with a well-oiled ease under the fine cotton shirt. She'd never seen him with his jacket off before, and without the formal wool silhouette masking the line of his body, his movements were controlled, powerful. She could now well believe how effortlessly he'd pinned her, held her.

"You broke into this room," he said. "Where'd you learn how to pick a lock?"

"Mercedes," she said, avoiding his gaze.

"What were you doing in here?" He put his suit jacket on a hanger and hung it on the closet rail with a click.

She said nothing. When in doubt, let the other person do all the talking.

He put a finger in his tie and eased it looser around his neck. "To be honest, I expected you to leave the room and try to get out through the kitchen in the back of the hotel. Or to hire someone to distract me so you could bolt out the front."

"Wish I'd thought of that," she said, half meaning it.

"I didn't expect you to ransack my room." He walked back to stand in front of her, staring down. "Did you take anything?"

His question sparked an idea. If she was as good an actress as she hoped, she might pull it off.

"No!" She made it a little too loud; the lady protesting too much. "I'm not a thief."

"I don't have any alcohol in here, Pagan," he said, exactly as she'd hoped. "While I'm on this assignment with you, I'm sober as a judge."

"Not the highest standard to measure yourself against," she

said, a shade too flippantly, and continued to avoid looking him in the eye.

"Why were you in my bathroom?" He circled around to look into that room, now in disarray.

"I..." She ducked her head in shame. "Nothing. Like you said, I was hoping to find your secret stash of scotch, but there was nothing. And then I heard you coming and I panicked. The bathroom was the only place to hide."

"You," he said. "*You* panicked."

She looked up, surprised at his skepticism. He eased one shoulder against the wall, the corner of his mouth curving up. "I don't believe you're capable of panic. Even in there—" he jerked his thumb back at the bathroom "—you were thinking with perfect clarity. You blocked my punch, and after I got you in a lock you had the presence of mind to stomp on my foot."

"Sorry about that," she said, not meaning it.

He lifted the foot and flexed it. "Where did you learn that?"

"Mercedes again," she said. "She taught me a lot."

He nodded, pursing his lips. "Mercedes Duran. Now there's a formidable individual. Joined the Avenidas gang when she was thirteen, stole her first car when she was fourteen, and got caught."

"That was her second, actually," Pagan said.

He smiled and dipped his head, acknowledging her superior expertise on the subject. "But they let her go a month later. Did she tell you she used to extort money from shop owners?" he asked. "Usually only the most intimidating men in the gang get that job."

Pagan nodded. "Her older brother was one of their top members," she said. "He taught Mercedes a lot before..." She broke off. Was she betraying Mercedes's trust by saying these things?

"Before he was killed by a rival gang." Devin raised one

dark eyebrow as she shot him a look. "Yes, I've done my homework."

Oh, he was so smug. "Did you know her best friend died of a heroin overdose when they were both fifteen?" Pagan asked. "Mercedes has seen so much, even I can't shock her. It made for a nice change after all those screaming headlines during the trial."

"You're not that shocking," he said. "Just surprising."

"Where did you learn to fight?" she said. "It isn't usually a skill on the résumés of studio flacks."

"Stop trying to change the subject," he said. "There's no alcohol in my bedroom or my bathroom, Pagan."

"No?" she said. "Ever look at the ingredients on a bottle of mouthwash? Or cough syrup?"

Comprehension dawned over his face, just as she'd hoped it would. She darted her gaze away and let her shoulders slump. She knew all too well how to act humiliated. The memory of real shame was ever present for her to tap into. "That's what I was looking for, okay? It's disgusting and awful, but after what Bennie said to me earlier, I just..." She broke off, knowing she didn't need to say more. People were so ready to believe you when you revealed some horrible fact about yourself.

He exhaled a long breath, nodding as if to himself. "Okay," he said. "I appreciate you telling me." He pulled his tie completely loose. "Maybe we should order lunch from room service today."

"Oh, no, please, can't we go out?" The question came straight from her heart. "I've been cooped up for nine months, and tomorrow I go back to work. Can't we just—I don't know—go for a walk somewhere green? Or even around the city, I don't care, I just want to see the sky and look at people who aren't in school uniforms."

"Fair enough." He undid his top button, and she caught a

glimpse of the smooth skin over his collarbone. He pointed at his bedroom door. "Let me change and I'll think about where we can walk around and find some food."

"That sounds boss!" she said, jumping up and darting out of his bedroom. "See you in a few!"

She ran into her room, shut the door, and leaned back against it.

Her head was spinning. Dang, that had been crazy, dangerous, and *fun*.

She hadn't felt this juiced since she and Nicky zoomed down Mullholland at midnight racing two guys in a Chrysler 300E. Vodka was child's play compared to this. She was higher than high.

What, she wondered, would happen next?

PAGAN JONES PROBES PROTECTOR'S PAST

Dark Secrets Disclosed!

The outdoor café where they ate lunch had delicious schnitzel, and after some ice cream, Devin pointed their driver to a huge yellow palace with a bronze-green dome. Devin had picked the location, but the idea had been Pagan's.

After privately deciding it was time to learn more about Devin, she'd suggested they visit a museum. She knew two strange things about him for sure: he'd admired and understood the Renoir in her parents' room, and he had a pistol hidden in his hotel toilet tank. She wasn't likely to persuade him to take her to a firing range, but maybe if she saw him around more art, he'd give something away. If not, she'd throw smart-aleck remarks at him till he did.

They walked through the gate past two statues of naked, armed men, into the large square courtyard, where tourists ambled or rested in the shade of a huge bronze guy on a horse. Although the butter-yellow facade of the building was clean and new, scaffolding clung to the outer wings of the building, which stretched for what seemed like miles to the left and right.

"Schloss Charlottenburg," Devin said. "Badly damaged in

the war, and still under reconstruction, but in decent enough shape for a visit. I hear the gardens are nice, too."

He babbled on about Queen Charlotte and baroque art as they entered the rather plain first floor and she caught a glimpse of the vast gardens beyond. Geometric paths wound through emerald grass, bordered by thick, strictly trimmed trees. A fountain shot water nearly three stories high in the middle, and in the distance glassy olive-green water hinted at a pond or river.

A sudden longing to hear the trickle of moving water pierced her. It wasn't the Pacific Ocean she was used to, but it was beautiful, and natural, and it had been months since she'd been surrounded by anything but concrete.

Devin was trotting up the grand staircase, though, having spoken to a guide, so she reminded herself of her mission to learn more about him and followed. Above, the ceiling was painted cerulean blue and festooned with pink cherubs. The hall upstairs was far grander, with a shiny parquet floor and huge windows reflected in the long wall of mirrors.

"And I thought Beverly Hills was ostentatious," she said.

As she watched, Devin moved up to one of the windows and scanned the frame, leaning close to squint down. She came over and craned her neck to look down with him. She saw only the outside walls and the courtyard. The guy on the horse looked a lot smaller from up here.

"I bet he had a bald spot in real life," she said of the statue.

"Hmm? Oh. Probably." Devin strode away from the window and down the hall past two older women reading a brochure, his tall slender form reflected in the mirrors. "Most of the restored rooms are up here. How about some Chinese porcelain?"

She tagged behind him through carved double doors into a golden room packed in every corner with porcelain plates and

pots decorated in graceful curves of blue. Very pretty, Pagan
supposed, but boring. She preferred the painted ceiling, which
was cloudier this time, with gods and plump women in capes
whooshing around, winking and beaming at each other as if
they knew that life in the sky was better than for the suckers
down below.

Devin was at the window again, looking straight up this
time. Why was he always at windows? The door opened to
admit a museum guard, who sighed heavily and went to stand
in the corner.

Devin gave him a sharp glance and moved to the next room,
which contained a huge gilt-covered bed and several dozen
paintings of fleshy people cavorting through faded landscapes
showing more skin than a beach movie. The clean white marble bust of a Roman with a receding hairline was a relief after
all the movement and color.

Devin's eyes swept the room and landed on the painting
of a picnic with lounging figures and a dog. The label said it
was by Antoine Watteau.

"Like that one, do you?" she asked. "The dog's not bad."

"Precursor to Impressionism, Watteau," Devin muttered.

She watched him closely. It was subtle, but his eyes traveled
over the edges of the painting's gilt frame rather than studying the painting itself.

He'd spent more time studying the windows and how the
painting was attached to the wall than he had the art itself.
Did that mean what she thought it meant? Time to find out.

He'd flirted with her a day or so ago before making himself stop. Let's see how he handled things when she really let
out the stops.

"They don't have a guard in here," she said. "We're all
alone. In someone else's bedroom."

He shot her a glance. Now that the sunglasses were off, she

thought she saw a fierce glint in his eyes. "With no one but the paintings to see what trouble we get into."

The room felt suddenly quite warm. She ignored it and pressed on. "We could steal something."

He cast his eyes up at the busy ceiling, hands clasped behind his back. "Why," he asked, "would we do that?"

"It's fun to think about, isn't it?" She glanced out the window. "I'd say let's toss the marble head out the window, but someone would see us."

"Not at night they wouldn't," he said. "The lighting conditions are deplorable. Still, I wouldn't advise it. The windows are alarmed."

So he *had* been scoping out the alarm system around the windows. "But you could disable those easily enough," she said as if that were a given.

He raised both eyebrows, face blank. "What makes you think that?"

She waved her hand at him, dismissing a joke. "We could sneak it out during the day if you insist." She moved over to the Roman bust. "I could come in here with a pillow under my dress..." she put a hand under her blouse to pouf it out near her stomach "...and make the switch when the guard steps out." She mimed grabbing the bust and stuffing it under her shirt.

He laughed. "That would be one advantage to having a female accomplice."

"You mean you didn't have one?" She slipped the question in as if they'd already discussed this. "All good art thieves should have a pretty female accomplice, to distract the police at crucial moments."

His face was blandly baffled. "At the studio we call them secretaries."

So he was sticking to the studio executive story. Time for drastic measures.

"This one's your favorite, right?" She strode over to the Watteau. "Probably the most valuable. It's a bit big, but we could just…"

She grabbed the frame and hoisted the painting up.

He lurched forward, eyes widening. "What the hell are you doing?"

She stayed where she was, not letting it go. "Testing to see if the painting was alarmed, of course. I figured it wouldn't be."

"You *never* touch the frame!" He grabbed the frame, brushing her hands away, and lowered it so that it hung straight once again from its hooks.

"Why not? Oh, fingerprints." She dusted her hands off. "How can anyone ever steal a painting if you don't touch the frame?"

His face had gone pale with anger and agitation. "Father said, you cut the painting out in four quick strokes." He zipped his hand inches from the painting around its four edges. "Fold it up, stick it in your bag, and walk out."

"You *cut and fold* the painting?" she asked in horror. "Doesn't that damage it?"

"The cutting might…" He broke off, mouthing a curse word.

"Do go on," she said, trying not to sound too triumphant.

His blue eyes were suddenly stormier than usual. "Time to go," he said, and walked out of the room.

She followed him, half running to keep up. "You were an art thief."

He didn't respond, but his shoulders tightened as he headed down the stairs.

So Devin Black had a past as disreputable as her own. It

explained his acting ability and his pickpocket skills. It might even explain the hidden gun.

It did not explain his interest in her family background or why he wanted her cast in *Neither Here Nor There*. In fact, nothing about Devin Black made sense.

They reached the bottom of the stairs, and she caught up to him, keeping her voice low. "Did you ever steal anything really valuable? Any jewels or Picassos?"

He said nothing, staying two steps ahead of her and lowering his sunglasses over his stony face as he walked out onto the groomed gravel path. She took the path to the right, branching away from him, and ambled next to the grass, listening to her saddle shoes crunch on the gravel and to the rustle of the breeze playing with the carefully trimmed rosebushes. Ahead, the fountain splashed, and she sped up to reach it then leaned over to dip her fingers in the sun-dappled water. A faint mist from it brushed her nose and forehead.

Devin Black stalked over to her, eyes masked by the sunglasses. "Let's go."

"Dare me to dip my toes in the water?" she asked.

"Let's not get arrested today."

She kept her voice light and asked, "How does one go from child bandit to working in Hollywood?"

She couldn't read his eyes behind the glasses. "You're the one with the criminal past," he said. "You tell me."

He didn't wait for her answering scowl but crunched his way over the gravel toward the car.

Back at the hotel, he disappeared into his room, while Pagan took a quick shower and tried to picture a young Devin Black stealing museum pieces with his no-doubt debonair father.

But as she dried off, the reality of what she faced the next day began to sink in. She had to be on set very early the next morning. In her previous life, the night before a shoot, she'd be well into her second martini by now, happily riding the buzz that drowned out any butterflies. It was unnerving to face the first day on a movie without that.

Filmmaking was an intricate, demanding process, a dance between actors, the camera, the lights, and the director. So much to remember. So many ways it could go horribly wrong.

Pagan walked out to the living area in her robe, toweling her hair with one hand, and picked up the phone to order something to drink. The image of an ice-cold martini swam through her thoughts, like a salmon battling upstream.

Something made her turn. Devin stood in the half-opened doorway to his bedroom, his shirt unbuttoned all the way. She looked up from the smooth muscles of his abdomen and flushed so hotly he had to see the blood in her cheeks.

He didn't smile. His lips parted, as if about to say something, his eyes like turbulent seas on a blustery night. She saw a question in his face, and a wordless answer rose inside her, beating against her heart.

But then Devin shut his lips and turned away, saying in a very clipped tone, "I'll order dinner in a minute."

What the hell was going on? She still loved Nicky. And this man was the enemy, her jailer, nothing else.

"All right." Her voice was distant to her own ears. Pagan put the phone handset back in its cradle.

She hadn't done it. She was safe. She was strong. She could do this.

Devin clicked his door shut. But her hands were trembling. She threaded her fingers together and headed back into her room.

When she was younger, before the drinking, the jitters of the night before a shoot would be stilled by spending time with her mother, running her lines, going over the names of the other actors, figuring out what her character really wanted and how to show that without saying it. Mama had been brilliant at taking apart a scene or a script to see what depths lay behind the facade.

"Most words are lies," Mama had said. "Small lies, big lies, slanted or bald-faced lies. They're what we use to disguise the wonder and terror we feel but can never say."

Those were some of Pagan's best memories of her mother, those nights before production started. Mama would pull out the script, put her arm around Pagan, and they'd pore over it together. It had made the next day seem less frightening, and they'd shared a common admiration of the complexity of life, and a common cause to be as good as possible at the job.

Mama could be frustrating and controlling, but she had understood that process. And at least Pagan had been safe with her. If Pagan was worried she'd mess up a scene, Mama would rehearse with her till she knew it cold. Just as when Ava got frustrated with a piano piece, Mama would break it down bit by bit for her until it flowed. The monsters under the bed were scared of Mama. Jerry Allenberg and most of the people at the studio had been, too.

But Mama had decided to go away. She would never come back.

The amorphous, smothering fear she'd first felt the night after her mother died filled her lungs and loomed over her, bearing down with its hulking, soul-crushing mass.

She sucked in air and clenched her fists. Yes, her eyes were leaking. But she wouldn't give the fear anything else.

You want a drink? Have a drink. Of water.

And then study your lines. That's what Mama would want.

Pagan poured herself a glass of water and drank it down as she wiped her eyes. The script lay waiting for her on the bedside table. She'd read it over twenty more times tonight if she had to.

The door behind her creaked. "Pagan? What would you like to me to order?"

Devin. She turned toward him without thinking and stopped, her red eyes staring right into his.

His face dropped. He took one hasty step into the room, then pulled up short. "I'm sorry. When you didn't answer my knock, I got worried…"

She hadn't heard a knock at all. She must've been too deep in thought. "I'm just tired," she said, pushing her lips up into a weary smile.

He took another unconscious step toward her. "Can I get you something…" He stopped himself. "We can run lines, if you want, over dinner," he continued, his voice more formal, but still warmer than it had ever been before. The kindness buried there nearly made her tear up again. "Or whatever you need."

She couldn't bask in any kindness now, or she'd crumble. She sniffed and shook her head. "Thanks, but I think I'll eat in my room tonight. Alone. So I can be ready for tomorrow."

He didn't move for a moment, looking at her. And that scared her more than anything, that he might say one more nice thing and destroy her completely. But he schooled his face into its usual nonchalance and nodded.

"All right," he said, backing out of the room. "I'll have your food brought to you in here."

"Thanks," she said, and the door clicked shut. She was alone with her doubts and an oh-so-inspirational glass of water. *Shoulders back, Pagan.* That's what Mama would have said. *Head high.*

She would be great tomorrow. She'd nail it. She had to. Her entire future depended on it.

CHAPTER TWELVE

TARNISHED TEEN STAR SHOOTS COMEDY IN BERLIN!

Oscar-Winning Director Very Demanding on Set

Pagan arrived on set with Devin a few minutes early, wearing no makeup and with her hair down and dirty. That was how the stylists liked it, and it made life a lot easier when you had to drag yourself out of bed at 5:00 a.m.

The quasi-domestic oddity of life in the suite with Devin had continued mostly in silence that morning. He hadn't said a word about the day before, and she still couldn't reconcile all the conflicting information she knew about him. Devin Black was shady, and she'd figure out exactly what was going on soon.

But today she had to focus. Today she had to be brilliant.

Makeup and hair done, dress fitted, she was called on set so that Bennie could walk her through the scene with Jimmy Brennan. Brennan was cold, but kept his skepticism of her in check in front of Bennie.

Bennie, meanwhile, was brisk, rattling out the blocking, guiding her from one mark to the next, expecting instant absorption. Afterward, Pagan scribbled notes on to her script so that she wouldn't forget, then went to seek out Matthew Smalls, the assistant director. She had two favors to ask him, but she decided to start with only one, because it, at least, might be important for the production of the film. The other one would keep until she could tell whether he liked her or not.

"I'm so sorry to trouble you," she said, putting a hand gently on his arm when no one else was within earshot. The grips were nearly done focusing the lights, and she didn't have much time.

"What can I do for you, Miss Jones?" Matthew asked, keeping one sharp eye on Bennie as he bickered with the gaffer and the DP over whether the set was overlit or not. Matthew's job was to make Bennie's job go as smoothly as possible, so he was never far from the director.

"This might be a drastic favor to ask," she said, feeling suddenly shy. It wasn't as if the whole world, particularly movie people, didn't know her history, but it still wasn't easy to confront. "It would be best for me if there wasn't any real alcohol on set. I know usually it's all iced tea and water, but sometimes actors ask for the real thing…"

The upcoming scene took place in the office of the character played by Jimmy Brennan, and like most executive offices, it had a bar, complete with ice bucket and tongs. In a later scene, Jimmy's character had a drink with his secretary/mistress while dictating a letter, and the thought of it had been in the back of Pagan's mind for a while.

Matthew's shrewd brown eyes assessed her. "There's no alcohol," he said. "Anywhere."

"Ah, good, thanks." She looked around for Devin, but he was nowhere to be seen. "Did that annoying Mister Black already ask you to do that for me?"

Matthew shook his head, his features registering no surprise, no curiosity of any kind at her rather odd question. "It's standard procedure on all of Bennie's movies."

"That's good to know." She couldn't help smiling ruefully. "I've got to say, you have the best poker face I've ever seen."

He breathed a laugh. "If only that was true when I actually played poker."

A few yards away, Bennie was walking, eyes narrowed and lips pursed in thought, over to the camera. "I think we're ready, Matthew."

"Places!" Matthew boomed.

Lounging crew members snapped to attention as Jimmy Brennan yawned and got out of his chair, moving to stand behind his character's desk. He nodded at Pagan, who smiled and made her way quickly over to stand behind the door that led into the office. A waiting grip smiled back at her in greeting.

"Door shut, please," Bennie said.

Pagan knew better than to touch the door. The grip leaned in and shut it behind her. A makeup assistant tiptoed over and freshened up her powder. Pagan had forgotten how the lights pressed down on you with palpable heat. Her nose got shiny fast in these conditions, but the makeup folks were never far away. She adjusted the fur-lined jacket she was wearing so that it hung haphazardly off one shoulder, showing more of the low scooped neckline of the tight flowered Nina Ricci dress they'd put her in, and shut her eyes, going over Violet's movements just prior to this scene in her head.

"Thank you all for being here, ladies and gentleman," Bennie said, hoisting himself up into his elevated director's chair. "We're going to do a rehearsal take of the master and go from there." The master was the long shot that showed the entire scene from start to finish, as if they were shooting a play. Bennie liked to start that way to let the actors find their rhythms. Later they'd break it down for the medium shots, inserts, and close-ups, if any. "I know you'll all act with consummate professionalism and talent, so that we finish today's scenes on time, on budget, and with something we can all be proud of. All right." Bennie gave Matthew the nod.

"Quiet on set," Matthew said.

Down the hall, the second assistant director shouted, "Quiet, please!"

Everyone stilled. Pagan tossed her head, becoming Violet, and pictured herself striding up to the door to L.T.'s office fresh from a long hot night spent with the world's most beautiful man. Pagan remembered well how empowering it was when she sneaked home after being with Nicky. How her whole body was relaxed yet energized. Every tiny thing in the world glowed, and she had emanated that reflected light.

Strangely, the sardonic face and strong graceful hands of Devin Black sprang to mind, and she hastily brushed that aside to replace him with the strong, square-jawed face of the man who was Violet's East German boyfriend, played by Thomas Kruger.

"Roll camera," said Bennie.

The camera whirred. "Rolling," said the camera operator. The second assistant cameraman, standing in the middle of the set, lifted his clapboard and waited.

"Sound," said Bennie.

The sound mixer flipped the Nagra recorder on, adjusting his headphones. "Speed," he said. Off to the side of the set, the boom operator lifted his microphone into position.

"Slate," Bennie said.

"*Neither Here Nor There*, scene 25, camera rehearsal," said the second AC, and slapped the clapperboard down sharply before he sidled off camera.

"And...action."

Pagan gave it a beat, and then sighed dreamily and opened the door. The blaring lights of the set fell full upon her. For

Violet Houlihan they were like the lights of heaven, and today she was wearing wings.

Jimmy Brennan, in character as L. T. Houlihan, had his back to her as he yelled into the phone. Beyond him, in the shadowy dark beyond the lights, the indistinguishable figures of the crew watched, utterly silent.

"I don't care if she's migrated with the kestrels to Greenland, we've got to find her, understand?" Brennan was yelling. "Get me the chief of police, get me Khrushchev, get me John F. Kennedy! Yes, all of them at once!"

Pagan sailed over toward the desk, removing her gloves, to land on her mark. "What's all the ruckus?"

Brennan shot her a cursory glance. "Violet's missing." Then into the phone: "Whaddaya mean we don't even recognize East Germany as a country? I can see it from my window!"

Pagan's mouth made a puzzled little moue. "But I'm right here." Her Southern accent gave the word *here* two, almost three, syllables.

"Quiet!" Brennan shouted, and then did an incredible double take at Pagan, who blinked at him, wide-eyed. "Violet!"

She could feel the stir of humor from the crew. During a rehearsal they were allowed to audibly react.

"Good morning," she said, splashing the widest, most innocent smile on the planet across her face.

"Where the blazes have you been?" Brennan slammed the phone into its cradle and rounded the corner of the desk toward her.

Pagan allowed her body to flood with love, lust, and excitement. "Well, you see, there's this boy over in East Berlin. And he's, well—what *isn't* he?"

"Boy?" Brennan's pouched eyes were alive with alarm and suspicion. His energetic frustration gave Pagan something solid to play off. "What boy?"

Pagan dreamily removed her coat and laid it on his desk. "Well, last week I was over in East Berlin to see what it was like and some boys started yelling at me to take my fur coat and go home."

"Yelling at you?" Brennan looked as if any second smoke would pour from his ears.

Pagan nodded. "And then Niklaus walked up and told them they shouldn't bother with me since I was just a poor bourgeois capitalist piglet who didn't know any better because I'd been raised in a corrupt society bereft of moral values." She shuddered a little with happiness, staring at Brennan as if she'd just seen the face of God. "It was love at first sight!"

The crew murmured appreciatively, and Pagan knew she'd nailed the joke.

The scene went on, over five minutes long, and by the time Pagan introduced her Communist boyfriend to Brennan, she was in the groove, bouncing her lines off both men as if they'd been doing it together onstage for weeks. When Bennie yelled "Cut!" the crew burst into applause.

"All right, all right," Bennie said. "So that went well. This time we do it for real."

"Places!" shouted Matthew Smalls, and they started all over again.

By lunch break, they'd done it thirty times, and everyone was ready to move on except Bennie. Jimmy Brennan was sweating and sending hot glares Pagan's way whenever she did a particularly funny take.

When Bennie announced they'd start the scene up again after lunch, Jimmy stomped over and pulled the director aside. He was trying to keep his voice low, but angry spurts of words spilled out as Pagan gave her purse back to the prop master.

"She's deliberately pulling focus from me," Jimmy spat. "It's unprofessional scene stealing, pure and simple!"

Bennie replied in soothing tones with something no one could hear, and, knowing Jimmy had to be ranting about her, Pagan blushed furiously and hustled away from them while the crew pretended to be busy.

The entire ninth floor of the building had been set aside as a makeshift cafeteria for the cast and crew. Pagan found a spot next to Thomas during the meal break, happy not to have to deal with the complicated Devin Black. Thomas gave her a wide dimpled smile as she set her tray down on the conference table.

"Jimmy hates me," she said under her breath to him.

Thomas didn't look surprised. "He's an excellent actor, but he must be the center of everything or he feels small."

"But I'm not the center of anything," she said. "He's the star of the movie."

"Not when you're in a scene with him," Thomas said. "And he knows it."

"Well, I hope Bennie talks some sense into him. I don't want him hating me the whole shoot."

"Just wait until he sees your fans in Berlin swarm you," Thomas said. "He'll have to hire someone to bump you off."

"Check out your English skills," she said as he smiled proudly. "You're sweet, but I doubt I have any fans left."

"Oh, but you do." Thomas pulled a magazine out of his jacket pocket and unfolded it to show her the cover. It was a newsprint rag, the kind that printed the nasty gossip rather than official studio news and interviews. On the cover was a huge photo of Pagan taken yesterday in the gardens of Schloss Charlottenburg as she dipped her fingers in the fountain. She surprised herself by easily reading the headline, which screamed the German version of: Tarnished Star Pagan Jones Free From Reform School, Shooting Film Comedy in Berlin!

Her heart sank. She'd hoped to escape the press for a little while longer, until she was more at ease out in the real world.

The photo looked innocent enough, but something was missing. She took a second to study it and it struck her. Devin had been right beside her most of the time. But in the photograph he simply wasn't there.

"Are there more shots?" she asked.

"Not many," Thomas said, opening up the magazine. He frowned at her, concerned. "Was I wrong to show you? It's quite flattering, really."

"No, of course it's all right." Pagan took the tabloid from him and scanned the three other photos of her, all taken at Schloss Charlottenburg. Devin was in none of them. It was as if he'd been erased.

She scanned the print, looking for clues. The more she read, the more easily the German words came back to her. At this rate it wouldn't be long before it became second nature to her, as it had been when she was a kid.

The article gave an accurate account of her conviction for manslaughter in the deaths of her father and sister, and her last nine months in the Lighthouse Reformatory for girls. It was told in the most sensational language, of course, but the facts were better than any story the magazine could have made up. The reporter finished by recounting how she seemed to be enjoying the beauty of the Schloss Charlottenburg, unconcerned about the past and no doubt looking forward to a second chance costarring in Benjamin Wexler's new movie, which would be shooting in Berlin for the next four weeks.

"Are you all right?" Thomas asked as she handed him back the magazine. "It is good publicity for the film. I'm sorry if I—"

"No, no, it's all right." She managed a smile at his worried face. "It's just a little strange, you know?"

He looked thoughtful. "The photos are of you, but are not actually you."

"Exactly," she said, relaxing a little. Despite the language barrier, it was clear Thomas Kruger was very kind, that he understood her life in a way that many people could not.

"Once I went fishing with some friends, and we took off our shirts to get, um, *die Bräune*..." He looked at her quizzically.

"To get a tan," she said.

"Yes, exactly! To get a tan, and we didn't know a photographer had followed us. The next day—photographs of me were in the paper." He lifted his arms in a weight lifter show-off pose and widened his smile into a grimace so silly, Pagan laughed out loud.

He nodded. "Exactly! I saw the photographs and thought, who is this ridiculous boy showing off for the camera? It didn't seem like me at all."

"You must be very popular," she said, "if there are photographers following you."

"Only in my own country, and maybe a little in the Soviet Union," he said. "I was like you. I started as a child, and after my father died, the money was very helpful for the family."

He was more like her than he knew. "I liked acting from the first, even though it was all my mother's idea," she said. "You probably took to it right away, as well."

He shook his head. "I always enjoy acting, but—" he lowered his voice "—to be very honest, until now the scripts have been so terrible that I had trouble forcing myself to truly *act* in them. The state film office in my country does not have directors and writers like Bennie working there. This..." He gestured around at the cast and crew, scattered around the large conference room they'd turned into a sort of cafeteria. "This is too good to be true."

"It is for me, too," she said. "Maybe we both have a second chance."

"I hope so." Thomas's gaze stopped on something behind her, and his face froze.

Pagan turned to see Devin by the conference room door, lean and intent as a panther, beckoning to Thomas with one imperious hand.

"Excuse me, please," Thomas said. "I'll be right back."

If Devin was going to take away her lunch companion, she would take advantage. With Thomas temporarily blocking Devin's view of her, Pagan slipped away.

She made her way quickly to her dressing room and grabbed the photo of her young grandmother in Berlin out of her purse. It was time to ask Matthew for that second favor.

She emerged from her dressing room to find Devin leaning one shoulder against the wall in the hallway outside. Thomas was nowhere to be seen.

"Going somewhere?" he asked with a casual indifference completely at odds with the fact that he was stalking her like prey.

"I just wanted to get this," she said, flourishing the photograph. "I'm going to ask Matthew to see if he can find out where it was taken."

"Matthew's from Chicago, not Berlin," Devin said.

"Watch and learn, genius," she said, and stomped off to find Matthew. Devin followed.

Matthew was eating with the grips and seemed receptive when she said she needed to ask a favor.

"Do you think there's any chance our location scouts might know where this building is?" she asked, showing him the photo. "That's my grandmother, you see, holding my mother when she was just a baby. I know very little about Mama's family, so I was hoping to find out where they lived while I was here."

Matthew took the photo from her, scanning it. "I can ask our location scout, sure, but this might be one of the buildings that got bombed during the war."

"I know it's a faint chance," she said. "I promise not to be disappointed if they don't recognize it."

"Okay," he said. "I'll get this photo back to you by the end of the day."

"Thanks so much, Matthew," she said. "I promise I'll return the favor."

"Got any tips for improving my poker game?" He allowed himself a smile.

"Hmm…" She gave it a moment of thought. "Well, if you want to bluff, it's all about the acting, right? And acting is all about lying to yourself. If you believe it, they'll believe it."

"So pretend I've got the best hand in the world?" he said. "I already do that, and it's not working."

"No, it's more than pretending." Pagan thought back to what she told herself before she did a scene. "You've had really good hands in the past, right? Well, when you want to bluff, remind yourself of how you felt when you had that royal flush or four aces or whatever it was. Bring that feeling back, even if you've only got eight high, sink deep into that feeling, and everyone around you will see it on your face. They'll believe you."

The grips were all listening intently along with Thomas. Several were nodding. One said, "So, if I wanted them to think I had a bad hand…"

"Just pull up that feeling you had when you first saw the crappiest hand you ever got in your life," she said.

They all laughed. Matthew shook his head at her. "It's no good. Now you've told them all the secret, too!"

"So sorry…" It was Thomas, hovering a little anxiously be-hind her. She hadn't seen him a moment ago, and Devin had disappeared. "But I couldn't help overhearing. You wanted to find a particular building in Berlin?"

Pagan's mouth fell open a little as she realized the obvious had completely bypassed her. "Yes! I— One second!" She slid the photo out from under Matthew's hand, smiling apolo-getically at him, and thrust it at Thomas. "Do you know it?"

Thomas raised his eyebrows, looking down at the small picture. "No, I'm sorry, I don't. But I was thinking, if you like, we could show this to my mother. She knows Berlin very well, both before and after the war, all of the sectors. Even if the building is now gone, she might know it."

"That would be great!" For the first time, she might actu-ally be making progress. The location scout idea had been a stab in the dark. "Maybe if your mother comes to visit the set one day, we could show her the photograph?"

"Or you could come to our house for lunch tomorrow." Thomas laughed at her surprised expression. "We both have the day off, you and I. They're shooting scenes without us, so I'd been thinking of inviting you anyway, selfishly, because my sister Karin is such a fan of yours. And I would enjoy your company." He flushed slightly, but his gaze was steady. "It would mean so much to Karin, and you'd have plenty of time to talk to my mother about this. "

"I'd love to!" The whole prospect was appealing—an ad-venture into the eastern sector, finding out about her mother's past, hanging out with the easygoing Thomas, getting away from Devin… Her stomach fell. "I'm not sure I can, though."

"Devin told me it was okay," he said as if he'd read her thoughts. "Perhaps I am presumptuous, but I know you're still underage, and I didn't want to cause any problems. So I asked him first."

"Oh!" She was taken aback and slightly confused. "You asked him just now?"

"Yes. I hope you don't mind."

But she'd seen Devin beckon Thomas over, not the other way around. Which meant their conversation had to have been about something other than an innocuous invitation to have lunch with Thomas's family, right? Why would Thomas lie about something so small? Or maybe Thomas had asked him after that. The latest revelations about Devin probably had her overthinking things. "If Devin says it's okay, then we're all set."

"Great!" Dimples showed in both of his cheeks as he grinned. He really did look quite pleased. Perhaps she'd imagined the dread in his eyes when he spoke to Devin. "I'll pick you up at eleven-thirty tomorrow. How is that?"

"I can't wait," she said.

CHAPTER THIRTEEN

SPOILED STARLET
VISITS SOCIALISM CENTRAL

Welcomed into Home of Red Movie Star

But when Pagan trotted down the front steps of the Hilton to meet Thomas the next day, she spotted Devin, ominous as a raven perched on a pigeon coop, talking to Thomas. They stood beside a red convertible Mercedes-Benz. The sight of it made her breath catch. Its low-slung silhouette was very like the cherry-red Corvette she'd driven off a cliff.

"Good morning," Devin said, smiling at her. It gave her time to gather her wits.

"How nice of you to see me off," she said to him. "I promise to be back before midnight."

"I'm going with you," he said, unperturbed. "Assuming I can fit in this poor excuse of a backseat."

"But…" She made a helpless gesture with her hands. A nice family lunch with the very manageable Thomas and his family, people who wanted nothing from her but conversation, would feel like a much-needed vacation.

"You can't think I won't be safe with Thomas," she said to Devin as she flashed a genuine smile past him at her costar, who looked glowingly handsome in a crisp white shirt, open slightly at the neck to show a peek of smooth tan skin, and casual cotton pants that fit ever so nicely over his hips.

"It's Thomas I'm here to protect," Devin said.

She put her hands on her hips. It was an attempt at a joke, but as usual, he was full of hooey. "Three's a crowd."

Devin nodded sympathetically but didn't budge. "Pretend I'm not here. Think of it as an acting exercise."

She leveled a *don't try to humor me* glare at him. "My talent stretches only so far."

Thomas had gotten out of the car and opened the passenger door for her. "My lady?" He bowed smartly at the waist, smiling.

She glared at Devin. He was unmoved.

"Gentlemen first," she said with a sour smile.

"Sure you don't want to try the backseat yourself?" Devin shoved the passenger seatback forward and squeezed his long legs into the narrow space that barely qualified as two backseats. If the soft top of the convertible had been up, he never would have fit.

Pagan stared at the car. The Benz was a little older than her Corvette had been, probably a '55 190sl, but well kept, with bigger side fins than her Chevy. It had red wall tires instead of white, and a slightly boxier profile. But the overall feel of the two cars was very similar—elegant, sporty, exciting.

The back of her neck was perspiring. Pagan forced herself to take a deep breath. "I didn't think decadent Western luxuries like this were allowed in your country," she said to Thomas.

He shrugged. "My father was a party official, and when this was confiscated from the original owner, he decided he'd better take possession. Anyone with less commitment to the Party might have been contaminated by it." He popped his eyebrows up with a crafty smile.

"Nice of him to do everyone else a favor." The car was beautiful, but Pagan's feet didn't want to move any closer to it. Devin had settled in, and Thomas pulled the seat back into place for her.

"Father rarely drove it, of course, and I don't much either since he passed away. It's too Western to be paraded around. But I thought I'd take it out just for you." He gestured to the open air above the car. "No roof means better sightseeing. Perhaps we'll spot that building in your photograph!"

"I'll keep my eyes peeled." She moved toward it and put her hand on the smooth crimson door. All that red. She took a deep breath, fanning herself with her Hermès clutch. "But if Devin really must come with us, hadn't we better take a bigger car?"

Devin was scrutinizing her as if she were a strange new life-form. "Since when do you care about my comfort?"

"I don't!" she said a little too loudly, then reined herself in. Waves of heat were washing over her, even though it couldn't have been more than seventy-five degrees. "But you look ridiculous folding yourself up like that. And your knees will poke me in the back the whole way there."

Thomas frowned. "I'm sorry. I didn't mean to inconvenience anyone…"

"No, no, it's not you." Pagan pushed a smile onto her lips for Thomas. The thought of getting in the sports car, of being behind that familiar swoop of dashboard, of sitting there helpless while it was moving, made her dizzy. She took two steps back from it, swallowing down the bile that was rising in her throat.

If she got in that thing, she'd die.

Some tiny part of her brain knew that wasn't true, but every other part of her body was about to riot if she got any closer.

Devin was still examining her. He probably saw every bead of sweat on her brow, but she couldn't care about that now.

She had to get out of this. She waved a hand toward Devin. "Everything would be fine if *he* didn't insist on coming along."

"I can be the villain in this story if you like," Devin said. His assessing gaze was gone, his face mild. He scooched his way back out of the car with relative grace.

"Give me a moment to arrange for our usual car and driver. How is that for you, Thomas? We can follow you as you drive your car back to East Berlin and meet you at your mother's house."

Thomas shrugged. "Of course, whatever is most comfortable."

Devin slammed the door of the Mercedes sports car shut, and in that moment, as he stood close to her, said in an undertone to Pagan, "I'm sorry. I should have realized."

Before she could reply, he was walking back into the hotel. She backed farther away from the car, relieved.

Within five minutes, the big black limousine pulled up in front of the Hilton, and she and Devin got comfortable in the back, then followed Thomas in his red convertible through the busy streets of West Berlin.

The columns of the Brandenburg Gate loomed as they drove through, slowing just long enough to be waved on by an East German policeman in his olive-green uniform.

"What a contrast," Devin said. "Back in Hitler's prime days, particularly on his birthday, this whole area was hung with Nazi flags. They installed extra columns with swastikas on top or eagles, leading up to the gate, and everything was red and black and white. Now look at it."

"Hitler's birthday," Pagan said to herself. Something niggled in the back of her brain, like a reminder of an event she had once thought important and then forgotten. "I think I remember seeing photos of them all goose-stepping past him and giving him presents."

"It was a national holiday in Germany while he was in power. Now people go out of their way to ignore it."

"When was his birthday?" Pagan asked. "I want to be sure not to bake a cake."

"April 20," Devin said. "He died ten days after his fifty-sixth birthday, on April 30."

Again came that strange, jumpy feeling that Pagan was forgetting something. Something significant. But why should Hitler's birthday have any special meaning for her?

"Welcome to East Germany," Devin said. "Where the people own everything, yet have so very little."

They entered Pariser Platz in East Berlin, and the bustle of the West faded into uneasy silence. Only one car other than theirs and Thomas's was driving down the Unter den Linden. Despite four rows of young trees, two of them lining a walk down the center of the street expressly made for a lovely stroll, the boulevard hosted few pedestrians, and fewer businesses.

Piles of rubble stood next to once-grand buildings with facades now pitted by bomb blasts, windows and sconces stripped of color, statues broken, their hands and noses gone. They passed two bicyclists and square-built Trabants parked by the curb. Scooting along in front of them, Thomas's red convertible looked too shiny and colorful for this gray, underpopulated place.

"It's a ghost town," Pagan said. She watched a little boy bounce a battered ball against the side of a building all by himself.

"Committing genocide takes a toll," Devin said in a dry tone that gave her a chill. "Many also died in the war, and in the past ten years, 20 percent more have fled for the West. Every day the numbers escaping into West Berlin get higher."

They passed a building halfway through reconstruction, but no one was working on it. Women in boxy dresses that didn't quite approximate fashion in the West wheeled perambulators or sat smoking at tiny tables outside cafés. Men in flat caps and utilitarian corduroy trousers hustled along the tree-lined sidewalk, heads down.

"There's the Soviet embassy." Devin pointed to a plain new edifice to their right. Two men in overalls were sweeping with large push brooms near a bust of Lenin as big as a boulder.

He pointed down a road as they passed. "That's Friedrich Strasse, once a main street in town. North, that way, if you go far enough, you'll hit the French sector. Go South—" he pointed to the right "—and you'll find yourself in the American sector."

"Must be confusing for the mailmen," Pagan said. She peered down Friedrich Strasse. Although the street itself was clear of debris, every building lining either side was a bombed-out skeleton, a series of vacant shells covered in dust, pointing jagged fingers of stone at the sky. "Holy cats!"

"In 1945, most of Berlin looked like that," Devin said. "Dresden was even worse."

"They've rebuilt way less than West Berlin over here," Pagan said. "Maybe East Germany should rethink what they're doing." Hanging down from the roof of a new building was a large black-and-white poster of Krushchev, bald and bull-dog stern, next to a smaller picture of a man with glasses and a goatee that failed to hide his prim, thin-lipped mouth.

"Walter Ulbricht," Devin said, following her gaze. "First Secretary of the Socialist Unity Party, which means he's the leader of East Germany. Behind his back they call him Comrade Ice. He's not the sort of man who will blame himself for the mass exodus. So he blames the West."

"He's got to do something soon, or he won't have any people to order around," she said.

A stationary tank with a Soviet red hammer and sickle

painted on it went by. Several soldiers in darker green with guns slung over their shoulders stood smoking next to it.

"That's what's got everyone worried," said Devin.

"But what can he do? *Time* magazine said the agreement with the West won't let them close the border inside Berlin."

Devin looked grim. "And if they closed the border anyway, what could we do about it?"

Pagan frowned. "We've got troops in West Berlin, right? So do the British and the French…"

"What do you think would happen if we sent tanks and soldiers to reopen the border?"

Pagan's hands were cold. "War. And both sides have the bomb."

Devin nodded. "It all depends on what Krushchev and Ulbricht think Kennedy is prepared to do."

A lone tram rumbled in front of them along its tracks between the blank facades of nameless buildings. They'd reached the wide-open Alexanderplatz, and their car turned to follow Thomas's north. More pedestrians were going about their business here, moving in and out of colorless stores around the circle of tram tracks with their shopping bags.

"Nuclear war to save Berlin?" Pagan asked, not really looking for an answer. "That would just wipe it off the map."

She caught a glimpse of Thomas's blond head ahead of them, shining in the sunlight. "If Ulbricht is so worried about people fleeing to the West, how did Thomas get permission to shoot a movie there? You'd think they'd crack down on things like that."

"They have," Devin said. "Permits to work in the West have been curtailed, and the remaining ones are under strict watch. But Thomas is special. Not only is he a big film star in East Germany, but his father was a hero of the Communist party and a good friend of Walter Ulbricht's."

"So not all of the proletariat are equal," she said.

"Karl Marx would not be pleased."

"When did Thomas's father die?" she asked.

"Two years ago, a car accident," Devin said.

"A car accident?" Sympathy sat heavy on Pagan. "Was the father driving, or...?"

"He was driving, alone. Nobody else was killed. He drove into a wall. They say he fell asleep at the wheel."

"They say?" She angled a questioning look at him.

"He was trying to become First Secretary of the Party at the time. He was very popular."

"So he died while campaigning against his good friend Walter Ulbricht?"

Devin's tone was heavy with sarcasm. "His very best friend in the world."

And Pagan had thought Hollywood was cutthroat. They'd moved onto smaller streets now, with fewer huge blank-faced buildings and more old apartments that had escaped the bombing.

Pagan stared out, searching for the winged griffin in her grandmother's photo. All she saw were curtained windows and a few brave flower boxes.

They passed a park, where women in faded dresses sat in the sun, watching children tumble on the grass, then turned right, slowing before a nondescript older building six stories high. An elderly man inching along with a cane turned to stare at their large black car.

"Where's Thomas?" She'd lost sight of the red convertible.

"He parks his car about a block away," Devin said. "Indoor garage space isn't easy to find. He'll be along."

How could Devin know exactly where Thomas parked his car? There was something strange going on between those two. As Devin settled back in his leather seat, Pagan clunked the door handle down and swung it open. "I'll keep an eye out," she said, and got out of the car.

Trees lined the street, shading the clean sidewalk. The entrance to the nondescript building was three steps up to a plain door. Pagan pushed the car door shut and scanned the six stories of windows.

On the second floor, or what Europeans called the first floor, a cute girl about twelve years old with her long blond hair in a ponytail was staring down at Pagan, her eyes wide, mouth open, as if she'd seen a ghost.

Pagan grinned and waved at her. The girl's face lit up. She flapped her hand back at Pagan furiously. A very pretty blonde middle-aged woman walked up behind her, saying something, and the girl pointed vigorously at Pagan, explaining.

The woman, who had to be her mother, arced her gaze out of the window, spotted Pagan, and she smiled with a familiar dimpled warmth. She had to be Thomas's mother.

She lifted the latch to angle the window open and put her face through the gap. "Hello, Fraulein Jones, is it? One moment and we'll be right down!" She put a hand on the girl's jittering head, laughing. "As you can see, Karin is very excited to meet you!"

Pagan waved again. "Hello, Karin! *Guten Tag!*"

Karin stopped bouncing, putting her hands to her mouth, suddenly self-conscious. "Hello," she said, barely audible, before her mother put her arm around her and led her away from the window.

"I bet Karin's been staring out of that window all morning, waiting." Thomas came striding up the sidewalk, fishing in his pocket to bring out a key. Devin still hadn't gotten out of the car.

"Just a minute." Pagan opened the car door and stuck her head in, squinting into the dark depths to find Devin still coiled there, deep in thought, hands steepled. He turned to her, removing his sunglasses. "Thomas is here," she said. "We can go in."

"You go on," Devin said. "I have to run an errand."

"An errand," she said flatly. "In East Berlin?"

His eyes, nearly black in the darkness of the car's interior, were preoccupied. "I'll be back in an hour or so."

"But…" She'd been longing to cast him off, and here he was casting her off. And not telling her why. Could he be more contrary?

He waited and said nothing.

"All right," she said, and withdrew to slam the door a little harder than she should have. Damned mysterious son of a…

Thomas took her hand. His square fingers were strong and warm. "Don't mind him," he said, and led her up the steps, unlocked the front door, and held it open for her. "Just up the stairs," he said.

Inside was a dark, plain hallway lined with doors leading toward the back of the building. A narrow stairway pungent with the smell of wood varnish interrupted it halfway down, and Karin was already thumping down it at top speed, ponytail swaying. She came to an abrupt stop at the bottom of the stairs as Pagan walked up, holding out her hand.

"So nice to meet you, Karin," she said.

Karin took Pagan's gloved hand, eyes wide, and shook it downward, hard, once. Pagan laughed and pulled her in to kiss her on the cheek.

"What have you been making?" Pagan asked. The scent of rubber cement was a dead giveaway.

"Something for you," Karin said, ducking her head, shy again.

"For me? Well, I have something for you, too." She reached

over Karin's head to shake her mother's hand. "Hello, Frau Kruger. Thank you so much for having me over."

The woman's hand was tiny, but her handshake was firm. "It is our great pleasure. Karin, step aside and let Miss Jones up the stairs, please."

Pagan glanced back. No sign of Devin. What was he up to? And did it involve his pistol? There was no way to know. She took Karin's hand and said, *"Komm mit mir die Treppe hinauf."* Come with me up the stairs. It was fun to speak German again. Her accent was pretty decent, given how long it had been.

Karin jumped up and down, squeezing her hand. *"Sie sprechen Deutsch!"*

"Almost as well as you speak English," said Pagan.

The apartment was a clean, modest two-bedroom with several bright windows overlooking the trees below. There was no peeling paint or crumbling brick, but it had a faded air, with doors that didn't quite shut all the way and unexpected dips in the wooden floor.

Cheerful watercolors of gardens and the sea were interspersed along the walls, fresh flowers had been arranged in several white vases in strategic spots, and a large banner hung over the table with hand-pasted crooked letters made of felt that spelled out, in English, Welcome to Our Home, Pagan Jones.

There were silver stars scattered over and under the words. Pagan removed her hat and hugged Karin, said *"Danke,"* and pulled out the box of Belgian chocolates and a Wonder Woman comic from May she'd found at a newsstand that morning.

Karin's eyes got round at the comic. "Skyscraper Wonder Woman!" She stared at the drawing of a huge woman in red, white, and blue climbing the Empire State Building. "Who is she?"

"I hope you don't mind," Pagan said over Karin's head to

Frau Kruger. "I'm corrupting her a little with Western non-sense and chocolate."

"Children need nonsense," Frau Kruger said, but she put her hand under Karin's chin to get her attention, and said in German, "You can read that, but only here in the apartment, you understand? Only family should see you reading that."

Karin nodded solemnly.

"Show Pagan around," Thomas said, and shot Pagan a smile over his shoulder. "Lunch won't take long."

"Nun," said Karin, looking around the small apartment, hands on her hips. "Of course here is where we eat." She made a cursory wave at the dining table.

"Where's the window where I first saw you?" Pagan asked. She needed to see if Devin and the car had left yet.

"Oh, in the *Wohnzimmer.* Here." Karin grabbed Pagan by the hand and walked her a few feet down the hall to a small but brightly decorated living room with three large windows facing the trees.

Pagan moved toward the mantel, where another vase of roses had been placed, close to the windows.

"What beautiful flowers!" She looked out at the street below. The black car was still there. That was odd. Was Devin still sitting inside?

"Come sit with me for a minute and I'll read a little to you." She plopped down in the chair and patted the cushion beside her. "It will help your English."

Karin came over willingly, but her mouth had turned down. "They want us to learn Russian in school instead."

"Here." As Karin sat next to her, Pagan took off her gloves and put her arm around her to help hold the comic. The bright blond hair under her chin smelled clean, and it was good to hold a little girl again. "Wonder Woman is a warrior princess, born to a race called the Amazons, where the women rule."

She began reading the comic out loud, throwing glances out the window whenever she could. About three pages in, the door of the limo opened and a very different Devin emerged. His hair was combed forward now, messier, and instead of his jacket and tie, he wore a battered high-collared peacoat that wouldn't have been out of place on a dock worker. He was barely recognizable, looking now more like a downtrodden handyman than a privileged Western capitalist. He stuck a cigarette between his lips, looked up and down the street, then trotted down the sidewalk, out of view.

MYSTERIOUS GUARDIAN DISAPPEARS INTO EAST BERLIN

Pagan Jones Investigates Old Family Stomping Grounds

Pagan put the comic onto Karin's lap and extricated herself from the girl. "Keep reading, honey. I forgot something in the car. I'll be right back."

"Okay," said Karin, eyes glued to the pages of the comic.

Pagan half ran down the hallway, shouted, "Just getting something from the car!" toward the kitchen, and bolted out the door before anyone could yell back.

What the hell was Devin doing? Was he just trying to fit into less fashionable East Berlin to meet a friend? Or a girlfriend?

Or was he in *disguise*? That was what it looked like. Otherwise, why not take the car? There was only one reason she could think of for Devin Black to don a disguise in East Berlin for an hour on a Friday afternoon.

Once a thief, always a thief. Pagan had no idea what art treasures might lie in this part of the city, but stealing one of them might be a good reason to change your clothes and skip a lunch at the Krugers'.

She slipped quietly out of the building and sped down the sidewalk, away from the limo. Fortunately, the driver was snoozing with the paper on his chest.

Sleep tight, Pagan thought, scanning the street. Devin was not in sight, so she trotted as fast as she could down the pitted pavement in her gray-blue kitten heels. Her gold-and-blue Balmain dress was a bit tight around the knees, forcing her to take many smaller steps. French fashion was perfect for a day party, but counterproductive for skullduggery.

Not that she was up to no good, of course. She was just curious.

She neared the corner and slowed, lowering her hat brim to cover her face as she peered down the cross street, first right and left.

No sign of Devin, just a large brownish patch of a park to the left, which she remembered seeing through the window of the Mercedes. Near the street, women were seated on benches, wearily watching as their children fought over marbles and played hopscotch. Farther inside the park, a gray stagnant pool of water that might once have been a pond lay, collecting algae.

When she first spotted the back of Devin's head above his bulky peacoat the silhouette seemed wrong. She was used to his long, elegant look. But that was him, walking away from her rapidly on the other side of the park.

She glanced back at the Kruger's empty street. She really ought to go back. They'd start to worry soon.

They'll live, she thought, and jogged across the street, past the warring children, into the park. Her heart was beating fast, and not just from the running. Every cell in her body was alive, excited, alert. Was Devin casing a museum or maybe a jewelry store today? Did they even have those things here in East Berlin?

Or maybe he was actually going to steal something this afternoon.

She had to know.

As she cantered past them, the women in the park stopped speaking to each other and stared. Pagan ignored them, hauled up the hem of her skirt past her knees, and picked up the pace. She jogged past the would-be lake in time to see Devin angle down a narrow street.

She skirted two girls playing jump rope and found herself face-to-face with two members of the uniformed *volkspolizei*.

"Oh!" She jerked backward, hand on her hat to keep it from flying off. "I beg your pardon," she said in German, and made to go around them.

But one of them, the older one, narrowed his eyes and stepped in her way. "Papers," he said, also in German, and held out his hand.

"Papers?" she repeated, favoring him with a blank stare to disguise the sudden acceleration of her pulse. Despite the warm summer day, both policemen were wearing double-breasted coats in olive wool with matching visored caps that had the red, yellow, and black compass emblem of the People's Police on the front.

The other policeman, taller and with the gauntness of a young man who'd just reached his full height, raised his eyebrows and unslung the rifle from his shoulder in what could only be a move to intimidate her.

"Yes," said the older man slowly as if speaking to an infant. "I need to see your papers."

She opened her gloved hands and then ran them over her hips to show she had no pockets. "I don't have identification on me at the moment. Sorry."

The younger one watched her hands slide over the bright fabric with interest. The older one smacked him in the shoulder with the back of his hand to focus his attention and said to her, "You must carry identification papers on your person at all times. That's the law. Here, we obey the law."

"We could arrest you for not having the right papers with you," the younger one said, a juvenile sneer distorting his face.

Pagan laughed and favored him with a dazzling smile accompanied with the barest hint of an eyelash flutter. "Oh, but you wouldn't do that to little me, would you?" She stumbled a bit with the German phrasing, agitation tangling her tongue, and could only hope her fluster was charming. "I'm a visitor from the West, as I'm sure you can tell, and I had no idea I needed to keep my identification with me. I should've known better, shouldn't I?"

"Well, perhaps this time..." began the young policeman.

"What are you doing here? What is your name?" the older one said, interrupting. "We must monitor all activity in this area."

This one wasn't caving in to her charms. She looked over their heads. No sign of Devin.

She caught sight of herself in a dirty window across the street. In her gold-and-blue dress, blue leather gloves, and blue straw hat in her hand, she vibrated with color against the gray stone like a peacock. Even the sunlight on her platinum hair was a beacon in this drab, dreary landscape.

She didn't want to go back to the Krugers', but she'd better. She was an alien in this dreary place, flown in from some frivolous planet faraway.

Time to bring out the big guns. She straightened and lowered a more astringent gaze upon the older policeman. "I'm getting a breath of air before I have a meal with Thomas Kruger and his family," she said. "You may have heard of his father. I believe he was high up in the Party."

"Thomas Kruger?" The older one's eyebrows shot up. He recognized the name.

The younger one was nodding. "The Krugers live just down the street," he said.

"What are your names and ranks, please?" Pagan asked with severe politeness. "In case I need to make a report."

The blood drained from the faces of both men. The younger one shouldered his rifle and wiped a sheen of sweat off his upper lip. "There is no need to make a report, *Fraulein*."

"No, no, no need," the older one said, backing away from her. "We're sorry to have troubled you."

She prevented herself from cackling like a Disney villain in triumph and kept up the hard, inquiring stare. "If you're sure. I thought you needed to see my papers."

They were nearly ten feet away from her now, fading fast. "Have a good day, *Fraulein*," the older one said, and as one they turned and marched away.

"Danke," she said, glancing past them one last time to make sure Devin wasn't on his way back. That dark head and pea-coat were nowhere to be seen. Dang it. She'd never catch up to him now or find out what he was up to. Best to look for other opportunities to uncover his secrets. She used her best confident model walk to stride across the street and back down the Kruger's road.

Inside their building on the ground floor, she leaned against the door, smiling, a strange feeling of elation taking hold. The looks on those soldiers' faces as they'd slunk away was more spine tingling than getting the Golden Globe.

And she had some ammunition against Devin Black in her arsenal now. He was here in Berlin for some reason that had nothing to do with her movie. Maybe it was all a cover so he could pull off a heist of some kind. Or maybe he'd used his abilities as a thief to gain power at the studio, pilfering personal information on powerful people to get what he wanted. Whatever that was. The studio job had given him a plausible cover story to get him here to Berlin, and even into East Berlin. Given his insistence on coming today, and now the disguise and the skulking around, he had his eye on something on the Communist side of the border. Once she had proof of some bad behavior, she'd have leverage over him and their power dynamic would change, dramatically.

She couldn't stall a second longer. She walked up the stairs to the Krugers' apartment with no idea what she was going to say to them. When telling a lie, it was best to stick to some version of the truth.

"I'm so sorry," she said as she opened the door, removing her hat and fanning herself. "I didn't mean to be so long."

"But..." Karin started to say something, and Frau Kruger put her hand on her shoulder and the girl stopped speaking. Thomas walked in from the kitchen, eyes wide, holding a bowl full of greens.

As if nothing was even slightly odd about her absence, she sailed over to the table, where a platter of delicious-smelling *sauerbraten* was waiting, along with cheesy potatoes and the French-looking salad Thomas was holding. "Everything looks delicious."

Thomas said, "We were beginning to get worried."

"I know. I'm so sorry." Pagan removed her gloves and set them on a side table with her hat, speaking with breezy ease. "But a woman on the corner of your street recognized me. Very surprising. And then she asked me to come meet her daughter, who was playing over at that little park around the corner. I played a game of hopscotch with her and her friends. It seemed to mean a lot to them. I hope you don't mind."

Thomas set his bowl down, visibly relaxing. "It's not surprising at all," he said. "Before they cracked down on travel, many over here would cross over to West Berlin and see the latest Hollywood movies."

"*Young Annie Oakley* was my favorite!" Karin said, and they all sat down to lunch and that was that.

Pagan had to pretend she was in a domestic scene in a movie to keep herself focused on the Krugers instead of drifting off into speculation about Devin. She kept wondering if he'd brought his gun. Most of all—how had an art thief become the legal guardian of Pagan Jones, disgraced teen movie star? Not knowing the answer was like having an itch in a place she couldn't reach.

As they came to the end of the meal and the chocolates were passed around, Pagan remembered the other reason she'd wanted to come here.

"Oh, Frau Kruger, I wanted to ask you something." She couldn't believe she'd almost forgotten. "I hope you don't mind, but Thomas said you might know where this is. Or was."

She pulled the photo out of her purse and handed it to Frau Kruger. The woman took it with careful fingers, peering at it closely.

"That's my grandmother," Pagan explained, pointing to the blonde smiling woman in the picture. "She's holding my mother, who was born in Berlin just the year before."

"Ja," Frau Kruger said. "It looks familiar."

"It does?" Pagan asked, goose bumps rising on her arms. "Is the building still here?"

"Yes," she said, looking at Pagan with bright green eyes so like her son's. "If this is the building I'm thinking of, it's only a few blocks from here."

Pagan opened her mouth, but no words came out. The blood was dancing in her veins, her mind a thrilled sea of confusion. After so long, would she finally really be able to stand in the place where her grandmother had been?

"We should go!" Thomas said. "Can you guide us there, Mother?"

"Now?" Frau Kruger looked mildly surprised, but not unhappily so. "Why not? It's good to take a little walk after the meal."

"Oh, would you?" Pagan held her chair as the woman got up. "There's no guarantee that they lived there, of course, but I would love to see it."

"And you never know," Thomas said, grabbing his hat and jacket. "Karin, put on some shoes, *Liebling*. If you want to come with us."

"Hurra!" Karin skittered down the hall to her room as Pagan hastily helped her mother heap the dishes in the sink.

Within a few minutes, they were walking down the street, past the limo. Pagan waved to the driver as he craned his neck out the window at her. "We'll be back soon!" she shouted.

The walk should have been pleasant, with sun dappling them through the trees, no traffic except for the occasional bicycle, and neighbors who nodded and smiled as they passed. But after her brush with the police, and now, each step bringing her closer to her family's history, Pagan was jumpy. She wouldn't get her hopes up, no. It's not as if the answer to her mother's suicide would be waiting for her outside the griffin building. If she got any kind of information, it would be one step down a long road.

Three blocks later, Pagan spotted the stone griffin carving rearing over a doorway, and she broke into a run, holding her hat on with one hand. A young woman with a shopping bag was emerging from the building, closing the door below the griffin, and she stared as Pagan came to an abrupt halt before her.

"Guten Tag," Pagan said, her eyes a little wild, continuing in German. "I beg your pardon."

"Guten Tag," the woman replied, puzzled. "May I be of help?"

"Do you live here?" she asked.

"*Ja*," said the woman, eyeing Frau Kruger, Thomas, and Karin as they walked up. "Are you English?"

"American, actually," Pagan said.

"*Guten Tag,*" Thomas said, walking up to the woman and shaking her hand as she slowly came down the steps.

"Thomas Kruger!" the woman said, her eyes widening in recognition.

He bowed. "We live in the neighborhood and my friend here…" He gestured at Pagan and went on to explain that she wanted to see the building where her grandmother had once lived.

Frau Kruger came up to stand beside Pagan as Thomas smiled his way into the woman's good graces. Given the woman's blushes and smiles, he must indeed be quite famous on this side of the border.

"She might wish to talk to Frau Nagel," the young woman was saying. "She has lived here since the first Great War." She reached back and opened the big wooden door leading into the building and smiled down at Pagan. "Come on in."

"*Danke,*" Pagan said, moving slowly up the steps. She wanted to burst in, to find answers now now now. At the same time, she didn't want to rush the moment. She might never come here again.

"We will stay out here," Frau Kruger said, taking Karin's hand, "so that we don't overwhelm the old woman."

Karin pouted at her mother while Thomas held open the door for Pagan with a comic flourish. They stepped through, into a large entryway with a high arched ceiling splotched with large patches of missing plaster.

The echoing space smelled of damp stone and dust. It was cooler than outside. A smaller version of the griffin had been carved over the doors to the left and the right. The stone banisters of the wide central staircase, going up, were intact except for where they began, where someone had broken off what might have been statues. The shallow steps sagged in the center, as if many decades of feet had tired them out.

Pagan gazed around, trying to absorb it all. The building must have been beautiful before the war. But like everything else in Berlin, it seemed weary, broken, melancholy. So much had happened here, so much death and pain. Even the buildings could take no more.

Fate was buzzing in her ear, and history, and hope. But as Devin had said, hope was dangerous. *Don't be a chump.* This might not be the building where Mama had lived. Grandmama might simply have been standing outside it when someone— who?—had taken her photograph.

"Frau Nagel lives there," the young woman said, pointing through the doorway at the door on the right. "Just knock and introduce yourselves. She's sure to be home." And she went back outside.

Thomas bowed slightly and swept his arm forward, inviting Pagan to go first.

"No, please," she said. "You are the famous one, the one fluent in German. If you don't mind…"

He considered her, his eyes crinkling with concern at the corners. She felt like, for the first time, Thomas was really seeing her. Not just the film star he'd heard about or the actress he worked with, but Pagan herself.

She blinked and gave him a little smile.

"You have anxiety," he said.

Pagan nodded. "There's something here. Maybe it's something good, maybe something terrible."

The single overhead light backlit Thomas's golden head, casting his normally bright eyes into shadow. Behind him, the stone staircase swept upward, almost like wings from this angle, and for a moment he seemed almost divine, like an angel—a weary angel who had seen too much.

"Before the war," Thomas said, "my father worked in the resistance against the Nazis until he was forced to flee to Russia. He used to say that if you scratched the mud and sweat off of them, every single person, every house, every inch of Germany would be covered in blood."

Pagan had never heard him talk this way before. It frightened her, but at least it was real. "Secrets kill," she said. "It's better to know."

Some emotion she could not name spasmed across his face, and it came to her that he had a secret.

Whatever it was, it was too painful to share. She put a hand on his arm. "What I mean is, we must not keep secrets from ourselves."

He blinked and put his hand over hers. "Then we will ask Frau Nagel whatever you like."

They walked up to Frau Nagel's apartment side by side, and he knocked on the door.

"Hallo?" came a creaky voice Pagan could barely decipher. "Who is it?" The door stayed closed.

"Hallo, Frau Nagel," Thomas said, also speaking German. "My name is Thomas Kruger. So sorry to bother you, but your neighbor told us you might be able to answer some questions about the history of this building."

The door edged open, and a watery blue eye crowned by a high wrinkled forehead and wispy silver hair peered out. She spoke, saying something like: "Are you from the government?"

Or that's what it sounded like. Pagan had a hard time understanding her. The words were similar to the German she knew, but different.

Poor woman, she looked afraid.

"*Nein,*" Thomas said with a reassuring smile. And added

quickly how Pagan's grandmother might have once lived in the building, which kept the woman from closing her door. Pagan understood every word he said. She probably could have asked the questions herself.

"What was your grandmother's name?" Thomas asked Pagan.

"Ursula," Pagan said. "Ursula Murnau. She was married to Emil Murnau."

Frau Nagel's attention sharpened when she heard Ursula's name. She listened closely as Thomas asked, very clearly, whether she remembered a young woman named Ursula Murnau living in the building, or perhaps somewhere nearby, back in the 1920s.

"Ja." Frau Nagel was nodding, and then she rattled off a series of words that meant nothing to Pagan.

Thomas, too, was frowning, head to one side. He asked the question again, and the woman got agitated and spurted out more strange sounds.

"What is she speaking?" Pagan asked. Her heart was hammering against her ribs. The woman had recognized her grandmother's name, she was sure of it.

"It's some dialect of German, an old one. Some of her words are in more modern German, but I fear she isn't quite, well, what she used to be, and I'm having trouble…" He broke off speaking English and tried again in German.

Frau Nagel shook her head vehemently and said something else unintelligible, though Pagan would've sworn the name Emil Murnau was in there somewhere.

"I'm sorry," Thomas said to Pagan. "I can't get it. Perhaps, if you don't mind, I could see if my mother understands her. She traveled quite a bit around Germany before the war and knows more of the different tongues than I do."

Horrible hope. "Yes! That would be wonderful."

"Okay. Stay here." He told Frau Nagel he was going to get someone who could help him understand. She gave a curt nod of assent, and he turned and half ran back out the front door of the building.

"I beg your pardon," Pagan said in German. "Thank you for your patience."

Frau Nagel harrumphed, her seamed eyes running up and down Pagan's pretty gold dress, her wide-brimmed hat. Her face relaxed a little, and she put out two fingers and flicked the brim of Pagan's hat, smiling, and said something that seemed to be about a hat she'd once had.

Thomas re-entered, towing his mother and Karin after, telling Karin to wait there by the door for a few minutes.

Pagan removed her hat and offered it to Frau Nagel. The old woman frowned, and rattled off something Pagan couldn't understand. Frau Kruger walked up, listening intently, and to Pagan's enormous relief, she began, haltingly, to respond.

Frau Nagel's face brightened. She spoke again, pointing to Pagan and the hat.

"She says your young skin needs shelter from the sun more than her wrinkles do," said Frau Kruger.

"Please tell her I have another hat, and I would be honored if she'd take this one." Pagan smiled as Frau Kruger translated, slowly.

Frau Nagel frowned again, but this time as if considering her words. Sensing an opening, Pagan reached up and placed the hat on Frau Nagel's head and held up the pin. "May I?" she asked in German.

Frau Nagel's drooping face split with the strength of her smile. She bowed her head and said something like *"Danke"* as she took the pin from Pagan and, shaking slightly, used it to pin the hat on her head. Then she spoke again.

"She says you are too kind, and she will treasure it, especially during her long walks to the store in the sun," Frau Kruger translated. "Very nice, my dear. Now I will ask her about your grandmother."

The two women spoke in spurts and fits with each other. Frau Kruger had to carefully reach for each word while Frau Nagel emitted her sentences in gruff eruptions. Pagan clearly heard the names Ursula and Emil Murnau mentioned, and once possibly her mother's first name, Eva.

Frau Kruger's tone sharpened, became more demanding. Frau Nagel shook her head and replied in the negative.

Finally, Frau Kruger nodded and thanked Frau Nagel. The old woman made a small sound like "harrumph," threw a smile at Pagan, and shut her door.

Pagan took two involuntary steps toward Frau Kruger, angling herself to get in front of the woman, who was frowning, her eyes on the floor, deep in thought. Pagan cast a helpless glance at Thomas, who looked equally frustrated. *"Mutter!"* he exclaimed. "What did she say?"

"Oh, I beg your pardon." Frau Kruger lifted her gaze, eyebrows still drawn together. "She says Ursula Murnau only lived here for about a year before she left for America with her daughter, Eva. Eva wasn't born here. They came from somewhere else. She couldn't remember where."

Frau Kruger started to move toward the door out of the building. "It's time we got Karin back to do her homework."

They trailed behind her through the entryway, confused. "But it's Friday," Karin said. "My homework isn't due till Monday."

"Did she know why Grandmama moved?" Pagan asked. She looked back at the door to Frau Nagel's apartment, wishing Frau Kruger hadn't ended the conversation so definitely. "Did my grandfather live here, too, before he died?"

Frau Kruger sniffed and blinked, pushing open the door.

"She said Ursula kept mostly to herself while she was here. She lived alone and worked in an office somewhere while a neighbor looked after her baby. Then she moved to America with little Eva."

"But why move? Did Frau Nagel ever meet my grandfather?"

Frau Kruger walked down the stairs, her back to Pagan. "No," she said as if a little irritated by the question. "Emil Murnau died before your Grandmother moved into the building. Frau Nagel seemed to think Ursula always wanted to move to America, so she moved here, got a job, saved her money, and she left."

"She got a job as a secretary in New York for a German-American lawyer who worked in the film business," Pagan said. They were all hustling after Frau Kruger along the sidewalk now. She seemed to suddenly be on a mission to walk home as fast as possible. "When he moved to Los Angeles, so did Grandmama, with my mother."

"Did she ever remarry?" Thomas asked. He, too, appeared a little bewildered at his mother's change of mood.

"No," Pagan said. "She died when I was ten, so I didn't have much of a chance to ask her about her life before I was born."

"Your grandmother was a very young mother, without a husband," Frau Kruger said. "Life here must have been difficult for her. After the First World War, Germany was troubled, with terrible inflation, trying to pay war reparations, and filled with so much shame. Many young people moved then to America. Most of those who remained succumbed to the disgusting policies of Adolf Hitler in order to erase their shame." She shook her head. "A terrible time."

"Like my father, Mother was also active in the Communist resistance in the thirties," Thomas said. "She and Father had to move to Russia before the War, or they would have been killed."

"The Communists were allies once with the United States," Frau Kruger said. "It is not fashionable to say so, but Comrade Stalin ruined all that with his policies, and I'm afraid the Party has not yet recovered."

"Mutter!" Thomas looked shocked, glancing around them to make sure no one was on the street nearby to overhear.

"There is no one here to object to me," Frau Kruger said. "My country is empty."

Thomas caught up with his mother. Pagan heard him ask her "Are you all right?" in an undertone.

Frau Kruger shook her head, her forehead creased, and said something back to him in German that Pagan couldn't quite hear except for "no place for women," and "what they did to your father." Thomas's face sagged a little as she said it, and he nodded.

She turned partway round to Pagan as they continued to walk along. "I'm sorry, Pagan," she said, pronouncing it the German way as *Pah-gahn*. "But I have been reminded of how far my country has to go."

Pagan didn't quite understand the link between a conversation about her grandmother and Germany's problems, but Frau Kruger's distress was palpable, and it would have been rude to question her emotions. Whatever else was going on, it seemed as if Frau Kruger and Thomas also suspected that Thomas's father's death wasn't an accident. And they were helpless to do anything about it.

Pagan glanced back at the griffin building as they rounded the corner, heading back to the Kruger apartment. She promised herself that she would go back, perhaps even find someone else there to talk to. Where had Grandmama gotten the money to move to America? Where was she living before, when her husband, Emil Murnau, died? There was still so much to learn.

As they turned onto the Krugers' street, Pagan spotted the

big black limousine, parked in the same spot, with a lean dark-suited figure leaning casually against the hood. Devin had returned, looking like he'd been born into his Savile Row suit and sunglasses.

Thomas moved up rapidly to meet Devin first, apologizing for keeping her out so long. Devin, however, appeared unperturbed, and told him not to worry about it. He added something in a lower voice she couldn't hear that made Thomas turn faintly red, straighten up, and nod.

Karin was tugging on her arm. "Can you wait for one more moment? I want to get something to write with so that I can get your autograph."

"Of course," Pagan said, and the girl took off running and vanished behind the main door to her apartment building.

"Did you find the griffin?" Devin asked Pagan as she got closer.

"Yes, but I'm afraid we didn't learn much," Pagan said. "Frau Kruger was kind enough to translate for a woman who lived in the building when my grandmother was there, but she didn't remember very much."

"That's a shame." Devin didn't appear particularly disappointed. She couldn't help scanning the line of his suit as he moved, but it wasn't marred by a shoulder holster bump. If he'd brought his gun, he must have stashed it in the car, along with the rest of his disguise. And maybe some loot.

"How was your outing?" Pagan asked.

"Nothing to write home about," he said, and turned to open the car door. As he did it, his elbow hit Thomas in the arm.

The bump looked accidental, but Thomas started, his tan face reddening again, and turned to her. "Pagan, before you go, I wanted to ask—would you have dinner with me this evening? On Fridays your hotel has dancing and dining on the roof, with a wonderful view of the city. I think you'd enjoy it. And since tomorrow is Saturday, we don't have to be up early for the shoot until Monday."

"I..." Confused, Pagan looked back and forth between Thomas and Devin. Devin's accidental bump into Thomas looked an awful lot like a prompt to get Thomas to ask her out to dinner.

Disappointment and anger made her flush. How dare Devin arrange her personal life? Damn him, for pawning her off on another man, even one as smart and fun as Thomas.

"It sounds great," she said.

It would be great. She hadn't had a night out since before the car accident, let alone a fancy dinner and dancing. There'd be alcohol around, sure. But so far she'd been able to resist temptation. Thomas would be good company, and a far less complicated date than Devin, or her ex, Nicky.

"Oh, good!" Thomas took her hand in his. His smile was genuine but oddly nervous. His hands were slightly damp with perspiration, which only increased her anger at Devin. "I was hoping you hadn't gotten sick of me yet."

"Not sick of *you*, no," she said with a pointed look at Devin. "Thank you so much for all your help today, Thomas. I can't tell you what your kindness, your real understanding of my feelings, means to me."

"I think we have more in common than just acting," Thomas said, and, heels together, he bowed at the waist to kiss her hand lightly. "Meet me at the rooftop restaurant. I'll make a reservation for eight."

She couldn't help smiling at him. "I'll see you there."

She turned and shook Frau Kruger's hand, thanking her. The woman's smile was tinged with sadness, and her eyes flicked away from Pagan's too quickly. It had something to do with that strange conversation with Frau Nagel, although Pagan still didn't understand what.

But then Karin cannoned into her, wrapping her skinny

arms around Pagan's waist, head back to stare up at her. "I wish you didn't have to go so soon."

Pagan laughed and smoothed the soft blond hair back from Karin's forehead, then leaned down and gave the girl a proper hug. The slender, lithe child's body, the smooth, damp satin skin…for a moment it was as if she was holding Ava again.

She said softly into Karin's ear, "You're a wonderful girl. I'm so lucky I got to meet you."

"I'm the lucky one!" Karin said, pulling back. "Look!" She thrust out a German tabloid. A photo of Pagan was on the cover. It showed her, head down, sunglasses on with the black Mercedes in the background as she headed into her hotel. From what she was wearing, Pagan could tell the photo had been taken the night before. Devin had been nearby, but again there was no sign of him in the shot.

The headline translated to Infamous Teen Star Pagan Jones Tries for a Comeback in a Film Shooting in Berlin.

"Will you sign this, please?" Karin asked, holding out a pen.

Pagan couldn't help a rueful smile. Would she be infamous for the rest of her life? She took the pen from Karin. "Anything for you." And she signed *To Karin with so much love. Pagan Jones*.

As she finished with a flourish, her eye traveled to a smaller headline, shoved in the corner, and her hand arrested in mid-air. It read Nicky Raven Heads to Europe for Honeymoon with His New Bride! See Page 2.

Pagan's throat closed up. She was turning to page two before the full sense of the headline had sunk in. The spread featured a large photo of Nicky and his wife, Donna, waving goodbye to well-wishers as they headed through a doorway onto an airport tarmac. Donna was wearing a lovely Chanel suit, her blond hair neatly curled under a pillbox hat, her kitten heels the twins of a pair in Pagan's closet. Nicky Raven and His Pagan Jones Look-Alike Bride Head to Paris for Honeymoon Bliss, the interior headline read.

The subhead sent her stomach plummeting. Next Stop, Berlin!

Her eyes searched the body of the article, mostly fluff and speculation, for the date of their departure. They'd gotten married nearly a week ago now, which meant they'd gone to Paris probably on Monday. This was Friday.

They could be in Berlin even now. It made her sick.

Her eyes lingered on a grainy newsprint photo, on Nicky's and Donna's smiling faces, their joined hands. Donna's hair was a little shorter than Pagan's now, her smile a bit wider, her waist a little longer. But staring at them was like a glimpse into the alternate version of Pagan's own life. The version where she hadn't ruined everything.

"Pagan?" Devin was at her side, a hand on her arm.

She blinked, lifting her head. She must have been staring at Nicky and Donna's photo for a while. "I'm sorry," she said blankly.

Devin's hand tightened on her arm as he glanced down at the paper. He took it from her and handed it back to Karin. "I'm sorry, too, but we really must be going."

Then he was guiding her toward the open door of their car, shaking Thomas's hand, propelling Pagan forward, for which she was grateful. She managed a smile back in the direction of the Krugers.

"Come back soon," Karin said, flapping her hand in an enthusiastic wave.

Pagan waved back and ducked into the limo, finding refuge in a deep pocket of the backseat.

She wished then, more than anything, not for a second chance at life, not for one last glimpse of her sister, not for forgiveness and peace of mind. No. What she wanted most in that moment was a full cocktail shaker and an ice-cold martini glass.

PAGAN JONES'S WILD NIGHT ON THE TOWN

Cuts a Rug with Handsome Commie Co-Star

"He's in Berlin," she said as she and Devin drove through the half-deserted streets of East Berlin. "Nicky and his stupid wife are here!" She laughed, not caring that it sounded hysterical. "What else can the gods of idiotic teenage girls fling at me right now? Nothing, right? Because that's it. That's everything!"

Devin didn't reply, just looked away from her out the window.

"Oh, I'm sorry." God, he was infuriating. So he wasn't going to talk to her? Well, she'd see about that. "Am I irritating you? Are my petty concerns no longer of interest? Well, excuse me for not being made of stone."

"You live and work in Hollywood," Devin said. His voice was flat, brusque. "So does Nicky. Did you not think that you might see him again?"

"No!" she said. "Sue me, but I didn't think about that! As of last weekend my thoughts were all about climbing over barbed wire and heading for Mexico, for crying out loud. Since then life's been a little full with memorizing a script, shooting a goddamn movie without a drink for the first time in four years, and making sure you haven't drilled any peepholes in the walls. So excuse me if I didn't make contingency plans for seeing my ex and his wife! Maybe I should draw up a response in case they ask me to babysit their firstborn."

"Nicky is nothing," Devin said. "He's a fool, and he's the past. He doesn't deserve one moment of your time or attention."

He was right, dang it. But that only enraged her more. "*Deserve* has nothing to do with it," Pagan said. "I'm human. I have feelings. I'm not perfect. God knows, I'm the opposite of perfect."

"You can't control where other people go, or what they do or say," Devin said. They'd passed through the Brandenburg Gate and were zooming along the edge of the wooded Tiergarten. "All you can control is your reaction."

"This *is* my controlled reaction!" Pagan said. "It's taking everything I've got not to scream!"

"You mean not to have a drink?"

It was only the second time he'd mentioned drinking to her, and it stung. She wished she still had her broad-brimmed hat so she could tilt it down and hide her face. Instead, she looked away and did not reply.

"You're such an excellent actress," he said, his voice unexpectedly kind. "It's easy to forget the battle going on inside."

The kindness nearly undid her. She stared at her gloves, wanting to tell him that she knew he was probably here to steal something. She wanted to hear from his own mouth exactly what he was doing, and why she was mixed up in it.

But what was she thinking, wanting reassurance from him? Cold reason told her that was stupid. This man was her legal guardian. They shared a suite. He was involved in something criminal and dangerous. If she showed him her hand, he'd win this round, and maybe the whole game.

Maybe her whole life.

First coldness, then anger, then kindness. She and Devin fenced with words, with secrets and lies. What was really going on between them?

Maybe it didn't matter. She was still stupidly in love with Nicky. The past few minutes had proven that.

"Are you going to be able to manage dinner with Thomas tonight?" he asked. "He knows not to order you any alcohol, but—"

"You're *so* kind to be concerned," she said, her voice dripping acid.

He considered her through the opaque lenses of his sunglasses. She braced herself for an explosion. She craved it—anything to pull her out of the pit she was drowning in.

"I think it's best if you go up to your room to rest before your date."

She uttered a short, derisive laugh. "You have a lot to learn if you think you can order me around."

He removed his sunglasses and studied her again with a clinical detachment that made her itch. When he spoke, his tone was reasonable but touched with steel. "You'll do as I ask, in this instance, because it's what's best for you. I realize that you've had a difficult morning, a tough week, and a terrible year. But you're not the only person with troubles in the world. The more you think about others and less about yourself, the easier your life will be."

He was right again, damn him. She hated him for being so right. She hated everyone and everything, particularly herself. She had to move, to escape, to find a way out of this car before she suffocated.

They were pulling up to the front of the Hilton. Thank God.

"I'm going to take your advice," she said, gathering her skirt around her knees as the doorman opened her door. "Instead of thinking about myself, I'll think about you. I'll think about how you, a complete stranger, took control of my life just five days ago, how you nearly killed me in a dark bathroom, and how you've now arranged for me to have dinner with another man so you can slink around West Berlin tonight the same way you crept around East Berlin this afternoon. I'll think about your burdens, my friend. Your troubles. Of which I am clearly the smallest one."

His clear, handsome face was a mask, but behind the un-quiet blue eyes she saw speculation, and, strangely, respect.

The door clicked open, and she stepped smoothly out of the car, thanked the doorman, and swept up the steps.

The phone in their suite was ringing harshly as she entered, alone.

"Hallo," she said, using the German greeting.

"One moment for Albert Dorskind," a nasal woman's voice said. Other phone lines buzzed in the background.

"But…"

The woman put Pagan on hold. Albert Dorskind was the head of Universal Pictures, her very own studio, and the man who must have approved her costarring in *Neither Here Nor There.*

"Devin, my boy!" Dorskind boomed through the receiver, sounding like he was next door instead of thousands of miles away. Pagan recognized his voice instantly. "How did shooting go yesterday?"

The head of Universal Pictures was calling Devin personally? How could that be if Devin was actually an art thief, a poser, a fake?

"Devin's not here, Mister Dorskind," Pagan said, and cleared her throat so that she didn't sound so small. "Can I take a message?"

"Pagan, is that you?" Dorskind's voice softened from male

bonhomie to a condescending tone reserved for starlets. "How are you, my dear? We're all thinking of you here back at the studio."

"I'm great, Mister Dorskind." Pagan had met the man many times over the years, and he never failed to treat her like she was still eight years old, although that hadn't stopped him from ordering the costume designer to make her bathing suit in *Beach Bound Beverly* more revealing. "The movie's going to be brilliant."

"Well, that goes without saying, my dear! We all know how gifted you are at comedy, and with Bennie to guide you, you can't go wrong. What?" he shouted, confusing her for a moment, until she realized he was yelling at someone in the room with him. "All right, all right. Pagan, just tell that rascal Devin I called to check in."

"Of course, sir," she said, stifling a desire to ask if Dorskind knew how much of a rascal Devin had been in his earlier life, that he might be more than a rascal now. The studio head wasn't likely to respond favorably.

"Be good, Pagan," he said, his mouth moving away from the receiver as he hung up. "Do what Devin says now."

Click. He was gone. Pagan put the receiver back in its cradle and stared at it, hands on her hips, for a solid minute.

Albert Dorskind, millionaire chairman and CEO of Universal, sure didn't sound like a man being blackmailed. And if he was happily calling Devin Black, that meant Devin was a legitimate studio executive, and that his role in the film had been approved at the highest levels by the studio.

What, then, had he been doing in disguise in East Berlin? Had she somehow imagined there was more to him than met the eye?

After double locking her bedroom door, Pagan changed into comfortable clothes and had a tall cool drink of water to calm herself down. Do something, anything, other than think about Devin Black, and Nicky and Donna Raven, so happy, so married… So she pulled out the envelope with the letters to her mother in it.

Okay, so the letters contained some kind of code, but what? She examined the first letter. All the sentences made grammatical sense, and all of the word spellings were, as far as she could tell, the proper German spelling. Which eliminated some kind of single-letter code, exchanging *A* for *Z* or some variation.

She took out a pencil and a blank sheet of hotel stationery and tried writing down every other word, then every third word, then every fourth. Nothing. She took the first letter of each word, then the first and last letters of each line of handwritten text, but they spelled out nothing remotely like actual words in any language.

Pagan didn't know much about codes, but she knew she was missing something. Some kind of key or clue that would help her figure out which words were significant in the letters and which were not. The key to the code could be anything from the two correspondents using pages and text from the same edition of a book, to a random series of numbers.

Or she could be reading too much into this innocuous stack of mind-numbing letters.

Why, then, had her father kept them locked in his safe, even after Mama had died?

At 6:00 p.m., Pagan called the Lighthouse Reformatory for Wayward Girls from the suite's phone, dragging it into her bedroom and carefully relocking the door behind her. It was eight in the morning in Los Angeles. Mercedes would be at breakfast. It took the secretary a few minutes to get her on the phone, but whatever instructions Devin had left behind remained in effect, and after a minute, her friend was there, listening closely to every word she said. Pagan kept her voice low.

"You think he's really some high-level art thief?" Mercedes asked when Pagan was done telling her everything.

"That call from Mister Dorskind makes me think he can't be. Maybe he's secretly a Communist or something," Pagan said. "He knows East Berlin pretty well."

"Either way, no offense, but what would he want with you?"

"I don't know, but he's going out of his way to push me and Thomas together, and Thomas is the son of a high-ranking Communist official who was probably killed off by the current leader of East Germany, Walter Ulbricht, because they were rivals for party leadership."

"Why would Devin want Thomas to date you?" The question was rhetorical. Pagan could practically hear the wheels turning in Mercedes's head. "You're a film star, a convicted killer, with a history of drinking."

"Convicted of manslaughter, thank you very much," Pagan said, half joking.

Mercedes had no time for equivocation. "I'm just trying to see you how they see you. Are you a distraction while he steals something? Or are you a tool for some Communist propaganda? If people in East Germany learned Thomas was dating you, what would their reaction be?"

Pagan shrugged, trying to think. "The government says the West is corrupt, so I guess they'd think I was corrupting him."

"So it would make Thomas look bad."

Pagan frowned. "You think they're using me to discredit Thomas, to keep him from maybe following in his father's footsteps as a leader of the Party?"

"I don't know," Mercedes said. "It's all I can think of. But the more I think about it, it seems a long way to go, to get you out of Lighthouse, get you cast in a movie, and bring you there just to make him look bad? They could just plant evidence on him and lock him up in half that time. It's not hard to frame people when you control everything."

"They could just kill him, like they killed his father," Pagan said.

"Way simpler than dealing with you, eh?" Mercedes said, her tone lightening.

Pagan laughed. "Poor Devin. Seeing that photo of Nicky with that stupid wife of his made me mental, and I took it out on him."

"Don't waste your time feeling sorry for Devin," Mercedes said. "He's lying to you, using you, too. We just don't know why."

"Yet," Pagan said.

"Exactly. Nicky's the sad one. He lost you and ended up with a washed-out, boring old copy instead. It's his loss, *Hereje*," said Mercedes. "If you do run into him, tell him from me that desperation's not a good look on him."

Pagan lay back on her bed, soaking in the pleasure Mercedes's words brought. It was petty, she knew, to want to hear bad things about Nicky. But right now it was giving her more comfort than a shot of tequila. "So I'm not crazy thinking Nicky's not over me," she said.

Mercedes exhaled a contemptuous grunt for Nicky. "He's showed the whole world he'll never get over you by marrying that girl. She's gotten the worst if it, chained to a guy who doesn't love her for the rest of her life because she kind of looks like you."

Pagan laughed. She wanted to believe that Nicky didn't really love Donna. She wanted to be able to feel sorry for Donna, to feel compassion. And maybe Mercedes was right. But for now Donna had the life Pagan had always wanted. The life she could never have because always the specters of her father and her sister were there, haunting her. And always the pressure not to drink.

"But if Donna's got problems, how am I supposed to hate her?"

Mercedes laughed shortly. "Hating her would be too easy. Since when did you ever do things the easy way?"

"How about never?" Pagan said, a bit sheepishly. "How's your arm, M?"

"It's no sweat," Mercedes said, her voice taking on a trill of excitement. "Hey good news. I'm up for parole in a month."

Pagan sat up. "What? But I thought you had to wait till you were eighteen to get out, which is, what, nine months, right?"

"Got a notice in the mail," Mercedes said. "The judge reconsidered my case. I have to go in and convince them I'm staying on the straight and narrow, but at least it's a chance."

"Which you will do, no sweat." Pagan was on her feet, bouncing like a pogo stick around her bed. "Holy cats, M, I'm gonna bust!"

"Don't get bunched up yet," Mercedes said. "*No hay garantías.* But I was wondering, if you're not too busy, you know…" She cleared her throat. Asking for favors came to her hard. "Would you come to the hearing? Maybe say a good word for me?"

"Are you kidding me?" Pagan practically yelled into the phone. "I'm hiring you the best lawyer in town. I'm bribing everyone I meet to come be a character witness for you. You are going to nail this!"

Mercedes was laughing wholeheartedly now. "Okay, okay!"

Pagan stopped bouncing as a thought hit her. "It's an awful big coincidence, don't you think?"

"What is?" Mercedes asked. "My parole hearing?"

"Coming so soon after I got out," Pagan said.

"Hmm." Mercedes exhaled. Pagan could almost see her, sticking her lips out in thought, eyes narrowed. "Not even a week since Devin Black took you out of here, and I get this letter."

"But why would Devin get you out, too?" Pagan's heart had begun beating loudly, unevenly.

"I'm no use to the Reds, if that's what he is," Mercedes said. "And I'm never stealing anything again. If he is behind my hearing, it probably means he's not a Commie, after all. He just wants to keep on your good side, for whatever he wants you for."

Pagan gulped. *Whatever he wants you for.* The phrase evoked more than one image that made her face hot. She rallied. "Maybe he just wanted to mess with Miss Edwards."

Mercedes laughed. "In that case, you have my permission to marry him."

Pagan pulled out a black Givenchy cocktail dress and her mother's vial of *L'Heure Bleue* perfume for dinner that night. Devin was reading the evening paper as she walked out of her bedroom on a puff of spicy-sweet aniseed resting on a dusky base of powdery violet, rose, and sandalwood. The perfume was a bit softer, more adult, and more romantic than she was, but tonight she would be softer, more adult. Tonight she would dance with a tall, handsome boy and put aside all thoughts of Nicky, of Devin, of the ghosts in her past.

It was nearly 8:00 p.m., and the full skirt of the dress swishing just above her knees put Pagan in a good mood. She hummed a little Ray Charles to herself as she emerged from her bedroom and headed for the door, arcing past Devin in his armchair.

"You look lovely." He'd put down the paper, hands quiet in his lap, long legs crossed, his jacket and tie gone, shirt unbuttoned to show that smooth line of collarbone she'd glimpsed before.

She turned toward him, catching a glimpse of herself in the hallway mirror, and paused to smooth a stray hair near her temple into place. The sleeveless dress had a low square neck and wide shoulder straps, and nipped in tight at her waist before blooming out at the hips. The back was cut even lower, also square, and featured a bow right at the valley where her shoulder blades flexed. Short white gloves, a patent black leather clutch from Chanel, matching black patent heels from Dior and her mother's double strand of champagne-colored pearls and diamond earrings completed a very elegant ensemble, if she did say so herself.

But to her own eyes, Pagan didn't look like Pagan. Who was she tonight? Actress or drunk? A movie star, or a villain? She'd hoped to be sophisticated, adult, if only just for this moment when Devin saw her.

"Thank you," she said, making sure her red lipstick wasn't smudged. Her nose was perfectly powdered, the black winged eyeliner exquisitely even on each eyelid.

"Give Thomas my best," he said.

"Better than that, I'll give him mine," she said, turning from the mirror finally to catch his expression.

His gaze traveled slowly up her legs, and he cocked one eyebrow in appreciation. It was as if he was sliding his hands unhurriedly up her calves, pushing aside the hem of her skirt to explore even higher. Her cheeks flared with heat. He swung his gaze up to her face, lips suppressing a smile, as if he'd been caught, but he didn't mind all that much.

"What disguise will *you* be donning tonight?" she asked airily, hoping to slap that smirk off his face and restore her own equanimity. "I can see you as a sailor, or maybe an organ grinder."

He nodded, pretending to give her suggestions real consideration. "With you as my monkey?"

"I've got plans, but thanks," she said.

"I hear a few others from the movie might be showing up on the roof tonight," he said. "It's the hot new place in town."

"And here you sit, all alone." She tsk-tsked, shaking her head. "Such a shame."

"Oh, I'll see you later," he said, his smile widening. "You know I can't stay away."

"I've noticed," she said, rallying, her skirt rustling. "Am I really free to go? Without you watching my every move?"

"If you don't come back, I'll call out the military police," he said. "No big deal."

"Nice to know you care," she said. "Good night and drop dead."

"Bis bald," he said as she closed the door behind her. She understood all too well what he meant: *see you soon.*

She stared at the back of the elevator operator's gray uniform as she took the elevator to the roof, fingers tapping impatiently against her pocketbook. It took every ounce of her self-control to stay here instead of heading downstairs and grabbing a cab to somewhere else, maybe even all the way to East Berlin.

Not that Thomas deserved to be ditched. But now that Pagan was alone, thoughts of the possibly coded letters to her mother, of elderly Frau Nagel and the many times she'd uttered the names Ursula and Emil Murnau, crept to the forefront of her thoughts. There had to be more to the story than Frau Kruger had told her.

As the doors swished open, the elevator operator put out a hand, gesturing grandly at a wide vestibule with doors to restrooms on either side, an unattended cloakroom in the corner, and a short flight of steps up. Strains of music drifted down those stairs, along with a cool brush of summer air.

"Just up the stairs to Die Sparren," he said. The name of the restaurant translated to The Rafters. "Have a lovely evening."

Pagan half ran up the stairs. The soft jazz swelled as she came out the doorway under a black velvet sky onto a broad rectangular rooftop rimmed with footlights. Laid out below, the lights of Berlin appeared to float. The city was a dark lake reflecting back the stars.

Thomas, in black tie, stood next to a podium where the maître d' was arguing with an older couple. Beyond him, two dozen round tables dotted the space, each lit by a single centered lamp, which cast uncertain shadows on the animated faces of the diners in their white dress shirts and dark bow ties, their pearl necklaces and low-cut gowns. Gray clouds of cigarette smoke wafted upward in single columns, as waiters hurried between tables, bearing gin and tonics, shrimp cocktails, and plates covered in crispy potato latkes, and mini tarts filled with blue cheese and pear.

The seating area opened up at the far end to allow space for dancing in front of the bandstand, where a jazz orchestra of ten musicians was swooning out a very romantic version of Gershwin's classic "Someone to Watch Over Me." No one was dancing yet. Too early, but that would change after suppers were eaten, drinks imbibed, and the night wore on.

"Good evening," Thomas said, bending his dimpled smile at her as he came forward. "You look exquisite." He leaned down and kissed her cheek. "Ah, Guerlain," he said, inhaling her perfume with real appreciation. "It is indeed the blue hour, when the night is transformed, and we shall be reunited."

"You smell pretty good yourself, bub," she said, throwing a little extra sass into the line.

"Thanks, *Küken*," he retorted with equal sass. The word

meant chick or young goose, and was often used for the baby of the family. He held out his elbow and she slipped her arm through his. *"Mein Herr,"* he said to the maître d', "the most beautiful girl in the city has arrived."

The maître d' bowed, his eyes taking in Pagan with a brief shock of recognition, which he smoothed over expertly within a blink. "Indeed, Herr Kruger. An honor, Fraulein Jones. This way, *bitte.*"

The space between tables was narrow, so Pagan released Thomas's arm to follow the maître d'. *Shoulders back*, she thought, weaving gracefully between the chair backs.

Sure enough, the woman at the table closest to her did a double take, which pulled the stares of the other three at her table. More heads turned, and the room's chatter first cooled, then escalated, rippling outward as she moved along, her eyes resolutely on the broad back of the maître d'.

"Is that Marilyn Monroe?" a man asked nearby in a very bad whisper.

His wife smacked him in the chest with the back of her hand. "No, dummy!"

Pagan laughed and slowed, angling back toward Thomas, who bent forward, his ear near her mouth. "I should be so lucky," she said.

He chuckled, and their interaction sparked further currents of comment. By the time they reached their table, right beside the dance floor, the place was buzzing, and Pagan settled into her chair, buzzing a bit herself.

"Let's go crazy and have some lemonade," she said quickly, as the waiter arrived to get their drink order. The dinner club atmosphere and sparkling trays of cold cocktails was all very enticing, and she needed to set the tone right from the start. So they toasted each other with tall frosty glasses of golden liquid. She even tried a bite of Thomas's dreadful herring and apple salad appetizer. She settled for sauerkraut balls and fried asparagus to start, followed by a delicious chicken Kiev.

Halfway through, a dapper Bennie Wexler came over with a somewhat sloppy Jimmy Brennan, exclaiming hellos. Hoping to forge a stronger bond with Jimmy after his temper tantrum on the set, Pagan invited both men to join them.

They sat down and the waiter appeared to get their drink order. "We can't stay long, but we may see you later on the dance floor," Bennie said. "They say this place has the best band in Berlin."

"Best, my eye," Jimmy said, slurring a bit, and ordered another scotch and soda.

"Jimmy, my dear, maybe you should have a little dinner first," Bennie said.

Jimmy fixed him with red-rimmed eyes. "It's not my job to set an example for your alcoholic little pets."

"Hey," said Thomas, frowning at Jimmy.

Pagan put a hand on Thomas's arm to show him she was okay. "Don't worry about me."

"I don't," Jimmy said. "Hey, isn't your ex in town? That Nicky what's-his-name?"

"Is he?" Pagan managed a look of faint surprise even as her stomach lurched.

"Time to go order our own dinners, I think," Bennie said. He looked at Pagan and mouthed *I'm sorry* at her. She shook her head back at him and made a *don't worry about it* gesture. Had she ever been that horrible when she was drinking? She hoped not, but she also didn't remember everything from those days.

"You order," Jimmy said, standing up and swaying a little as he buttoned his jacket. "I'm going to make a call."

Bennie watched him walk unsteadily away through the crowd. "At least he doesn't do it on set," he said with a sigh, and stood up. "I'm very sorry to have inflicted him on you, my darlings. Please have a wonderful night. Perhaps we'll see you later."

He kissed Pagan on the cheek, shook Thomas by the hand, and took off toward his table.

During dessert Pagan noticed a familiar dark head tilted down to speak to a pretty brunette in fuchsia satin in his arms as they skirted the dance floor in a stately manner. Her full stomach fluttered uncomfortably and she put her fork down. So he was making good on his threat to keep an eye on her, only he had his own date. A very attractive one.

"Is that Devin Black?" she asked Thomas, knowing the answer.

Thomas frowned over at the couple. "What's he doing here? And who's that he's with?"

Pagan watched Devin move easily to the music, his hand on the woman's narrow waist, their other fingers intertwined. From her teased updo to her shiny nails, the woman was effortlessly sophisticated, older than Devin by at least ten years, and darkly beautiful, with Elizabeth Taylor eyebrows and ropes of pearls lustering against her creamy skin.

"Whoever she is, she's ancient," Pagan said, and put a hand over her mouth. "Oops, did I say that out loud?"

Thomas slid her an appreciative glance. "She's practically on her deathbed. We need to show them how proper dancing is done."

As the female singer sent her contralto swinging along with the band, Thomas led Pagan onto the dance floor with a flourish. For a broad-shouldered boy, Thomas was surprisingly deft with his dance steps, swinging her into a smooth fox-trot as the band went into "I've Got a Crush on You," and switching easily to a rhumba when they started up "Just Another Rhumba."

They passed Devin, swaying. Thomas kept them hovering effortlessly in place for a moment as they nodded and smiled his way. Devin swept them up and down with a measuring look, smiled hello, and whispered something in his date's ear. She laughed, and they swept off to the other side of the dance floor.

"What a witch," Pagan said.

"With her warlock," Thomas said.

She smiled up at him. It was fun hanging out with someone as ready to dig on Devin as she was. She really wished she could feel something more than friendship for him. "Can you believe he's my legal guardian? He's barely two and a half years older than I am."

"That must be a temporary arrangement only," Thomas said. "For the duration of the movie, right?"

"I hope so. Ugh." She threw another glare at Devin and his date. Was this why he'd arranged for her to have a date with Thomas? So he could have his own date and keep an eye on her at the same time? Or was he up to some other criminal enterprise? "Do you hate him for my sake, or are there other reasons?"

"He was my first contact with the studio," Thomas said. "I didn't want to do the movie at first. I was worried it might displease the Party. But Devin persuaded me it would be good for my career. He's the whole reason I'm in the movie, really. So I'm grateful to him for that."

"But?" She could feel a twist in the story coming up.

Thomas opened his mouth, closed it, and shook his head. "It's not very interesting. At first he was very nice. I thought we were becoming friends. But as soon as I got the part— fft!" Thomas let go of her hand to make a gesture with his fingers. "He was gone."

"To make sure I got in the movie," Pagan said. If Thomas's

recruitment by Devin was anything like hers had been, she could understand his resentment, even if Thomas didn't want to give the details.

"Yes. He left me for you," Thomas said with a sly smile.

"And now he's with her!" Pagan said. "So fickle."

"With any luck he'll leave her for someone else by the end of the evening, then she can join our little club," he said, and twirled her around for emphasis.

"What if," Pagan asked as he took her hand again, "the band played something from this decade? Think Devin and his darling could keep up?"

"There's one way to find out," Thomas said. "Not sure this is the right crowd for the Twist, but hang on."

He lifted her hand and twirled her toward her chair, releasing her so he could walk over to the band leader. The man dipped his head to listen as Thomas slid a bill into his hand and asked him a question.

The leader slipped the bill into the pocket of his white dinner jacket, shrugged, and nodded. After the rhumba, there was a brief pause as the band leader consulted with his musicians and the singer, who was grinning as she sauntered up to the microphone. The guitarist put down his acoustic instrument and picked up an electric one. Pagan took a big sip of her lemonade and got ready as the crowd parted for Thomas and he extended his hand to her. Out of the corner of her eye, Pagan could see Devin's head turn their way. She was ready to show him just how good a time she could have without him.

The drummer counted off, "One, two…" and tapped his snare *ba-dum bum!*

"One, two, three o'clock…" the singer belted out, and the band ripped into "Rock Around the Clock."

The crowd stirred, and someone laughed. Thomas made

a funny face, and shrugged. "An oldie but a goldie," he said, and grabbed her hand to twirl her around twice.

"Woooo!" Pagan shouted, and Thomas swung her out, then pulled her back into a breakaway. He twirled her again, and her skirts flared out. She let go, only to catch his hand behind her back on the beat. She'd like to see Devin's lady-like date top that.

Unless...unless the woman was more than a date, and more than a girlfriend. If Devin was a thief, his date might be, too. That female accomplice she'd joked about back at Schloss Charlottenburg.

She tried not to slow down as the thought hit her. The crowd on the floor was growing, forming a circle around Pagan and Thomas as he led her in a left side pass. She couldn't see Devin or his date in the throng, but there was no doubt who the star dancing couple on the floor was.

In no time, the song was over, and the band went right into Buddy Holly's "That'll Be the Day." Pagan and Thomas slowed the pace slightly to accommodate the song.

Still no sign of her keeper. She wondered if she'd be able to leave Thomas for a moment and find them in the press of people, maybe overhear what they were talking about.

Thomas had spotted the assistant director, Matthew Smalls, with a petite round woman on his arm, dancing confidently nearby. He led Pagan close to catch Matthew's eye and shout their hellos.

"My wife, Elisa!" Matthew said over the guitar, pointing to his partner, who flashed a smile, her feet moving in perfect time with her husband's. They were swinging pretty hard.

Thomas cocked a glance at Pagan, who knew instantly what he was thinking, and nodded. The band segued into "Long Tall Sally," with the female vocalist doing a nicely shredded imitation of Little Richard, and Thomas sent Pagan out, releasing her, and triple-stepped up to Elisa Smalls, asking her, "May I?"

With Pagan ready to be Matthew's partner, Mrs. Smalls threw up her hands in a *why not?* gesture and let Thomas take her hands to send her out in a left-hand pass. Pagan grinned at Matthew and he, thick brows frowning, hesitated, then grabbed Pagan's hands and threw her expertly out and whipped her back in a furious series of under-arm passes and twirls that had her whooping with delight. The room was spinning in the best possible way, and for a tiny while she forgot all about Devin Black and his double life.

They danced through a surprisingly raucous version of "Roll Over, Beethoven," until Matthew, breathless, begged off and led her back to her table for a long drink of lemonade, while he gathered up his wife and thanked them both.

Still no sign of Devin Black. It was irrational to resent him for *not* hovering over her every second of the evening, but wasn't he supposed to be keeping an eye on her? He was really falling down on the job. She could've downed a drink any number of times by now without anyone the wiser.

Thomas took his seat, ordering them both more lemonade and water. A shadow crossed his face, and she tilted her head at him inquiringly.

"I have a favor to ask," he admitted, dabbing at his high forehead with a napkin, his cheeks flushed from the dance. "I've been invited to a garden party tomorrow at First Secretary Ulbricht's hunting lodge out in Döllnsee, about twenty-five miles northeast of the city. They say it's lovely out there, right on the lake and surrounded by woods. It won't last for more than a couple of hours for an early dinner, and it would be so much more fun if you came with me."

Pagan fanned herself with her napkin. The night was cool for August, and the sky was starting to cloud over, but the dancing had left her breathless. "You're so kind to invite me," she said, to give herself time to think about it. An afternoon party with Communist party leaders sounded like the stuffiest event since her last mixer with the Hollywood Chamber of Commerce, but Thomas inviting her flew right in the face of Mercedes's speculation that being seen with Pagan would tarnish Thomas's reputation in East Germany. And that made her curious.

"Are you sure they won't mind being in the company of a capitalist tool like me?"

"They may squawk a little amongst themselves in order not to seem too starstruck," he said. "But I have it on good authority that the First Secretary's daughter is a fan of yours, and secretly they'll all feel very important because they got to meet a real film star from the West."

An idea was forming in Pagan's mind. "Well, I must say it doesn't sound like two tons of fun, with the exception of being in your company. But I wouldn't mind getting out of the city for a few hours. I'll go if we can stop off and see your sister afterward, even just to drop off some more presents I have for her."

She didn't have more presents for Karin, not yet, although it would be wonderful to see the girl again. But if Thomas agreed, getting back to the Krugers' neighborhood might give Pagan a chance to sneak back to the griffin building and maybe talk to some of the other residents, perhaps even to chat with Frau Nagel again. Somehow she'd find a way to communicate, this time without Frau Kruger's strange reaction interfering with the interview.

"Karin would love that! Oh, and—" Thomas paused, looking a little sheepish "—I already asked Devin, to make sure it was okay, because you're still underage."

"You asked him tonight?" She hadn't seen the two of them talk. "Does that mean we'll be a happy threesome again?"

"No, actually." Thomas brightened. "He said it would be fine for just the two of us. Perhaps he thinks I'm trustworthy, after all."

"Oh, great!" Pagan faked a smile over a strange feeling of deflation. An expedition into the countryside without the smothering presence of her minder should've been a victory. Instead, it felt like a snub. And what illegal no-goodery was he planning to execute while she hung out with boring, movie-star-despising socialists?

"Excellent!" Thomas downed the last of his lemonade as the waiter brought them two more large glasses. "I'll swing by around four o'clock, so that we can be sure to get there by five. I'll see if my mother can allow Karin to stay up until we get back to the apartment. Perhaps we can be there by eight."

"We don't have to stay long," Pagan said. A tall, elfin figure weaved toward them through the crowd. "Oh, look, Bennie's back."

"At least Jimmy Brennan's not with him," Thomas said.

"Hello, hello, my spectacular stars!" Bennie said. "You two are the picture of youth and beauty out there on the dance floor."

"Thomas can cut a rug," Pagan said. "He's wearing me out, as you can tell from all the empty glasses of lemonade."

Bennie eyed her shrewdly through his thick glasses. He seemed pleased. "Would it be too much to ask you to have this dance with this old man?"

"I'd be honored!" Pagan took his hand. The band was murmuring a hypnotic version of "Begin the Beguine," and Bennie led her out for an easy stroll around the floor.

"It's good to see you out and having fun, as every young person should," he said. "While keeping it wholesome."

He meant that she wasn't drinking, of course. She could see how her being out at a dinner club might worry him, but she pretended he was talking about something else. "Oh, I think you can trust Thomas," she said. "He's always been the perfect gentleman."

Bennie gave a great cackle, throwing his head back as he shuffled her, with surprising lightness, back and around. "Yes, of course! With you he would be."

"What does that mean?" Pagan asked. Bennie was an odd old duck.

"You have seen too much already in your young life, my dear. But there is even more for you to learn, I fear. Hey, that rhymes!" He spun her around, and she followed adeptly, laughing.

The night was going far better than she'd hoped. She'd thought it would be more difficult to see so many people drinking, to watch glasses full of alcohol passing her on trays, ice clinking enticingly on every side. But dancing was even more fun when she was sober. Even Bennie seemed to have relaxed around her.

As the song ended, Bennie put one arm expertly behind her back and dipped her with a quick, practiced move. She was giggling as he righted her, and he beamed back with fatherly pride and escorted her back toward her table.

Jimmy Brennan materialized out of the milling throng. His pouched face was creased with some secret happiness, his tufted eyebrows lifted like devilish accent marks over his dark eyes. "Pagan, my darling, I have such a surprise for you," he said, and gestured to someone else moving toward them through the press of bodies. "Look who I called to come join us for a drink!"

He turned around and pulled from the press of people a good-looking young man of medium height, his thick brown hair combed back and gelled into place. He had sharp hazel eyes; a slightly crooked nose; and a wide, sweet, flexible mouth she knew all too well.

Pagan's fingertips went cold. She must have turned a strange color, because she was vaguely aware of Thomas taking her hand and saying, "Are you all right?"

The young man stopped in his tracks when he saw her, face slackening with surprise, with loss, with longing. He swallowed hard. "Hello, Pigeon."

"Hello, Nicky," Pagan said.

CHAPTER SIXTEEN

PAGAN JONES/NICKY RAVEN MEET FOR FIRST TIME IN TEN MONTHS

Was His Serenade for Her?

In spite of the growing mass of diners, dancers, and gawkers pressing in from every side, regardless of Thomas looming helpfully by her side, Jimmy Brennan smirking on the fringe, and Bennie's look of alarm, the world had narrowed down to the empty corridor of space between Pagan and Nicky.

He'd lost some weight. His cheeks were more hollow than she remembered, his once-beefy shoulders leaner, his waist narrower in a tight black Oleg Cassini tuxedo. The thick brown hair, however much gel he used, still threatened to break loose over his forehead, dark eyebrows like commas over his heavy-lidded eyes, He had a strong, once-broken nose and a sensuously full lower lip she could well remember nibbling on. It was a friendly face, open, casual, and usually so at ease. Every inch of him was like coming home.

Only he wasn't hers to come home to. Not anymore.

"How are you?" he asked, and looked over his shoulder nervously. "It's good to see you."

A lie. And yet, she hadn't imagined that look of desire in his eyes when he had first seen her.

"I'm great," Pagan said automatically. "How—"

A tall blonde woman in a powder-blue Empire-waist gown

squeezed past Jimmy Brennan and took Nicky's arm, glancing around with a smile until her eyes, pale blue like the dress, stopped on Pagan. Her happy expression suspended, like an unanswered question, over the halted conversation.

"My wife, Donna Raven," Nicky said into the silence. "Donna, you know Bennie Wexler, of course. And this is Pagan Jones. I'm sorry, I don't know this gentleman." He nodded toward Thomas.

"Thomas Kruger," Pagan blurted out, slipping her arm into the crook of Thomas's elbow for support. So this was Donna. She was more lushly fleshed out than Pagan, with opulent cleavage, a heart-shaped face and plump lips shining in their glossy red paint.

"I apologize for not introducing him sooner," Pagan continued, forcing herself to smile and skating her gaze over Nicky's face, over the pair of them, over the drink in Nicky's hand, over the shiny diamond and narrow gold band on Donna's ring finger. "Thomas is my costar in Bennie's movie, and quite a celebrity here in Europe."

"Glad to meet you," Thomas said, holding out his hand.

After a brief hesitation, Nicky shook it, eyes darting back and forth between Thomas and Pagan. Bennie also greeted him, and to break the tension, turned to Donna, taking her gloved hand in his.

"Donna, my dear. We weren't expecting you, but how nice," Bennie said, casting a brief glare at Jimmy. "You're glowing."

"We flew in from Paris yesterday," Donna said. Her voice was higher than Pagan's, more girlish, but sweet. "Never thought we'd run into people we know." She managed a smile that wasn't sour, but Pagan could see she wasn't thrilled to be standing in front of her husband's ex. That made two of them. "On Monday we head off to Venice, then Rome."

"Gotta pay homage to the family homeland," Nicky said. "Might visit my cousins in Naples."

An awkward pause developed. Pagan reached deep, trying to find something to say that would be completely innocuous, something to show that she didn't give a fig about how happy they were, how *married* they were...

"So you must be the lucky girl who got my role in Bennie's movie," Donna said, turning her fixed smile on Pagan. "I hope you're having fun."

It took a moment for the sense of her words to sink in.

Jerry Allenberg had said the actress up for the role of Violet in *Neither Here Nor There* had to be replaced because she got pregnant. Pagan's eyes lowered to Donna's gown, belted with a sequined band under her bust, skating over the slightest swell of her stomach to the floor.

Pagan swayed. The girl was pregnant. By Nicky.

Thomas steadied her, his head dipping low to look at her face with concern. But she wasn't going to faint or make excuses now. She was going to show them that she was doing great, better than ever. That she was happy for them even, that she didn't give a damn.

"I am very lucky," she said, her voice lilting in a good approximation of happiness. "And may I offer you both—" she couldn't help meeting Nicky's anxious gaze; the knuckles holding his glass were white "—my hearty congratulations."

Nicky dipped his head in acknowledgment as Donna leaned into him possessively. "We have so much to be grateful for," she said.

"Ladies and gentlemen," the band leader's voice broke through the awkwardness in English with a clipped German accent. "We have a genuine recording star visiting us here tonight. Please give a warm round of applause for Nicky Raven!"

The spotlight swiveled from the band leader to pick Nicky

out of the throng, glinting off Donna's blue sequins. Nicky, caught off guard, jerked his eyes off Pagan and plastered a big smile on his face as the audience clapped.

"I know it's a bit much to ask a man on his honeymoon to work, but, Nicky—is there any chance you'll grace us with a song?"

The ovation escalated to cheering, and people seated at tables stood up, nodding and smiling. Nicky shook his head, putting up a hand in protest to the band leader, as if to say, don't let me interrupt.

The volume of the clapping increased. Men whistled. Nicky ducked his head modestly. Pagan had watched him in concert from backstage, heard the girls swooning, but she'd never seen an adult crowd so enthusiastic about him. He must have become even more popular since she'd gone to reform school.

"How about this?" the band leader said, swinging his baton in a gentle rhythm. "We'll start to play "The Fairest Stars," and see what happens…"

As the violin and cello sang out the first phrases of a song Pagan didn't recognize, cheers swelled so loudly they briefly blotted out the music. People all around Nicky were waving him up toward the stage, patting him on the back, shouting encouragement. Nicky bent his head, saying something low to Donna, who smiled permission. So he gave her back her arm, bowing, and half ran up to the bandstand steps, slowing as the female vocalist curtsied and handed him the microphone.

"Thanks, everybody," Nicky said in his smooth, performer's voice. "It's an honor to be here, in this beautiful city, with all of you."

Applause rose around her as Pagan, unsteady, moved to get out, to leave, but her knees were weak, and Thomas misinterpreted her movements and pulled out her chair. She sank into it, and clutched her glass, still half-full of lemonade, like a ward against evil.

Jimmy Brennan was leading Donna back to her table with care. As she walked, her dress flowed against her body, and Pagan couldn't help staring again at the convex curve of her belly. The girl *was pregnant*. She was having *Nicky's baby*.

An unworthy thought came to her. Was that why Nicky had married her? What if they'd *had* to get married because of the pregnancy?

The music swelled, then dipped in volume to allow the singer to step in. "I am too bold," Nicky sang, his round baritone cozy but grand, confident yet intimate. "'Tis not to me she speaks."

Pagan hadn't heard the song before, but she knew the lyrics instantly. On their first date alone together at the Brown Derby, Nicky had quoted Romeo's speech to Pagan while he stood under Juliet's balcony. She'd told him it sounded like a song. He'd started singing it to her then and there, improvising, and here he was, sixteen months later, with a swinging hit. It was typical Nicky, an almost-radical interpretation of something classical that instantly became a classic itself.

It had once been their intimate little secret. Now it belonged to the world.

It all came swooping back to Pagan, the powdery smell of Nicky's pomade mixing with his own musky scent, the opulent zest of his voice, the tiny rhythmic movements of his hands and his shoulders as he sang. After the first concert she'd attended with him, he'd come offstage, stooped, and wrapped his arms around her thighs to pick her up off the ground. Her head had been higher than his, forearms resting on his shoulders, and he'd buried his face between her breasts, breath warm on her skin.

It had shocked and thrilled her; they'd only kissed once be-

fore that, but Nicky wasn't one to wait for proprieties, to follow the usual steps. Nicky lived for now, now, now, damn it.
It had been exhilarating. That was why he'd run up onstage
now, during his honeymoon. He really believed that tomorrow he might not be alive to do it.

The song ramped up to a crescendo, and Nicky's voice
soared over the rapt men and women in their summer finery,
cigarettes smoldering forgotten between their fingers, hands
entwined under the table.

Pagan applauded briefly with everyone else and took a long
drink of her lemonade. Thomas's green eyes were dark with
concern. "I'm all right," she said. "It was a bit of a shock." She
laughed at her own understatement. "But I'm okay."

Thomas put his hand over hers. "Would you like me to take
you somewhere else? I know a wonderful little club where no
one famous ever goes."

Thank God for Thomas. Devin Black, wherever the hell
he was, not looking out for her, could whistle up a rope wondering where she'd gone.

"You know what?" she said. "That would be great." She put
her glass down. "Just let me powder my nose, and we'll go."

He smiled. "I'll be here."

The band was starting up another song, something in
4/4 time with a slow shuffle beat. Pagan turned her back
to the bandstand, grabbed her purse, and began to wind
her way toward the vestibule near the elevator, where the
restrooms were located.

"This is a new hit song from a wonderful singer named
Patsy Cline, back in my home country," Nicky said into the
microphone. "It's called 'I Fall to Pieces.'"

Pagan kept going as Nicky launched his baritone into a tor-
chy country song she hadn't heard. Around her, people were
standing to see Nicky better, swaying to the beat. A few cou-

ples were dancing in small circles right next to their tables, arms draped dreamily around each other's necks. That was the kind of impact Nicky's singing always had, a hypnotic excuse to act like you were the only two people in the universe.

Pagan neared the maître d's podium as the lyrics began to sink in. The singer's lover didn't want them to be together, yet the singer didn't understand it. He still fell to pieces every time he saw her.

Pagan stopped walking. As Nicky sang about how he couldn't act as if they'd never kissed, she turned slowly around, heart beating hard against her ribs. It couldn't be a coincidence he'd chosen to sing this song here and now.

Across the rooftop under the cloudy skies, over the heads of all the other listeners, Pagan's eyes met Nicky's. He was staring right at her. His wife in her pregnant powder blue was at a table off to his right. But Nicky's gaze was fixed on Pagan as he sang about how when he went out with someone new, he'd still fall to pieces when she walked by.

Pagan was pinned in place. The love that Nicky had always had for her was blazing out of him.

And she… She loved him still. She always would.

The song came to its sad conclusion, and the room erupted in applause again. "Thank you," Nicky said, handing the microphone off to the female vocalist and bowing once more to the audience.

Pagan put her head down and made it down the stairs and into the ladies' room. There weren't many women in there, thanks to Nicky's serenade, and she quickly checked her makeup in the plush front lounge area after washing her hands, refreshing the lipstick and repowdering her nose. Her hair had gotten a little wild, but the way it curled around her forehead wasn't awful, so she let it stay. Who gave a hoot how her hair looked? Nicky still loved her.

It felt so good to know it was true. She wasn't just telling herself lies to feel better. But what did it mean? Maybe she should stay after all. Except—oh, God, Nicky was married. What was *wrong* with her?

She emerged from the ladies' room, not sure what to do, when someone lurking near the cloakroom put a hand on her arm and pulled her against him and into the dark forest of hangers, wool, and fur.

Instinctively, she twisted her arm against the grip and tore herself free, inhaling deeply, getting ready to scream.

"Pigeon, it's me!" It was Nicky's voice. In the indirect light she picked out his familiar silhouette. He took a step back, his hands up. "I'm sorry. I forgot…"

He looked down guiltily and didn't finish his sentence.

She exhaled carefully, trying to leash all the emotion rising inside her. What came out was anger.

"You forgot—what? That I'm no longer the carefree girl from last year? I was convicted of manslaughter, Nicky. I spent the past nine months in a reform school for girls, so don't jump at me in dark corners or I might gut you with my shiv."

"Yeah, no," he said, dropping his hands dejectedly. "I just see you and it's like I've gone back in time to last year and all I can think about is when can I take you out again."

"Take me *out* again?" She stood up on her toes in disbelief. "All I can think about is how my entire family is dead and my boyfriend never returned my calls."

"I'm so sorry, Pidge." Nicky had both hands in his pants pockets, shoulders stooped. She could see the pain in his posture. "That's really why I'm here. To tell you how sorry I am. I failed you. I know. But if I'd known you were going to get sober, get your life back like this, I never would have ended it at all. I would've waited for you."

"If you had known…" She broke off, helpless. He must be

muddled from seeing her. He couldn't be that blind. "You never even gave me a chance!"

"I know." He nodded. "I should have. But the truth is—I can't stop thinking about you."

Pagan stared at him. She wanted to throw her arms around his neck and kiss him. She wanted to sock him in the jaw. "I never stopped loving you, Nicky."

Nicky lurched forward, hands reaching, but she stepped back, fending him off.

"I never stopped dreaming I'd see you in court or that you'd come by on visitors day in the reform school—something, anything! But you ran away from me the second my life went bad. You couldn't even be bothered to say goodbye. My father and sister are dead, Nick, and you didn't even send me a stupid sympathy card." Her eyes filled, but she would not cry, damn it. "That's not love!"

He tore his hands out of his pockets and grabbed her arms, the grip strong yet gentle, the touch so familiar. She shook her head and pulled away again, and he let her go.

Nicky's touch. The thing she'd longed for most all those months. She had to ask. "Did you ever love me?"

Horror dawned behind his eyes. "Yes, of course! You've got to believe me! Oh, God, it's my own damned fault." He ran one hand over his gelled hair. "Everything's my fault. But see, it was my publicist who told me about the accident, and afterward he wouldn't let me near the phone. I wanted to call you, but he didn't give me your messages until after your trial. He kept saying I wasn't thinking straight, so he'd do it for me. He kept talking about my career. How I was about to hit it really big, and I couldn't let anything get in the way of that."

"Not even the girl you loved." It wasn't a question.

"It killed me, Pidge. He took all the phones out of my house, and only brought one back in so that Momma could call and tell me the same things he was saying. That's what really threw me. I thought she of all people would understand, but she kept talking about how young we are, how I didn't have to make any decisions now. She told me to wait. But I know now that I made a bad choice."

Her throat was too tight for her to speak. She could feel her lower lip trembling. Treacherous tears pooled in her eyes, and one dripped hot on her cheek.

Nicky reached out and brushed her cheek softly with his thumb, wiping the tear away. "I was wrong. I want to make it up to you."

She shivered at his touch. She remembered how his arms used to enfold her, how safe she'd felt there once upon a time. He was only inches away from her now. So close, but so far.

"I don't see how you can," she said.

His hand traced the curve of her wet cheekbone and sketched a warm trail down her jaw to her chin. "I'll do anything you want," he said.

She was trembling. Here he was, the boy she'd loved more than anything, begging for her forgiveness, admitting he had been wrong—everything she'd dreamed but told herself would never happen. But was it a dream come true, or a nightmare?

With the tip of his finger he outlined the curve of her bottom lip. "Anything, Pagan. Name it, and I'll do it."

A low, menacing voice reached out from the dark near the stairs. "Get your hands off her."

A blur of movement. Shadows parted as a figure laid hands on Nicky, yanked him out of the cloakroom, and sent him slamming into the opposite wall. Grimacing, Nicky kept his feet, turning on his attacker, who had his back to Pagan. But from the set of the shoulders, from the coiled power in the stance, she knew who it was.

The elevator in the vestibule creaked, and the doors opened to throw a shaft of yellow light on Devin Black.

Two late-arriving guests emerged from the elevator, chattering in French, and walked obliviously between the two men up the stairs to the restaurant.

The moment they were out of sight, Nicky pushed himself away from the wall, fists clenched, ready to fight.

"Your wife is looking for you," Devin said, his voice sharp as a dagger.

Those words cracked something in two. Pagan was shaking but she held her chin up. "Your pregnant wife."

Nicky pulled himself up sharp. From the set of his mouth, Pagan knew he was angry. He'd been in his share of fights. His broken nose was evidence of that. He wanted to throw a punch at Devin, but he knew it wouldn't do him any good. He unclenched his fists and brushed off the shoulder of his jacket that had hit the wall.

"I'm sorry, Pagan," he muttered, and ran up the stairs. He paused at the top, silhouetted there, the whole line of his body tense, head half turned as if about to look back at her. Then, with clear effort, he pushed one hand off against the door frame, and he disappeared.

Devin turned to Pagan, adjusting his tie. "You should go back to the suite," he said, and held out his hand. "I'll take you."

Pagan shook her head mutely. Devin's eyes held a question, but she didn't want to answer. She broke away and slammed through the ladies' room door. A woman on her way out swore in German as Pagan barreled past her and into a stall.

The terrible weight of her failures was there, waiting. Overhead, and on every side of her, looming like a tidal wave, the familiar smothering horror threatened to suffocate, annihilate.

She concentrated on each breath, counting as the analysts

had taught her, for each inhale and exhale, until the choking weight retreated enough for the shaking to subside. The
chattering voices in the front lounge drifted into the distance.

Pagan emerged, dry-eyed, and examined herself in the mirror. A bit of mascara under the eyes, dealt with easily enough.
The lipstick along the lower edge of her mouth smudged
where Nicky had touched her. Wiped away. A touch of powder, an adjustment of hairpins. She walked into the ladies'
lounge, wishing she could somehow fly instantly back to her
cozy cell with Mercedes.

Then she saw the nearly full martini glass sitting on the
counter.

She looked over her shoulder, even though she knew she
was alone. The glass was still frosted with cold, a lone olive
bobbing lazily in the vodka like a bather in a lake. Pagan
drifted toward it, her mind blank.

That martini sure was going to waste here in the ladies'
lounge.

If she had a sip, just one little taste, no one would ever know.
She needed it, and she'd earned it, God knew. She'd had a
night to end all nights, and she deserved a rest.

The glass was cool and smooth in her hand. The vodka,
tinged with salty olive, blazed a piquant trail down her throat.
The familiar burn, the starry taste of it loosened the knots in
her shoulders and unknit the tangles in her mind. She downed
the entire glass. For all the terrible things alcohol had done to
her, it had never failed her in this.

Before long she'd forget all about the shame of this terrible
evening. For a little while, she'd be free. The heaviness hanging
above her softened, lightened, and feathered into smoke. Soon
it would blow away. Light as a summer breeze, Pagan gave one
last adjustment to her garters and sailed out of the ladies' room,
ready to see what the rest of the night would bring.

CHAPTER SEVENTEEN

PAGAN JONES FLEES NIGHT CLUB

Starlet Takes Wrong Turn on the Road to Redemption

She'd been braced to encounter Devin, waiting for her impatiently outside the ladies' room. But there was no sign of him. It was strange he hadn't stayed to see how she was doing.

Who cares? She didn't need Devin Black. She walked steadily back up to the restaurant, to an entire rooftop alive with dancing bodies. The tables had mostly been abandoned, useful only as drink holders and coat hangers, as the band gushed out one lush rhythm after another. There was no sign of Nicky or his wife as Pagan snaked through the laughing, swaying couples, found Thomas and, before he could ask a question, yanked him up for a dance.

Obediently, he put one hand on her waist, the other lightly holding her hand, and squired her around the floor. "Sorry!" Pagan said over the noise. "I just had the urge to move again."

"I'm happy if you're happy," Thomas said, but she caught him glancing over her shoulder. Nicky and Donna were there, also dancing, on the other side of the floor.

"They can't ruin our good time," Pagan said, wiggling her hips closer to Thomas's. "Maybe we should stay here after all."

"Whatever you want, *Küken*." He jiggled his eyebrows up and down at her and picked up the pace as they rounded the floor. They neared the bandstand, and he sent her out with one hand, pulled some German marks from his pocket, and thrust them at the bandleader. "Come on," he said, in German. "You must know 'The Twist'!"

"And 'Tossin' and Turnin'!" Pagan shouted. The band leader nodded and kept the money, and she raised her hand in victory as Thomas tugged her back to dance.

The moment the saxophone dug into its lead-in and the drums smacked to "The Twist," a general whoop of excitement ran through the younger members of the crowd. Pagan and Thomas were at the center of the dance floor, ready, and began twirling in perfect time as the other kids circled around and followed suit.

Ladies in furs and gray-haired gentlemen drifted off the floor, sharing confused looks, but Pagan saw Matthew Smalls and his wife in there, rotating their torsos, heads thrown back in laughter. As hips and butts twisted and ground, circled and shook, the puzzled looks on the faces of the older people became expressions of shock.

Pagan laughed. She knew what they were saying behind their gloved hands. "Young people today are such degenerates!" But for her the twist was liberating. No longer tied to a partner, no longer forced to respond to him, she could move however she liked. She could dance her own dance.

Her full skirt allowed Pagan to sink especially low as she twisted, and Thomas mimicked her, his long, muscular legs bending deeply at the knees as he put one toe forward and gyrated downward. The segue to "Tossin' and Turnin'" brought more people to the dance floor, and by the time they started up "Shop Around," everyone was clapping to the beat.

Out of breath, Pagan and Thomas took a break, and when Thomas excused himself to go to the men's room, Pagan couldn't help looking around for Nicky.

Through the swiveling bodies and banks of cigarette smoke, she found him, looking at her.

Her vision swam. Heat rose up from the soles of her feet, and she stumbled to an empty table, found a glass half-full of someone else's drink, and downed it.

She set it down with an unsteady hand. Two different colors of lipstick tinted the rim. One was hers. The other...wasn't. She'd drunk another person's drink without a thought of how wrong, or how disgusting, that was.

Mortified, she swayed over to her own table again and guzzled what remained of her lemonade. Water. If she drank nothing but water and sat still for a little while, no one would ever know.

"Just came by to say good-night." It was Bennie Wexler, his coat over his arm, smiling at her. The thick lenses of his black-rimmed glasses turned his eyes into huge watery puddles of blue.

She stood up, wobbled, and steadied herself with one hand on the table. "Thank you so much for the dance earlier," she said, enunciating each word. She hadn't slurred, had she? "And for everything."

Bennie's gaze grew more pointed. His endless forehead furrowed. He leaned into her, inhaled, then reared back. "You've been drinking."

"What?" Goose bumps rose on Pagan's suddenly cold skin. "Don't be silly, Bennie. Someone spilled their drink on me. That's why I was in the ladies' room, cleaning up."

"Don't kid a kidder, kid." Bennie's voice quivered with disappointment, with anger. "I can smell it on your breath. You're fired."

"But..." She didn't know what she was going to say, but she had to say something, anything. He couldn't mean it. Think of the delays it would cause in filming, the extra expense. Think what it would mean to her career...

Bennie didn't give her a chance to beg. "I told you—one drink and I'd throw you off the picture, and I'm a man of my word. Don't bother coming in on Monday."

"Bennie, please, it's just one slip!"

He glared at her, his lips pressed together. "I should never have hired you. Do you know the real reason I threw your mother off the set of *Anne of Green Gables*, back when you were eleven years old?"

She shook her head, mute.

"Your mother was an anti-Semite." Bennie spat out the word. "She was too smart to say it around Hollywood much. But she hated Jews. When I cut a few of your lines two weeks into the shoot, she told me that I was a typical stingy, manipulative kike, that it was too bad they hadn't gassed my parents before I was born. Oh, you gasp, but she wasn't the first, and she won't be the last to say these disgusting things.

"So I got rid of her. Just as I'm getting rid of you. I hope she didn't poison you with her lies, but I guess it doesn't matter now. You're out."

Pagan fled. She left Bennie glowering, grabbed her purse from her table, and ran for the elevator, not caring who saw.

Thomas emerged from the men's room as she stepped into the elevator. He frowned, puzzled, extending a hand, about to ask a question.

"I'm sorry." Her voice was more like a croak. It made the elevator operator jump. "I have to go."

The doors closed on his mystified expression, and she huddled into the back corner of the elevator until it released her to run down the endless hallway to her suite.

The place was empty. God knew where Devin was. She slammed the door to her bedroom and, without turning on the light, shed her clothing and got into the shower, head spinning, cursing Bennie Wexler as she cried.

It had been only one drink! And Mama had been protective, argumentative, yes, but a bigot? Bennie was wrong, so wrong about everything.

As the hot water cooled to lukewarm, she remembered—it hadn't been only one drink.

It had been two.

She could lie to Bennie, lie to Devin, lie to the whole world and say that she was fine. But she'd told Thomas they shouldn't keep secrets from themselves. The truth was that abandoned martini in the ladies' room had dissolved all her cares like magic. And then she'd grabbed someone else's drink and downed it, too.

And it had—*she had* gotten fired off her best film role since *Leopard Bay.*

Oh, God, she really was an alcoholic.

Even thinking that word about herself made her wince. Drunks were disgusting, pathetic. She was Pagan Jones, actress, smart aleck, singer, sister, daughter. People thought of her as the notorious, the bad girl, the killer. All of those identities, from good to horrible, carried a grain or more of truth she could own up to. The one label she'd never accepted was Pagan Jones, the alcoholic.

"I'm a drunk," she said out loud. "I'm an alcoholic."

Mercedes had known. She'd practically begged Pagan to go to an A.A. meeting. But Pagan had thought she was strong enough to go it alone. She used the staring eyes and boring stories at those meetings as an excuse. She assumed she'd suffered the worst the world could dish out, that she was past it.

But the world kept churning out challenges. It would never stop. And all that made her want to do was drink.

She'd been lying to herself about her own drinking. What other secrets had she kept from herself?

With a dark flash she remembered something else.

Hitler's birthday was April 20. That was the date her father had written in the margins of those letters from Rolf von Albrecht to her mother.

She got out of the shower, wrapping herself in a thick hotel robe, and fished the packet of letters from her luggage again. By the light of the lamp on her nightstand, she found the date in the margin in her father's round, neat hand. 20 April, 1889.

The exact date and year of Hitler's birth.

Pagan had speculated that there was some key to the code in these letters to her mother. What if...

She got her pencil and a blank sheet and wrote down the second word after the letter's greeting, then the fourth word, then the first, eighth, eighth, and ninth. 20-04-1889. She went through the entire first letter, picking out the words that corresponded to those numbers, not wanting to see the sentences as they formed. Her own handwriting was uneven, wandering nervously over the page.

She stared down and read:

Our friend says you sympathize. May I stay with you November. Write back same way if you agree.

Simple boring words, which, put together, still weren't very interesting, unless you knew they'd been put together with a code key based on Adolf Hitler's birthday. Unless that code had been used by your very own mother. The mother Bennie Wexler said was anti-Semitic.

May I stay with you November.

The very month Doctor Someone had come to stay with them when Pagan was eight. Which meant Doctor Someone had to be letter-writer Rolf von Albrecht.

And whoever von Albrecht was, he'd corresponded in code, using Hitler's birthday as its key.

Her mother must have written him back, because there were nineteen more letters to her, and he'd come to stay until the night of her parents' terrible argument.

Arthur Jones had fought in the war against Hitler. He'd abhorred the Nazis and everything they stood for. When he'd found the letters and broken the code using Hitler's birthday as the key, he would have been very angry indeed.

Not that he could've been completely ignorant about Eva Jones before that. He must have suspected something. After all, he'd figured out the key to the code. To do that, he must have known that his wife had a connection to Hitler's birthday.

But Daddy had been an expert in avoiding conflict. He'd excelled at denial. The warning signs that Pagan was drinking too much had been everywhere, for years, after her mother's suicide. Eva would never have let her get away with it, but Daddy had preferred to remain ignorant. So much so that he'd allowed Pagan to drive him and his younger daughter while she was plastered. Daddy's willingness to deny reality was epic.

Whatever he'd suspected about Mama, he'd probably ignored it, or pretended it wasn't true as long as he possibly could.

Then Rolf von Albrecht had come to stay, Arthur had decoded the letters, and he could no longer refuse to see the truth about the mother of his children.

Bennie was right. About her drinking. And about Mama.

Pagan shoved the letters into her nightstand drawer, turned off the light, and sat on her bed in the dark for she didn't know how long.

The loving, controlling, ambitious Eva Jones had been a bigot. She'd probably learned it from her own mother, who no doubt had brought it with her all the way from the griffin building now in East Berlin.

A thought made Pagan stop breathing. Had Mama messed up again somehow four years after these letters had been written? If she had, and Daddy had threatened to leave again with the girls, could that be why she'd decided to kill herself?

She thought back. There had been no fights, not that Pagan had seen. No visitors.

The day before Eva Jones hung herself, she'd sung a German lullaby to Ava to get her to sleep.

The morning of her death, Daddy had kissed Mama goodbye before he headed off to drive Ava to school and Pagan to the studio. He'd seemed perfectly contented on that drive. It had been when Pagan got in that evening that the world had fallen apart. So whatever had spurred her mother to her death remained a mystery.

And what of the shadowy Rolf von Albrecht? Was he a member of Mama's extended family who had needed help because he was some kind of criminal?

Or was he something worse than a criminal?

Pagan shoved the thought and all its implications from her mind. It was too much. She was still tipsy and not making good decisions. She needed help. She needed perspective.

Call Mercedes. That's what she had to do. She was padding across the darkened bedroom toward her door when she heard the front door to the suite open.

Devin. It all came rushing back—the fight with Nicky, her drinking, Bennie's banishment. She'd failed Devin, too. He'd tried to keep her sober and moved heaven and earth to get her on this film, and now that was gone. Everything was gone.

"Pagan?" Devin said loudly.

She backed away from the door until she bumped into the edge of her bed.

"Are you here?" His voice was getting closer. "It's okay. I know what happened."

Something rang, loud and jarring. She jumped, heart skittering.

The ring came again. The phone in their suite. She paused. Would he keep walking toward her room, or…?

Click, and Devin picked up the receiver. "*Hallo?* Yes, sir."

Sir? Who did Devin Black call "sir"? Could it be studio head Albert Dorskind?

"Yes, sir. Can you wait for a moment while I check?" The headset clicked on the table, and his footsteps moved toward her bedroom again.

Panicking, not wanting to face him, she darted into her closet and shut the door. Maybe he'd get his phone call over with quickly and leave her alone again. That's all she wanted, a few minutes alone to talk to Mercedes.

Her bedroom door clunked open, and the lights flicked on. "Pagan?"

His shadow crossed her bedroom to the bathroom. He flicked the light on there, too, then crossed back rapidly to the phone, leaving her bedroom door half-open. "She's not here, sir, but she was. From the wet towel and water on the floor, it looks as if she took a shower and left again."

Why was he discussing Pagan with whomever? Also, his voice now held a distinct accent. Not exactly an English one, but more of a Scottish burr, with rolled *R*s, softer vowels, and crisper consonants. As if answering a question, he said, "No, I have no idea why. I'll find out now if you let me go look for her."

He sighed, listening. Pagan would have given her left kidney to hear what was being said on the other end of the line.

"I have been reporting in precisely on schedule," Devin said, irritation creeping into voice. The Scottish accent grew thicker the angrier he got. "I'd be with Pagan now, but you insisted I meet up with Felfe's girl only to have her tell me precisely nothing. Yes, Felfe's got nothing new, and I spent all night finding that out. Nothing on troop movements, police preparations, or new supplies being brought in. No offense, sir, but Felfe's a great useless pile of dung." He paused, and when he spoke again, his voice was crisper. "Yes, sir. I understand."

Troop movements? That wasn't something an art thief reported to someone about, and on a schedule, too. It wasn't something a studio head like Albert Dorskind would give a damn about. There was only one explanation that fit all the facts.

Devin Black was a spy.

But for whom? And was "Felfe's girl" the same one he'd been dancing with just a little while ago? It sounded as if she was some sort of contact for information rather than a true date. Pagan might even be able to like the girl now.

"No, sir, I haven't heard back from my contact yet, but of course he can't call from over there with all their phones tapped."

Over there? Phones tapped? That had to mean he was waiting to hear from someone in East Berlin. He must've been going to meet that contact when she'd tried to follow him.

And if Devin was worried about the East Germans overhearing—did that make him a spy for the West? Her brain was spinning too fast for her to work it all out, but that made the most sense.

"I'll see him tomorrow if I can, while the girl's at that party with Kruger."

The girl. He was talking about Pagan again. Is that why he'd given her permission to go to that stupid garden party? So he could meet up freely with that East German contact?

Devin paused and then replied, "That's all going very well.

She's not falling for him, not in the way you mean. Which is just as well. But she's agreed to go tomorrow, so he's in. Yes." He waited, listening. "There was a bit of a close call today when Kruger's mother talked to someone about her grandparents. It's been useful to have her so driven to find out more, but perhaps we've manipulated that piece of intelligence enough. She's been through so much. We could just let her uncover the truth now."

Pagan's chest was thumping like the snare drum during "Rock Around the Clock." So Devin did know something about her grandparents. He'd found it useful. He wanted her to try to find it out, but not yet.

But why? Was it somehow connected to what she'd just learned about her mother?

"No, but she's clever, brave, and extremely determined, so we might as well... No, sir!" This last protestation was startled and vehement. "No, that's just an honest assessment. Of course I'm objective enough to continue."

Pagan strained, but could hear nothing of the other end of the conversation. She heard Devin exhale, as if deeply agitated.

"Have you heard anything specific, sir?" A pause. "That's disappointing. Yes, I'll report in tomorrow. I'd better go find her now. Good night, sir." He hung up the receiver and said in the thickest Scottish burr she'd ever heard: "Ya glaikit skelly old tosser."

He left, slamming the door behind him. She was alone again.

DEVIN BLACK: COMPLETE GENTLEMAN OR DEVIOUS SCOUNDREL?

Pagan Jones: Charming Young Lady or Accomplished Liar?

Pagan exited the closet fizzing with confusion and apprehension. Who was Devin working for? He'd yakked about gathering information on East German troop movements. That and his Scottish accent implied that he worked for the West, probably the British.

But maybe the accent was a fake. Maybe that conversation was a double bluff and he was actually working for the East Germans, trying to find out how much the West knew.

Her head hurt thinking up all the possible angles. Or maybe that was the alcohol. She took some aspirin and hastily donned a cotton skirt and blouse. She stared at her bare face in the mirror. Dark circles had lodged under her eyes.

She'd seen them there before, after a long night of drinking. They were a sign of her mistake. She'd lost the tasty role of a lifetime in Violet Houlihan. She'd be facing the consequences for years to come, maybe the rest of her life.

But hearing Devin's phone conversation was a reminder that she and her troubles were tiny things, dust mite in the air of the grand theater of life. She was in a city split between world powers, the epicenter of conflict where information about troop movements and supplies could trigger a war. Nuclear war.

Somehow she was connected to that. Overhearing Devin's conversation on the phone just now was a strange gift. Now she had a reason to sober up and try again. She had to know the truth.

She wished she could call Mercedes, but Devin could be back any second and she had to decide what to do before he returned. She could either confront Devin with everything she knew, or she could make her own plans, play this out, and see where it went.

The answer was obvious. She donned a bulky coat, tied a dark scarf over her messy bright hair, and slunk out of the suite. Down in the lobby, she passed the unmanned front desk, lurked behind a pillar until the doorman came inside for a bathroom break, and trotted out of the hotel.

The night air was cool but not cold. It did little to clear her head. Clouds covered the stars, shrouding the city in a murky darkness. She didn't like the heaviness in the air, the long shadows cast by the streetlights, the anonymous cars with blinding headlights rushing past.

Pagan walked briskly around the block unmolested, then took off her scarf and bounced up the stairs through the Hilton's front doors. The doorman, back from his break, hastened to get the door for her.

"Miss Jones," he said, touching his cap.

So far so good. She made her way up to the suite and found Devin still gone. She deposited her coat on her bed, repacked the scarf in her luggage, and made herself a big glass of ice water. By then the door had clicked open, and Devin was back.

"There you are," he said. His hair was ruffled, as if he'd been out in the wind. "I was out looking for you. Everything okay?"

His accent was once again perfectly, blandly American. The difference was startling. As an actress who'd mastered a few accents herself, Pagan knew real talent when she heard it, and this boy was good.

"If by okay you mean horrible, then yeah, sure," she said.

"Where have you been?" he asked, shedding his jacket. "I've been trying to find you."

"Sorry." She took a long drink. "I went for a walk. Had to clear my head."

"Yeah, the doorman told me he saw you come in a couple minutes ago," he said, removing his jacket. His eyes went to the half-open door of her bedroom, where he could see her coat lying on the bed. "That's all you did? Go for a walk?"

Time for her confession. She cast herself back to the time, just a few hours ago, when Bennie had confronted her. Her eyes filled.

"I got fired," she said, her voice thick. It was all too true. "I had a couple of drinks and messed everything up, Devin. I'm sorry. The studio's never going to put me on another picture, are they?"

He set his jacket down on the back of an armchair and took a few steps toward her. "Bennie told me."

She glanced up through wet eyelashes and saw his face. The firm mouth and expressive eyebrows were calm, controlled. But his eyes were ablaze.

"So you know." She set her water glass down. "I had two drinks. Well, more like two halves of two drinks. Not that it matters. I drank the first one after what happened with Nicky, and then I couldn't stop."

"You could have," he said, his voice carefully neutral. "But you didn't."

"Yes." She blinked and tears spilled out of each eye. She brushed them away with an angry swipe of her hand. "Yes,

yes to all of the proper A.A. terminology. Time for a fearless moral inventory." She took a deep breath. If she really was going to be fearless about this, she knew all too well the one thing she really needed to do. "Mercedes told me I should attend a meeting. She was right. Do you think they have them in Berlin? Or maybe I should just pack my bags."

"Don't pack yet," he said. "Let Bennie cool down."

He took a clean linen handkerchief out of his pocket and offered it to her. She took it and blew her nose. "He's not going to change his mind."

"Probably not," Devin said. "But we should sleep on this before we make any drastic decisions."

"So you're not sticking me on a plane first thing tomorrow?" She knew damned well he wasn't. He wanted her to go to that stupid garden party with Thomas so that he could head into East Berlin and do whatever secret things he did there. Meanwhile, she could do her own secret things without him hovering around.

"There's no rush," he said, and turned away from her, easing his tie loose and heading for his own bedroom door. "Besides—" his voice was oh, so casual "—you're going out with Thomas tomorrow."

You bet she was. But she couldn't seem enthusiastic about that. "He won't mind if I cancel on him. He'll understand."

"Cancel?" He disappeared into his room, calling out behind him. "Why?"

"Because I'm not feeling up to it!" She let it spout out of her angrily. "After tonight I don't want to ever go anywhere again."

Devin stuck his head out of his bedroom. "See how you feel in the morning," he said as if it were just a suggestion. "Don't make any big decisions now."

Subtle and thoughtful all at once. He knew just how to

play this. He didn't know she was playing, too. She nodded. "Fine. See you in the morning."

He stepped fully out of his room. "It's going to work out, Pagan," he said. "It'll be all right."

She looked at him, standing there with his shirt half-unbuttoned, his belt off, his long-lidded eyes shadowed with fatigue and concern.

They were alone in their suite together, tired after a terrible day, and it would be so easy to walk over and kiss him. She imagined how it would feel as she stood on her bare tiptoes and set her lips softly against his. He'd want to pull away; he'd tell her it was wrong; and then he'd wrap his arms around her and hold her all night long until they were out of breath.

Except that wasn't how it would go. However much he might like it, Devin Black wouldn't bed her tonight. He wouldn't even allow her to kiss him, because right now it was wrong.

Maybe it was something connected to that souvenir bullet he kept with his gun. Maybe it was the shame she'd seen in his face when he spoke of his criminal past. But Devin was trying to make up for something, and he wouldn't do the wrong thing, however right it might feel at the time. That self-control of his, that need to do the decent thing, was one of the reasons she wanted to kiss him now. That and his knowing, unhappy blue eyes, his warm elegant hands, and the way the long muscles in his shoulders slanted up the line of his neck.

That...and because he wasn't Nicky.

Which was why she shouldn't kiss him. Not yet.

"You made a mistake tonight," he said. "But you can start over again. You can do this."

She set her empty water glass on the table with a click. "At least nobody died," she said, and went to her bedroom and shut the door.

★ ★ ★

She slept in the next day and had breakfast in her room, nursing the expected hangover headache until the aspirin and coffee kicked in. When Devin yelled out that she better be dressed by noon, she told him to sit on a duck, but threw on some clothes.

Around twelve o'clock, someone tapped on the door, and when Devin let them in it turned out to be Matthew Smalls and the actor Hans Petermann, dressed in casual pants and crisp white shirts for a summer's day out.

"Someone here to see you," Devin said, and departed the suite.

Pagan stared at the two men, taken aback. "Gentlemen. Hello," she said. "What can I do for you?"

"We were hoping to have a meeting," Matthew said. "But we don't know where to go in Berlin."

"A meeting?" They were both looking at her expectantly, as if she should know what they were talking about.

"Matthew and I are in the program," Hans said. "Your friend Mister Black said we could have a meeting in here."

Her mouth had fallen open. She shut it, blushing as the sense of what they were saying sank in. "You're both…"

"Drunks," Matthew said, and laughed. "Sober three years, two months, and five days now."

"Six months, twenty days," Hans said.

Pagan gulped. Devin had arranged this. He must have. For her. "Twelve hours."

"Is it okay if we have a seat?" Matthew asked, his voice gentle.

They left an hour later. Pagan watched them walk toward the elevator, then went back inside the suite, smiling. Maybe it was knowing she wasn't the only one who wanted a drink. Or maybe it was the fact that Devin had gone out of his way to do her the best favor in the world. But she felt like she just might make it through the day without repeating last night's mistake. Devin came back a little while later with two tall iced teas and some takeout. The French fries were congealing a bit, but the chicken kebabs on little wooden sticks were delicious.

"Thanks," she said. "For arranging that meeting today."

His eyes rested on her face, smiling faintly. "You're welcome."

"I wasn't sure you'd still be nice to me," she said. "Now that I'm off the movie."

"You don't really think that's why I'm nice to you," he said.

"I guess." She studied him. "I know you're using me to get something else, something important."

He got very still, eyes narrowing as he studied her. "Just as you're using me," he said. "To get to Berlin and learn more about your mother, and to try to revive your career."

"And to get out of reform school," she said. "Is that all relationships are? Using each other?"

He shook his head. "At that reform school last week, you could've left Mercedes behind and gotten away. Instead, you climbed back over the fence to help her fight those other girls. That wasn't in your best interest. But you did it anyway, because you care about her."

"Yeah, but I need her," she said. "It was selfish because I can't imagine life without her."

"Is that what you were thinking when you climbed back over the fence?" he asked. When she didn't answer, he continued, "I'll bet you Miss Edwards's Zippo lighter it wasn't."

She snorted and shook her head. "This garden party. It seems innocuous, but it isn't really, is it?"

He didn't say anything for a moment, weighing her question. "Anytime you're in the same building as the leadership of a country on the brink of nuclear war, it's anything but innocuous. But if you remain harmless, they shouldn't harm you."

Shouldn't, he had said. Not *wouldn't*. But she would have gone even if he'd said it was dangerous. She needed to question Frau Nagel again, and Devin and Thomas were up to something.

"What about Thomas?" she asked. "If the leaders of the Party killed his father, he could be in danger. It could be a trap for him."

"Thomas is the least of Walter Ulbricht's concerns right now," Devin said. "Ulbricht's focus is on President Kennedy. And you'd be surprised. Thomas can take care of himself."

They ate in silence, until she said, "I'm going to find out what's really going on, you know."

He looked at her thoughtfully and didn't appear alarmed by what she'd said, even though it was the closest she'd come to telling him she knew that he was more than he seemed.

"I know," he said. "That's one of the things I like most about you."

She blushed but didn't look away. He smiled. The silence between them was oddly comfortable, as if they both knew where they stood at last.

"I spoke to Thomas," he said, in a more businesslike tone. "He's assuming he can pick you up around three-thirty this afternoon."

She sighed and threw down the soggy French fry she was holding.

"Yeah, okay," she said. "A boring bunch of elderly government officials out drinking in the woods shouldn't be too much for me to handle."

"It's a garden party," Devin said, his voice light and mocking. "What could happen?"

EAST GERMAN LEADERS GATHER AT THE HOUSE OF THE BIRCHES

East and West Berlin Savor a Summery Saturday Night

She was perfumed, coifed, and outfitted in her recently cleaned chocolate-brown Dior suit dress by the time Thomas rolled up in the long black limousine Pagan had been using since the beginning of her stay. Her brief foray around East Berlin in bright colors the day before had been the deciding factor in her choice of clothing, but also, after last night, she needed to feel confident and graceful.

Thomas was driving, with no sign of the usual chauffeur. He popped out and opened the front passenger door for her. "Do you like my borrowed car?" he asked, helping her inside. "Devin let me borrow it. Better not bring the sports car or chauffeur, or all the partygoers will think I've been contaminated with capitalism."

"As long as it doesn't change into a pumpkin, we'll be fine," she said.

Thomas climbed into the driver's seat and closed the heavy side door with a *whump*. He was in his shirtsleeves, no tie, summer-weight wool trousers and shiny oxblood shoes. His suit jacket lay on the seat between them. He looked as wholesomely handsome as a young ranger in a park brochure.

He stepped on the accelerator and they cruised away from

the hotel, east toward the Brandenburg Gate. "You're a life-saver for me today. The Party Secretary's assistant told me he was looking forward to meeting you, and as a faithful citizen of the Deutsche Demokratische Republik, I'm relieved not to disappoint him."

"Walter Ulbricht wants to meet *me*?" She wrinkled her nose. "This should be interesting."

"And my mother's making a lovely strudel for us to try when we stop by after," he said. "Not that we'll need it after the party really, but mother couldn't let you come by without offering you something."

A thin ivory scrim of cloud veiled the sky. It kept the summer temperature down to a lovely seventy-five degrees. Pagan's spirits lifted as she gazed out at the pale blue heavens. She might not have a movie to work on, but she'd attended an A.A. meeting without wanting to bolt and was headed to East Germany to find out more about her family after this weird little political gathering.

The signs about leaving the British sector flashed past, then the *volkspolizei* were waving them through the gate.

"That's new," Pagan said against the sudden tension in her throat. A large camouflaged tank stood parked half a block down a side street. Its large main gun was pointed toward them.

She spotted another tank through the trees, sitting on the pedestrian walkway down the middle of the street. Soldiers in dark green uniforms stood smoking in shady spots, rifles glinting. "So's that."

Thomas's hands were clamped hard on the steering wheel. "Always some military maneuver or another going on," he said.

"They're wearing different uniforms than the men at the gate," she said. "Are they not *volkspolizei*?"

"Not *vopos*," he said. "*Grentztruppen*. Border police. Different uniforms, but they all think the same."

"One city at war with itself." Pagan pushed down the urge to tell Thomas to turn the car around, to run back to the hotel and make sure Devin knew about the tanks. "Like a person with a split personality."

"Sometimes I feel I'm like that—at war with myself," Thomas said. "There are things about me…if I could kill them off, I would."

"Me, too." She looked at his profile, strong and handsome as a Norse god, wondering what he could mean. "But you can't kill only the things you don't like. It's all or nothing."

"And death is very final," he said. "It's better to stay alive, even if you are at war."

They continued down the Unter den Linden, past Friedrich Strasse and two tour buses from the West. Things couldn't be that bad if they were still allowing tourists across, she told herself. It was just another Saturday.

They passed over the blue-gray River Spree again, which curved through the city at many points.

"The Nazis blew up the original bridge that was here in 1945, trying to stop the Soviet advance," Thomas said. "We rebuilt it later, but we're still rebuilding the street."

She had thought the Unter den Linden looked forsaken, but the wide street that curved slightly north from it, Liebknecht Strasse, was barren of anything but bombed-out buildings, a few lots cleared of rubble, and a lone bicyclist pedaling his way somewhere else. Under an endless faded sky, the street stretched on and on, vacant and ruined. Only a few brave trees were pushing their way through the rock-strewn dirt.

"My father was injured in Germany when he was serving in the army," Pagan said. "I wonder if he saw this place after the bombing."

"My father was at the front most of the war, too," Thomas said. "While my mother and I tried not to starve in Moscow."

"My dad never talked about it."

"No one wants to talk about their scars," Thomas said. "We just want to forget."

In ten minutes they were driving through a forest, shaded by pine trees. Pagan rolled down the windows and breathed in the sweet scent. It reminded her of summer in Maine with her grandmother, and gave her strength to finally give Thomas the news.

"Bennie fired me last night," she said.

Thomas's head whipped around, his eyes wide. "But why? That can't be true!"

"I've been trying to think how to tell you," she said. "That's why I ran off like that at the end. I'm sorry, because it's going to affect you, too. It's all my fault." She gave him an abbreviated version of the events from the night before, omitting the part where Devin had slammed Nicky into a wall.

"We must prevail upon Bennie to change his mind," Thomas said. "Anyone can make a mistake, and he knows you are excellent in this role."

"He told me if I had one drink I'd be off the movie," she said. "I don't blame him. I should've known better."

"You had a bad night," Thomas said. "Well, other than when you were dancing with me." He flashed her a mischievous smile. "Bennie should fire Jimmy for bringing Nicky to meet you so unexpectedly. He wanted to make you feel bad."

"The old goat enjoyed seeing me squirm," Pagan said. "But I need to learn to deal with jerks like him, and with surprises like running into Nicky and his wife." The word *wife* stuck in her throat.

"It will get easier with time," Thomas said. "You are strong and intelligent. You will learn."

Pagan leaned against the door of the car, gazing at him with a smile. "Have I told you lately how great you are, Thomas? No matter what happens with me on the movie, I hope it does great things for you, because you deserve them."

"*Danke,*" he said. "But if I remain in East Germany, I fear this movie may only hurt me."

"Move West," she said. "I know your mother is a member of the Communist party and all…"

"I know I can trust you not to tell anyone else this…" He shot her a sideways glance and a smile. "But we have a plan for me to bring mother and Karin to the West after the movie is done. We may even go all the way to America."

"That would be great!" She sat up straighter. "You should come to Hollywood. They'd eat you up there, you're so hand-some."

He flushed, smiling. "You're too kind. I've wanted to move for a while now. So much has happened to change how I feel about the Party. Mother, too."

He was probably thinking about his father's suspicious acci-dent. There was no delicate way to bring that up, so she didn't.

"Yet here we go off to a garden party being thrown by the leader of the Party," she said.

"Secretary Ulbricht is not someone you can refuse," Thomas said. "Believe me, if I didn't have to go to this, I wouldn't. And I'm grateful you're bearing it with me."

They'd broken free of the city and were driving through true countryside now. Trees grew more tightly spaced, inter-rupted every now and then by a small brick house or an old church with a tiny graveyard beside it. They slowed as they wound through a village where some kids were playing soc-cer in the public square with a ball that looked too small. A few fields surrounded the town, dotted with cows, then the trees closed in again, and they wound through some low hills.

"Not far now," Thomas said as he turned onto a smaller road and slowed to a stop by a guardhouse manned by five armed men in brownish-gray uniforms bearing dark red flag insignias she hadn't seen before.

"*Hallo,*" Thomas said in a subdued tone, and handed over his ID and a paper invitation that bore Ulbricht's name and the name of the estate, *Haus der Birken.* The House of the Birches. Beyond the guardhouse the pine forest did indeed give way to groves of white-barked birches sequined with the dark green leaves of midsummer.

The soldier did not reply but examined the documents and Thomas closely. Pagan startled as another soldier, rifle in both hands, peered at her through her half-open window. She glimpsed the black script on his shoulder insignia: *Ministerium für Staatssicherheit.* Ministry for State Security, which meant they weren't regular army, but special troops for an arm of the government.

She smiled at the soldier. He didn't smile back. If the man examining Thomas's papers recognized him, he did not show it.

"Pagan Jones?" the man by Thomas's door asked, eyes sweeping over her Dior suit and down her stockinged legs to her shiny heels.

"*Ja,*" she said, adding brightly in German, "That's me."

The guard took his time assessing her, blank-faced, then with an abrupt motion, handed Thomas his papers and pointed up the tree-lined drive. "You may go."

Thomas rolled up his window and stepped slowly on the gas. When they were well away, he said in a low voice, "Those are the guards from Feliz Dzerzhisnky regiment. The enforcers for the Stasi."

"Oh." Pagan resisted the urge to turn around and look back at the men at the guard post. She'd heard of the Stasi, the infamous intelligence service and secret police agency in East Germany known to be even more ruthless and effective than the KGB in the Soviet Union. It was said they had spies in every building and on every street in East Germany, making sure the citizens weren't trying to undermine the state. But like the CIA and the KGB, they also operated internationally, spying on rival states and friendly ones alike.

"Look," she said, pointing at six more men in the same uniforms marching between the trees. She spotted movement on the other side of the road. "And more over there."

"They're everywhere," Thomas said as they passed another clutch of soldiers lined up along the road. "It must be to guard the First Secretary and his ministers."

"I'm glad we're not trying to sneak in," she said. "Or out."

They pulled into the sweeping half circle of a drive leading up to a series of buildings next to an open front lawn. Just beyond, a lake lay flat and gray blue in the dim late-afternoon sunshine. Long fingers of shadow cast by the birch trees reached across the aggressively trimmed lawn and cut dark lines in the rigidly carved hedges.

"This used to be where Hermann Göring's huntsman lived," Thomas said. "You know—one of Hitler's chief ministers and founder of the Gestapo. Göring burned down his own house nearby, but this one remained. Our own leaders built the two adjacent buildings."

Pagan unrolled her window to crane her neck out and get a look. The central three-story building with its sloping red roof did look older than the two complementary ones that winged it. The rows of windows on the lower floor were tall and narrow, almost like French doors, with ivy crowding in between. Even on a warm summer day like this, every window was closed and curtained.

The side buildings were done in a more subdued gray-white

stone, but their roofs sloped in a similar steep manner. Cars, mostly Trabants, Mercedes-Benzes, and Volkswagens, were parked on the lawn.

"It's lovely," said Pagan. And that was almost true. The place would have had a quiet, gracious air of a bygone era if not for the armed guards and curtained windows. At least it was different from the stern, pragmatic style of East Berlin's new buildings.

By Pagan's watch it was just coming on five o'clock. "And we're exactly on time."

"Wouldn't be a good idea to come late to your leader's garden party," he said. "Not if you want to keep acting in his terrible state-sponsored films."

She laughed, and he pulled the car to a stop in front of the central building's front door. A male servant in gray trotted down the steps to open her door as Thomas got out and tossed him the keys.

"It's not my car," he told the man in German. "So be kind to it."

The man didn't crack a smile, but bowed sharply at the waist as she stepped out and gestured toward the door. "The Secretary is expecting you, Herr Kruger," he said. "Please go in."

Pagan straightened her skirt as Thomas came around to let her take his arm. His usual smooth walk was jumpier than usual, his grip on her hand tense.

"I think I'm actually a bit nervous," she said, so that he didn't feel he was the only one. "It's not every day you meet a Communist leader surrounded by armed troops."

"Just imagine them all naked," he said with a grin, and she laughed as they walked up the stairs past flanking bronze statues of rams to the half-open white door.

"Thomas Kruger!" The door jerked open all the way to reveal a balding man of medium height with a crisply trimmed graying goatee. Pagan recognized him from the oversize poster she'd seen hanging next to Stalin's portrait. "You have done as I asked, I see."

Walter Ulbricht had such a prim, self-righteous face that he would've looked at home wearing a big black hat with a buckle on the front, the kind worn by men who burned witches. His permanently disapproving expression had carved deep marionette lines from nose to mouth. Even in happy greeting he didn't smile, just quirked the outer corners of his mouth up, lips closed. His drab, nearly round glasses magnified the dark gray furrows under his restless pale blue eyes—eyes that were fixed on Pagan.

"*Guten Tag*, Comrade Secretary," Thomas said, ushering Pagan to go before him. In English, he continued, "May I introduce you to Pagan Jones, from Hollywood in the United States. Fraulein Jones, this is Walter Ulbricht, General Secretary of the Central Committee of the Socialist Unity Party."

The dark foyer was a study in dictator clichés, beset with stuffed deer heads, mounted guns, and heavy red drapery. What was it about oppression that was so incompatible with chic?

Pagan suppressed a desire to fling open all the windows and gave the leader of East Germany a demure smile as she held out her hand.

"But this is excellent, Thomas, well done," he said in German, switching to English as he ignored Pagan's hand and took her by the elbow, leading her with a rushed, stiff-legged walk past wood-paneled walls toward a hallway. "Welcome, Miss Jones. My daughter is eager to meet you."

"Thank you for inviting me," she said, also in English, a little alarmed at how quickly he was hustling her toward some lace-curtained glass doors. Thomas trailed behind. "Your estate is lovely."

Ulbricht opened the French doors and put one meaty hand on her back impersonally to push her outward. "Beate!" he shouted.

The doors opened onto a large cement patio dotted with tables draped in white cloths. A plump girl with dark blond hair turned from talking to two older women in large flowered dresses.

What should have been an idyllic scene was instead sad and creepy. Armed soldiers marched by the sparkling lake. Closer by, squinting in the golden light of late afternoon, several dozen grim-faced, middle-aged men slouched by the laden food tables, smoking and downing tiny tumblers of clear liquid that was probably vodka.

One thing the Communists had plenty of was her favorite alcohol. She pulled her eyes away and made herself smile at East Germany's leader.

But Walter Ulbricht wasn't looking at her. He was motioning impatiently to the blonde girl. "My daughter heard you were in Berlin, Fraulein Jones. And she asked me especially if she could meet you. Beate! Come, please."

So that's why Pagan was here. Not just as Thomas's date, but because Walter Ulbricht had a daughter who was a fan. Beate, for that must be her name, clapped her hands together at the sight of Pagan.

"Oh, *Vater!*" she exclaimed in German. "It's true. She's here!"

"Yes, yes." Ulbricht gave Pagan a little shove toward Beate. "I have brought you Pagan Jones, just as I promised."

Pagan felt like a pony with a bow in its mane being presented to a spoiled child. She plastered a confused smile on her face to cover up her resentment, pretending she didn't understand the German.

"Fraulein Jones," Beate said, blushing slightly as she moved

up and held out her ungloved hand. Maybe gloves were bourgeois. Beate couldn't have been more than seventeen years
old herself. Her crisp white cotton shirt was meticulously
buttoned up to the top, tucked into a well-made circle skirt
in a dull flowered print. The style had gone out of fashion in
the fifties. "You are my favorite movie star. I have seen all of
your films!" She spoke English almost as well as Thomas did.

"What a lovely way to start a party, meeting you," Pagan
said, and her outstretched gloved hand was pumped up and
down enthusiastically.

Beate didn't look at all like her pasty-faced father. Her
ruddy skin was clear and firm, her eyes much rounder than
her father's, her nose a cute snub turned up at the end. Pagan
recalled vaguely having read that Ulbricht and his wife had
adopted a daughter. Beate must be the one.

His job done, Ulbricht abandoned them, leaving Thomas
to stand forgotten behind Pagan so he could whisper something to a stout woman with short curly blond hair. Pagan
recognized her from the *Time* magazine photo spread as Ulbricht's wife, Lotte.

Beate was speaking. "I saw your performance in *My Brother
Michael* last month. Father obtained the movie for me especially when I came back from school in Leningrad, and I enjoyed it very much."

"It was kind of your father to get it for you," Pagan said.
"But that wasn't my best effort."

"Oh, no, you are mistaken, the movie is delightful!" Beate
slipped her arm through Pagan's, drawing her over to a table
as heads turned. Thomas trailed two paces behind them.

Fans always wanted to touch Pagan, as if somehow they
could absorb what they loved about her through their skin. But
she was here for Thomas, so Pagan nodded and smiled, letting Beate chatter on about the movie, one she barely remem-

bered because she'd been drinking so heavily, as she scanned the crowd. Ulbricht's wife wandered over to join a clutch of women while Ulbricht was joined by a very short, powerfully built brick wall of a man with heavy jowls, a receding hairline, and a lipless, downturned mouth that sank even more deeply into disapproval as he surveyed Pagan and Beate.

Pagan tugged Beate a little closer to her and lowered her voice conspiratorially. "Who is that man staring at me over there, next to your father? You must help me. I know no one here but you and Thomas."

"Oh, that's Erich Mielke," Beate said. "Head of the Stasi. He works for father and has a football team. Don't worry. He frowns like that at everyone."

Head of the Stasi. So that was the man in charge of East Germany's dreaded secret police, the man tracking tens of thousands of spies and commander of the soldiers they'd passed outside. The West Berlin newspapers referred to him as "the master of fear," because his ministry kept the East Germans quiescent after the labor uprisings in 1953 had been violently crushed.

"Can I meet him?" Pagan asked impulsively. It wasn't every day you got the chance to annoy an evil mastermind.

Beate shrank back. She obviously didn't like Mielke. But she quickly pushed a smile onto her lips. "Of course," she said, and led Pagan to where her father and Mielke were talking in low tones. They stopped speaking abruptly as the girls approached.

Mielke was shorter than Pagan, barely five foot four, but even in his midfifties, he'd taken care to remain in top physical shape. He didn't blink as she came up, topping him by several inches in her heels. He was not a man who could be intimidated. Behind her, Pagan could feel Thomas, tight as a piano wire, staying well back.

Ulbricht attempted a smile at his daughter, but Mielke's narrow, slitted eyes glittered with open contempt.

Pagan had seen that look before, on the face of the judge as he sentenced her and on Bennie's face as he told her she was fired from the movie. But the head of the Stasi emanated the confidence of a man with far greater power than those men would ever know. He held an entire country in the grip of fear, and he had no time for stupid capitalist little girls like her. For kicks, she decided to prove him right.

"Herr Mielke," Beate said, keeping to her stilted but excellent English. "May I present Fraulein Pagan Jones. She is one of my favorite actresses."

"An actress," Mielke said, also in English, lips forming precisely around the syllables. "I have heard of you and your recent difficulties."

"Oh, you are too kind!" Pagan fluttered her eyelashes at him and took hold of the square, powerful hand he was not extending to her and shook it heartily. "Which of my movies is your favorite?"

Mielke withdrew his hand, one side of his nose wrinkling as if he smelled something bad. "I have not seen any," he said. "I have a job to do."

"No doubt you are as busy as a little bee," Pagan said. His frown deepened at the word *little*, but Pagan pretended not to notice. "My poor head can't even begin to fathom what you men have to deal with, running a country, keeping track of everyone, and all. It's just marvelous!"

Mielke almost sniggered to her face. How easy it was to be exactly what they wanted her to be.

"It must seem marvelous," Mielke said, "to one who dwells in a decaying and frivolous industry in a country that values only greed."

Pagan frowned and shook her head. "Oh, no, didn't you know? We also value beauty and fame."

Mielke's eyebrows came together in a sort of wondering pity. "Can you not see how all those qualities demonstrate your worship of the individual over the collective? Where is your love for humanity? Your sacrifice for the greater good? That is why your society is as rotten as a three-day-old fish."

She could tell from his voice that he genuinely wished to enlighten her, to help her understand where her values were awry. It sounded strangely naive coming from a man who kept his people in line through surveillance and terror. But it meant he was a true believer, a man who tortured, killed, and spied for what he thought was "the greater good."

She managed a girlish giggle, as if he'd made a joke. "Well, it smells like piles of cold hard cash to me!"

"Tea and hors d'oeuvres are over by the view of the water," Ulbricht interrupted, dismissing them. "Perhaps it would be best if you partook of them now."

Beate, taking her father's cue, tugged on Pagan's arm. Pagan waved and smiled at the two men as she allowed herself to be led slowly away. "You all are just so gracious," she said, and made her attempt at German deliberately lame. "*Danke* so much!"

Frau Ulbricht and her contingent of matrons also turned to watch them move through the stiff-necked crowd of graying male bureaucrats. The men and women weren't mingling much. The women fetched food for the men and then retreated to talk in low voices among themselves. The men gathered around ashtrays, nodding as they exhaled smoke through their nostrils at each other like posturing bulls on a crisp day in the pasture.

Pagan had to be the youngest person there, with Beate and Thomas the only other teenagers. There were no children, no families, even though the patio opened onto a grassy lawn leading to a beautiful still lake with a boathouse on the shore. It screamed out for crazy games of croquet and volleyball, for motorboats and inflatable rafts, for waterskiing and toddlers splashing in the rocky shallows.

Instead a sour-faced bunch of officials in ill-fitting suits were picking tobacco leaves off their lower lips and talking in hushed tones as patrols of Stasi soldiers marched past the boat-house. All eyes glanced furtively toward Ulbricht and Mielke, as if waiting for an execution.

Maybe they were.

The table covered with shiny bottles of vodka was surprisingly easy to ignore. Pagan's growing sense of unease made her want to stay alert. She tried to pay attention as Beate launched into a glowing assessment of her award-winning role in *Leopard Bay*. Fortunately, the girl didn't need much encouragement to chatter on, nervous and eager to impress.

When she got up to fetch tea and finger sandwiches for Pagan, Thomas leaned and said, low, "What in heaven's name were you doing with Erich Mielke?"

"Giving the audience what they want," she said.

"I thought he was going to put you in a cell and give you the full Marxist indoctrination," he said.

"This place is scary enough without imagining that, thanks," she said. "Everyone looks like they think my capitalist cooties are catching."

"At least Beate loves you."

"You could have told me she's the reason Ulbricht wanted me here," Pagan said.

Thomas looked abashed. "I know. That's the only reason he asked me to come—so that I could bring you to meet Beate. I'm sorry I couldn't tell you earlier."

"I would have come anyway," she said.

"I know." A mutinous look crossed his face. "But Devin Black told me not to tell you."

"That boy Devin," she said, "is at the center of every web, and he's caught you in it, too." She fixed Thomas with a serious eye and asked, "What's really going on here?"

A million thoughts blazed behind Thomas's eyes. "Pagan," he said, and put his hand on her arm. His fingers were trembling. "If you can't find me for a little while this evening, don't worry. And please don't point out to anyone that I'm gone."

She opened her mouth to demand to know why. But the strange urgency in his eyes made her choke it down. She wanted to ask if he was okay, if she could help in any way, but she could tell now was not the time.

"All right," she said.

He looked as if he was about to say more, but pulled his hand away and looked down again. "Thank you," he said.

"Look what I have for you!" Beate was approaching, holding a pot of tea and a cup.

Pagan worked up to a smile. "You're so kind, Beate."

Beate set the teapot down, eyes aglow. "Now I must tell you what my favorite movie of yours is."

"Please!" Pagan said.

The sun set into a crimson and violet haze in the western sky. Harsh electric lights along the roof of the house glared down at them, and an overboiled dinner was served. Pagan decided to keep speaking English, throwing in awkwardly phrased attempts at German to whomever she met as a game to see if anyone could tell. But nobody cared enough to probe beneath her bright, shiny surface. One man openly rolled his eyes at her and spoke in German to his friend about the rampant corruption of youth in capitalist countries, and an elderly woman took her hand and pulled her in close to sniff, as if she were a carton of milk that might have gone bad.

Thomas was pulled away into other, more genuinely admiring conversations as a few of the attendees revealed themselves to be fans of his work. At one point Pagan looked around and realized she hadn't seen him in the past ten minutes.

He'd warned her he might have to step away, but what for? Did he have someone he needed to meet with in secret? She hoped it was someone he cared about, something sweet and positive. But she couldn't help thinking it was the exact opposite. That he was stepping into something dangerous. And she couldn't help, because she was flying in the dark without a compass.

By then Venus was sparkling on the horizon, and the sky had turned a deep indigo that made her think of Devin Black's troubled eyes.

She was furious at him for engineering this long, awkward evening, but perversely she missed him, too. Her own fakery was going splendidly. Everyone but Thomas and Beate thought she was an empty-headed child with nothing more than her own fame to discuss. But that diversion had lost its flavor hours ago. She opened her purse to get out her lipstick and found instead keys with the Mercedes-Benz symbol on them.

She kept them in her lap so that no one else could see as she tried to think. These had to be the keys to the car. She'd seen Thomas give one set to the servant outside. Had he put this second set in her purse before he went off to do whatever it was?

She looked around for Thomas. He hadn't come back to the patio. It was tempting to say goodbye, walk out the door, and drive away then and there. She was itching to get out. But she couldn't ditch Thomas.

She walked toward the lake to see if he was there, but two Stasi soldiers patrolling the shore waved her back.

So she made an extra trip to the dessert table. Cake could

only be helpful now. Not far away, two men spoke in German, their heads close, their voices low. Pagan could understand almost every word.

"Is this why we fought the Nazis?" a thin man with a thinner mustache was asking rhetorically. "To stand around and wait for Walter Ulbricht to tell us what to do?"

Strange to think these men who hated her and all she supposedly stood for had fought the Nazis, like her father, while Pagan's own mother had...what, exactly? Sympathized with them? Or had Eva Jones done more than that?

"It's something big this time," a tall man with a double chin said, also in German. "He's never invited me here before, let alone every member of the Central Committee."

"And where's Honecker?" the thin man asked, deeply annoyed. "Everyone's here except Honecker."

Pagan pretended to be deciding between a chocolate cake and a pastry topped with streusel, edging slightly nearer to catch their rapid back-and-forth. She probably should've known who Honecker was, but the words *something big* peaked her interest.

"He was here early," double-chin said. "But he left. Business to attend to."

"Why does he get to leave while the rest of us must stay here, trapped?"

Trapped? Pagan did not like the sound of that.

"Whatever Honecker's up to, there's no one with any power left in Berlin to challenge it," thin mustache said.

Double-chin cast a dubious look at Pagan.

"Don't worry," the thin mustache said. "That silly slut couldn't speak German if she'd been born here."

Pagan held herself very still and began humming "Gee, Officer Krupke" under her breath to hide the surge of anger that flooded her at his words. She'd worked hard at making them think she was silly. His comments were a tribute to her acting ability, really. And, as the analyst she'd briefly visited had told her, whatever people said of her was a reflection on them, not on her.

Still, she wanted to punch him in the throat. Thanks to Mercedes, she knew exactly how to visualize it.

Double-chin nodded and leaned into his friend to whisper rather loudly, "I think it's happening tonight. Honecker's in charge. You know what I mean. The event we've all been…" He uttered a German word she didn't know. But he'd given *the event* a particular emphasis.

Pagan eyed a sweet roll and was glad no one but herself could hear the sudden acceleration of her heartbeat. She should know what event he meant, but it was eluding her. She picked up a piece of Black Forest cake and eyed the layers.

"I had the same thought," said thin mustache. "Yesterday, Parliament voted to allow the Secretary to do whatever he thinks best to address the situation in Berlin."

The "situation in Berlin" probably referred to the fact that East Germany was losing thousands of citizens to the West every day across the porous border to West Berlin. What, then, would Ulbricht do to "address" that situation tonight?

Double-chin pulled his chins in tighter. "What if Kennedy is more stubborn or more foolish than we think?"

"Then, my friend," thin mustache said sourly, "we all die in the service of our Party."

"As long as Mielke dies with us," double-chin said with a dark look toward the head of the Stasi.

Thin mustache shook his head. "He's like a cockroach. He'd survive a hundred atom bombs."

Pagan widened her eyes and tilted her head, increasing the blankness of her look to counteract the contraction of her throat. Two East German officials were talking about the possibility of nuclear war here, tonight, as a result of an event in Berlin happening now, while she stuck her fork in a *sachertorte*.

"We'll be here all night, I suppose," said double-chin.

"Why do you think the Secretary had Mielke post so many soldiers around this place? It's to keep us here until we all give our consent. As if we wouldn't."

"Even if we didn't, it would make no difference." Double-chin set down his cake in disgust. "The event is already in motion, and we must go along or be swept aside."

He caught Pagan's eye and frowned. Pagan waved her piece of cake at him. "I declare," she said in English with just a touch of Violet Houlihan's Southern accent. "You all have the best desserts."

They peered at her as if she was some molting creature at the zoo. "What is an American doing here?" double-chin asked, in German.

"I'm sorry?" Pagan said, blinking uncomprehendingly at him.

"The Secretary's daughter likes the foolish films the actress makes," thin mustache said, ignoring her. They were turning away, heading back to their table, desserts in hand. Pagan trailed along ten feet behind, eyes back at the desserts as if rethinking her choice. "Comrade Ice feels so guilty for having sent his only daughter to boarding school in Leningrad that he made Thomas Kruger invite her favorite Hollywood actress to dinner."

"How much longer do you think that boy will be around?"

Thin mustache shrugged. "He only wants to be an actor. So far he's harmless."

"So far," double-chin said with a fleshy, ominous smile, and they settled in at their table.

Pagan had a hard time swallowing her cake. She played with it, hoping Thomas would reappear so they could leave.

At least Beate was happy to jabber on about anything without much encouragement.

"Excuse me, ladies and gentlemen." The servant in gray who had taken the keys to Thomas's car had emerged from the house and was speaking in German by the back door. "The General Secretary will now be screening the latest comedy film from the Soviet Union for your enjoyment in the screening room inside."

The crowd murmured, getting up from their seats. Pagan looked at Beate expectantly. "What did he say?"

"Father's screening a movie inside, a comedy from the Soviet Union."

Pagan stood up. "Well, if there's anyone who knows comedy, it's the Soviets. Maybe after I see it I can give Bennie Wexler some pointers."

Beate smiled uncertainly, not quite able to pinpoint the sarcasm. "Come, I'll show you. Where's Thomas?"

Pagan managed to shrug nonchalantly, gathering her things. "I'm sure he'll be right back."

They were led into a large screening room lined with thick red curtains and filled with hard wooden chairs. According to Pagan's watch it was nearly ten in the evening as they turned down the lights and the screen lit up with a Russian farce called *Each Man for Himself*. As the film wore on, the captive audience drank until the room reeked of schnapps.

And Thomas was still missing. She ran the East German officials' conversation over and over through her mind.

Whatever Honecker's up to, there's no one with any power left in Berlin to stop him.

It had something to do with the border. That was why the tanks had been stationed near the Brandenburg Gate. That was why Devin had wanted information on troop movements.

Devin. More than anything she wished he was here. He

would know exactly what was going on, and how to get safely away.

And what about Thomas? She craned her neck around the darkened room looking for him. It had been hours now since he'd left her alone. Her skin was crawling with anxiety.

Something was terribly wrong. How the hell had she, Pagan Jones, teenage starlet—*alcoholic* teenage starlet—gotten here? Somehow she, of all people, was alone in a house with the leaders of East Germany. The relative safety of West Berlin was an hour's drive away. The armed troops of the most feared security service in the Europe stood in the way.

Unless, of course, Ulbricht's plan got President Kennedy riled up enough to press the red button and send them all up in a mushroom cloud.

No, no. She couldn't believe the President would let that happen. And she couldn't allow that to shadow her thinking. She had to figure out what the hell she was going to do. She was trapped, and for Pagan that meant only one thing. One way or another, she was getting out.

The movie was about half over when Pagan got up and sidled toward a side door. She knew where the nearest ladies' room was. Now she just had to look as if she'd forgotten while she took a good look around for Thomas. She had the key to the car, which Thomas must have put there. If she could find him, they could damned well get the hell out.

If they could get past the armed Stasi troops.

She didn't let herself think that far ahead. One thing at a time, like they said in A.A.

The flicker on the screen covered her movements and washed the staring faces of the crowd white with its reflected glow. Pagan put her hand on the doorknob and turned it very slowly, making no sound.

But the knob turned by itself under her fingers. She jumped

back as Walter Ulbricht flung open the door and strode through. Erich Mielke, head of the Stasi, was right behind him.

Pagan sat down fast in an empty chair just as the lights went on and the film froze on a frame of a woman screaming in terror as some poor tiger bared its teeth.

"Comrades," Ulbricht said in German, positioning himself at the front of the screen. The projector was clicked off, and the image behind him vanished. "I have an important announcement to make."

The room was dead silent. Pagan eyed the door, but Mielke's broad frame was blocking it. The man in the chair in front of her swayed drunkenly, and his neighbor put a hand on his shoulder to keep him upright.

Ulbricht's glasses glinted as he took in the room, plump hands clasped in front of him, tight mouth pursed in satisfaction. "In a mere two hours time, the border between East and West Berlin will be closed."

Pagan gulped down a gasp. A disbelieving murmur vibrated through the room and died as Ulbricht continued. "All the ministers here will sign a printed edict that authorizes action by our security forces to place under proper control the still-open border between socialist and capitalist Europe."

Ulbricht took a moment to assess the silent assembly and continued, "At last, the corrupting influence of the West will be removed. At last the kidnappings and deceptions that have taken so many of our population will stop forever. Comrade Krushchev of the Soviet Union is in agreement, so I know the rest of you cannot fail to see that this is the best course of action."

Again, that glinting gaze swept the room. *"Alle einverstandert?"*

All agreed?

Pagan had no doubt of the answer.

"*Ja,*" muttered the man in front of her. Around the room, people were nodding, forcing smiles. There was no enthusiasm, no sense of victory in the audience to echo Ulbricht's. But Ulbricht didn't care. They were agreed.

"Just as I'd hoped," he said. "Visitors from other countries will be allowed to cross the border back to the West. We will not interfere with them. Our own citizens will be kept within the borders of the fatherland. For your own safety, none of you will leave this place until the operation is well under way. Until then, there is plenty of food and alcohol left for you to enjoy."

Walter Ulbricht spread his hands, smiling with the upturned corners of his constricted mouth, and walked toward the door through which he'd entered.

As if released from a spell, the men and women in the room began to fidget and cautiously converse. Pagan unclasped her fingers, which had tightened painfully around her purse. Ulbricht had said foreigners could go home, right? So she was trapped here for now, but eventually she could cross back into West Berlin.

Ulbricht stopped in front of Mielke a few feet from Pagan, cocking his head as his security minister said something too low for her to catch.

"Ah, yes," Ulbricht said. "This is your moment, my friend. Tell them."

He stepped back and the head of the Stasi took center stage, opening up the door behind him. "Comrades," Mielke said. "I have one more little surprise for you here tonight."

Pagan's jittery stomach plummeted. Mielke was smiling with a ferocity that the trained animals in *Each Man For Himself* had lacked.

"We know that all of you here are loyal champions of the Party, ready to do what is right here tonight. You will all be rewarded, of course. But traitors…" Mielke paused, his eyes moving over the still, silent crowd. His gaze landed on Pagan, and his sneer widened. "Traitors will be punished."

He snapped his gaze back through the opened door. "Bring him!"

Heavy booted steps answered. Something dragged along the wooden floor. Pagan's hand was at her throat. She stood up without thinking, not wanting to see what was coming through the door.

"Traitors like this," Mielke said, and stepped aside as two Stasi soldiers dragged in the limp body of Thomas Kruger.

CHAPTER TWENTY

THE HOUSE OF THE BIRCHES

ACTRESS INTERROGATED BY STASI CHIEF

Hunky Co-Star's Espionage Exposed

A collective inhale of shock flew through the screening room. The soldiers half threw Thomas's body on the floor. He fell with a horrible, loose-jointed thud. A woman in the back of the room screamed.

Pagan lurched toward Thomas, eyes traveling frantically over his blood-smeared head, torn shirt, and jacket, looking for signs of life. Mielke stepped in her way, and, before she could react, put one hand on her collarbone and shoved her. She yelped, stumbling backward into her chair to sit down hard.

She looked up, heat rising up from her heart. Her hands curled into fists. She gathered her feet under her, eyes on Mielke's throat.

Mielke snapped his fingers, and the two guards who had hauled Thomas's body were on her. They each took her by an arm and pulled her to her feet. She tugged against them, trying to pull free. "What the…"

One soldier released his grip on her right arm and slapped her across the face.

She heard it before she felt it, like the sound of a stick snapping in two. Stinging pain erupted from her cheek as her head rolled to the side; her left ear rang. Her vision darkened. She would have fallen if the other soldier hadn't held her up.

She blinked as her eyesight righted and tried to feel her jaw. Her knees were weak with fear, but she focused first on her face. Nothing broken. She still had all her teeth, but she tasted blood.

She looked up into the eyes of the stone-faced soldier who had hit her. "Oh, please," she said in English. "Lana Turner hits harder than that."

A faint line of puzzlement between the soldier's eyebrows was the only answer.

It was a bad idea, pushing down her terror to be her smart-aleck self. She'd just spent hours reinforcing her reputation as a featherbrain. Such a person would be no threat to anyone here, and more likely to fly under the radar. Better to seem helpless and overwhelmed, which was close enough to the reality, than act tough. This wasn't reform school.

As the soldier gripped her arm again, she allowed herself to cry. It wasn't hard to do as she stared at Thomas's body. He was lying on his side, clothes dirtied, blood-spattered, and torn. At least she didn't see any devastating wounds. Was that his back expanding and falling with breath? Her own body was shaking too hard to tell.

Two more soldiers entered and moved in on either side of Mielke, awaiting orders. Mielke kicked Thomas's leg and watched Pagan closely as she winced.

"Your escort is still alive," Mielke said to her in English, and smirked as she sagged in relief. "We could have killed him outright, but we had a few questions, as you can see. We caught him in the act of espionage, going through papers in the Comrade Secretary's private office."

More whispers from the crowd. Pagan popped her own

eyebrows up and blinked in fake astonishment. She couldn't look as if she'd suspected Thomas was up to something.

So Thomas *was* a spy. Working with Devin Black, and against Ulbricht and Mielke. That had to mean Devin was working for the West and not the Communists.

Mielke was a smug malevolent little jerk, but he was right. Her date was a spy, and he'd used her popularity with Beate Ulbricht to get here.

Mielke stepped one leg over Thomas so that he stood astride his body and slapped the boy in the face three times, hard. "Wake up, Thomas."

Thomas didn't stir. Mielke held out a hand to the solider to his right. The man put a vial in Mielke's hand, and Mielke snapped the top off under Thomas's nose. "I said, wake up!"

Smelling salts. Pagan had seen them only in movies. The sharp odor of ammonia stabbed at her sinuses. Thomas's eyelids fluttered, his head arching back.

Mielke's voice boomed through the room in German again. "This man we know as actor Thomas Kruger is a collaborator with the West. He will pay the ultimate price, as will any coconspirators."

Thomas rolled over, and Pagan could see his injuries more clearly. Someone had dabbed most of the blood off his face, but a swatch of it was still smeared under his nose, trickling out one ear, and oozing from a cut on his forehead. The flesh around his left eye was swollen and purplish black. He kept both hands close to his chest, but she could see that the fingers on his left hand had been taped together, and the skin under them was puffy and red, as if someone had broken them.

Another surge of rage swept through her. She closed her eyes to contain it. She must keep her head clear if they were going to survive.

Thomas clutched his side as he sat up, eyes blearily searching the space around him. Mielke stooped over and thrust his face close, jowls shaking. Thomas flinched back.

"Your mother and sister will be taken in for questioning, Comrade Spy," said Mielke in German. "We will find out how far they have been compromised."

Tears leaked out of Thomas's eyes, but he didn't pull away. "It is you who have been compromised. My father fought fascism only to die as it found another form in the country he loved."

Mielke stood up, puffing out his chest, his face reddening. "You know nothing about the evil we fought. The Party saved Germany and will keep it safe. Everything we do is to keep oppression from returning to the fatherland."

"Oppression doesn't know which party you belong to," Thomas said. "All it requires is blind certainty and fear."

Ulbricht walked up to stand beside Mielke. "Don't argue with a child. Take him back to my office. We have more questions for him."

As the other two soldiers closed in on him, Thomas caught sight of Pagan standing between her two captors. His swollen eyes flared open. He shook his head back and forth, blood flying from his lips. "No, no, she doesn't know anything about this. I told you. I just used her to get here, I promise you..."

Mielke punched him casually in the jaw. He didn't put much force behind it, but the ease with which he did it told Pagan he knew how to use his fists. Thomas fell to one elbow with a grunt, but didn't lose consciousness. His green eyes, cloudy with pain, sought Pagan's face almost blindly. It took every fiber of her self-control not to get down on the floor and wrap her arms around him.

Instead she steadied her voice for him. He needed her to be strong. "I'm here, Thomas," she said. "I'm okay."

Mielke stepped back, speaking to his soldiers in German.

"Do as Comrade Secretary told you and take him back to his office."

The soldiers hauled Thomas to his feet. He reeled, shoes scraping at the floor till they had him fully upright. "I'm so sorry, Pagan," he said.

"Stay strong," she said, almost choking on her next words. "Don't worry about me."

They led Thomas out the door, one unsteady step at a time. Pagan wanted to scream at Mielke, to cajole, to plead, but some instinct told her that would only entertain him. She pressed her lips together to keep them shut.

"And you, Fraulein Jones," Mielke said, in a tone that made all the blood drain from her heart. "I think first we will speak with you." He gestured to the soldiers. *"Nimm sie in mein Büro."*

Take her to my office.

Mielke was still speaking to Pagan in English, then switching to German for everyone else, which meant he and everyone else truly believed she didn't understand his language. She didn't know how that might be helpful, but she decided to let him keep thinking that. She needed any leverage she could get.

Her life might depend upon it.

She couldn't think that way. If she did, she might curl up into a ball of fear and never come out of it. She was an inconvenienced Hollywood star, a privileged dingbat, and if she believed that, these dangerous men might keep on believing it, too.

The two soldiers took her through the door, both hands on her upper arms gripping hard. She pictured kicking them, or stomping on their insteps. She thought about faking a faint. Instead she walked quickly with them to see if she could catch a glimpse of where Thomas was being taken.

She got lucky. The hallway was long, all gleaming dark

wood and mounted swords and boars' heads. She got there in time to see Thomas being led through a door at the end on the right.

Not that she could do anything about it with two soldiers on either side of her. But it calmed her, knowing where he was.

The soldiers took her down the same hall to a room two doors from Thomas. Mielke unlocked the heavy wooden door himself, and the guards marched her over to sit in a red leather wingback chair. Ulbricht followed them in.

"Leave us," Mielke said to the guards in German. She was alone with the leader of East Germany and the commander of the Stasi.

Bone-deep trembling threatened to take over her body. Anxiety was making her light-headed, pushing at the edges of her control. A nice frosty martini would blanket it with a comforting fog. Never in her life had she wanted a drink more.

Never had her sobriety been so important.

She forced herself to look around, to keep thinking, assessing, planning. Mielke's office was spacious, with high ceilings and the same long windows she'd noted earlier. It would have been cozy if he hadn't decorated it exclusively with large East German flags, more dead animals, and photos of soccer players. Beate had said Mielke had a "football team," which meant soccer to an American like Pagan. If the number of pictures of him standing next to a bunch of buff young men in uniform or holding up trophies was any indication, soccer was his obsession. Soccer and spying.

Mielke positioned himself behind a heavy dark wood desk and rolled a soccer ball off a wooden pedestal to bounce it in his hands. Ulbricht came to stand in front of Pagan, hands clasped behind him.

She crossed her ankles and clasped her shaking gloved hands in her lap. This was a scene in the movie of her life. How would Violet Houlihan feel about being here? She'd be scared, sure. These ugly old men were being unnecessarily mean. But they were interfering with her life. It was late. She needed her beauty sleep.

"Your friend has been found to be a spy," Ulbricht said to her in English. "What do you have to say about that?"

"Um—wow?" Pagan shrugged. "I'm flabbergasted. Are you sure it isn't a mistake? Because as nice as Thomas is, he doesn't strike me as all that brainy, if you know what I mean. He doesn't have the jets for that kind of thing."

"Flabbergasted?" Ulbricht frowned, looking at Mielke and pronouncing it wrong. "Jets?"

"Flabbergasted. That means blown away," Pagan said helpfully. "Brains about to explode from the unholy surprise of it all. Which mine are." She rubbed her left cheek and gave them both a little frown. "When am I going to get an apology for that slap your guard gave me? I'll be bruised for a week!"

Mielke tossed the soccer ball from one hand to the other. "Perhaps if you report it to your embassy, they'll try to extract further reparations from our country."

Ulbricht barked a short, humorless laugh.

Pagan sulked, as if she took him seriously. "You can bet they're going to get an earful from me about this whole stupid evening!"

Mielke's face flattened into something so cold it made her shiver. In German, he said, "If you survive the evening."

Pagan rubbed her upper arms to disguise her trembling. If only she were as brainless as the persona she was faking. "And tell your thugs not to squeeze so hard next time. I'm going to have to wear bracelet sleeves at the very least for weeks—in the middle of summer!"

Ulbricht stared at her, stroking his trim little beard. "You must have known what Thomas was planning to do before you came here," he said in English. "Why else would you come here, if not to help him spy?"

"'Cause he's a flutter bum, of course, and I wanted to make good, not that it's any of your business." Pagan flushed and fanned herself as the two men exchanged puzzled looks. "He's a golden god hot rod for sure. Not the usual subterranean type I meet. A real square shooter, you know?" She frowned, as if searching for a more easily translated turn of phrase. "He's a cute boy and I like him."

Mielke sat down heavily in the chair behind his desk. Ulbricht looked down and massaged his forehead with one hand.

Pagan allowed herself to feel a twinge of actor's pride. So far so good. If she didn't jump out of her skin, this could work.

Mielke asked Ulbricht, in German, "Did she say he's not the normal underground?" Watching him try to make sense of her hepcat use of *subterranean* was a good distraction from her terror. "Do you think she means that he's not a spy or not the usual kind of spy?"

"I have no idea what she means," Ulbricht said. "I'd wager good money she doesn't know herself."

"Whoever decorated this place is trying a little too hard," Pagan said, glancing around to get a better idea of where she was. "You know what Freud would say about that." The long front windows were draped with heavy dark red curtains, but her internal sense of direction told her they must look out onto the front lawn of the estate, where the cars were parked. Other than the door to the hallway, there was a narrower door behind her, which looked like it might lead to a bathroom, and another next to Mielke's desk. Both were closed.

Mielke ignored her comment and tried again, one square hand drumming fingers on his desk. "Fraulein Jones, think back carefully. What did Thomas tell you about his reasons for coming to this party?"

Pagan blinked, as if trying to recall. "Well, he said that Mister Secretary here had a daughter who was a fan of my films and would I like to come meet her? So I said sure, of course, anything for you, Daddy-O." She looked at Mielke, wide-eyed and slightly hopeful. "Do you think that means he likes me?"

Mielke rolled his eyes. In German, he said, "It doesn't seem possible, but her head is even more vacant than I thought."

"It's likely that Kruger saw my request to bring her here as his chance to go through my papers. Apparently he used his good looks to get her to say yes," Ulbricht replied in German.

Pagan lowered her eyebrows in faint puzzlement to make sure they kept on thinking she had no idea what they were saying.

Mielke narrowed his already pinched eyes at Ulbricht, thinking. "Was it you who asked Kruger to invite her?"

Pagan's gaze darted to Ulbricht. Was Mielke challenging his boss, accusing him of bringing in the spy?

Ulbricht pursed his lips at Mielke, overgrown eyebrows lowering in anger. "Beate suggested it to me after she read in the paper that this stupid girl was in Berlin making a movie with him. It seemed harmless."

Blame it on your daughter. What a nice father. Pagan waited for Mielke to question his boss's judgment. But after a flash of calculation, Mielke shook his head and looked down, backing away from the conflict. Pagan couldn't help thinking he'd made a note of his boss's weakness. If the tide turned against Walter Ulbricht at some point, it might come in handy.

"Beate read it in one of our papers?" Mielke made a sort of *tsk-tsking* sound. "I need to have a talk with the editors."

"No," Ulbricht said. "She got hold of one of those West German rags somehow while she was out shopping."

Mielke leaned back in his chair as if that answered everything and waved his hand at Pagan. "The ones obsessed with celebrities."

Pagan sat up straighter, as if responding to his gesture and waiting for an explanation in English. When neither of them bothered to even look her way, she sagged in puzzled frustration and began picking at the heavy leather on the arm of her chair like a bored child.

But she would've bet the Renoir hanging over her parents' bed that Devin Black had arranged for those "West German rags" to fall into Beate Ulbricht's shopping bags.

God, what a genius, ridiculous, convoluted plan. Somehow, Devin must have uncovered that Walter Ulbricht's only daughter, Beate, was Pagan Jones's biggest fan. So he'd engineered to get Pagan to act in a film in Berlin with an East German costar. Then he'd arranged for Beate to ask her father to get Pagan to attend a private party. How to get Pagan there? Have the East German costar invite her, a costar Devin had already recruited to spy for the West.

If it wasn't for Devin Black, Beate Ulbricht's fandom, and the cold war tensions in Berlin, Pagan would still be sharing a cell in Lighthouse Reformatory with Mercedes. She should be grateful to the CIA or MI6 or whatever institution Devin was working for, but right now she wanted to smack him.

To keep up her act, she shifted uneasily in her chair, as if worried by all the chatter she supposedly couldn't understand.

"Just as well this girl's not involved," Ulbricht was saying. "We don't need any incidents to further rile the West while Operation Rose is in play."

Operation Rose—a lovely name for a plan to cut off the last piece of freedom their citizens had.

Mielke nodded, leaning forward in his seat to grab a paper from a neat pile on the desk. "True. Kennedy's just the type to start a war because we mussed up a pretty little actress."

"Kruger's the key," Ulbricht said. "If we can get him to name his contacts..."

"Even he matters little," Mielke said. "Nothing can stop Operation Rose now."

A phone rang, shrill and high. It brought Pagan, fists clenched, to her feet. Realizing what it was, she quickly sat back down and put a hand on her heart, smiling as if at her own foolishness.

But neither man was paying her any mind. Mielke stood and opened the door next to his desk to reveal a whole other office behind it. The ringing came again, much louder. Mielke moved into the other office and picked up the receiver. *"Allo? Ja.* Ah." He motioned to Ulbricht, who joined him and shut the door.

Pagan was alone in the office of the head of the Stasi. She had to think, to act—now. While Ulbricht and Mielke were out.

She stood up cautiously. Not only were East Germany's leaders on the other side of one door, but two guards stood behind the other.

She darted silently over to the narrow side door and gently opened it to see a small but very clean bathroom, as she'd suspected. It had its own door out to the hallway, where the guards were watching, and a big window covered with drapes.

She stepped in and shoved the drapes aside to examine the window. Carefully, so as not to draw attention from any patrols who might see the light from outside, she ran her hands over the sill and found the latch. She lifted it and pressed on the glass. The window slid open. Fresh air rushed over her face. There was no screen. She stuck her head out and saw that the ground was only three feet below the bottom of the window. If she turned sideways and took off her heels, she could slip out and jump down to the ground.

But should she? She peered out at the dark lawn. The porch light from the building's front door to her right was dim. It glinted off the bumpers of the cars parked on the lawn but revealed little else. The cloud-veiled sky showed no stars.

The patrols of Stasi soldiers were still out there. Ulbricht and Mielke wanted to keep them all bottled up until the border was completely closed. She glanced at her watch. Eleven forty-five. From what Ulbricht had said in the screening, the border would be closed at one in the morning. Less than an hour and fifteen minutes away.

She thought of Frau Kruger and little Karin and her stomach clenched. They'd been questioning Thomas for hours by the look of it. If Mielke had called his office in East Berlin, the Stasi might have already taken his mother and sister away to be questioned, too.

A shout of what sounded like victory came through the walls to her. She pulled her head out from behind the curtain to stare at the closed door where Ulbricht and Miclke had gone. Although the free air was telling every nervous cell in her body to jump through the window now, she had a chance here to learn more before deciding what to do.

Pagan slid the window shut, rearranged the curtains, and closed up the bathroom before tiptoeing over to press her ear against the other door.

The sounds on the other side were muffled but audible. Ulbricht's higher-pitched voice was saying in German, "What about the Bernauer Strasse station?" A pause before he remarked, probably to Mielke, "Ah, good, that is also now closed."

He lifted his voice louder, as if yelling into the phone receiver. "Excellent work, Honecker. Soon all the metro connections will be cut off. Any resistance yet? Good. And all of those on the border know to fire blanks at first? That should be enough to keep most citizens in line. Yes. Good. Keep us informed."

So they were shutting down all the underground metro stations and connections between East and West Berlin. They'd also have to block up the hundreds of streets that crossed the border, not to mention all the buildings that straddled it. The scale of the endeavor was mind-bending.

The receiver thunked down. Pagan, about to pull away, paused long enough to hear Mielke say, chortling, "Not a whisper from the West. They have no idea what's going on right next door!"

"It's splendid, splendid!" Ulbricht said, equally gleeful. "Even now the troops are moving into place with the barbed wire. Felfe has kept them from discovering anything."

Felfe. Where had she heard that name before?

"I told you recruiting him would pay off." Mielke's voice was alarmingly close. Pagan stomach leaped into her throat, and she sprinted over to the wingback chair to throw herself into it as the two men emerged, still talking.

Mielke continued speaking in German. "Operation Rose is keeping my soldiers very busy, Comrade Secretary. It may be a few hours before I have enough men free to collect the Krugers. We have to prioritize our assets tonight of all nights."

"The Krugers can wait," Ulbricht said. "It's not as if they can go anywhere."

Both men laughed heartily. Pagan's tormented gut burned with fury. She channeled it by fidgeting impatiently like a toddler about to have a tantrum.

"We have some more calls to make, no?" Ulbricht walked over to the big door and opened it up. The two guards there turned on their heels and saluted. "One of you. Take this girl back to sit with the others. We're done with her."

Pagan looked at her nails and hoped they couldn't see her

hands tremble. "I'm kind of hungry again," she said. "Can I get room service or something?"

"You will leave now," Ulbricht said in English, waving her out the door as a guard stepped forward.

"All rightee, then," Pagan said, getting to her feet. Dang. How was she going to sneak out the window now if the guard took her back to that windowless screening room with all the others?

As she swept toward the hallway, Pagan took hold of the handle on the big oak door, as if to shut it behind her in a grand exit. At the last minute she paused and peeked around the edge back into the office.

Ulbricht and Mielke turned to stare at her as if she'd grown an extra head.

She favored them with a big sweet smile. "If I don't get to say it later, thanks for throwing the craziest party ever. And I've been to Frank Sinatra's."

She shut the door with a click and pulled up the edges of her gloves, keeping her smile at its highest wattage for the guards. "Which one of you lovely gentlemen is my escort?"

The guards exchanged perplexed looks and the taller one stepped forward to take her upper arm in his hand to push her down the hallway.

She paced two steps with him and then halted. "I'm so sorry, but where's your nearest little girls' room?" As he stared and tugged on her arm, she shook him off and said, "The *Klosett, bitte?*" She pointed toward the door next to Mielke's office, which she knew led to his private bathroom. "I'll just be a minute."

She almost made it to the door, but his hand on her shoulder brought her up short. *"Nein,"* he said, shaking his head. *"Hier, bitte."*

He pointed toward a larger door across the hall from

Mielke's office. Damn. So much for that plan. She smiled, said, *"Danke,"* and went in.

Her heart jolted with happiness as she saw it was the same layout as Mielke's bathroom, only this one had no second door adjoining it to a personal office.

From what Mielke said, because they needed all their troops for the huge job of closing the border, it would take a while before they could arrest Karin and Frau Kruger. If she was lucky, she might get to them before the Stasi did. She had no idea how she'd get them safely past the troops into West Berlin. She was better with a script, but this time she'd have to improvise.

She clicked the light on, locked the door behind her, turned on the tap to cover other noises, and paused for a moment. She was in no danger herself anymore. They'd decided she knew nothing and was no threat. If she wanted, she could wait it out in the screening room with the drunks and bootlickers.

She stared at her face in the bathroom mirror. Her crimson lipstick was still perfect from her postdessert application; the liquid liner winging her eyelids had not yet faded. The rich chocolate-brown wool of the Dior suit dress was unstained, the fit a marvel. Was she just wearing it because it brought out her brown eyes and narrow waist? Or was she wearing it to put it to good use, to be the girl of action and grace the suit clamored for?

She flashed on Karin Kruger's bright blond head bent over the Wonder Woman comic, the warmth and eagerness of those skinny little arms wrapped around her as they hugged goodbye. The thought of Karin being dragged away by men in uniforms made her fists curl up inside their leather gloves. She couldn't live with herself if she didn't do everything within her power to prevent that.

Her power. That was funny. She was an actress, a screwup.

Hell, she was powerless against alcohol. What possible ammunition could she bring against the East German army?

One thing at a time. She left the water running and sidled
between the heavy drapes and the window. The architec-
ture here was the same, only overlooking the backyard and
the lake. The cement patio where they'd eaten dinner was
twenty yards to the left, lit only by a single porch light near
the central back doors. The food and trash had been cleared
away long ago. Nothing moved except the black shadows cast
by the birch trees.

She had to leave the bathroom light on, or the guard in the
hallway might wonder. So she wrapped the curtain around
her body to block the light, cupped her hands around her eyes
again, and peered through the glass.

Two men with rifles in hand walked by her, not five feet
away. She stifled a yelp of surprise and the urge to step back,
which would have sent the light streaming past her and allowed them to see her silhouette in the window. As it was,
they walked past without turning their heads, feet marching
in rhythm. They turned onto the lawn and moved toward the
boathouse on the lake. Each set of guards probably had an area
to patrol. They would be back in a few minutes.

Pagan removed her shoes and clutched them in one hand.
The drop down from this window was farther than on the
other side of the house, and landing in kitten heels on wet grass
was a recipe for a broken ankle. With one last look around to
make sure no other guards had wandered into view, Pagan
opened the latch and slid the window open. Cold lake air sent
the drape behind her billowing. A sliver of light cut a waver-
ing shape on the grass.

Was she really going to do this? She could close the window now and no one would be the wiser.

Instead she slung her purse crossways over her chest, slipped through the opening, and jumped down. Her feet hit cold wet grass and a stone half buried beneath it. With a muffled "Mmf!" she fell on her side, the arch of her left foot pulsating with pain.

So landing without the kitten heels was terrible, too. The menu tonight didn't hold a lot of great choices. She rolled to her feet, slipping the shoes on over wet stockings, thankful for the somewhat water-repelling wool of her dress, and got to her feet.

She crouched, waiting to see if her fall or the brief peek of light from behind the drape had drawn any attention. She heard only the leaves rustling and the far-off lapping of small waves on the lakeshore. To a city girl, all was ridiculously quiet. The nature-dampened hush and the sharp scent of pine reminded Pagan of her grandmother's little house in Maine.

The natural stillness around her was strengthening. Her grandmother wouldn't have approved of anyone slapping her granddaughter, of threatening Thomas's mother and sister, of slicing a city in two.

Hugging the building, she crept toward the corner, looking down to make sure she wasn't going to trip on a pipe or a rock, then up to check for more patrols. She rounded the corner, visualizing the layout of the grounds in her head. She was now on the short side of the rectangular building. If she rounded one more corner she'd be at the front, with its lawn and parked cars. She walked carefully, staying close to the vigorous growth of ivy. It helped camouflage her as she got to the second corner and peered around to see what obstacles might stand between her and the car.

The lawn lay empty as far as the weak porch light could illuminate. She could just see the fender of their car parked about fifty yards away.

She debated—sprinting across the lawn in heels versus no

heels. Landing on the rock had convinced her that going a little slower might be worth not jamming her foot.

Eyeballing her route, she cast a glance back and around. All clear—but wait. She'd failed to notice a square of light slanted on the narrow path and strip of grass that ran along the front of the building. Someone had pulled aside the curtains in the room closest to where Pagan stood.

If she ran through the light, she was more likely to be spotted. She'd have to run straight out first, then angle right to avoid it. Was the light coming from Mielke's office? She looked down the facade of the building, to see that the light was actually pouring out of the window closest to her. If her assessment of the building was right, it came from the room where they were holding Thomas.

After one more look at the empty lawn, Pagan crept along the front of the building, staying close to the ivy. The bottom of the lit window was three feet off the ground, above her waist. Careful to keep most of her body out of sight, she peered in.

Another office, larger than Mielke's, spread out behind the windowpane, lit by two lamps on the large black desk. The floor was carpeted in lush Turkish rugs, the walls studded with antique revolvers and a particularly large stag's head with impressive antlers and sad, dead eyes.

Beside the fireplace, in a large wingback chair like the one she'd sat in, was Thomas, nearly unrecognizable under the bruises. His bright gold hair was dark with sweat and blood, his left hand still taped and clutched close to his chest. But he was awake, eyes lost in thought, facing her direction.

Pagan was about to step out and wave so that he'd see her when she realized she was looking at him through the legs of one of the Stasi guards. The soldier stood, back to the window, hands on his rifle, facing Thomas. The backs of his trouser legs were just inches away on the other side of the glass.

Breath ragged, Pagan forced herself to inspect the room more carefully. Thomas and his guard were indeed the only ones in the room.

She looked over her shoulder at the car. Even if she reached it, there was no guarantee she'd make it past the guard posts and get to Berlin. But if she tried to help get Thomas out, the odds against her increased dramatically. Her own guard would shortly lose patience and force open the bathroom door to find her gone. And Ulbricht and Mielke could walk in any second to question Thomas further.

It was stupid, foolish to try to get him out, to escape with her. Thomas was a spy. He'd known the risks. It was his fault, not hers, that his family was going to be imprisoned, and probably worse, for what he'd done.

But how the hell was she supposed to go on living her life if she left Thomas behind to be tortured and executed?

She didn't have a family of her own anymore. That was her fault. She couldn't save them by helping the Krugers.

But she might save the Krugers.

Pagan moved into full view of the window. Thomas continued to stare into the middle distance, lost in his thoughts.

Pagan put one finger to her lips and waved, jumping up and down.

Thomas's eyes snapped fully open, uninjured hand tightening on the armrest.

Pagan shook her head, tapping her lips with her index finger.

Thomas's eyes moved up to the guard looming above her, then back down to her. His expression resolved into a bored blank. Casually, he turned his head to look at the fire.

Pagan followed his gaze and saw an upright iron stand of fireplace tools next to the fire screen.

Thomas turned slowly back to look at her. She nodded and raised her fist to the window.

Thomas dipped his chin. A nod.

Pagan rapped on the glass with her knuckles. In the country quiet, the sound echoed in her ears loud as a gunshot.

The guard inside the room whirled, staring out the window right over Pagan's head.

Behind him, Thomas grabbed the poker out of its iron stand. To keep the guard from turning back around, Pagan tapped the window again and backed up a step.

The guard's gaze zoomed down to find her smiling up at him.

Thomas had the poker in both hands. He lifted it like a baseball bat and took two careful steps toward the guard.

Incredulous, the guard frowned down at Pagan, reaching for the pistol in the holster at his waist.

Pagan put up her palm in a *wait wait!* gesture, and mimed unlatching and opening the window.

The guard's frown deepened, but he leaned down, hand reaching for the latch.

Thomas swung the poker. It whacked into the guard's head with an awful thud. He tottered and dropped in an awkward heap, hopefully out cold.

Thomas hit him again, to be sure. Pagan jumped up and down, miming applause. Thomas blinked down at her, a smile starting to take over his mouth. He dropped the poker and leaned over the guard's body to unlatch and slide the window open.

"Pagan! What…"

"I've got the keys to the car!" Pagan said. "Come on!"

Thomas didn't need to be told twice. He pushed the window open as wide as possible and stepped onto the sill, his body sideways, about to jump down.

"Wait!" Pagan said, seized by a thought. "Take his gun."

Thomas halted his progress through the window, staring at her wildly. "What?"

"His pistol." She pointed. "We might need it."

Disbelief battled with shock on his face, but he grabbed the pistol out of the guard's unconscious hand and jumped out the window.

Pagan was already running across the grass toward their car, one hand in her purse fumbling for the keys. God, where were they? Had she lost them? Her fingers closed around the cool metal and her heart found its place in her chest again.

Thomas caught up with her as they got close. "You put the keys in my purse," she said, panting. "We might as well use them."

"You better drive," he said, holding up his taped hand.

She stared at the car, cold sweat beading on her forehead. She hadn't driven since the accident. It was a big black boat of a car, not a sleek red convertible, but she'd have to hold the wheel in her hands. She'd have to shift.

"Pagan?" Thomas stopped halfway into the passenger seat, frowning at her.

Thomas's fingers were broken. She had to do this. She wasn't drunk this time. She was helping now, not hurting.

Helping now, not hurting. She repeated that phrase to herself and hefted the keys.

"God help us both," she said, unlocking the driver's side door and ducking in to pull the lock up on the passenger door.

"Don't turn on the lights," he said, climbing in and shutting his own door quietly.

"Don't worry." She pulled her own door shut with a muffled clunk. "We'll be lucky if I can get the thing started. Keep your eyes peeled for guards."

He rolled down his window, peering out at the velvet dark of the lawn. "Nobody."

Pagan put the car into Neutral, fingers shaking only slightly, and cautiously turned the key, foot on the accelerator. The engine coughed, then thrummed to life. She closed her eyes and leaned her head back in relief, forcing herself to take deep, even breaths.

Big black boat-car. Helping, not hurting. She could do this.

"Are you okay?" Thomas asked.

She forced her eyes open, stepped on the clutch, and shoved the car into first. "Yeah. I'm fine."

Her stomach heaved as she stepped on the gas and the car rolled forward. But she could shift gears and turn on the wheel, so she concentrated on that. She'd known how to drive since she was thirteen, when they gave her lessons for her bank robbing role in *The Tiny Outlaw* at Disney. It was ingrained in her muscle memory, like riding a bike.

Or a car. Off a cliff.

Shut up, brain.

They rolled forward in relative quiet onto the circular drive. Pagan accelerated slowly to keep the noise down, peering through the windshield to avoid the bushes. "Dang, it is dark out here."

"How are we going to get past the guards at the front gate?" Thomas said. "Maybe we should leave the car when we get close and find a place in the hedge to get through on foot."

"And walk to Berlin?" Pagan shook her head. "We can't waste time flagging someone down or hitchhiking."

"This is insane, Pagan," he said, putting his hand on the steering wheel. "You can't risk yourself like this. They won't hurt you if you go back and make it sound like maybe I kid-napped you. They'll send you home. It's me they want."

Pagan brushed his hand off he wheel and shook her head. "I heard Mielke say he won't have enough men to arrest your mother and Karin for a few more hours. And you can't drive with that broken hand. If we get there soon, we might be able to save them."

Thomas inhaled a sob that made her stall the car. She looked at him in concern as she threw the stick into Neutral again and turned the key. "Are you okay?"

He had his chin pressed to his chest, good hand over his eyes, shoulders shuddering. He lifted his head to look at her, the outline of his swollen face limned very faintly in the near dark.

"I thought I'd killed them," he said. "I thought they were dead."

Pagan put one hand on his arm before using it to push the car into gear again. "I know exactly how you feel. But there's still a chance, and I'll be damned if we don't take it."

Thomas wiped his eyes. His bruised jaw squared. "Then we drive through the gate."

"We smash through the gate," Pagan said. "Guns—or rather gun—blazing. Ready?"

Thomas slipped his hand around the pistol and clicked off the safety. "Let's go."

TANKS ROLL INTO EAST BERLIN

Military Build-Up Heightens Nuclear Tension with the West

Pagan slowed the car as soon as they spotted the lights of the gatehouse up ahead. "Get down low," she said to Thomas. "In case they start shooting."

"What about you?" he asked, scooching down the leather seat, his long legs folding up beneath him.

"I'm a lot shorter than you are," she said, sliding down, too, so that she could barely see over the dashboard. "This is a better idea than trying to talk our way out, right?"

"They won't let us through until they get orders to do so," he said. "If we pull up with our lights on, trying to seem normal, they'll shoot the second we take off. Surprise is better."

"That's what I figured," she said. "Ready?"

He set the point of the stolen pistol on the sill of his open window, sighting down the barrel. "Ready."

Pagan downshifted, revving the engine, and let fly. The Mercedes wasn't as fleet as a Corvette, but it had a large engine and a light load. They accelerated briskly, bumping and jostling over the dirt road. Pagan pumped it into second gear, then third, hitting around forty miles per hour before the guard standing outside the shack turned in their direction, both hands on his rifle.

"Here we go," Pagan said over the engine's growl, stomping on the accelerator.

The guard yelled something toward the shack, and two more heads popped out, peering from their lit area into the darkness.

"I think there's only three," Thomas said.

"Only!" Pagan said, and a great nervous laugh erupted out of her.

The guard outside shouted "Halt!" and fired in the air. The gunshots cracked like fireworks. Pagan winced but aimed right for him. The other two guards were shouldering their rifles, using the shack for cover.

"Halt! Halt!"

All three were shouting. The outside guard shouldered his rifle, and the others lowered their heads to aim.

Thomas squeezed his trigger, once, twice. His hand recoiled each time, but stayed steady. The blasts slammed into Pagan's ears as the wood frame of the guard shack exploded outward in two places.

The guards in the shack ducked back inside, yelling at their comrade. The Mercedes rocketed toward him, twenty yards away, fifteen. He fired his rifle, and the report was like a slap in the face. The side mirror attached to Pagan's door popped off and soared into the trees.

Five yards away. The outside guard dived for the bushes as the Mercedes bore down, bounced heavily over the makeshift dirt bump they'd shoveled there, and flew past.

Pagan sat up to haul the wheel hard to the right to make the turn onto the road, downshifting. They skidded, but she kept doggedly pulling. The back end of the car smacked into some bushes with a leafy crunch.

Thomas pivoted in his seat, hair falling into his eyes as he aimed the pistol toward the shack and fired again. More bangs, and something whizzed overhead, breaking off a branch. Another dinged their bumper.

Then the tires found their grip. Pagan downshifted again and gunned it. The car shot forward. Distance swallowed the light from the shack and the guards' shouts.

"I guess they know we're out now," Pagan said. She'd kept the car's lights off, so she had to bend forward over the steering wheel, following the nearly invisible right edge of the road where it vanished into the slightly blacker line of the forest.

"They know *someone's* out," Thomas said, pushing his hair back and leaning back in his seat in relief. "That was some incredible driving, Pagan. No offense, but they'll probably think it was me."

She grinned. Her heart was beating fast but steady, her hands had stopped shaking, and a strange euphoria was taking hold. She shifted into third and laughed out loud. "You drive pretty well for a man with a broken hand!"

He answered with his own laugh, teeth flashing in the dark. "*Mein Gott*, that was crazy. *You* are crazy!"

"Nicky taught me a few tricks," she said. "We used to go cruising. Got in a few races dragging down the Strip late at night."

"Maybe I don't want to move to California after all," Thomas said, and Pagan burst out laughing.

They were alive. They'd made it out.

"Now, tell me—" Thomas went on. "How do you know Mielke doesn't have the manpower to get Mother and Karin yet? Did he question you? Did he hurt you?"

She shook her head, turning the wheel slightly as they curved down the empty road. Up ahead she caught the lonely silhouette of a barn against the charcoal-gray sky. "They took me to Mielke's office and asked me a bunch of questions, trying to get me to admit I knew what you were up to." She paused, flashing him a look. "Thomas, you're a spy. You're working with Devin Black."

He exhaled wearily. "Did you tell them you knew that?"

"Are you kidding?" She couldn't help smiling at the memory. "You should've seen them trying to make sense of my teenage gibberish. I told them I was only there because you were so handsome I couldn't resist you. I acted like such a dizzy Chiclet they couldn't help believing me."

"So you didn't tell them about Devin, or anything else?"

"Well, I don't know much of anything else, but no, I didn't mention him or how he wandered off in East Berlin while we were visiting your family, or how he's actually Scottish, or…" She flicked on the lights to avoid crashing off the road. "Here's the deal. You tell me everything you know about him. I'll tell you what I know."

"What you know?" He cast her a sidelong look. "What have you two been doing in that hotel?"

"Now, now, Thomas, don't be jealous!" she said, teasing.

Thomas didn't reply. She threw him a concerned look and saw that he was looking down, the tendons on either side of his throat standing out like cords.

An outrageous realization glimmered inside her head. He had told her before that he had a secret. But could she say out loud what she was thinking? Would he hate her if she did?

"*Are* you jealous? Of him. I mean, of me. I mean…"

He inhaled sharply and shot her a look of such terror that she put her hand on his arm. He shook his head, lips pressed angrily together, as if he wanted to say no, and his own longing to deny it incensed him.

"Don't hate me." The words came out clipped, almost paralyzed.

So it was true. She contained her surprise, her questions. She'd never seen anyone so scared, so full of self-disgust, but she knew the signs. She experienced it herself, all the time, for different reasons.

"I could never hate you, Thomas," she said, and couldn't resist a question. "Did Devin… Did you and he…?"

"I met him before I auditioned for Bennie," Thomas said, looking down at the gun in his hand. "They said someone from the studio needed to see me before Bennie did, and there he was waiting for me outside a café, leaning against a newsstand, reading the paper. He looked up at me and smiled. You know that smile he has, when only one side of his mouth goes up, and his eyes move up and down your body like he can't wait to put his hands on you."

Pagan's throat was tight. "I know that smile."

"It was like lightning hit me, or a tidal wave." He turned his head to stare out the window. "I swear to you I couldn't help it. I've had friends before that I wanted to spend every day, every hour with. I told myself it was just friendship, and it was, mostly. I didn't want to think about it too much, until I saw him that day. Then I couldn't stop thinking about it. Thinking about him."

"Did he…" She didn't know how to say this, but suddenly the answer felt very important. "Did he feel the same way about you?"

Thomas shook his head. "No, but for the longest time I wasn't sure. About him or about anything. So I kept hoping, stupidly hoping."

Guilty relief washed over her, followed by anger. At Devin. "I wouldn't put it past Devin Black to encourage you, to keep you hoping so he could get you to do what he wanted."

"That may be so," Thomas said. "He didn't flirt with me, exactly, but…" His gaze flicked over to her. "You're not surprised? About me?"

"A little, maybe," she admitted. "I had no idea, if that's what you're asking."

"But it doesn't bother you?" He slid his good hand around his own shoulder as if he'd gotten a chill. "Knowing that I'm...that way?"

"Oh, please," she said, keeping her voice light. "Move to Hollywood. I'll introduce you to Monty Clift and Tab Hunter. They don't advertise it, but everybody kind of knows."

"Montgomery Clift?" He sat up straighter. "He's like me?"

She nodded. "I heard similar things about James Dean."

"I don't want to be like this, I don't." Thomas pounded his right fist on the armrest. "I've tried so hard not to be. But these feelings, they just keep..." He gripped the front of his shirt, as if to keep his heart from spilling out of his body. "I'm so sorry if I misled you, Pagan, or made you think that you and I..."

"Don't apologize," she said. "I like you, Thomas, but I might be where you were not long ago with Devin Black. Stupidly hoping."

"He's a brilliant bastard," he said. "I think he likes you."

Her heart did a soft-shoe. "If we get through this," she said, "I'm going to slap Devin Black just like that stupid Stasi soldier slapped me. We'll see how much he likes that."

The road branched before them. "Go right, here," Thomas said, and pulled out the magazine of the pistol. "Four bullets left."

"Let's hope we don't need them," Pagan said. "The border is officially closing at 1:00 a.m. If we're lucky..."

"It's twelve-thirty now," Thomas said, peering at his watch. "They must have posted checkpoints on the way into the city."

"Maybe not," she said. "They want to keep people from going to West Berlin. It sounded like they were concentrating their soldiers on all the points where the two halves of the cities meet. You and I are just two silly kids returning from a delightful party on a Saturday night." She glanced over at him. "A party where you got punched a lot. Here." She tossed her purse onto his lap. "I've got some pancake in there that might cover up your bruises. Probably not exactly your shade, but…"

"…still better than my current shade of purple," he said, fishing her makeup out of her purse. "Brilliant."

"Part of every good spy's tool kit," she said. "Or it should be."

Thomas turned her rearview mirror toward him and began applying the makeup. "Easy to say when you carry a purse."

The trees were thinning around them, buildings cropping up more frequently, changing from barns and sheds to homes and stores, all shuttered and dark for the night. But something up ahead was growling like heavy machinery. A line of lights bobbed over the road.

They started passing tanks.

The first one loomed ahead of them, taking up most of the left-hand side of the road, so they cautiously passed on the right. The treads rumbled ominously, and something near the main turret squeaked like a giant sewing machine in need of oil. The air was choked with gasoline and dust.

Pagan looked up as the young man sitting in the open hatch glanced down. He had his hand on the machine gun perched there. His helmet shaded his eyes, and he wore some kind of earmuffs that gave his head a funny shape. Tank guns must be very loud when they fired. Pagan hoped she wouldn't find out firsthand.

Pagan didn't wave or smile, because she had to look ahead at the road and to the dozens of tanks trundling slowly down the street toward East Berlin.

"*Mein Gott,*" Thomas said under his breath.

Between the tanks were trucks filled with armed soldiers, cement blocks, and wheels of coiled barbed wire. The men glanced at them as they passed by, but no one tried to stop them. They had their orders to close off the city. Two teenagers were of no concern.

Pagan and Thomas encountered no checkpoints as they entered East Berlin. They didn't speak much, as if holding their breath lest the spell be broken. Thomas quietly told Pagan to turn right as soon as possible, to get away from the tanks, jeeps, trucks, and soldiers marching endlessly down the main streets.

As the adrenaline of their escape drained away, a cold stillness took its place. Goose bumps crawled over Pagan's skin. Her wet feet in their battered heels were colder than a frozen martini shaker.

Pagan glanced at her watch and managed to find its hands in the dark. It was five minutes to one.

"Your apartment isn't far from the northern border of East Berlin," Pagan said. "Ulbricht said they've closed down all the metro lines that link to the West, so we can't go underground. There must be a lot of little streets that cross into West Berlin nearby. Once we get your mother and Karin in the car, maybe we can sneak down one of those, or go on foot if we have to."

"Leaving our whole lives behind," Thomas said, staring out at the bomb-damaged buildings and empty streets. "But it's better than what the Stasi has planned."

"I wish we could stop and call to warn your mother," said Pagan.

Thomas shook his head. "All the lines are tapped. And they've probably cut off all the phone exchanges until the job is done. Turn left here."

They wound through the smaller streets of East Berlin, passing ragged silhouettes of damaged buildings and blocky newer construction, all cloaked in an eerie middle-of-the-night silence.

"It's like the witch from Snow White gave the whole city a bite of the poison apple," Pagan said.

"Except tomorrow they will wake and find not a prince, but a prison," Thomas said.

"I guess that makes us two of the seven dwarves," Pagan said. "I'm Dopey."

"Don't be foolish," Thomas said. "You're Doc, the only one with any brains."

She grinned at him. "I think you just said I was smart."

"I knew you were a wonderful girl the first day we met," he said. "But tonight..." The headlights reflected off a glass window and lit his somber face, staring at her. "You saved my life by distracting that guard and kept your head while they were shooting at us. I can't quite believe you're real."

It was embarrassing to hear such things, to hear someone she respected say that she was smart, although it made her chilled flesh glow with warmth. But this wasn't about her. This was about something more important than her sad, silly life.

"We can't let them win, Thomas," she said. "To them, you and your family are just one tiny skirmish in a much bigger war. But for you and me, they're everything."

Thomas put his hand on her arm. "Thank you for saying that. Here's my street up ahead. Turn left."

"Lights off, I think," she said, turning off the headlights. "In case anyone's watching."

She slowed as they coasted around the corner. At the end of the block, a tan Trabant sat parked, lights pointing away from them. Between the trees, near the main door to their apartment building, shadows moved down the steps.

Thomas gasped. *"Nein! Zu spät!"*

Too late? Pagan jerked the car to a stop, peering through the windshield.

Human shapes moved onto the sidewalk. A man in a Stasi

uniform had his hand on Frau Kruger's arm. She was half turned around yelling at the soldier behind her, who was struggling with a smaller blonde figure. Karin. He tried to wrangle her legs, cursing, as she kicked and scratched at him.

Rage sent the iciness in Pagan's body fleeing, clearing her head. She shoved her hands into the depths of her seat, found the unused lap belt and clicked it over her. "Brace yourself," she said.

"No, no, we're too late!" Thomas moaned, head in his hands. "They have them!"

"Only two soldiers," Pagan said shortly. Her stomach lurched, but she pushed the car into first gear and gunned the motor.

Thomas looked at her, not comprehending, then fumbled between the front seat and the door, pulling up the strap of the belt and clicking it into place. "But—"

"It's our only chance. Get ready!" They were half a block away, hurtling forward.

The Stasi soldier escorting Frau Kruger lifted his head to peer down the street toward them. He must have heard the engine.

Thomas grabbed his pistol, shoving the magazine into place. "Four bullets."

"Make them count." Pagan pushed the car into second and aimed it at the Trabant.

The soldier let go of Frau Kruger, pulling his rifle off his back, and stepped off the curb into the street to get a better look at the engine roaring toward him.

Pagan smiled tightly. She was about to deliberately crash a car. She who had killed her father and sister in a car crash. But this time she wasn't drunk. It was her choice, and her passenger's choice, too.

The soldier was between her and the back end of his Trabant, lowering his rifle and shouting, "Halt!"

"Better get out of the way, you son of a bitch," she said, and flipped on the headlights.

The soldier shielded his eyes from the sudden glare, letting go of the rifle with one hand.

The Mercedes-Benz bore down. Beside Pagan, Thomas braced himself. Caught in the brilliance of the lights, Frau Kruger's face contorted with fear. The other soldier threw Karin to the ground to reach for his own gun.

The soldier in front of the Trabant scrambled toward the cover of the trees, shouting. Pagan gritted her teeth and kept the accelerator pressed down. He needed to move faster if he was going to make it. She hoped he did.

"*Zu spät,*" she said.

Too late.

The bumper clipped his legs, and he went flying. Pagan braced her hands against the steering wheel, and the Benz slammed into the Trabant. The upper half of Pagan's body jerked forward. Her forehead bonked against the wheel.

As Thomas hurtled forward, he torqued so that his shoulder hit the dashboard instead of his head. Pagan heard him grunt in pain, then he was out of the seat belt, shoving his door open, gun in his good right hand.

A man moaned in agony nearby. A loud pop, and Frau Kruger screamed. Something warm trickled down Pagan's forehead between her eyes as she peered over the dashboard, unbuckling her seat belt.

Lit by the one remaining headlight of the Mercedes, the soldier she'd clipped lay on his back on the sidewalk. His right leg was splayed out at an unnatural angle that made her wince. Blood spread outward from his knees, soaking his pants. His rifle had been flung several yards away, where it lay beside a tree. As Pagan watched, he stopped moving. She could only hope he'd passed out instead of something worse.

Another crack. The Mercedes' windshield spider-webbed as a bullet thwacked into the back of the seat where Thomas had just been sitting.

The remaining soldier wasn't using blanks first, even though Ulbricht had told Honecker to make that happen. Maybe those instructions were only for the soldiers manning the border posts.

A train-whistle scream split the night.

Karin.

Pagan had to shove her car door hard to open it. The entire front end of the Mercedes was pushed in, warping the car's frame. Using the door for cover, Pagan rolled onto the street, trying to spot Karin and the remaining soldier.

She fell against the body of the man she'd hit with the car. She put one hand on his chest and relief rushed over her as it rose and fell.

Another gunshot, coming from the sidewalk. Pagan crawled up to the narrow trunk of a tree beside the walkway and peered around it. The glare of the headlights lit a strange tableau.

The remaining Stasi soldier was using Karin as a shield, his left arm around her waist, holding her against his body, while his right hand pointed a pistol at her temple.

The impact from the crash had pushed the Trabant forward, smashing its hood into a thick tree, which tilted at a dangerous angle over the soldier's head. Steam rose from its engine.

A few yards past the streaming veil of vapor crouched Thomas, pistol pointed at the soldier holding his little sister. His mother stood behind him, her arms outstretched toward her daughter, her face a mask of terror.

The solider had his back to Pagan. She was unarmed.

"Surrender yourselves!" he shouted.

Any moment, more soldiers could come running to his aid. That's probably what he was hoping for.

Pagan dug her nails into the bark of the tree in front of her. Now or never. Focusing on the back of the soldier's knees, She scuttled out from behind the tree, keeping low.

In the periphery of her vision, she saw Thomas point his pistol at her, waver for half a second, then turn it back on the soldier.

"You will surrender!" Thomas shouted back in German. "She's better off dead than in your hands, so don't think I won't shoot."

Every detail of the Stasi soldier's uniform came weirdly into focus as Pagan rushed toward him: the torn hem of his long coat; the scuff marks on his boots; the tension drawn in the tendons at the back of his neck.

At the last moment, he must have heard her because he made an "Oop!" sound and began to pivot.

She cannoned into him, arms hooking around his knees. He kicked, but her weight and momentum slammed through. All three, Pagan, the soldier, and Karin, fell hard to the ground.

Pagan's left shoulder banged into the sidewalk, and her arm went numb. She heard the air whoosh out of the soldier as Karin cried out. Running footsteps moving toward them. Somehow Karin was up, free of the man's hold.

The soldier's legs scrambled near Pagan's head as he tried to get up. Remembering something Mercedes had taught her, Pagan shoved herself single-mindedly to her raw knees, pulled her right arm back, and punched the soldier in the crotch.

The man let out a coarse shriek. His knees jerked up into a fetal position, his hands grabbing between his legs.

Thomas loomed over them. The pistol glinted as he smacked it into the side of the soldier's head once, twice. The man stopped moving.

Pagan was on her feet, breath coming hard. Thomas was

listing to his left, blood running down his right leg, but his green eyes were sharp and focused.

"Remind me not to make you angry," he said.

"Are you shot?" Pagan asked, pushing the hair out of her eyes.

"It's not deep," he said, beckoning with his injured left hand. *"Mutter!"*

Behind him, Frau Kruger walked Karin toward them, inspecting her for wounds as they came. Karin broke free and flung herself at her brother, arms wrapping around his waist.

Thomas staggered a little. "I'm all right, Liebling."

"Both cars are useless." Pagan leaned over to grab the pistol still clutched in the unconscious soldier's hand. "And I don't think you can walk far with your leg—"

A gunshot popped down the street. Flashlights bounced toward them as running steps echoed between the stone buildings. "Halt!"

"Stasi," Frau Kruger said. "Run, Karin!" She grabbed her daughter's hand and bolted past Pagan down the sidewalk.

Thomas fired a shot at the soldiers. Their boots thumped to a stop. "That's my last bullet."

"They're under orders to fire blanks at first," Pagan said, throwing him the unconscious soldier's gun. "I got you a backup, now go!"

Thomas grabbed it out of the air and threw down the empty pistol. He lurched around the body on the sidewalk toward her. She took his right elbow. "Lean on me, come on!"

They ran in an awkward rhythm down the sidewalk. "My car's a block away, in a garage," Thomas said. He was panting.

Pagan glanced over her shoulder. The flashlights were scanning the wreckage, moving cautiously. Ahead, Frau Kruger darted to the right down an alley.

"Your car?" Something inside Pagan stirred sickeningly. "I don't think I can—"

A soldier behind them shouted in German, "There! Down the street!"

He stood in silhouette, his arm an accusing slash of shadow. Beside him, another aimed his flashlight. The glare lit up the sidewalk at their feet.

"This way!" Thomas tugged Pagan down the alley where Frau Kruger had vanished. It cut a narrow valley between buildings, dark as a cellar. Ahead, feet scuffled, and a cry from Frau Kruger pulled them forward even faster.

"Stop it, stop it!" Karin was yelling in German.

The alley turned left, and Thomas almost barreled into a soldier grappling with Frau Kruger. Karin was kicking at him, pounding his back with her little firsts. He wrenched Frau Kruger's arm, and she screamed, falling to her knees. Without hesitation, Thomas aimed his pistol at the man's head and fired.

Blood sprayed like a fountain out of the back of his head. He fell back, stiff as a board.

Pagan grabbed Karin in her arms. "Are you all right?"

"Mama!" Karin yelled, pulling Pagan toward Frau Kruger.

Thomas was helping his mother to her feet, but touching only her left arm. The right shoulder was hanging at a very wrong angle, the arm useless. Sweat covered Frau Kruger's pale face, pain written in every muscle.

"I think it's dislocated," Pagan said. "You need to…"

Frau Kruger put her left hand over her own mouth and rammed her right shoulder into the wall of the building beside her. The joint cracked audibly into place. She screamed into her hand, the harsh sound muffled.

Pagan stared at her as Thomas took Frau Kruger's left arm again. "Mother saw far worse during the war in Moscow," he said as Frau Kruger leaned against him, sucking in air.

"Remind me not to make your mother angry," Pagan said.

Thomas breathed a faint laugh. Frau Kruger's lips curled

upward a little between gasps. Thomas eased her a step or two, holding her around the waist. "The car's not far, *Mutter*."

The car. Pagan didn't let herself think about it, running behind Thomas and Frau Kruger, holding Karin's hand. Thomas led them down some steps and opened an iron grate with a rusty squeal.

They all froze, waiting. Shouting voices bounced toward them from the street, but they weren't cries of discovery. Thomas stuck his head into the unlit basement area. No sounds other than his own harsh breathing came back to them.

"I don't need the light to find the car," he whispered. "Mother, take my hand. Karin, you hold on to Mother's skirt and hold Pagan's hand."

Aligned like that, they stepped into the pitch-black underground garage, the *clip-clop* of their shoes rebounding off the walls around them. Pagan shuffled her feet, worried that she might trip over something in the dark, sticking close to Karin.

"We could steal someone else's car," she whispered. "Yours isn't big enough for all of us."

"Mine is the only one here," Thomas said. "And the only one where I know to find the keys. It narrows here."

"Hardly anyone owns a car here," Frau Kruger said. "You have to wait years even to buy a very old Trabant. Thomas is lucky his father was able to keep hold of this one."

"Lucky," Pagan muttered to herself. She put out a hand. Cold cement walls rose to both her right and left. "That's one way to look at it."

"Mostly they store construction equipment down here," Thomas said. "It's here to the left. Yes, come. Not far now."

He flicked on a light to reveal a narrow space between piles of cement blocks and boxes just wide enough to fit the sleek red Mercedes convertible. Behind it a narrow driveway sloped up to a closed metal door, which could be hoisted up to access the street.

Pagan forced herself to take a long deep inhale, counting to ten. Just the sight of the car made her woozy. Every cell in her body screamed for her to run. She made herself hold still, made herself breathe. Maybe she could be a passenger in the stupid thing for a few blocks.

The thought darkened her vision. She leaned against the cement blocks so as not to fall down.

Okay, so the Krugers could take the car without her and she would find her own way back to West Berlin. No way was she getting in that car. She didn't want to hold them back, and as a US citizen she could probably get back to her side of the border alone without much interference.

Thomas limped over to the boxes and reached behind them to fish out a hidden metal container with his one good hand. Frau Kruger was already opening the unlocked passenger door of the sports car and helping Karin into the narrow backseat with her left hand. She held her right arm close to her body. Her face was still gray with pain.

The keys jangled in Thomas's hand. He took a step, wincing, then threw the keys toward Pagan. They landed with a clang at her feet.

She looked down at them, not understanding.

"My right foot isn't working properly and my left hand's broken," Thomas said. "Mother can't use her right hand to shift. Pagan, you're going to have to drive."

Her already churning stomach heaved. The last time she'd driven a car like this she'd killed everyone inside it, except herself.

Pagan gazed at Karin's long blond ponytail and her big green eyes, and all she could think of was her sister, Ava, her little neck bloody and broken, eyes wide-open in death.

EAST GERMAN TROOPS TURN GUNS ON THEIR OWN PEOPLE

Escaping Refugees Encounter Deadly Resistance

Thomas limped slowly up the ramp toward the garage door as Pagan stared down at the car keys.

Her knees were made of water. She stooped for the keys and stayed there, head down to stop it from spinning.

"Pagan, are you okay?"

Frau Kruger had put the top down on the red Mercedes convertible so that she could fit in the tiny backseat along with her daughter. Karin half sat, half lay on her mother's lap, staring at Pagan. "Did you get shot?" Karin asked.

Pagan breathed in, breathed out, and stood up, shaking her head. "No, honey. I'm fine."

She forced her feet to walk toward the car.

Yes, it was red. Yes it was sleek and sporty. But it wasn't the Corvette she'd driven over the edge of Mulholland Drive the night of her sixteenth birthday, killing her father and younger sister.

This was a different car, a different night.

She was a different girl.

That got her as far as the driver's seat. She put the key into the ignition and grabbed the wheel. Her whole body quivered uncontrollably, but she put up one hand and adjusted the rearview mirror. Reflected there she saw Thomas standing by the door to the garage.

"I'm going to turn out the light and pull up the door," he said. "Then you back up the car."

What choice did she have? "Yep," she said, spitting the word out before she could think too much. "Hang on."

She put the car into Neutral. This was no different than driving the bigger Mercedes-Benz, damn it. One car was just like another.

She turned the key and stepped on the accelerator. But she pressed too hard and the engine revved like a rocket.

She snatched her foot away as if the pedal had burned it. At least the car didn't stall. She sucked in air, trying to ignore the churning of her stomach and leaned her head against the steering wheel for a moment. Sweat trickled down her temples.

A small warm hand rested itself on her shoulder. "It's okay," Karin said in English. Her voice was very small. She cleared her throat and said it again, more firmly. "It's okay, Pagan."

Pagan loosed a shaky laugh. A little girl was comforting her. A girl who'd been wrested from her home and shot at tonight, whose mother had been manhandled and injured, whose brother had been tortured and shot.

And here she, Pagan, was undone by a stupid sports car. It was ridiculous. Pagan herself was ridiculous. She laughed again and raised her head, swallowing her nausea.

"Thanks," she said, and stepped on the clutch so she could put the car in Reverse. "Ready?" she called out to Thomas.

"Ready," he said, and flicked off the garage light.

Darkness fell like a curtain. The garage door rattled under Thomas's grip and then clattered upward. Pagan twisted in the driver's seat, one arm over the back of the seat, and saw a square of charcoal night sky cut faintly out of the blackness around her.

"Just go straight back," Thomas said. "And I'll hop in."

"Okay." Pagan's mouth was dry. Something lodged hard in her throat like a chunk of underchewed apple. She reached her hand to the backseat and found Karin's skinny leg. She patted it. "Ready, Karin?"

"Ready," the little girl whispered, and put her hand over Pagan's.

That helped her to ease the car into gear. As the car rolled backward, the monster in Pagan's gut rose up. She choked, swallowed it down, and kept going. So what if she threw up? So what if her heart was tap-dancing like Gene Kelly on cocaine and she was covered in a cold sweat? Nothing mattered but how she drove.

The car purred backward up the ramp. Pagan aimed for the square of charcoal sky. As it got closer, her eyes found more light. Thomas's form resolved itself out of the dark beside the open door, waiting.

They were out. The small street was quiet. No soldiers yet.

She jerked the car to a stop beside Thomas and gulped the night air as he climbed in. "You okay?" he asked.

"No," she said. "But that doesn't matter. What's the fastest way to the border?"

"There," he said, pointing to her left. "Then right on Fehrbelliner Strasse. The French sector is just on the other side of Bernauer Strasse, to the north."

"Not far now," she said, and backed onto the street, pushed the car into first gear, and started off slowly.

The cool night air on her face was a blessing. Her eyes skidded over the barren street, trying to listen over her own engine for the rumble of trucks, the shouts of guards. She turned right onto the quiet, tree-lined Fehrbelliner Strasse. They crossed a tiny street and made it a full block before her gaze came to rest on the red dashboard.

Red as fresh blood.

She gagged, coughing. She couldn't breathe. Blood was pouring down her throat, tasting of salt and metal, covering her nose and mouth, smothering her. She was buried beneath the bodies. They crushed the breath from her, pressing her face in a river of gore.

Her vision narrowed down to a black-red tunnel. Hot blood coated her skin, burning like acid.

She tried to stomp on the brake. Tried to swerve, but she was too late. Palm trees and scrub on the horizon tilted like a handheld movie camera. The hood of the car dipped down sharply over the cliff.

They fell, like a suicide off the Empire State Building, straight down. Ava screamed, sobbing out for help, trying to climb over Daddy's shoulders to the backseat to get out of the car as it plunged. Daddy grabbed Ava with one arm, the other braced on the red red dashboard, shouting for Pagan to stop, please stop, Oh, God, stop!

The car pounded into a tree or a rock and kept going. The jolt shook Pagan loose. She flew sideways. The red steering wheel and the cherry leather seats ran with darker crimson as the car blew past her and kept falling and falling and falling...

She hit the pavement and rolled. Her stomach heaved. She was lying on her side in the middle of the street, throwing up so hard it hurt. All the tea, the black forest cake, all the stroganoff, spewed out of her and still she was hacking up bile.

The spasms subsided, and she pushed herself away to see the red convertible, still rolling down the street, driver's door swinging wide. Karin's wide-eyed face popped up over the back edge, staring at her.

She hadn't gone over the cliff off Mulholland Drive. She was in East Berlin.

Not far away, men were shouting. Footsteps hammered closer.

Pagan fell onto her back on the road and stared up at the sky.

There was no way she could drive that car. The soldiers were coming. She was going to die here tonight.

She deserved it.

A breeze caressed her perspiring face, blowing away the sour odor of half-digested food. The fresh earthy aroma of soil, of grass, of living things washed over her.

A memory, sweet as the scents, stirred. She half sat up and turned her head to see a park to her right. The benches and young trees looked familiar. It was the same park she'd walked through when she'd followed the peacoat-clad Devin Black, empty now of mothers and children, still oddly barren and more brown than green.

But there was life there, trying to grow. She could smell it.

Her grandmother's garden had held that scent of life, too. Her father had told Pagan once that she had a laugh just like his mother's. He'd loved hearing it for that and so many other reasons.

Her grandmother's laugh deserved to live, even if Pagan didn't. Karin and Thomas and their mother deserved to live. And Pagan's grandmother certainly would not have approved of Pagan lying in the middle of the road, indulging in thoughts of death when there was work to be done, work saving a girl a lot like Pagan's little sister.

Mama had given up. So Pagan had sworn that she never would.

It was up to her now.

She sat up. The terrible shaking quieted to a low-grade tremor.

She looked over her shoulder. The shouts and footsteps weren't far, but the soldiers hadn't turned down this little street yet. The Krugers had a chance.

Thomas was limping painfully toward her, blood soaking his pant leg, green eyes owlish with concern. "Pagan?"

"Thomas." She got to her feet. "Sorry about that."

"You were screaming and then you just jumped out of the car!"

So that's how she'd ended up on the pavement. It was all a horrible blur.

"I'm okay now." She touched his outstretched hand briefly and sped back toward the car. She felt empty, like the shell of a ruined building after the bombing was over. She was in pieces, but at least the explosions had stopped. "We better get going. They're coming."

"I can try to drive if you can't..."

"Don't be silly," she said briskly. It's what her grandmother would have said. "Sit down and put pressure on that leg wound this instant. Karin, get down, please."

She thumped down in the red leather seat, slammed the heavy door shut, and turned the key. The engine roared to life. "Where to?"

Thomas was staring at her. "Past the park, then stop at the next cross street, Anklamer Strasse. That will be a block south of the border. We should check down it to both the left and the right because there will be more soldiers there."

"The good news is that the guys already looking for us won't expect us to move toward the troops." Pagan stepped gently on the accelerator, past the park. The car drove easily. A deep vibration still buzzed inside her, but she was driving.

As they approached Anklamer Strasse she slowed to drive the car between trees up onto the sidewalk where the trunks and leafy branches made the shadows deeper. She stopped just short of the corner.

She climbed out of the car, keeping her voice low. "Stay quiet. I'll check down to the right and the left. The streets parallel to ours will cross the border, right?"

"Yes. Let me help you." Thomas began to hoist himself painfully out of the car.

"Sit down!" Pagan snapped. "If you bleed to death it will be very inconvenient."

"I can help!" Karin pushed off the back of the seat in front of her, standing up in the backseat. "I'll go right and you go left."

"Nein!" Frau Kruger said, grabbing her daughter with her good arm.

"One foot outside this car, and you'll regret it!" Pagan whispered at Karin vehemently. "Now stay quiet and help put the top up. I'll be right back."

It was a relief to trot away from the red convertible, to make her legs move and get her heart thumping in a steady rhythm. Staying near the trees along the sidewalk, she looked carefully left down Anklamer Strasse. It was a very short block down to the cross street, Brunnen Strasse. Running lightly on her toes, Pagan hugged the buildings to move even closer.

A tank lumbered by, heading north. She pulled up short as a truck full of barbed wire tagged behind it. She got to the corner of Anklamer and Brunnen Strasse and peered around to the right, up the long block to the border between East and West Berlin.

Another truck was already there, at the corner of Brunnen and a Bernauer Strasse, which marked the border. A manned machine gun sat in the middle of the road, pointing toward West Berlin.

Machine gun and tank. Bad.

Pagan took a moment to make sure no one else was coming down either street before she skulked back down Anklamer Strasse, past the intersection where the convertible sat waiting, and up the slight curve of the street to the intersection on the right.

The street sign here said Ruppiner Strasse. It was a relief

to find it much narrower than Brunnen Strasse, where she'd seen the tank, with no soldiers visible yet. She crept down it half a block before she saw another machine gun in the middle of the intersection with Bernauer Strasse, again pointed at the border.

Two other soldiers, rifles in hand, watched the street, focused for now on the French sector on the other side of the border. Two soldiers moved slowly down the middle of Bernauer Strasse, a roller of barbed wire held between them as it unraveled, leaving spiked cable in their wake.

All around, the windows in the bullet-scarred buildings remained dark. Even if the citizens of East Berlin had been awakened by the sounds of a wall going up around their city, they were probably keeping their heads down and their lights off. There was nothing to distract the soldiers from their job.

Which gave Pagan a terrible, desperate idea.

Breathlessly, she ran back and reported in. "I don't think we're going to find a border street without soldiers on it," she said, putting the car in gear. They'd put the soft top of the convertible up, as she'd said, "But Ruppiner Strasse has no tanks or trucks and only one machine gun."

"Machine gun?" Frau Kruger asked weakly from the backseat.

"A total of five soldiers that I could see. The tank and trucks are a long block farther down. If we can surprise them and get you through, they won't have time to react." She turned the car onto Ruppiner Strasse, slowing to keep the engine's growl low. Beside her, Thomas was peering up ahead. She said, "They've only laid down one layer of barbed wire so far. You have to go now."

"You?" he asked. "You mean *we*."

She didn't answer but brought the convertible to a halt, throwing on the emergency brake, to do a quick check of her face in the review mirror. She wiped away a smear of dirt along her cheek and the bloodstain on her forehead. Not close-up ready, but pretty good given the night she'd had. She opened the door.

"You're coming with us," Thomas said, reaching for her but missing as she slipped out.

Pagan slid around the hood of the car, keeping to the shadows, glad that her Dior suit dress was a dark chocolate brown. It hid so much. She dusted off her skirt, adjusting her purse strap across her chest. "I'm sorry, but, Frau Kruger, you're going to have to drive. Not far, just a little more than a block."

"But…" Thomas shook his head as Karin moved out of the way to let her mother up into the driver's seat. "Where are you going?"

Pagan kept her voice firm but light, optimistic. "Thomas, maybe you can help her shift or steer with your good hand. That's it." She nodded as Frau Kruger put in the clutch and Thomas put his unbroken right hand awkwardly on the gearshift. "Then when the soldiers move out of the way, all your mother has to do is floor it and smash through the barbed wire. Once you're on the other side, just keep driving. Turn the corner as soon as you can to get out of sight, out of gun range."

"Wait—what do you mean, when the soldiers move out of the way?" Thomas asked.

Pagan backed down the dark sidewalk along Ruppiner Strasse, heading toward the border. "When the guy at the machine gun steps away, that's probably when you should gun it."

Thomas poked his head and shoulders out of the window, blond eyebrows frowning dangerously. "What's going to make him move away?"

Pagan shrugged and gave him a what-the-hell smile. "Me."

EAST GERMAN TROOPS SEAL BORDER WITH WEST BERLIN

To Block Refugee Escape

The soldier at the machine gun sat in a puddle of light in the middle of the intersection.

Pagan sidled closer, focusing on not letting her heels click on the sidewalk. Given what she was about to try, that was the only way to keep incapacitating dread from seizing her. One step at a time, one breath at time, she approached, taking mental notes as the two soldiers in their thick brown-gray coats on either side of the machine gun paced up and down the paving stones of Bernauer Strasse to her left and right.

The headlights of a jeep, parked in the middle of Bernauer Strasse, illuminated the scene, casting the warped shadow of the machine gun's tripod over the thin white line painted down the middle of the street which marked East from West.

The Stasi soldiers weren't goose-stepping the way they did in parades or in front of Communist monuments. This was a military perimeter, not a show. The darkness, the guns, the wire were all too grim, too real.

The soldiers kept their rifles tightly clenched in both hands in front of them. Their necks swiveled constantly this way and that, scanning the Western side for movement. Most of their attention was across the street in the French sector. The machine gun was pointed that way, too. Their main concern for now must be resistance from the West.

But the pacing soldiers also sometimes looked down Ruppiner Strasse, in Pagan's direction, and scanned the upper windows of the buildings overlooking their street. Good thing she'd skulked so carefully this far. She did a quick check of her purse, battered but still strapped across her body. It was dark, but she could feel the leathery cover of her passport inside. She hoped she lived long enough to need it.

Something about the whorls of barbed wire, anchored by heavy cement barriers, edged Pagan's dread to the side to allow the anger in. The whole situation was weirdly familiar and horribly wrong. Just last week Pagan had tried to get over the fence around Lighthouse Reformatory. But she'd been duly convicted of a crime she'd actually committed. She deserved to be a prisoner.

The Krugers and the people of East Germany had done nothing to justify this. This wall cutting them off from the rest of the world treated them as if they were all criminals. The entire country had become a prison; the citizens were now inmates, incarcerated without trial.

Her anger gave her strength and focus to think. Where were the guys unspooling the barbed wire? She got close to the corner, hugging the building, and peered down Bernauer Strasse to her right. She found them heading back toward the machine gun, still rolling out a curved wave of spiked wire behind them. They were on their second trip along this stretch of road. If these men passed the mouth of Ruppiner Strasse again, the Krugers would have to bust through two layers of barbed wire instead of one.

Both soldiers holding the wire were young, tall, and strong. One had a tired, resentful look on his face as he half hobbled along, as the other one, more upright and focused, kept telling him to check the strand behind them. Of the two, he was more in charge.

A year ago, Pagan would have been drunk by this time of night. She closed her eyes for a moment and cast herself back to that late-night tipsiness she remembered all too well. How her fingertips had buzzed, and her joints had loosened. How the alcohol made her stupid and fearless.

Now there was no alcohol to ease her fright. She missed that foolish certainty, but she was an actress. She wasn't brave, but she could pretend to be.

She opened her eyes and, smiling and humming, stepped out of the dark. She walked right in front of the headlights of the East German jeep, casting a curvy shadow that stretched all the way across Bernauer Strasse.

"Hey!" The man at the machine gun jerked his capped head her way.

She ignored him, swaying toward the two men bearing the barbed wire, away from the intersection. The fine wool of her dress brushed against her knees. She could feel the holes in her stockings. Hell, she should have taken them off before she tried this. They were in a sorry state, just like her nerves.

"Yoo-hoo!" she called, waving at the soldiers and sashaying closer. "Excuse me."

They stopped dead, eyes zeroed in on her like gun sights. The resentful one's mouth fell slightly open.

"Halt!" called the soldier at the machine gun.

She glanced back. He was trying to swivel the gun her way, but she was still too far behind it. He'd have to pick up the tripod and turn it around to aim at her. He gave up and pulled his rifle off his back.

Pagan's knees were shaking. Adrenaline flooded through every cell in her body, telling her to run.

But she was a drunk right now, or at least channeling her

old drunken self. Drunks didn't feel adrenaline. She let herself roll off her heels, ankles bowing. "I'm so sorry, but I'm lost. Oh, gosh darn it, you probably don't speak English. Um, *ich habe mich verlaufen*. Is that right? *Ich bin Amerikaner*."

She smiled and expelled a hiccup. The resentful soldier's gape reversed into a condescending smile. He muttered something to the more focused soldier beside him, but that one didn't respond, running wary gray eyes up and down her body.

He'd been telling his partner what to do, and he hadn't taken her immediately at face value, so he was probably the smarter of the two. She couldn't see much of his hair under his helmet, but his nose was long and commanding, his lower lip was full, with a deep, sensuous dent between it and his strong chin. Handsome.

He was her target. If she could convince the cute, clever, suspicious one, she could convince them all.

"Halt!" yelled another voice behind her. She nearly leaped into the air in surprise, but somehow maintained her relaxed, slightly sloppy stance. But now she knew that the pacing soldiers had spotted her, along with the machine gunner.

To make sure they were all fixated on her, she pretended to spot the huge gash in her stocking and came to an unsteady halt. "Dang it all," she said, and hauled her skirt up a good five inches to inspect how high the tear went, running a hand over her knee and thigh. "Can't get through a night without ruining them!"

"You're American?" the cute soldier said in accented English.

Both he and his partner were staring at her legs. Good. And good thing they couldn't see the tremor of terror just beneath her skin.

"Aren't you clever?" she said. "That's right!"

"You have come to the wrong place, Fraulein," he said.

"Get out of the street!" One of the guards behind her yelled in German. "Get back or we may have to shoot!"

"She's American, wait!" the cute soldier said in German.

"*Amerikaner*," a soldier behind her said with disgust, as if that explained everything.

Pagan was only ten feet away from the cute soldier. She wobbled closer, frowning. "Would you mind helping a lady out? I can't find my friends anywhere. I mean, all I did was look up at this big old statue of a guy on a horse, and when I looked back down—poof! They were gone. Like magic!"

She stumbled and pitched toward him. Instinctively, he dropped the handle of the barbed wire spool and caught her.

"Oop!" As she fell, her arms dropped around his shoulders.

He leaned toward her to keep his own balance, his hands seizing her by her rib cage. The strength in his grip was terrifying. But for her right now, this was all just a scene in a movie, one she could act the hell out of. So she still let her breasts bump against his chest. Her hair brushed his mouth.

"*Vorsicht!*" he said, one hand sliding down to grab her waist, trying to right her. "Watch yourself, Fraulein."

"Oh, my goodness!" She leaned her whole body against his for a moment longer, as if trying to get her balance back. "I must have tripped over that nasty wire of yours."

"*Gott im Himmel*, she's cute!" the resentful soldier said in German, pushing his cap back in wonder. "Even if she's drunk off her little derriere."

Pagan kept one hand on the cute soldier's chest, wobbling until he put his hands on both her shoulders to keep her steady. "What did he say?"

Amusement finally turned his lips up. "He said, you're pretty far away from your friends, I think."

Liar. He was attracted to her. She could tell from the way his fingers tightened, the way his pupils dilated as his eyes moved down her neck. But something behind his eyes remained cold and distant. She repressed a shudder and the desire to shove him away. She needed him for one more minute.

"I'm starting to think I ended up in exactly the right place," she said, and stepped into him again, one hand on his waist, the other still against his chest.

He smiled and slid his hands down to her hips.

"You lucky son of a bitch," the resentful soldier muttered.

She couldn't feel much through the cute soldier's thick wool, but he was tall and well-muscled. His heavy leather belt bore a flashlight and his pistol. The pistol was secured in its holster by a leather flap with metal snaps.

"It isn't proper to take advantage of a female comrade in distress," he said. His lips twitched. "Are you in distress, Fraulein?"

She stepped back and pointed his own pistol at his chest. Her hands were shockingly steady. "Not anymore."

A startled shout erupted from the resentful soldier.

The cute one's smile soured. His eyes glinted dangerously, giving her the faintest warning before he lunged.

She skittered back, aimed, and pulled the trigger.

The gun recoiled in her hand, giving off a loud crack. She'd sighted perfectly thanks to her *Young Annie Oakley* training.

The cute soldier stopped in his tracks, paling, eyes wide. The other Stasi men hollered in alarm, and lifted their rifles at her.

But no splotch of blood appeared on the cute soldier's uniform, or anywhere else. His face cleared in relief. Anger followed.

"Blanks," said Pagan in German. She remembered the exact right word because she'd heard Ulbricht use it during his phone call to Honecker. "Your friends have them loaded, too. How many more before I get down to the real bullets?"

The cute soldier took a furious step toward her. The others began to close in.

Pagan fired again.

He pulled himself up, fury twisting his handsome face. It felt good and right to frighten him. Finally she had a proper venue for her fury.

"How many more blanks?" she demanded.

He was thinking, hard. "They're all blanks," he said.

"Oh, please," she said in English, and spared a glance to her left and saw that all three soldiers blocking the intersection of Ruppiner Strasse and Bernauer Strasse had left their posts to curve around her in a semicircle, rifles at the ready. "One more move and your friend is dead," she told them.

The cute soldier reached for his own rifle, slung across his back.

She fired his pistol at him again.

He flinched and dropped his hands, unhurt, but sweating.

"I don't think they're all blanks," she said, smiling, and sighted down the pistol to aim at his head. "How many?"

He shook his head, lips white with rage, eyes on the pistol in her hand.

Her finger tightened on the trigger.

"Three!" the cute soldier said. "Three blanks. The rest are real bullets!"

Pagan backed up a step, farther from the intersection. As if pulled by a string, they all followed her a single pace. Good.

"So the next bullet will work," she said. She was still speaking German, so they could all understand her.

"You won't be able to kill us all," her target said. His hands were slowly clenching into fists.

"Probably not," she admitted. "So make no mistake. If any of your friends so much as flicks an eyelash at me, I'll kill you. Let's find out which of them hates you the most."

Silence. Behind the cute soldier, the resentful one swallowed audibly.

An engine snarled like a buzz saw, coming fast. A blur of red tore down Ruppiner Strasse, tires smoking, and smashed into the barbed wire. Metal scraped over metal with a hair-raising screech.

Every head but Pagan's swiveled to follow. The car slowed but didn't stop, dragging the heavy concrete blocks used to anchor the wire over the worn cobblestones.

"Halt!" one of the pacing sentries shouted, lowering his rifle toward the car.

The machine gunner ran for his emplacement. "Halt!"

A barrage of gunfire assaulted her ears. Or what sounded like real gunfire.

Pagan was sprinting for the cover of the trees along Ruppiner Strasse, praying that those first shots were blanks.

She made it to a tiny cross street and spared a glance over her shoulder. The red convertible was on the West Berlin side of Bernauer Strasse, zooming deeper into the safety of the French sector, dragging barbed wire behind it. As she watched, the wire rolled up and over the car's roof, ripping a jagged hole in the soft material before striking sparks off the back trunk and falling free.

She had time for one huge grin.

"Stop now or I'll shoot!" a voice called clearly in English. A familiar figure was racing toward her.

The cute one. He lowered his rifle and fired, but no bullet whizzed past her or slammed into her body, no leaves were knocked from the trees.

"Blanks!" she shouted at him in German, and, powered by a spurt of excitement and fear, she darted down the lane.

She was grateful for how dark it was here. She ran full-out, pumping her arms hard. As she reached the end another shot rang out behind her. Above her head, a brick exploded.

Her heart nearly stopped. So much for the blanks.

She didn't spare a moment to fire back, although she still had the pistol in her hand. She rounded the corner and zigged immediately down another alley to her right, leaping over piles of rubbish. She turned down the next street and dismay nearly overcame her. He was driving her deeper into East Berlin.

The cute soldier's footsteps followed as she scurried across the next street toward the roofless ruin of a structure standing empty in the early morning darkness.

Her breath was coming in short, irregular gasps. She stumbled over a fallen block of stone and fell, scraping her hands and jarring her wrists.

"I see you!" the soldier shouted in English, appearing at the mouth of the last alley she'd traversed, raising his rifle to his shoulder again.

Her breathing was frayed. Her chest hurt, and her burning thighs trembled. An armed soldier was hunting her in the dark through a city she didn't know. She was nothing but a whirring, mindless tangle of panic. But she'd die in her tracks before she gave the son of a bitch the satisfaction of giving up.

She half dived through the crumbling frame of a large window and fell hard onto a clump of damp weeds. A bullet ricocheted past her.

Heavy treads sprinted toward her. He wasn't a cute soldier; he was a goddamned relentless one. She loped carefully over the debris-strewn landscape. A gaping hole yawned in some rotting wood at her feet and she leaped over it. From there she sprang onto the stone frame of another window, crouching to look back.

The relentless one was stomping around, searching for her. Another stomp, and his foot plunged through the rotting wood. He yelled and dropped his rifle, plunging into a jagged hole up to his waist.

Pagan let out a whispered "Ha!" and slipped off her window ledge, angling down a passage between buildings. Her pursuer was noisily hauling himself out of his pit, cursing as wood snapped against him.

She lost count of how many blocks she pelted down, how many random turns she made. She'd lost all sense of direction when she heard him behind her again. At the familiar thump of his boots, she reached for a random doorknob.

Miraculously, it turned under her hand. She slid inside, shut the door behind her, and turned to look down the long nave of an abandoned church. Above, the roof vanished over where the altar had once been.

She had no idea whether she'd find a way out, but Pagan picked her way through smashed statues and broken pews on wobbly legs. She found an intact wooden doorway in the back and paused, listening, waiting to be discovered. But the room lay dark and still. She left the door open to let in the moonlight and glided through another room and outside into a back alley. Behind her the wall was combed with scaffolding.

Back inside the shambles of the church, something clattered. She whirled.

Another heavy click. The relentless soldier must have seen her enter.

She took two steps down the alley and stopped. The blank wall of a building closed it at one end, the windows of an apartment complex shut it off at the other.

She was trapped, the thing she hated most in the world. There were always options, a way out. There had to be, or she was dead.

She looked down at the gun in her unsteady hand. She

could try to shoot him in the dark, but even if she could hit him, gunshots would probably bring other soldiers.

Still, it was better than letting him shoot her.

But it was best if nobody got shot. That was her goal for the rest of the evening. That and getting across the border and telling Devin Black what she thought of him.

Picturing Devin roused a profound ache in her chest. At the very least, she needed to see him once more, to brush her fingers over his face. Then she could die from all this anxiety.

The door to the artist's studio groaned. She had to decide now. Her only advantage was that he was progressing slowly, exploring every hiding place before he moved on.

Hiding place.

She looked up.

Delicately, she reached for the metal pipe above her head that supported the scaffold. Placing the toe of one shoe on the cross brace below it, she hoisted herself up.

The platform didn't move, squeak, or rattle under her weight, thank God.

Her hands were slippery from the oozing scrapes from her fall. She wiped them on her suit dress before strong-arming her way up to the next level, hips to the bar like a gymnast before she fell forward and crawled onto the platform.

A cold breeze hit her. Shivering, she found the embedded rungs of a ladder and scaled it quickly. Her shoes made tiny, hollow metal noises as she ascended. She prayed to the goddess of alcoholic actresses that the relentless soldier wouldn't hear.

She reached the third and last level of the platform, hands throbbing, and had to pick her way carefully through bizarre arrays of broken gargoyles and praying stone figures arranged in rows. She knelt down to keep her profile low as she looked over the edge.

A footfall landed on the cobblestones of the alley below.

She craned her neck without moving other muscles to see over the edge of the scaffold, looking down on the relentless Stasi soldier.

He was breathing hard, fighting to keep his panting quiet. His nose and cheekbones glinted with sweat. He had the rifle in both hands, swinging it this way and that as he peered down the alley in both directions.

Her own hands were slick with perspiration and blood. She set the gun on her knees and wiped her hands on her skirt again. If he turned around and went back inside now, it might save his—and her—life. Even if she killed him before he could fire back, she really didn't want to bring anyone running.

But really, she'd killed enough people for one lifetime.

She picked up a piece of broken stone in one hand and steadied it with the other, and saw with an odd clarity that it was a small bust of Karl Marx, placed here somehow among the other broken creatures.

Thanks for volunteering, Karl. She peered over the edge of the scaffold again.

The soldier was underneath her, not centered exactly, but if her aim was true and her hands not too shaky...

The Stasi soldier turned, about to go. But he halted, staring at the metal frame of the scaffolding in front of him. As she watched, he followed the line of pipes up, his head tilting back.

His gaze met Pagan's with a shock.

Then he smiled. "There you are," he said with satisfaction, and raised his rifle.

His helmet protected the top of his head, but he was looking up. Pagan hefted Karl Marx in both hands and dropped it.

It struck him between his eyes with a thunk like a hammer striking heavy cloth, and cracked in two.

The soldier's eyes rolled back. Blood poured down his scalp. He staggered, reaching blindly toward the scaffold for support.

Pagan scrabbled around her platform for another statue, grabbing something, anything, in case she needed to hit him again.

But the soldier dropped to his knees. His unfocused eyes scanned the air above in confusion and anger, as if trying to find her. Then his face smoothed to a serene blank, and he toppled to the ground.

She didn't believe it at first. She stayed frozen, the wind whistling between the metal pipes of the scaffold, staring down at his still body until her trembling started to rattle the stone monsters around her. With her hands shaking, it took her longer to descend the scaffold than it had to climb up.

The soldier lay on his side, blood pooling in his helmet. His hair, she could see now, was dark auburn. Lying there he looked very young and vulnerable, not relentless at all.

She hunkered down and put her hand on his neck. It was warm. His pulse thudded under the skin, and the bleeding was slowing. Good. He'd live to fight capitalism another day.

She sat back on her heels and took a deep breath, considering his bloody profile. She should feel sorry for him, she supposed. But she couldn't summon up any feeling now beyond exhaustion and an all-consuming desire to get "home" to the Hilton in West Berlin. It was tempting to steal his heavy coat and get warm, but it was far too large for her, and the moment someone realized there was a girl inside it, she'd get arrested for spying or something.

She did take his rifle and his walkie-talkie and dropped them both in a large barrel of the scummiest water she'd ever seen, along with the pistol she'd taken from him earlier. She kept his flashlight for herself, since it might come in handy, and went through his outer pockets to see if he had anything else she could use. She came back with a wallet, a stick of gum, a pack of filthy-smelling Russian cigarettes, and a very nice steel lighter bearing the flag/rifle seal of the Stasi in red, yellow, and black.

She unwrapped the gum and thought of Devin Black, snagging Miss Edwards's Zippo lighter back at Lighthouse Reformatory. That seemed like aeons ago, yet it had been just last week.

She stuck the gum in her mouth and looked inside the wallet—a few notes of currency and an ID card bearing the name Alaric Vogel. She tossed it onto the ground beside his head.

"Well, Alaric," she said, standing up and putting his lighter in her purse. "You owe me, so I'm taking your lighter. There's someone I want to show it to, and you can always get another one."

She flicked on the flashlight and left him, following the beam through the warm artist's studio, through the fallen church, back out to the street. Her watch said it was just past two in the morning, and her footsteps sounded a lonely dead-of-night echo down the deserted street.

With no idea where she was, she turned the nearest corner. Lifting the flashlight, she could finally read the street sign. Not that she knew many street names, but what the hell.

"Friedrich Strasse." She said it out loud and looked up at the rising sliver of moon, her spirit rising, too, in triumph. "Friedrich Strasse!"

This was the very street she'd looked down while riding in the backseat of the Mercedes-Benz limo, Devin Black at her side. She'd remarked on how badly destroyed it still was from the war. This same street Devin had said was one of the few which bisected the city. It began in West Berlin, cut south through a bulge of East Berlin, and came out in West Berlin again.

She scanned Friedrich Strasse in both directions with no

idea which was north or south. The good news was that, if she walked far enough in either direction, she'd get to a crossing back into West Berlin, one where she hadn't just abetted an East German escape.

She clicked the flashlight off, and set off at a good clip down the sidewalk. It, at least, was clear of rubble. But the buildings on either side of her reminded her of a line of plastic skulls her father used to set up along the mantelpiece for Hallow-een, with decrepit windows instead of empty eyes and uneven protrusions of brick poking up like broken teeth.

She had no idea how far she walked down Friedrich Strasse, but her feet were throbbing nearly an hour later when she heard the roar of big engines and spotted a line of tanks lurch-ing out of a ruined theater.

"Jeez Louise!" A man across the street shouted in English. He wore a Hawaiian shirt over khaki trousers and was just emerging from a small side street. "Tanks out the wazoo!"

The flat American voice, slightly slurred from a night out on the town, was music to Pagan's ears. Three other men in similar casual clothes staggered sloppily out of the darkness behind him and stared at the procession of armed might.

"Hoo, boy," one said, leaning on a hand wearily against the ruined building beside him. "This can't be good news."

Pagan trotted across the street toward them. "Are you guys American?"

All four heads turned to her. Eyes lit up. "Hey, little lady!"

She skittered to a stop in front of them. "Boy, am I happy to see you!"

The tallest one peered down at her, mouth twisting with speculation to one side. "What is a nice girl like you doing in a place like this?"

"Trying to get back to civilization," she said. "But I keep

bumping into things like that." She pointed at the tanks. "I'm Pagan, by the way."

"Pagan *Jones*?" the shortest one said, leaning in a bit too close, then jerking himself away as if realizing he'd been rude. She could smell the beer on him, but his smile was bemused and benign. "Why, so you are. Will wonders never cease. A real live movie star."

"Nice to meet you," the tall one said, shaking her hand. "I'm Bob. Don't mind Dickie. He's harmless."

They all introduced themselves, and in short order, Pagan was strolling down Friedrich Strasse surrounded by four US army soldiers who'd used one of their off-duty days to explore what Dickie called East Berlin's "less savory bits."

"They say it's less savory," Dickie added. "But I found it pretty tasty myself!"

So Pagan approached the border of East and West Berlin in a guffawing clump of American goodwill. The men were amazed at the newly installed barbed wire and conglomeration of trucks and tanks, but quietly critical of the formation of the armed troops.

An East German captain marched up, yelling, but Bob handled him with a self-deprecating smile and some decent German. After a brief display of their passports and consultation with another officer, the captain had his men push a cement barrier aside wide enough to let them through single file.

There were no American troops waiting on the other side, but a few West German police had gathered in the shadows. One stepped out nervously and waved them forward, asking for their passports in a rattled mixture of German and English that showed just how bananas the situation was.

"Does the army know what's going on?" her new friends asked, but the policeman shook his head and waved them down the street.

He examined Pagan's passport for what seemed like forever, checking it against a handwritten list. She asked to make a call, but he shrugged, looking helplessly around the dark deserted street fronted with tanks, and then he let her go.

Bob, Dickie, and friends had gone. Any possible taxi cab had been frightened off by the tanks. So Pagan started walking again, looking for a pay phone or a cab.

Unlike deadly quiet East Berlin, here heads were poking out of windows, staring toward the border. Voices called to each other across narrow streets, spreading the news. Pagan forced herself onward on legs made of egg noodles, her head buzzing with fatigue, craning her neck for a taxi, and stumbling over cracked paving stones.

The streetlights blurred in front of her watering eyes. She hugged herself, the shaking from the cold penetrating to the bone. She stopped and leaned against a lamppost. Maybe if she just sat down here for a while to rest, she'd gather enough strength to go on.

Here in the West, at least, there was life and noise. Here, if she lay down on the sidewalk in a coma, someone kind would eventually call an ambulance. Here she would not be shot or forced to run for her life.

She barely registered a car doing a U-turn in the street next to her. Someone was shouting, and it pulled up beside her with a screech.

Was it a cab? No, just another black Mercedes. She leaned against the lamppost again, her friend in need, and tried to keep herself from falling into a sickening blackness. Her knees gave. Her head fell back.

But she didn't hit the ground. The world swooped around her as strong arms caught her and cradled her close. A coat flicked around her shoulders, and a voice she knew was whispering her name in a thick Scottish accent.

"Pagan," he said. "Pagan, thank God."

"Devin." Curling into his delicious warmth, she looked up and saw stormy blue eyes staring starkly down at her. She didn't know how he'd found her, but somehow it didn't surprise her that he had.

She brushed her cold fingers over his cheek, just as she'd imagined doing back in that ruined church. "Devin."

"They made it out," Devin said, his arms tightening around her with an intensity that would have frightened her if she wasn't so happy. "Because of you, Thomas and his sister and his mother are all safe, Pagan. And now so are you."

She closed her eyes, smiling.

Something warm and soft brushed her forehead. She wondered if it was his lips. She was indeed safe now, and as he picked her up in his arms to take her to the car, she fell without regret into the blackness.

BERLINERS WAKE TO A DIVIDED CITY

"They are, and remain, our German brothers and sisters."
—Konrad Adenauer, West German Chancellor

Pagan woke up in her big cozy bed in the Hilton. A sliver of golden daylight cut past the blackout curtains across her tattered Dior suit dress, hanging over the back of a chair. She doubted even a good cleaning would be enough to make it wearable again, but that didn't matter much now. It had been a true and loyal ally during her long night. Perhaps Dior would consider featuring her in a campaign for "grace under fire" fashion.

She stretched lazily and turned over to find Devin Black asleep beside her. Her heart jumped like a startled cat, but she stayed very still, not wanting to wake him. He looked so young and innocent with his lips slightly parted, his eyelashes dark smudges on his tanned cheeks.

She was lying warm under the covers, but Devin lay on top of them, still wearing his shirt and pants from the night before. She double-checked herself and flushed as she realized she was in her bra and panties. She pulled her knees up to her chest. Had Devin been the one that put her to bed?

He inhaled a long breath and opened densely blue eyes.

"Good morning," she said.

He blinked and abruptly sat up, looking over her shoulder at the clock in alarm. "Crivens! I'm so sorry."

"Crivens?" she said.

He hoisted himself off the bed, running a hand through his hair, which had spiked up along the top of his head as he slept. His long eyelids were heavy with embarrassment and fatigue. "I didna mean to fall asleep here. Nothing happened, I swear to you. I was just—" he made a sweeping motion with his hand at her lying there on the bed "—making sure you were all right, and I must have been very tired."

He scratched the back of his head, looking uncomfortable and adorable.

"You're very Scottish when you're sleepy," she said.

He relaxed and shook his head. "I'm always Scottish, as you can see. I'm sorry for lying to you about that."

"And about a lot of other things," she said.

"Yes, yes." He dropped his hands with resignation to his sides. "Will a blanket apology do?"

"I'm not sure yet," she said. It was fun, this discomfited version of Devin. She sat up and let the sheet fall to her waist. It was just a bra, after all. She'd revealed more in *Beach Bound Beverly*. "Was it you who undressed me last night?"

"Oh, dear God." He stared at her for a split second, his cheeks reddening, eyes wide until, with visible effort, he turned his back. "Yes. But I promise you it was just to make sure you weren't seriously wounded. I considered taking you to the hospital, but there was no need, and you would have been recognized. It's better if nobody else knows what happened. And before we go anywhere, I need to debrief you."

"Looks like you've de-briefed me already," she said. "Took my garters off and everything."

His shoulders slumped and he rubbed one hand over his forehead. "You were just so beaten up. I am sorry, but I needed to be sure you were all right. I dressed some cuts on your legs, too."

She lifted the coverlet and saw that indeed, there were bandages taped over her clean, sore knees and down one calf. She didn't even remember hurting herself there, but she could feel the sting of the wound now. Warmth expanded through her chest, knowing that he'd taken such good care of her.

But she was still kind of mad at him, for all the lies, the manipulations. She couldn't let him off the hook yet. "So you're a doctor as well as a studio executive and a spy?" she asked.

He exhaled and moved toward the half-open door to her bedroom, averting his eyes. "I owe you a lot of explaining, and some breakfast. Or possibly lunch. So how about I order some food and we both get ready for the day."

"But I want to lie in bed all day." She lay back on her pillow, clutching the coverlet to her chest, her hair spread out around her head, and pouted. "I think I've earned it." She made sure to roll her Rs, getting very Scottish on *earned it*.

He turned in the doorway to survey her, and a devilish look overtook him, as if he was about to say something scandalous. But he caught himself, ducked his head, smiling, and said, "As your legal guardian, I'm not allowed to have an opinion on what you do in bed, but you should know Thomas asked to see you when you were ready. He's all right, but he's in the hospital with a broken leg."

"Oh, my God, Thomas! What about Karin and Frau Kruger?"

"They're exhausted and shaken up, but fine. Get ready and you can see for yourself."

"All right, all right!" She whipped back the covers as he departed the bedroom, softly closing the door behind him.

Over lunch she told Devin about her night. He didn't take notes, but she could see he was logging all of the details in his mind as she spoke. The conversation continued as they called for a car and got into the new black limousine to visit Thomas in the hospital.

"Alaric Vogel," Devin repeated after she described going through the pockets of the soldier she'd beaned into unconsciousness. "Did he recognize you as Pagan Jones, the movie actress?"

"I don't think so," she said. "None of the soldiers seemed to know me."

He nodded, looking satisfied. "Better for the East Germans to think you had as little to do with the Krugers' escape as possible."

"Well, that one guard at the House of the Birches saw me outside the window, waving at him, just before Thomas whacked him with the poker."

"Hmm." Devin seemed to be making a mental note. "I'll see if I can find out what they know about you."

"Oh, I have a present for you." She reached into her purse and pulled out the Zippo lighter with its red-and-black insignia. "I took it off Alaric Vogel."

He looked down at the battered silver case, and his lips twitched. "I'm honored," he said. "But it's a souvenir of your adventure. You keep it."

She nodded, stroking the lighter with her thumb. "Speaking of souvenirs. Why do you keep a used bullet with your gun?" As his eyebrows rose, she grinned. "I found them in your toilet tank."

His jaw dropped, and then he laughed. "That's what you were doing there! You bloody sneak."

"You're one to talk," she said. "So. Where's the bullet from?"

His eyelids dropped like shutters over his eyes. She could feel him withdrawing. "Maybe someday," he said.

She wasn't going to let him off the hook just yet. "Aren't you a bit young to be running some espionage scheme for MI6? Did they recruit you when you were twelve or something?"

"Fourteen," he said, staring out the car window. "Well, that's when they started grooming me. Something about how my early training as a thief would be—" he hesitated, then said the last word with bite "—*advantageous*. And I'm not running this lovely scheme alone."

"You're not in charge." She gave him a half smile as he turned his head to stare at her. "I overheard you talking on the phone to someone the night before the garden party. That's when I figured out what you were, and that you were talking to your boss."

"I searched your room before I said a word!" he said, and shook his head. "You dodgy monkey."

"Fourteen." She imagined Devin five years younger, smaller and skinnier, all knees and wary blue eyes. "Even younger than me. What happened when you were fourteen that made them recruit you?"

A jeep full of red-hatted British military police passed by. Devin turned to look at them, his face devoid of emotion.

"A lot," he said. "A lot happened."

And he said no more. She decided to respect his privacy. For the moment.

They'd seen more soldiers about than usual on their drive, but no tanks or trucks full of troops were heading toward the new wall. The Allies had mustered no organized armed military response to the closing of the border. But the streets were buzzing. Their car passed a number of angry pedestrians, flocks of bicyclists, and cars full of West Berliners, heading toward the border with the East. The official response had been to stay quiet and let Ulbricht's new wall go into effect. It looked as if Kennedy and the other Allied leaders might not start a nuclear war over Berlin, at least not today.

The civilians had other ideas. Devin had heard about growing crowds gathering near the Brandenburg Gate and other former border crossings. The Westerners were demonstrating, chanting, demanding that the Allied armies stand up to the Communists, even as East German troops reinforced the barbed wire with bricks and mortar. Buildings had been divided down the middle; families torn in half.

A swarm of young people on motorcycles buzzed past, heading toward the border, probably to throw rocks over the wire at the *vopos* and the Stasi. Devin had received reports of other last-minute escapes, of babies handed across the Wall to their mothers, of East German soldiers themselves hopping over to freedom.

But most of the population had been trapped like water in a dam. The East German troops, tanks, and water cannons lined up along the border had turned toward their own people now. They weren't worried about the Western response anymore. And the flood of refugees had stopped.

"What will happen to the East Berliners now?" she asked. Devin shook his head and said nothing. They'd reached the hospital.

Thomas grinned like a school kid on summer holiday as Pagan ran into his hospital room and threw her arms around him. He had a row of stitches in his broad forehead, a leg cast, and a brace on his left hand, but he was otherwise healthy. She took her gloves off to sign her name on the cast. His mother and Karin, he explained, were safe in a hotel nearby. They'd both been released from the hospital early that morning.

Devin said hello, shook Thomas's unbroken hand, and then faded down the hallway to let them speak together alone.

"Thanks to you, my family is safe. And we're free," Thomas

said to Pagan. "I'll be forever grateful. If you need anything from me, you have only to ask and it will be done."

She smiled at his very German phrasing. "I wouldn't say last night was fun, exactly." She paused as Thomas laughed incredulously. "But I feel different this morning. I haven't thought about having a drink in at least an hour. Maybe it was good for me in some strange way."

She didn't say it out loud, but she suspected she knew the reason for the difference in her. For the past ten months she'd been nothing but a killer, someone who brought only pain and suffering to others. As of last night she was a person who helped people, too.

"For me and my family, your life is a symphony of hope," Thomas said, echoing her thoughts. "I wish I could do as much for my poor countrymen."

Pagan's heart sank, thinking about the East Berliners. She remembered with a sad flash the building with the griffin. "Whatever I might have learned about my mother by talking to her neighbors is gone now," she said. "Unless the wall falls, I can't go back and talk to anyone over there about her."

Thomas's eyebrows crowded over his nose, and he shifted uneasily in the narrow hospital bed. "I have something you should know. This morning my mother told me that Frau Nagel said something interesting that day, about Emil Murnau. Something my mother didn't share with us then."

"The old lady said something about my grandfather?" Pagan sat up straighter. "Why didn't your mother tell me?"

"She was embarrassed, I think. It's something looked down upon, particularly for women. It made her angry, to think that your grandmother needed to lie. She thought maybe she should keep your grandmother's secrets for her and not embarrass her or you."

"Embarrass me?" Pagan had no idea what he could be saying. "About what?"

"Frau Nagel said that Emil Murnau could not have been your grandfather. Emil Murnau was an elderly veteran of the 1870 Franco-Prussian war who lived in that building, but he passed away a few days after your grandmother moved there with her baby, your mother. At the time, he was a widower of ninety-three with no living children."

"But..." Pagan's brain was a cloud of confusion. "Why would my grandmother say he was the father of her baby if he wasn't?"

"Frau Nagel said that your grandmother bore her child out of wedlock, and to hide the shame, she used the name of a dead man to make your mother seem legitimate."

"Grandmama was never married?" Pagan conjured up the stiff, aging, self-righteous face of her grandmother, and struggled to believe it. "But she was so proper!"

"Mother said that sometimes women use a mask of propriety to cover up their sins. Or what others see as their sins. Mother herself thinks women are unfairly labeled when it comes to their sexual activity, but she is quite modern that way."

Pagan nodded. "Your mother's amazing. And it's still difficult to have a baby out of wedlock. I knew some girls in reform school who had to give up their babies for adoption. Back in the twenties it would have been even worse."

"Mother told me last night, here in the hospital," Thomas said. "She felt guilty for having kept it from you. She just didn't want you to hate your grandmother."

"No, that's all right," she said. "But I can't help wondering..."

"Who your real grandfather is." Thomas nodded. "Of course."

"And did my mother know?" Pagan asked. Was this somehow connected to Mama's suicide? Clearly, her family had its secrets. She'd managed to uncover a few. More than ever, she wanted to dig deeper, to find out more. Something somewhere would clue her in on the reason for Mama's death.

She spent the next hour rehashing their crazy night together with Thomas, until Devin came to get her. She kissed Thomas on the forehead and told him that if his family moved to California, they could stay with her in her big empty house in the Hollywood Hills as long as they liked. She truly hoped they would take her up on the offer, and Thomas said it was possible.

Out in the strangely deserted hallway, Devin wasn't alone. A stooped, balding man with a sagging belly and wan blue eyes had joined him. The man wore a long gray raincoat belted over a gray suit and a stained gray hat that covered up his thinning hair.

Devin said, "Pagan Jones, this is my boss, Frank Ballantyne."

"Miss Jones." Ballantyne looked down his pinched nose at her and shook her hand with a limp grip. His voice was smooth, educated, and very English. "I wanted to thank you for all you did to save Thomas last night, and to apologize. We had thought only to use you to get Thomas invited to that garden party. We had not imagined your involvement would go any further than that."

"Your imagination department might need some new recruits, Mister Ballantyne," she said. "But I managed."

Ballantyne smiled, looking like nothing more than a genteel, dotty old man happy to look at a pretty girl. Only his shrewd eyes revealed that there was more to him than that. "You managed quite splendidly, Miss Jones. Our hats are off to you this day. I think you should know why we put you in such danger. You see, we had no idea the wall was scheduled to go up. Unfortunately, Erich Mielke's secret service outsmarted us in that. We wanted Thomas to go through Ulbricht and Mielke's papers for quite another reason. We believe our organization, or one of those we work with closely, has a mole."

"Mole?" She hadn't heard the term used except to describe garden pests.

"A double agent, planted within our ranks to report our every move to the East Germans. We've been so sorely uninformed about their activities and so thwarted at every turn that we know someone inside our own ranks, or inside our allies, has to be giving the East Germans information." Ballantyne spread his age-splotched, veiny hands open. "Thomas was not able to find out who the mole is. But we are nonetheless grateful to you for keeping him out of the hands of the Stasi. Otherwise, they may have learned even more about us."

"A double agent." A memory stirred in Pagan's brain from the night before. "I heard Ulbricht and Mielke say something after they hung up the phone with Honecker last night."

"Honecker." Ballantyne's tissue paper eyelids drooped in thought. "No doubt he was the architect behind the border operations last night."

"They were congratulating him, and after they hung up, Ulbricht said something to Mielke about how recruiting Felfe was worth it, how Felfe had kept you all in the dark."

Ballantyne's nearly nonexistent eyebrows arced toward his vanishing hairline. His rheumy eyes sparkled.

"Goddamn Heinz Felfe," Devin said, anger clouding his face. "It would explain a lot."

"Indeed," Ballantyne said, and in the steel behind that single word Pagan glimpsed an incisive, implacable will. Grayman Ballantayne was more formidable than he seemed. Pagan wasn't the only one who knew how to act harmless.

Then before her eyes he seemed to shrink again into a silly

old codger. He took her hand softly in his and shook it again. "We shall look into what you've told us, Miss Jones. Our counterparts in the CIA are aware of your actions, and they've spoken to Benjamin Wexler about your role in his movie."

Pagan's grip on Ballantyne's hand tightened, her heart skipping a beat. "What did Bennie say?"

"You're back on the film," Devin said, grinning widely as she gasped. "Bennie was pretty touched to hear how you helped Thomas and his family, so you're getting another chance."

Ballantyne nodded. He removed his hand from Pagan's death grip, smiling with sagging basset hound eyes. "Because of the wall going up, and Thomas's injury, they're probably going to postpone shooting for a little while and move production to the studios in Munich. It would best if you flew there as soon as possible."

Pagan didn't care how English and uptight the old man was. She shouted "Hurray!" and threw her arms around his neck, squeezing him tight.

"I say, I say," he said, standing stiffly until she released him. He adjusted his coat, his drooping cheeks burning with spots of red. "Very kind, I'm sure."

"Thank you, Mister Ballantyne," she said.

"Thank *you*, Miss Jones." He tipped his gray hat at her and shuffled away, humming a little under his breath.

Pagan and Devin watched him go. "Is he…" she started to ask.

"Whatever you're about to ask," he said, "I won't be able to confirm or deny."

Pagan rounded on him. "But you can confirm that you and Mister Ballantyne and this organization of yours used me to get Thomas to a garden party to hunt for evidence on a mole. Information I got for you instead, by accident!"

"Yes," he said. "I can confirm that."

"What a circus," she said with a derisive snort. "Did you blackmail the judge into giving me parole? Is that how you got Mercedes a parole hearing?"

"That's classified," he said, but his smirk was confirmation enough. "Right along with how I convinced the studio to push Bennie to give you and Thomas your parts in his movie."

"You are such a schemer!" She gave him a little shove. "Were you ever an art thief, or was that another bluff?"

He captured her hand in both of his, his expression quite sober. "All that was true."

"Redemption." The memory of him saying that word to her back at Lighthouse now made all kinds of sense. "You jumped at the chance for it."

He pulled her hand to his chest, reeling her in closer. His heart beat steadily beneath her palm. "I'm sorry I lied to you, Pagan. But I'm not sorry it happened. If it weren't for you, Thomas and his family would be trapped in East Germany, and we'd know nothing about Felfe being the mole."

She stared at his elegant fingers, wrapped around her own. When he spoke again, his voice was low and intimate.

"And I'm not sorry I got to meet you."

She slid her other hand around his. "Should a legal guardian be holding hands with his underage ward?"

He chortled softly, but he didn't let go of her, leaning in close until his forehead touched hers. His indigo eyes were all she could see. "That was always meant as a temporary measure."

"To give you control over me," she said, but she didn't pull away. The warmth of his body was so close, like glowing coals behind a fire grate

"When has anyone, ever, had control over you?" he asked.

She smiled. "Who gets to try now that you're stepping down?"

He slowly, deliberately slid his hand down her arm and around her shoulder, drawing her against him.

She gasped, her heartbeat skyrocketing, but didn't resist. His other hand stroked her hair, sinking his fingers between the soft strands, then tracing the outline of her ear. "Steps are already being taken to transfer guardianship to your family attorney."

Her insteps and her knees were melting. She had to lean against him to stay upright, her head on his shoulder, but he didn't seem to mind. His breath was warm on her cheek.

"Poor Mister Shevitz," she said. "Do you think he'll want to share my suite?"

"If he does, I'll have him killed," Devin said, and pressed his mouth to hers.

She'd been kissed before—stiff, closed-mouth kisses on a movie set, fumbling first kisses with boys she never saw again, and finally Nicky Raven's eager puppy-dog smooches. She'd made out in cars, in beds, on couches, and on a blanket spread over the grass. She'd gone farther with Nicky than nice girls were supposed to go. She thought she knew all about kissing and lovemaking.

But no kiss had ever burned her lips like Devin's. No hands had ever blazed such a trail of fire on her skin, or ever gripped her so expertly, so ruthlessly. She pressed close, near swooning as his arms crushed her to him. She needed that strength, needed his solid weight pressing down on her. She forgot everything she ever knew as the boundaries of her body melted away in a rush of near-volcanic heat.

A long silence followed, during which his suit and shirt came unbuttoned and her hair was mussed.

He finally pulled away, his lips half-open, blue eyes turned black with desire. "Pagan," he said.

"Mmm," she said, and gently bit his neck.

She thought his knees buckled a little, and she laughed softly against his skin.

He put a hand to her cheek, thumb stroking her lower lip, tender now where a moment ago he'd been almost brutal. "Pagan, we're still in a hospital. Now that Ballantyne's gone, the staff are free to walk through here. There's a nurse coming down the hallway."

She forced her thoughts into something like order and pressed her feet back on the ground. "You're being prudent again, damn you."

He laughed quietly, lips against her hair. "Someone has to. I never should have let it go this far."

She exhaled shakily. "Anyone ever tell you you're the world's biggest tease?"

He put both hands on her shoulders and pushed her farther away, as if her closeness was too much of a temptation. "Everything changed last night when the Wall went up. The world is different, and I have a lot work to do."

She ran her index finger over his lips, wiping away traces of her lipstick as a nurse clomped by. "I could put you to work," she said.

His fingers on her shoulders tightened, but then he dropped his hands. "You're good, you know."

"At kissing?" She smiled slyly.

"Well, yes." His eyes fell to her lips, and it took him a moment to lift them back up to meet her gaze. "But I meant last night. You were good out there, better than good. So there's one more thing I need to tell you."

"Tell me," she said, and stepped back from him, straightening her skirt.

He took a deep breath and ran a hand through his own hair to put it to rights. "The CIA has a file on your mother."

Surprise opened up inside her. "But—why?"

He shook his head. "I wish I knew. The fact that such a file exists tells you there must be more for you to find out. They won't let me or anyone at MI6 see it. They only shared a few facts when we talked to them about this operation—that your mother was born here in Berlin, that perhaps her father wasn't Emil Murnau."

"So you did know that," she said, resentment of him rising. "You could have told me instead of stringing me along."

"No," he said. "My mission was to keep you here, interested in finding out more about your mother. If I'd told you what little I knew, you never would have gone to that garden party with Thomas. For your sake, part of me wishes I had told you so that none of this had ever happened, but I had to do my job. People's lives depended on it."

"Maybe I'm a little glad it happened this way," she said. "Not just because the Krugers are safe. But because of your lies, Mercedes will get out of Lighthouse soon. Because you were a manipulative jerk, I'm getting a second chance at a movie career and an opportunity to find out why Mama killed herself. Because of you, I've got two men on the movie set I can turn to whenever the need for a drink takes over."

What she couldn't quite say was that now, finally, she had real reasons to stay sober, reasons to live. Because of what Devin had helped make happen.

He was smiling. "You're the one who turned it around, not me. Now…" His voice became more clipped and English, more distant and efficient. "The only way the CIA will ever show you the file on your mother is if you help them out in some way. I believe at some point they or we or one of our allies will come asking, now that everyone knows what you're capable of."

"But I'm an actress," she said. "What would they ever want with me?"

"Fame is a key that opens many doors," he said. "So I wanted to warn you."

Her back stiffened. "Warn me?"

"I know you," he said. "You won't stop until you learn all there is to know about your mother. They'll use that."

"I'll use them right back," she said.

"Yes, but they're better at it," he said. "It's what they do. Just…be careful. Don't trust them."

The wall between them was going up again. He was putting it there, against his will, because he had to.

She had to help him build that wall. That was the only way she could bear its existence.

So much division. So many boundaries and restrictions between people, between countries, between two halves of a now sadly divided city. Pagan took her gloves out of her purse and pulled them on, armoring herself with their formality, layering another barrier between them.

"Why should I trust you?" she asked.

His smile was tinged with regret. "You shouldn't."

This really was goodbye. "You're not coming back to the suite, are you?"

His eyes were troubled. He tried, without success, to mask it. "There's a nice young lady named Patty waiting for you back at the car with the driver. She'll take you to see Karin and Frau Kruger before you go to the Hilton to pack. Given the current situation, you should leave the city today. Patty will make sure you get on the right plane. Only please don't tell her, or anyone, about last night, or about Mister Ballantyne and Heinz Felfe."

"When…" She stopped herself. She wanted to know when she would see him again, when she might touch him again. But he was telling her, in his own way, that he didn't know. He was going to be very busy now that the Wall had gone up, and she was off to Munich to finish shooting the movie. Without him.

He took her hand and kissed it. The heat from his lips seared through her white silk glove. "Thank you," he said, looking at her with those damned blue eyes. "For everything."

She took her hand back slowly. She didn't want it back, but it was clear: they were parting.

Chin up, Mama had always said. Shoulders back. Good posture could get you through anything. She even managed a smile. "Goodbye, Devin Black."

She turned and strode away, her heels clicking steadily on the hospital tile.

"I have a feeling we'll meet again, Pagan Jones," he said, his voice echoing down the hall.

She swiveled around on one foot and shot him a smile.

"If you're lucky," she said, and walked on.

She didn't look back at him again. She didn't need to. She knew that he stood there watching her until she was out of sight.

★ ★ ★ ★ ★

ACKNOWLEDGMENTS

I want to thank my talented critique partner and friend Elisa Nader for giving me such excellent notes on all the versions of Pagan Jones as the story developed over the years. Big thanks as well to brilliant writer and good friend Jen Klein, who helped hone the book with her writing expertise and insight.

My marvelous agent Tamar Rydzinski gave me invaluable creative guidance and immediately understood the potential in this character. My first editor, Annie Stone, poured her love for the book into terrific notes on the manuscript. I owe a huge thanks to the entire amazing team at Harlequin Teen, including the marvelous Natashya Wilson and T. S. Ferguson.

My parents, Jackie Berry and Paul "Doc" Berry, exhibited their usual supportive, loving behavior throughout the long process of writing and editing this book. How lucky I am to be able to say that, for me, this is the norm.

My friends put up with me bailing on plans because I had to write and found encouraging words whenever I wanted to bang my head against the wall. They are my family, and they include John Mark Godocik, Brian Pope, Valerie Ahern, Maria de la Torre, Maritza Suarez, Michael Musa, Scott and Pam Paterra, Peter Shultz, Roger Alt, Matt Chapman and family, Jennifer Frankl, Diane Stengle, Katherine Munchmeyer, Geoff and Emma Chapman, Lisa Moore, Cathy Kliegel, Chris Campbell, Frank Woodward, Jim Myers, Meriam Harvey,

Cheri Waterhouse, Cathleen Alexander, Kathleen, Tay and Kasey Bass, and Joe and Sharon Salas. A shout-out to cats Lucy and Marlowe for being good company during the long hours of writing.

Special thanks to close friend and travel buddy Wendy Viellenave, who offered to get me to Berlin to do hands-on research for this book, and then to Buenos Aires for Pagan's next adventure. I only wish I could have found the time between drafts to go! Here's to more eye-opening journeys together.

THE HISTORY BEHIND PAGAN JONES

"Berlin is the most dangerous place in the world."
—Premier Nikita Krushchev of the Soviet Union, June 1961

I grew up during the Cold War, so I can remember being at school, watching jumpy 16mm films instructing us how to duck and cover under our desks if a nuclear bomb went off nearby. Even in second grade, I knew this had to be a fantasy. If nuclear war started, we were all dead. It was perversely reassuring to know that my home town of Honolulu was a primary military target. I and everyone I loved would be annihilated in the first wave of bombs, turned into dust or a shadow. None of us would linger and suffer from the fallout.

Thoughts of nuclear war didn't consume me as a child. Life was good. But during the Cold War, that threat lurked on the borders of everyone's life. There were nights when I'd lie awake, listening to a jet flying overhead, and wonder vaguely if the war had started after I went to bed. In that case, maybe the jet was actually a missile carrying the bomb with my name on it. When I got a little older, my friends and I would joke about whether you could get a sunburn during nuclear winter.

I'm happy to say that those who came of age after 1991 didn't have to deal with pointless duck and cover drills or imagine inventing SPF five-million. They may not even know what "nuclear winter" means. So when I decided to write a book set during the height of the Cold War, I knew I had to get the basic facts right, even though I was going to embellish them to suit my story. I owed it to all those who grew up after the Berlin Wall came down, and to all those who died trying to cross it before it fell.

The truth behind my fiction starts with the character of Pagan herself, who came into being after I learned about famous people who were also spies at some point in their career. Casanova, Julia Child, Josephine Baker, writers Roald Dahl and Ian Fleming, Mata Hari, mobster Charles "Lucky" Luciano, Shi Pei Pu (aka M. Butterfly), Harry Houdini, and baseball player Moe Berg were all well-known public figures who did clandestine work for their countries. When we think of spies, we usually think of people working under the cover of a false identity, but many of these people used their fame, in one way or another, to help their cause. I decided that my teenage version would be a child movie star whose fame, family, and bad reputation would give her unique access to people and places, access which might come in handy to a spy agency.

But which Cold War story to tell? I found the answer when I read that East German leader Walter Ulbricht threw a deceptive little garden party at a hunting lodge once owned by Hermann Göring the night the Berlin Wall went up. The idea of East German leaders keeping possible opponents locked down at a supposedly festive event as they also imprisoned an entire city was horribly twisted, and thus perfect for a story. Even better, the party gave me a way to fit fictional disgraced movie star Pagan Jones into real Cold War events.

The more I learned about how the Wall went up, how the Western powers were taken by surprise, and the horrible consequences for the East German people, the more compelling the story became. For, just as Pagan witnesses, the divide that became the Berlin Wall did go up at approximately 1:00 a.m. local time on August 13, 1961. There were no protests or shows of force by the armed forces in West Berlin. (Although the citizens did protest vehemently later that morning.) Even though Berlin was teeming with spies of every kind, the West was blindsided. Walter Ulbricht and his head of state security, Stasi chief Erich Mielke, had succeeded beyond their wildest dreams.

Pagan arrives in a city already divided. After Western and Soviet troops overtook Berlin, defeated Hitler's Germany, and ended the Second World War in Europe, the city was divided into four factions—French, English, American, and Soviet. The four Allied powers had an agreement to keep that arrangement while Germany was rebuilt.

But by 1961, the Soviets were no longer allies with the other three countries and had swallowed up all of Eastern Europe, including the Eastern chunk of Germany which included Berlin. The partition of Berlin remained, but the "Soviet" sector had become part of the new state of East Germany, aka the German Democratic Republic, a Soviet satellite state as yet unrecognized formally by the Western powers.

At that point, the East German economy was in tatters, even as Western Europe experienced dramatic growth. Lack of jobs, lack of freedom, and the brutality of their Communist regime sent East Germans fleeing to the West in record numbers. By 1961, because of the presence of Western forces still in sections of the city, Berlin was the only place from which East Germans could sneak into the West. The rest of their country was cut off.

In June of 1961, 630 refugees entered West Berlin from East Berlin every day. July averaged 1,000 per day, and the numbers kept rising. On August 8, for example, 1,741 people fled East Germany into West Berlin. These refugees are the people Pagan sees on her way from the airport to her hotel with Devin, clutching their suitcases and their children, leaving everything else behind. East Germany's best and brightest were fleeing, and the Communist regime was determined to put a stop to it.

This mass exodus helped turn Berlin into a hot spot for intrigue and danger. Because of it, the Western intelligence services expected some kind of action from the East Germans, but they mistakenly thought Soviet premier Krushchev, without whom the East German leaders would never make such a bold move, hadn't yet given his permission for a wall. He had.

Also, the Western committee to coordinate intelligence in Berlin couldn't decide if a Wall going up between East and West Berlin was even feasible. They waited, thinking that drastic action by the East would take place after a separate peace treaty was signed between the two Germanys, probably in the fall of 1961.

They were wrong.

On Friday, August 11, 1961, the East German Parliament gave its approval for whatever measures were deemed necessary to stop the exodus. The official name for that plan was, as Pagan overhears, Operation Rose.

Because the Western espionage agencies were so clueless about the plan to put up the Wall, I couldn't make Devin's need to use Pagan to be about the Wall, specifically. Instead, he uses her to get his spy, Thomas, into Walter Ulbricht's private hunting lodge. Western agencies suspect someone working for the them is acting as a mole, or double agent, and Devin hopes that Thomas will be able to search Ulbricht's private office to find out who that agent might be.

The identity of this mole, too, is based on fact. Someone within the Western ranks was indeed sending sensitive information to the East Germans and Soviets. I gave the discovery to Pagan, who overhears the agent's name while being questioned by Ulbricht and Mielke. His name: Heinz Felfe.

Historically, Heinz Felfe was an Obersturmfuhrer (senior assault leader) in the Nazi SS during World War II, captured by the British in 1945. Later, he went to work for the US intelligence-supported Gehlen Organization in West Germany in their counterespionage department. Both East and West had few qualms about hiring former Nazis and using them to their advantage. Felfe had a high rate of uncovering Soviet spies in West Germany, until it was discovered in 1961, after the Wall went up, that he was in fact working for the Communists. He was convicted of espionage in 1963, and served 14 years until he was exchanged for three West German students being held by the East Germans. He spent the rest of his days teaching criminalistics at East Germany's Humboldt University.

The book is sprinkled with many details based on what actually occurred. Ulbricht did have an adopted daughter named Beate. He did screen the Soviet film comedy *Each Man for Himself* (which I suspect from the title was a parody of capitalist doctrine) during his garden party even as Stasi guards patrolled the surrounding woods, more to keep the guests in than to keep anyone else out.

Around 10:00 p.m. Ulbricht announced the plan to put up a Wall in Berlin, asking "Everyone agreed?" No one dared to disagree, and he informed them they would all have to stay at the House of the Birches until Operation Rose was complete.

Under the direction of Erich Honecker, the Berlin Wall began to go up around 1:00 a.m. on August 13, 1961, mostly using barbed wire and concrete blocks. That night was very cold for that time of year in Berlin. The waxing moon was just a sliver.

My research lead to other fluffier facts making their way into the book. The Dior suit dress Pagan lusts after and wears was a brand-new design from that house for Fall of 1961. The Berlin Hilton on Budapester Strasse was brand-new that year,

and often featured dinner and dancing on its roof. It over-
looked the nearby parkland of the Tiergarten. Throughout
this book, I've used actual street names, like Bernauer Strasse,
whenever I could, and I've tried to stick to the actual geogra-
phy of Berlin and its buildings wherever possible.

The movies Pagan starred in are all fictional, including *Neither Here Nor There*, the one shooting in Berlin. But I came
up with the idea of her costarring in a film shot in that city
when I learned about a film directed by the late great Billy
Wilder, titled *One, Two Three*. That film was shooting in West
Berlin when the Wall went up. You can still see footage of
the pre-Wall border crossing at the Brandenburg Gate in its
opening minutes.

However, *Neither Here Nor There* is its own film, with a
different plot, characters, and dialogue. The actors and crew
members working on it are entirely fictional. The actions of
the spiteful Jimmy Brennan are in no way intended to reflect
upon *One, Two, Three's* star, James Cagney, who is brilliant
in the film and was notoriously kind to everyone, including
his fellow actors.

Billy Wilder, one of my favorite film directors, fled his
homeland of Austria before World War II, and some of his
relatives died in Hitler's concentration camps. Those facts in-
spired me to give those attributes to the director Bennie Wexler. But Bennie is fictional. Billy Wilder is not.

The one detail the fictional movie shares with an actual
movie is that after the Wall went up, production of *One, Two,
Three* moved from West Berlin to studios in Munich, a safe
distance from the hotbed of danger that was Berlin.

As far as I know, no one on the real movie was involved
in espionage.

Suggested books and links for further reading about Berlin,
the Wall, and other historical elements in this book:

Berlin 1961: Kennedy, Krushchev, and the Most Dangerous Place on Earth by Frederick Kempe, Berkeley Trade, 2012.

The Berlin Wall: A World Divided by Frederick Taylor, Harper Perennial, 2008.

Stasi: The Untold Story of the East German Secret Police by John O. Koehler, Westview Press, 2000.

Conversations with Wilder by Cameron Crowe, Knopf, 2001.

For a comprehensive overview online of the Berlin Wall, including interactive maps, timelines, history, and photographs: *http://www.berlin.de/mauer/index.en.html*. Versions in German, French, Italian, Chinese, Russian, Polish, and Turkish are also available.

For photographs related to Berlin in 1961, both East and West, you can visit my own Pinterest board here: *http://www.pinterest.com/ninaberry/berlin-and-the-wall/*

For photographs of historical characters in the book, like Walter Ulbricht, and for my inspiration for the fictional characters and details in this book and future Pagan Jones books, including fashion, cars, music, dancing, and more, go to my Pagan Jones Pinterest board here: *http://www.pinterest.com/ninaberry/pagan-jones/*

*Turn the page for a sneak peek
at the next adventure
starring Pagan Jones
CITY OF SPIES
Available now!*

BAILAMOS

More of a statement than a question the man asks a woman: Shall we dance?

"Devin." She breathed it more than said it. Had she conjured him with her thoughts? She took two steps toward him, on her tiptoes. "Are you real?"

"That's a matter for debate." He smiled at her with a delicious fondness that sent blood rushing to her cheeks. "You, however, look very real."

The impulse to obliterate the distance between them, to throw her arms around him, was almost irresistible. The fierce way he'd kissed her the last time they met was imprinted on her body like a brand. But something made her pull herself up short.

His gaze may have been more than friendly, but he hadn't walked up to her or taken her in his arms. He stood at a distance, all coiled grace in his custom-made suit, keeping a good six feet between them.

It had been four months and two days since they last saw each other. Anything could've happened. She needed to reverse the overeager impression she'd given him, and fast.

"Delighted to see you haven't been slaughtered in the line of duty," she said, keeping her tone light. Years of actor training came in handy at times like this. "Last thing I needed was to be haunted by your ghost."

He took a step toward her. "It's good to see you."

His natural Scottish accent, which he could turn off or on, depending on which persona he needed to be, warmed as he spoke more personally. It fanned the tiny flames dancing inside her heart.

"Took you long enough, laddie," she said, using her own deadly accurate Scottish accent. "I was in your neighborhood a little over a month ago."

"Shooting *Daughter of Silence* in London." His voice flattened into a flawless American accent, as if answering an unspoken challenge. "Becoming an emancipated minor and turning seventeen. Happy belated birthday."

"Thanks," she said, dropping the accent. "I got the flowers you didn't send."

He winced. "I'm sorry. I was rather busy. I promise."

It sounded like the truth, but with Devin you could never tell. "Oh, that whole 'I was away serving my country doing unspeakable things' excuse. Very handy." She smiled.

"I hear that the director is so happy with the movie, and with your performance, that he's submitting it to the Cannes Film Festival."

"So you're still pretending to be in the movie business?" she asked.

"I've stepped back in, actually. That's why I'm here."

"And you're keeping tabs on me," she said. "Should I be scared?"

"*Could* you be scared?" His smile was knowing.

"Don't ask me to drive a red convertible." The only way to deal with the paralyzing anxiety brought on by memories of the accident was to puncture it with jokes. "Or wear something off the rack."

"How's your Spanish?" he asked.

It sounded like a non sequitur, but all at once she knew why he was here. It felt so good that it scared her. She took a moment before replying to steady her voice. "Why don't you ask the real question you came all this way to ask me?"

Admiration shone in his eyes. "No more facade between us, is that it?"

Of course he'd understood her immediately. But she hadn't been prepared for him to look at her like that. She clasped her hands to stop them from trembling. "We've pretended with each other enough for one lifetime."

He dipped his head in acknowledgment. "I've come to ask you to help us out, one more time."

"Us?" she asked. "Are you an American now? The last time I saw you…"

"I work for MI6, the British secret service," he said. "The CIA has asked to borrow me for this particular mission. I'm on loan."

"Because they think you have some kind of power over me." It was half question, half assertion.

"To be fair," he said with a smirk, "that's only one of my many valuable skills."

Her eyes fell to his lips. "I remember."

It was hard to tell in the dark, but she could've sworn he flushed. "It would be better if you didn't."

Her throat tightened. He was pushing her away, all right. But she'd gotten a reaction, however much he might try to deny it. "Who is she?"

He glanced away from her briefly. His expression didn't change, but it was enough to make her feel like someone had stabbed her in the gut.

Carefully, he said, "What matters is that I never should have…done what I did the last time we met. I truly thought

I'd never see you again. I thought…" He broke off and tilted his head back, eyes heavenward, inhaling a deep breath. "I'm not here to renew our acquaintance."

So after all they'd been through together in Berlin, after they'd shared a kiss that nearly burned down a hospital, he wasn't here to be with her. It shouldn't have surprised her or hurt her. She should've been over him by now, on to some new sweetheart who didn't come and go like a thief. But it hurt so bad she had to shore up her face with a sarcastic look she'd overused in *Beach Bound Beverly*.

"You mean the CIA didn't send you all the way to Los Angeles to make out with me?" She raised her eyebrows. "But what better way to spend our tax dollars?"

He exhaled a small laugh. "If you're interested in helping us out, then you should accept a starring part in a movie shooting in Buenos Aires, which will be offered to you very soon."

"Argentina?" She knew very little about the country. Something about grasslands and cattle and Eva Perón. "I do all right in Spanish, but there's no way I could pass for a native speaker, even with all of Mercedes's coaching." Her best friend, Mercedes Duran, had grown up in a Spanish-speaking house and was fluent. Pagan, who had learned some French and Italian during her lessons on set and grew up speaking German and English, had picked Spanish up from her fast.

"You won't need to be anyone but yourself," Devin said.

Argentina. Something in her memory was stirring about that country. "Why send Pagan Jones to South America?"

He shook his head, regretful. "I'll tell you after you say yes."

"So I'm going to say yes?"

He paused, lips twisting sardonically. "Yes."

She eyed him. If he was that annoyingly certain about it, he was probably right. "Why?"

"Because you want to," he said.

He was right about that. Even her disappointment at him keeping his distance hadn't dulled the buzz in her fingertips, the lift to her ego at the thought that they wanted her back, that they needed her. No one before had ever thought she could make the world a better place, even in the smallest way.

"I *am* a glutton for punishment," she said. *Or maybe she was addicted to it.*

He took a step toward her now, his eyes intent. "But mostly you'll say yes because it has to do with the man from Germany who stayed with your family back when you were eight."

A chill ran down the back of her neck. That man, her mother's so-called "friend," had come to stay with the Jones family for a few weeks and then vanished. She couldn't remember his name, but he'd been some kind of doctor, a scientist, and this past August she'd discovered that he'd written letters to her mother in a code based on Adolf Hitler's birthday. "You mean Dr. Someone?"

Devin nodded. "The same man who gave your mother that painting by Renoir. You told me you remembered what he looked like, what he sounded like."

"Oh, yes, I remember." She did easily recall the man's angular height, shiny balding head, arrogant nose and sharp brown eyes draped with dark circles. His voice had been the most distinctive thing about him—high-pitched, nasal, commanding, speaking to her mother in rapid German behind closed doors.

Devin was watching her closely. "The Americans think they've found him in Buenos Aires. But photographs and living witnesses are scarce. They need someone to identify him. You may be the only one left alive and willing to help."

"*May be* willing to help," she said, but it was an automatic response. Her thoughts were a cyclone of questions and confusion. She hadn't told Devin about the coded letters. They'd been signed by Rolf Von Albrecht, who had to be the same person as Dr. Someone.

"Why would they want to track him down?" She had her suspicions, but they were too horrible, too unproved. So she let them stay unexamined in the darkest recesses of her mind. She'd recently discovered that her own mother hated Jews, and that she'd helped this German Dr. Someone quietly leave the United States nine years ago. There were only so many reasons the CIA would bother to find such a man.

The thought of Mama, the bedrock of the family, hiding her bigotry and helping Germans illegally kept Pagan up late many nights, trying to untie the knot that was her mother. She'd kept it all from her family and then unexpectedly hanged herself in the family garage one afternoon while everyone else was out. Pagan still didn't know why Mama had decided to die, and more than anything—well, looking at Devin, she realized more than *almost* anything—she longed to find out.

"I'll tell you why," he said. "After you accept the job."

She glared at him. "We said no more lies between us."

"An omission," he said. "Which I'm telling the truth about."

Damn him. She was going to do it—because it made her feel good to be trusted, it was the right thing to do and because it involved Mama. It was Mama's death that triggered Pagan's alcoholic spiral, and it was Pagan's decision to keep drinking for years after that which led to the accident that killed her father and sister.

Mama hadn't left a note; she'd shown no sign of distress or depression. Pagan still had no idea why she'd taken her own life, why she'd left her two daughters without their fierce, controlling, adoring mother. A mother with her own dark secrets.

Thinking about it made it hard to breathe. But more than anything else, Pagan wanted the answer to that question. All the other terrible events had been her own damned fault. She couldn't help feeling responsible for Mama leaving, as well. But maybe, if she found an explanation, one corner of the smothering blanket of guilt and self-recrimination would lift.

"By taking the job," Devin said, "you'll help persuade the CIA to let you see that file they have on your mother. It may be the thing that does the trick."

"'Help persuade'?" she quoted, voice arching with skepticism. "It 'may' do the trick? You're the one who told me to be cautious if they asked me to help them again."

"Glad to see my warning sunk in," he said. "And I stand by it. But I know how badly you want to know more. And I'll be going with you, so I can be a buffer."

She lifted her head to stare up at him, her heart leaping into her throat. "You…"

"I will act as your liaison to the agency while you're in Buenos Aires," he said.

So that was why… "And there'll be no fraternizing because you'll technically be my supervisor," she said.

"It's not technical," he said. "I will be your boss while we're down there, and it's important that nothing get in the way of that. Your life might depend upon it."

"You're such a rule-follower," she said. "What if the rules are wrong?"

"You're such a rule-breaker," he retorted. "What if you're too blind to see why the rules exist?"

"That's what rule-makers always say," she said. "Rules are made to be broken."

"Rules are made for the obedience of fools and the guidance of wise men," he said in an exasperated tone that secretly delighted her. "Guess which one you are?"

She paused. "Was that Shakespeare?"

"Douglas Bader, fighter pilot," he said abruptly. "Those are the terms of the deal. If you say yes, a script for the movie will be sent to you tomorrow. All you have to do is call your agent and tell him you want the part. The movie starts shooting after New Year's. When you get to Buenos Aires, I'll contact you."

"Hmm." Two could play at being distant. And it might help keep her sane while she was working with him.

With her heels still dangling from one hand, she stepped carefully around him in her stocking feet, making it clear she was keeping at least an arm's length between them as she headed back toward the mansion. "I can't make decisions when my toes are wet and cold," she said. "Send me the script."

She paused, turning to look over her shoulder at him. "Maybe I'll say yes."

"Very well." He nodded curtly. The English accent was back, and a veil of formality fell between them. "Say hello to Thomas for me. I look forward to seeing you again soon."

She shrugged. "Maybe."

"There you are!" a voice called through the moist night air.

Pagan whirled to see Thomas's golden-blond head bright under the low lights of the poolside arcade, moving toward her. "I've been wondering where you went," he said, striding over the grass now. "Are you all right?"

"Remember this old friend?" Pagan gestured toward Devin. But Devin Black was gone.

Again.

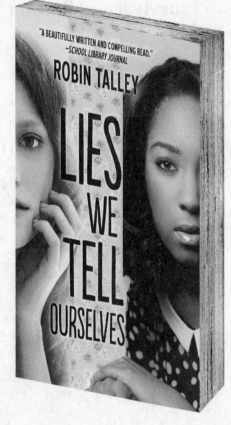

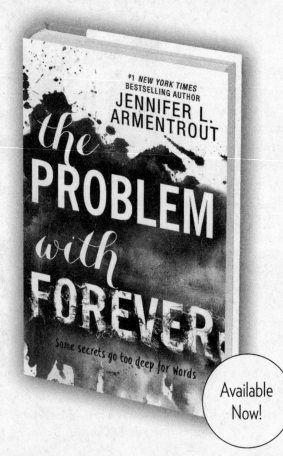

From the critically acclaimed author of the
Pushing the Limits series
KATIE McGARRY
RESPECT THE RULES.
RESPECT THE CLUB.

An unforgettable new series about taking risks, opening your heart and ending up in a place you never imagined possible.

Available wherever books are sold!

www.HarlequinTEEN.com

HTKMNBHTR4

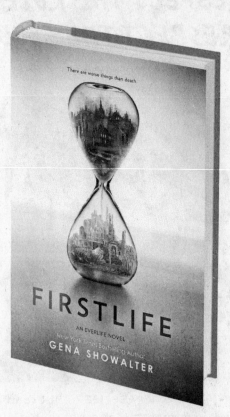